Terro[illegible]

and

City of Ghosts

TWO CLASSIC ADVENTURES OF

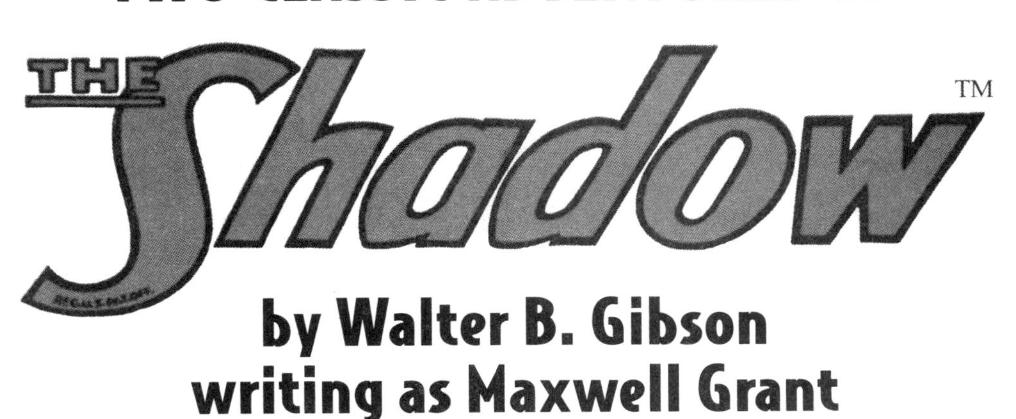

by Walter B. Gibson
writing as Maxwell Grant

and new historical essays
by Will Murray and Anthony Tollin

SANCTUM BOOKS

This Sanctum Books edition is an unabridged republication of the text and illustrations of three stories from *The Shadow Magazine,* as originally published by Street & Smith Publications, Inc., N.Y.: *Terror Island* from the August 15, 1936 issue, *City of Ghosts* from the November 15, 1939 issue and "The Green Light" from the April 1931 issue. These stories are works of their time. Consequently, the text is reprinted intact in its original historical form, including occasional out-of-date ethnic and cultural stereotyping. Typographical errors have been tacitly corrected in this edition.

International Standard Book Number:
978-1-60877-044-1

First printing: January 2011

Series editor: Anthony Tollin
anthonytollin@shadowsanctum.com

Consulting editor: Will Murray

Copy editor: Joseph Wrzos

Cover and photo restoration: Michael Piper

Published by Sanctum Books
P.O. Box 761474, San Antonio, TX 78245-1474

Visit The Shadow at www.shadowsanctum.com.

Volume 45

CONTENTS

Thrilling Tales and Features

Cover painting by George Rozen
Back cover art by George Rozen and Graves Gladney
Interior illustrations by Tom Lovell and Edd Cartier

Mile by mile, a pleasure yacht nears the hideout of a mastermind of evil who startled all Europe with his wave of terror! But aboard was The Shadow, arch-foe of crime, who had in his power the means to crush the danger that lurked on

TERROR ISLAND

From the Private Annals of The Shadow, as told to

Maxwell Grant

CHAPTER I
A CROOK IS TRAPPED

AN elderly man was seated, stoop-shouldered, at a massive desk. Behind him was a closed safe; to his left, a pair of French windows, wide open, that led to a screened veranda. The room was lighted, for it was after dusk; and there was a reason for the open windows, because the night was excessively warm. When occasional breezes came, they floated in from the veranda.

The light from the room repaid that service by casting its soft glow beyond the outside screen. The illumination revealed the long, crinkly leafed branches of palm trees against the porch.

The man at the desk was James Tolwig, a New York millionaire. The room in which he sat was the study of his spacious Florida bungalow. Though less than a dozen miles from Miami, James Tolwig enjoyed a most secluded location; and that

fact pleased him. It was one reason why he had chosen to stay in Florida during the off season.

James Tolwig's forehead was furrowed in a puzzled frown. The elderly man was studying a telegram; he stroked his chin as he read the message. The wire was from Havana; its message simply read:

> POSTPONE PURCHASE UNTIL NINE O'CLOCK.
>
> S.

There were footsteps from the hallway. Tolwig pushed the telegram beneath a book; he looked up to see a stolid-faced servant enter, bringing a tray with two tall glasses. Ice clinked as the servant approached the desk. Tolwig gestured.

"Place the tray here, Lovett," he ordered, in a testy tone, "then tell Mr. Bagland that I want to see him. Where is Bagland, anyway? Bah! He claims to be an efficient secretary, but he is never about when I need him -"

Tolwig cut his denunciation short as a tall, smiling-faced man stepped in from the veranda. The arrival was the missing secretary; out for a stroll, Bagland had arrived just in time to hear his employer's words. Tolwig indulged in a slight smile of his own; he motioned for Bagland to be seated.

Lovett stopped at the door; there, the servant turned about and adjusted his rumpled white jacket. He was waiting for further orders. Tolwig dismissed him with a wave of his hand. As soon as the servant's footsteps had faded in the hallway, Tolwig pointed to the door.

Without a word, Bagland arose and closed the door; the secretary came back to the desk and picked up one of the tall glasses. Tolwig took the other glass.

APPARENTLY, Tolwig and his secretary were on most friendly terms, despite the millionaire's harsh statement a few minutes before. As further proof of their accord, Tolwig produced the telegram that he had hidden from Lovett's view. Handing the wire to Bagland, Tolwig spoke.

"This arrived while you were out," stated the millionaire quietly. "What do you make of it, Bagland?"

The secretary studied the telegram. He smiled.

"You must have talked too much," decided Bagland, "when you made that short trip to Havana a few days ago."

"I did mention my intended purchase," nodded Tolwig, "but I did not state from whom I intended to buy. I said nothing concerning George Dalavan."

"Neither does this telegram," observed Bagland. "Probably the man who sent it has never heard of Dalavan. But he may know about the Lamballe tiara; if so, he knows that someone intends to swindle you."

"Unless the telegram is a hoax," rejoined Tolwig. "What should I do about it, Bagland?"

For reply, the secretary crumpled the telegram and threw it into the wastebasket.

"Forget it," he declared. "We already have the goods on Dalavan. We can handle him ourselves. It is after half past eight; Dalavan is already overdue. If we happen to wait until nine o'clock, all right. If not—"

Bagland paused. A bell was tingling; Lovett's footsteps answered, outside the door. The servant was on his way to the front door to admit the visitor. Bagland's smile broadened; in low tones, the secretary whispered:

"George Dalavan."

TWO minutes later, Lovett ushered the visitor into the study. George Dalavan was a man of heavy build, brisk in manner and of military appearance. His hair was short clipped; so was the black mustache that he wore. His whole face was ruddy; the color was natural and not the effect of sunburn. Most conspicuous, however, was the narrowness of his eyes.

They peered sharply from each side of a thin-bridged nose, as Dalavan darted a look toward Bagland, who was now seated at a table in the corner. Then Dalavan concentrated upon Tolwig; he gave a cheery smile as he reached across the desk to shake hands with the millionaire.

"I've brought it," announced Dalavan, in a smooth tone. He lifted a square-shaped suitcase and placed it upon the desk. "The tiara once owned by the Princess de Lamballe, favorite of Marie Antoinette."

Opening the case, Dalavan removed a glittering coronet. Diamonds gleamed brightly in the light. Tolwig received the tiara with both hands; he nodded as he studied the magnificent crown-like object.

"I saw this tiara once before," remarked Tolwig, dryly. "That was in Paris, when the tiara was the property of the Duke of Abragoyne. I doubted that he would ever part with it."

"You know those French nobility," returned Dalavan. "They hang on to their jewels, until they go broke. Then they part with them for a song. Fifty thousand dollars is small money for a piece like this one, Mr. Tolwig."

"Quite true," agreed Tolwig. He opened a desk drawer and drew out a sheaf of bills. "Here is the exact amount. Count the money, Dalavan, and give me a receipt for it."

Dalavan counted the money, which was all in bills of high denomination. He threw a restless glance toward Bagland. The secretary's back was turned; for Bagland was busy at his table.

Dalavan reached into his pocket and pulled out a sheet of paper. Hurriedly, he thrust it out of sight; found another sheet and used it to write a receipt. Tolwig received the written paper and slowly shook his head.

"This is not sufficient," declared the millionaire. "The receipt merely states that you have received fifty thousand dollars for a jeweled tiara. You should specify more than that, Dalavan. You should call it the Lamballe tiara."

"Why?" laughed Dalavan. "You, yourself, know that it *is* the Lamballe tiara."

"Suppose," conjectured Tolwig, "that I should show the tiara to the Duke of Abragoyne? Suppose that he should tell me that it had been stolen from him?"

DALAVAN'S lips tightened; then the mustached man demanded:

"Why should you show the tiara to the duke?"

"Ah!" exclaimed Tolwig. "You admit, then, that the tiara *was* stolen?"

"I admit nothing, Mr. Tolwig. I have sold numerous curios. People never question *where* and *how* I obtained them."

GEORGE DALAVAN —go between for Purvis Elger.

Dalavan paused, then resumed in a purring tone.

"Listen, Mr. Tolwig," he urged, "you're not the first big buyer that I've reasoned with. You want this tiara. You'd never have had a dog's chance to get it, if someone hadn't lifted it from the French duke's strongbox. It's yours now; bought and paid for, at less than half its value.

"I've convinced others before you. You've heard, no doubt, of Cholmley Clayborne, the big steel man from Chicago. He bought a swell tapestry that came straight from Buckingham Palace. He's keeping mum. Tyler Loman, the movie magnate, bought a collection of rare gold coins from me. They came from the Munich Museum, and he knows it. That doesn't matter.

"I didn't steal this tiara. I saved it. The fellows who had it were going to smash it up and sell the chunks. What you are actually doing, Mr. Tolwig, is to save this fine tiara from destruction. You should thank me for giving you the opportunity."

Dalavan's smooth talk had no effect upon Tolwig. Hunched behind his desk, the millionaire clasped both hands and tilted his head. Quietly, he put a single question:

"Then you admit that the tiara was stolen?"

"Sure," returned Dalavan. "I admit it. I've told you what other collectors do. They keep what they know to themselves—"

James Tolwig gestured an interruption. He swung about in his swivel chair, snapped quick words to the corner where Bagland was seated. The secretary spun about; his face showed a wise smile.

Before Dalavan could guess what was due, Bagland pulled a revolver from his coat pocket and leveled it straight at the visitor.

"You have met Bagland before," chuckled Tolwig, to Dalavan. "You took him for what he pretended to be—an ordinary private secretary, and a rather dull one. Actually, he is a private investigator, who has been looking for gentlemen of your ilk."

"I'm not such a bad secretary, either," added Bagland, using his free hand to hold a sheaf of papers in front of Dalavan's ugly eyes. "I've taken shorthand notes on all this conversation, Dalavan. All right, Mr. Tolwig"—Bagland nodded briskly to the millionaire—"you can call the police."

Chuckling, glad that he had trapped a rogue, James Tolwig reached for the telephone on his desk. To gain the telephone, his hand was forced to brush a small desk clock that showed the time as ten minutes before nine.

Tolwig scarcely noticed the clock. Hence, he did not think of the telegram that had specified the hour of nine. Even if he had recalled the telegram, it would scarcely have mattered at this moment. James Tolwig had ignored that message, to act on his own initiative.

The time was past when proper recognition of that telegram could have proven of vital value to James Tolwig.

CHAPTER II
A POSTPONED TRAIL

IF ever a man behaved as a cornered rat, George Dalavan displayed the part when James Tolwig placed a hand upon the telephone receiver. All of Dalavan's smoothness wilted; the fellow cowered away from the desk and raised trembling hands, as he looked toward the muzzle of Bagland's gun.

"You can't arrest me!" whined Dalavan. "I've done nothing. I sold you the tiara. That's all."

"That was enough!" announced Tolwig, sternly. "Your racket is finished, Dalavan."

The narrow-eyed rogue turned his beady gaze toward Bagland; in despairing fashion, Dalavan pleaded with the investigator.

"Don't turn me over!" he gasped. "Maybe—maybe I can help you out with other facts! Give me a chance, Bagland!"

The investigator nodded. Tolwig let the telephone receiver drop back upon its hook. With a quick, wise look toward Bagland, Tolwig returned the nod, then leaned forward to hear what Dalavan might have to say. The crook started in with the promised facts.

"This racket is bigger than you think!" blurted Dalavan. "It goes into millions of dollars! I'm only a front for it—sort of a mouthpiece. I freeze the stuff that's hot. You've probably guessed that, Bagland."

"I have," returned Bagland, steadily. Then, to Tolwig, the investigator added: "We'll hear all that he has to say. This stolen tiara represents but one item, Mr. Tolwig. The racket must involve huge robberies abroad; some smuggling system in addition; a perfect hideout, where the stuff is stored."

Dalavan nodded at each point. Bagland saw it and made a final statement.

"Behind it all," declared Bagland, "must be a master crook, far more dangerous than you, Dalavan. Wait a moment! I have an idea!"

Planting his notebook on the desk, Bagland stepped forward. Dalavan's arms went higher; Bagland shoved the revolver's muzzle against the crook's ribs. Reaching into Dalavan's pocket, Bagland whisked out the piece of paper that the crook had so hurriedly thrust from view, just before writing his receipt.

"Take a look at this, Mr. Tolwig."

WHILE Bagland continued to cover Dalavan at close range, Tolwig studied the paper. It was a piece of stationery; it bore no writing, but at the top was an embossed seal. The imprint represented a pair of gryphons, each supporting a side of a white shield.

Bagland managed a side glance that enabled him to see the gryphon shield. Facing Dalavan, he snapped the question:

"Who did that come from?"

"The big shot," returned Dalavan. "He used it, as sort of a coat of arms. Perhaps you'd like to know his name, and where he can be found?"

"I would!" snapped out Bagland. "You're going to spill it, Dalavan, without getting any promises from us—"

A sharp interruption came from Tolwig. Looking up from the sheet of paper with the gryphon shield, the millionaire saw straight beyond Bagland and Dalavan.

Tolwig's eyes caught a flash of white in the doorway; with it, the glitter of an aiming revolver. Tolwig's cry was a warning; heeding it, Bagland spun about. The investigator was too late.

A revolver barked. It was aimed straight at Bagland. The man who gripped the gun was Tolwig's own servant, Lovett. The white-coated arrival had taken accurate aim. He fired a second shot; a third. A fourth was unnecessary.

The first bullet had dropped Bagland; the other shots were vicious additions that Lovett gave to insure Bagland's prompt death. Staring across the desk, Tolwig saw the investigator twist in agony and lie still.

Madly, Tolwig bounded from behind the desk. In his left hand, he clutched the sheet of paper with the gryphon shield. With his right, he made a wild grab for the revolver that had dropped from Bagland's hand. Tolwig was a perfect target for Lovett; but the servant added no bullets. It was Dalavan who acted.

The mustached man whipped out a gun of his own. He let Tolwig get hold of Bagland's revolver; then with a vicious snarl, Dalavan opened fire. At a four-foot range, he delivered three bullets into Tolwig's body. The effect of those shots were immediate. James Tolwig sprawled dead across Bagland's body.

George Dalavan's ruddy face showed demonish as the murderer leaned within the focused area of the desk lamp. With eager hands, Dalavan snatched the Lamballe tiara and placed that treasure back into its case. Bundling the fifty thousand dollars, Dalavan added it with the tiara. His hand slid against the desk clock; the timepiece had almost reached nine o'clock.

It was not that fact, however, that made Dalavan turn about. The murderer knew nothing of the telegram that Tolwig had received from Havana. Dalavan's ears caught a faint sound. On that account, the murderer swung toward Lovett.

"Did you hear that?" demanded Dalavan, in a tense tone. "It sounded like a motor, somewhere outside the house."

Lovett listened, then shook his head.

"Nobody would be going by here," remarked the accomplice. "What's more, the main road is too far for anyone to have heard the shots."

"Was Tolwig expecting any other visitors?"

"None that I know about. I kept close tabs on him, like you told me to. There was a telegram that came for him, from Havana—"

"That wouldn't mean anything."

DALAVAN'S tenseness lessened. The murderer was confident that Lovett had kept good check on Tolwig. Dalavan had used Lovett as the inside man before; it was a precaution that he always adopted. The fact that Lovett had not learned that Bagland was an investigator did not detract from Dalavan's opinion. He guessed that Bagland had been careful enough to keep his real identity a secret.

"You'd better slide out and take a gander," decided Dalavan. "Peek from the front door; if anyone comes in by the gate, meet them like nothing happened. Tell them Tolwig is out."

Lovett nodded. He walked from the study. Dalavan snatched up Bagland's notes, put them into the case that held the tiara and the money. He found the receipt that he had given Tolwig; he put that with the other objects.

Looking toward the bodies, Dalavan grinned. He stooped and carefully placed his fingers upon the sheet of stationery that still rested in Tolwig's grasp. Dalavan was prepared to pluck away that bit of evidence.

Dalavan's right hand held its revolver; his left was on the paper that bore the imprint of the gryphon shield. Suddenly, his motion ceased. Rigid in his stooped position, Dalavan listened. With a sudden snarl of alarm, he spun about, to face the opened French windows that led to the porch.

Dalavan was too late in his move.

On the threshold stood a figure that froze the murderer. Dalavan's lips widened; his arms were chilled to numbness. His right hand released its hold upon the revolver; the weapon clanked to the floor. Dalavan's left hand opened also; but it dropped nothing, for the murderer had postponed his effort to pluck away the paper that Tolwig's fingers held in a death grip.

There was ample reason for Dalavan's new rigidity.

The figure on the threshold was clad in black—a cloaked arrival whose identity was unmistakable. To Dalavan, a crook by trade, the presence of that weird intruder was more formidable than a squad of police.

Eyes burned from beneath the brim of a slouch hat. Below was a thin-gloved fist that held a leveled automatic. Light showed the barrel of the .45, a looming tube that was ready to deliver withering blasts. The being on the threshold was The Shadow.

Superfoe of crime, The Shadow had learned of Tolwig's intended purchase. The Shadow had sent the telegram from Havana, confident that Tolwig would heed the warning and delay the purchase of the tiara until his unknown advisor had arrived. Tolwig had not done so; The Shadow saw the result as he surveyed the two bodies at Dalavan's feet.

SLOWLY, The Shadow stepped in from the threshold. Shivering, Dalavan backed away, almost stumbling over the bodies. The Shadow saw the object that the murderer had tried to gain; that telltale paper in Tolwig's grasp. He also spied the packed case on the desk. With a gliding side-step, The Shadow edged between Dalavan and the desk; his move forced the murderer toward the front door of the room.

Dalavan's lips moved helplessly. With Tolwig and Bagland, Dalavan had staged a bluff; but with The Shadow, his fear was unfeigned. Dalavan knew why The Shadow had cornered him toward the door. The Shadow suspected an accomplice, such as Lovett. He would be ready for the man when he returned. Dalavan saw The Shadow's left hand go to his cloak, to draw forth a second automatic.

Then came the unexpected countermove, for which Dalavan had not dared to hope. There was a sudden clatter from the veranda. An attacker hurtled into the room. It was Lovett; the servant had gone out by the front door, to return by way of the veranda.

Gun in hand, Lovett had spotted The Shadow; but the accomplice had been too wise to take out time for aim. Instead, he had launched into a driving attack, covering the dozen feet from the veranda to the desk.

The Shadow's move was proof that Lovett had played the best bet. Wheeling instantly, The Shadow whipped forth his left-hand gun, pulling the trigger as he made the draw. The .45 boomed; its bullet would have dropped Lovett, had the servant been the fraction of a second slower. As it was, Lovett was making a dive as The Shadow fired. The bullet seared the top of the crook's left shoulder.

Lovett landed on The Shadow. Viciously, the servant swung his revolver. The Shadow parried it; drove a blow toward Lovett's head. Only a lucky bob saved Lovett at that instant. Clutching The Shadow, the crook skidded away from the desk, dragging his black-clad foeman with him.

Dalavan saw instantly what the result would be. Despite Lovett's fury, The Shadow had full control. He was swinging the servant about, in order to take aim at Dalavan. A lucky twist of the servant gave Dalavan a second's chance. The murderer took it. He leaped for the desk; grabbed up the suitcase that held the tiara, money and incriminating evidence.

The Shadow's right-hand gun spoke.

A bullet chipped woodwork from the desk's edge. Dalavan dived for the French windows. Twice, a .45 responded, shattering glass from the open windows. Lovett, fighting like a fiend, had managed to offset The Shadow's aim. Dalavan gained the clear.

Balked by Lovett's tenacity, The Shadow wrenched away from the servant, spilling the fellow to the floor. Twisting, he made after Dalavan. His first step brought trouble. The Shadow's foot caught upon one of Bagland's outstretched ankles.

Head foremost, The Shadow hit the floor. Lovett, coming to hands and knees, saw the disaster. Wildly, the crook pounced upon The Shadow, swinging his gun as he came.

The Shadow rolled as Lovett struck. Face upward, he shifted his head to the right. Lovett's blow glanced from the side of the slouch hat; simultaneously, The Shadow pulled a trigger. Lovett's lips coughed a gasp; the servant rolled from The Shadow's shoulder.

GROGGILY, The Shadow came to his feet; swung toward the veranda, ready with a gun.

Lovett's blow had partly dazed the cloaked fighter. The Shadow was steadying himself, to take up the pursuit of Dalavan. As he stood by the desk, The Shadow heard a motor's rising roar, some distance from the bungalow.

It was the sound of a departing plane. Dalavan had come here by air, taking advantage of a clearing that must have given him an excellent landing field. The murderous crook was off to a speedy getaway, carrying his spoils with him. Pursuit was useless.

Looking past Lovett's body, The Shadow saw the form of James Tolwig. Stooping, he plucked the paper that Dalavan had wanted. The Shadow's lips phrased a whispered laugh as his eyes saw the gryphon shield. The sheet of paper went beneath The Shadow's cloak.

Though The Shadow did not know the name of the murderer who had escaped, he had seen George Dalavan face to face; hence he would know the man when he met him again. Moreover, The Shadow knew Dalavan's part; that the man was merely the representative of a hidden big shot. The paper with the gryphon shield must have some bearing upon the mastermind who had given Dalavan orders for tonight's crime.

From this single shred of evidence, The Shadow could hunt down evil men. It was a quest that would challenge his full ability; but The Shadow had met such tests before. For the present, however, he was forced to postpone the quest.

Striding from the room of death, The Shadow departed by the veranda. He found his parked car, boarded it, then set out in the direction of Miami. Present plans called for The Shadow's return to Havana, where he had left one mission in order to make his expedition to Tolwig's Florida home.

The Shadow had postponed a trail. He intended to return to it as soon as a definite mission was accomplished. That return would come sooner than The Shadow supposed. Oddly, his postponement was to prove the shortest route by which The Shadow could reach George Dalavan and the supercrook who ruled that man of murder.

CHAPTER III
OUTBOUND FROM HAVANA

IT was the next afternoon in Havana. A trim yacht was docked beside a harbor pier; on the deck stood a firm-faced man whose shocky, black hair was streaked with gray. He was Kingdon Feldworth, owner of the yacht; the vessel was the *Maldah*, from New York, as the name on the stern testified.

Trucks had pulled up at the pier. Dark-faced Cubans were unloading crates and boxes. As stevedores took charge of these objects, Feldworth called an order in English. The stevedores were acquainted well enough with the language to understand that they were to take the boxes to the main cabin.

While the boxes were being carried aboard, a man strolled up to the pier. He was an American, about forty years of age, dressed in youthful style. His eyes were sharp and quick of glance; his lips wore a smile that looked like a fixed expression. This arrival peered upward toward the deck, saw Feldworth go below.

Hands in his pockets, the man with the fixed smile waited until the boxes were all aboard; then he went up the gangplank. He was a guest aboard the yacht—one who had taken the cruise from New York.

His name was Bram Jalway; he was a business promoter who had traveled to many places in the world. Because of that experience, he had easily formed an acquaintance with Kingdon Feldworth. The yacht owner was a great traveler, and always made friends with other globe-trotters.

Not long after Jalway had gone aboard, the stevedores reappeared with empty boxes. These were loaded back upon the trucks; as the vehicles pulled away, two other persons arrived at the pier. One was a quiet, solemn-faced man who was puffing at a cigarette. The other was a girl, a striking brunette, whose eyes were large and dark.

The man was Seth Hadlow, a sportsman who was reputed to be a millionaire. Like Bram Jalway, Seth Hadlow was a guest aboard the yacht. The girl was Francine Feldworth, niece of Kingdon Feldworth. She always accompanied her uncle when he made a cruise aboard the *Maldah*.

Hadlow and Francine stopped when they reached the deck. The sportsman lighted another cigarette; the girl looked ruefully across the rail and studied the Havana skyline.

"We'll be leaving Cuba soon," declared Francine. "I wish we could stay longer here, Seth."

"So do I," agreed Hadlow.

Sailors were coming to the deck. They began to prepare the yacht for departure. It was Francine who spoke suddenly. The girl was looking across the rail. She laughed as she pointed.

"There goes Professor Marcolm, Seth."

An elderly man was jogging toward the pier, panting as he ran. His chin was tilted against his chest; his white hair was shaggy beneath the old felt hat he was wearing. In one hand he had a large carpetbag; in the other, he was lugging a cylindrical bundle rolled in oilskin.

Professor Marcolm gained the top of the gangplank. The old man smiled as he nodded to Hadlow and Francine. Puffing, he went below.

VARIOUS delays prevented the prompt

Crime fighter—master of darkness—elusive as the night from which he comes—such is The Shadow. The knowledge of all pending crime is his, and thus does he thwart the master crooks of crime. From the depths of San Francisco's Chinatown to the underworld of New York; from the dark dives of New Orleans to the Boston waterfront; wherever crime brews—crooks quail at the name of The Shadow.

To The Shadow with news of crime and criminals come his agents, men who under the guise of professions have been trained by the master of darkness to see crime in the making and report such immediately. None know The Shadow's identity, but faithful are they in serving him to the end that crime must be nipped in the bud. For agents all, they owe their lives to The Shadow.

There is Moe Shrevnitz, taxi driver without peer, who carries The Shadow on many of his dangerous missions; Clyde Burke, star reporter of the *Classic,* who because of his newspaper contacts furnishes many unknown facts; Burbank, through whom all the agents make their reports to The Shadow; Rutledge Mann, quiet-spoken broker of insurance, who is invaluable to the master-fighter; Cliff Marsland, known to mobland as a killer, but to The Shadow as his underworld contact man; Jericho, giant Negro, whose strength is equalled only by his devotion to The Shadow; Hawkeye, insignificant in appearance, but who can follow a trail until his man is run to earth; Harry Vincent, youthful and with a keenness that brings him into most of The Shadow's cases as the master of darkness's key man. These and others are the agents on which The Shadow relies, and never do they fail him.

The Shadow himself at times assumes the role of a globe-trotting millionaire—Lamont Cranston—when Cranston is on his many travels, and in this guise meets crooks face to face.

Such are the methods of The Shadow.

departure of the yacht. The sun had set when the *Maldah* finally started from its pier. Hadlow and Francine went below, for the girl said that she felt unhappy about leaving Havana and did not care to be on deck when the yacht cleared port. They came to the door of the main cabin. It was closed. Francine knocked; she heard her uncle give the word to come in.

Entering, Francine and Hadlow found Kingdon Feldworth seated in a chair at the end of the elegant cabin. His back was toward a wall that displayed a series of heavy oak panels. With the grizzled yacht owner was Bram Jalway. The sharp-eyed promoter was puffing at a briar pipe; his lips, as they held the pipe's stem, still kept their half-smile.

Francine looked anxiously toward her uncle. She noticed that his face was grim.

"What is the trouble?" inquired the girl. "You look worried, Uncle."

"Nothing at all," protested Feldworth.

"I don't believe you, uncle."

Feldworth seemed at a loss for another statement. Bram Jalway supplied one. Removing his briar pipe from his lips, the promoter remarked:

"Your uncle has reason to be worried, Francine. Storm warnings are being posted. The captain gave us the news a short while ago."

Feldworth managed a pleased smile.

"Yes," he agreed, "that is the trouble, Francine. We may run into a hurricane. I did not want to tell you, to alarm you. That is the real trouble."

The statement satisfied Francine. Kingdon Feldworth looked relieved; to Bram Jalway, he nodded his head in appreciation. The promoter smiled in response and went back to puffing his briar pipe.

IN proof of the weather prophecies, the *Maldah* encountered heavy swells just a little before dinner. When the meal was over, passengers retired somewhat early.

Kingdon Feldworth, however, remained in the main cabin. He stood there alone; his face showed signs of nervous twitching. Finally satisfied that he was unwatched, the yacht owner went to the heavy oak panels at the end of the room; he found a catch and opened the woodwork.

A fabulous sight was revealed. Hanging within the compartment were jeweled tapestries—shimmering decorations done in cloths of gold. Feldworth opened a small chest; the raised lid revealed gold itself, in the form of coins. Feldworth opened another box; jewels sparkled. Suddenly, the yacht owner turned about; he eyed the door suspiciously.

Feldworth had fancied that he heard a noise at the door. Finally satisfied that it was his imagination, he closed the boxes. Shutting the panel, Feldworth eyed it; then, reluctantly, he turned out the light. He opened the door in darkness and went through a dimly lighted passage.

A few minutes after Feldworth was gone, a blackened shape materialized from a corner of the passage. A cloaked figure came into view. There, in this portion of the heaving yacht, stood The Shadow.

With a gloved hand, The Shadow opened the door of the main cabin. He entered, closed the door behind him. Using a flashlight, The Shadow approached the panels at the end of the room.

The woodwork clicked under the touch of a skilled hand. The panels came back; The Shadow's light revealed the interior of the secret compartment. The Shadow eyed Feldworth's treasures; he studied the contents of the boxes. A brief estimate told him that these belongings were worth in excess of a million dollars.

There was a small, flat box that Feldworth had not opened. In it, The Shadow found letters and other documents that carried signatures. He studied these carefully; he was satisfied with his scrutiny. The papers explained the wealth that Feldworth had brought aboard.

All these valuables had belonged to a Cuban who had fled Havana at the time of the revolution. The Cuban had sold them to Feldworth for two hundred thousand dollars. With the sale, the Cuban had supplied information, telling where the wealth was hidden in Havana. Feldworth had managed to obtain the valuables, but only after an enforced delay.

With the documents were customs blanks. It was plain that Feldworth intended to follow an honest course to declare his wealth once the *Maldah* reached New York. He had bought the property in good faith; his reason for keeping it hidden was to avoid any trouble on the yacht.

Feldworth trusted his guests. The Shadow knew that fact, for he was one of them. Evidently, Feldworth feared followers from Cuba; or possible trouble from the crew, if it should be learned that a million dollars' worth of valuables happened to be on board. Therefore, to The Shadow, Kingdon Feldworth was a man who needed protection.

THE SHADOW had known this for a long while; from the time when he had come aboard the yacht in New York, for a cruise to Havana and return. He had not, however, learned what Feldworth planned until tonight.

That was why The Shadow had decided to return to New York on the *Maldah*; why he had made a hurried flight back to Havana from Miami, instead of taking up the trail of the murderer, George Dalavan.

The Shadow extinguished his flashlight. He moved in darkness from the main cabin. He followed the dim passage, then merged with other blackness. Soon, a door closed behind him. The Shadow was in his own quarters. His visit to Feldworth's treasure chest would never be known.

The *Maldah* was ploughing northward through heavy seas, carrying its secret cargo of wealth. Where treasure lay, intrigue could always follow. Perhaps there was someone on board who planned to capture Kingdon Feldworth's newly acquired wealth. That could be a matter of speculation. One fact, however, was evident.

The Shadow was aboard the *Maldah*. Camouflaged as a guest, he had undertaken a campaign of vigilance. Once he was sure the treasure was safe, he would be willing to leave and undertake other tasks. Should crime come, either on the yacht or elsewhere, The Shadow would reveal himself.

Until that hour, he would remain in the disguise that he had chosen for this adventure. No one would suspect his presence. To the world, The Shadow was a being cloaked in black. When he chose to appear in some ordinary guise, he did so without the knowledge of enemy or friend.

Should strife strike aboard the *Maldah*, The Shadow would be prepared for it. There was one peril, however, against which The Shadow could not cope. That was the hazard of the hurricane that threatened the yacht's course.

CHAPTER IV
THE STORM STRIKES

SLEEK and speedy, the *Maldah* kept ahead of the rising hurricane for many hours. Kingdon Feldworth congratulated himself as the next day passed. He was confident that the yacht would escape the worst weather. His surmise, however, proved wrong.

Sweeping up from the West Indies, the storm overtook the *Maldah* off the Florida coast. The blow increased; from then on, it was a battle for existence. The crisis came when the *Maldah* was swept in toward the Georgia coast. Surrounded by darkness, pounded by huge waves, the yacht was making a last struggle.

The fact that the *Maldah* had neared the shore was proven by a strange phenomenon. The captain believed that his ship was near a desolate location. The wireless was out of commission; it seemed impossible that anyone would sight the rising and falling line of the yacht's lights, as they glimmered pitifully above the waves. It was a sailor, stationed at the bow, who first learned otherwise.

A sudden line of sparks flashed from a mile distant on the lee of the yacht. A sizzling rocket whizzed upward from the shore, to burst into a myriad of colored sparks that were swept into instant oblivion. Word went to the captain of the *Maldah*; he ordered an answering signal. Soon, a streaking rocket shot up from the yacht's deck into the night.

While this was happening above, the passengers were assembled in the main cabin. Kingdon Feldworth was seated with his back to the oak panels that hid his treasure; but his thoughts were far from the Cuban wealth. Feldworth had cause for greater concern tonight. He was deeply anxious about the safety of those aboard his yacht.

NONE of the passengers showed great worriment. Bram Jalway was seated near Feldworth, a traveler who had been everywhere. Jalway was undisturbed by the storm. His lips had their usual smile; his eyes were sharp as they roved about the cabin. Jalway seemed to consider the storm with a half-amused indulgence.

Professor Thaddeus Marcolm was half asleep. The white-haired professor's head was drooped toward his chest; it bobbed with the heaving motion of the yacht. Marcolm's fists were tight upon the arms of his chair; but only for the purpose of holding himself in position.

Seth Hadlow was solemnly puffing a cigarette. His face looked anxious; but it usually had something of that expression. Hadlow's manner was proof that he was untroubled by the elements. A sportsman always, Hadlow was taking the hurricane as a game.

Francine Feldworth actually felt worried; but the composure of her companions quelled her alarm. Though her face was troubled, Francine's lips were set; her dark eyes sparkled their trust in the men about her.

Kingdon Feldworth surveyed his guests with approval. The yacht owner was pleased with the stoutness that three men had shown during the storm. Feldworth would hardly have been surprised had he learned that one of the trio was The Shadow, who was used to dangerous adventures. But Feldworth would have had trouble in picking out The Shadow, had he known of that master's presence. Since all had confidence and quiet courage, there was no way to choose between them.

Kingdon Feldworth had come to a decision. Whatever might occur, he would stay aboard the yacht. As owner, he felt that he had that privilege. Because of the Cuban wealth, he was determined upon his purpose. Should occasion come to take for the shore, Feldworth intended to insist that the others go while he remain.

Meanwhile, The Shadow had come to an opposite decision. He had not been idle during the voyage north from Havana. He had come to the conclusion that all of Feldworth's crew stood loyal to the master of the yacht. Feldworth's treasure would be safe on board.

Should persons seek the shore, however, they might encounter danger there. They would need The Shadow's aid; hence, he was prepared to go along with any party that might be ordered to the lifeboats.

Conversation had lulled when the door of the cabin swung open. The captain heaved through the doorway, with rolling gait; he caught himself and thrust the door shut. He turned a rugged face toward Feldworth.

"What is it, Captain?" questioned the yacht owner. "Is the hurricane increasing?"

"Yes," returned the captain. "We're in for it. I'm counting on the engines, though. Maybe we'll pull through."

A SIGH of relief came from Feldworth. The owner looked anxiously over his shoulder, toward the paneled wall. Hadlow puffed his cigarette and watched Feldworth. Jalway also eyed the yacht owner, then turned to speak to Francine. Professor Marcolm awoke from his doze and blinked.

"We're off the Georgia coast," informed the captain. "You know what that means, Mr. Feldworth. Islands. Sand. If we beach the ship, she'll be pounded to pieces. But if we can limp to any kind of an inlet, I can beach her where she won't break up."

"Good!" exclaimed Feldworth. "We must save the yacht, Captain! This ship means much to me—"

"Not as much as human lives," put in the officer. "Remember this, Mr. Feldworth: the storm is increasing. The longer we stand by the ship, the greater the danger. We can launch the small boats at present. But later on—"

"You mean we should abandon the yacht?" interrupted Feldworth. "I refuse to do so, Captain. As for you, it is your duty to remain."

"That is what I intend to do," retorted the captain. "Likewise the crew. I am speaking for the safety of the passengers. This will be their last chance to get ashore. With the engines working"—the speaker paused as the ship quivered with increased throbs—"I'm going to drive away from shore."

"But this coast is desolate!" exclaimed Feldworth. "If the small boat should survive the waves, where would it land?"

"Near human habitation," assured the captain. "We have seen lights on the shore. The yacht has been observed. We received a rocket signal from the beach."

"You answered it?"

"Yes. Rescuers are waiting. Our lifeboats are unsinkable. That is why I propose that you and your passengers should take this opportunity for safety. I shall stand by the ship."

FELDWORTH arose. Swaying unsteadily with the motion of the yacht, he clapped his hand upon the captain's shoulder.

"Fine news," declared the owner. "You are

The *Maldah* answered the rocket signal from the beach.

right, Captain. We shall launch the small boat for the passengers. But I, like you, intend to remain aboard."

"No, Uncle!" exclaimed Francine. "You must come with us!"

"I shall stand by," returned Feldworth.

"Then I shall remain," decided the girl. "And I believe"—she looked about the cabin—"that the others will do the same."

"What about it, Captain?" queried Feldworth, with a smile.

"The lifeboat will be ready in ten minutes," asserted the officer, steadily. "All passengers will go ashore. That is my order. It must be obeyed!"

"But my uncle!" protested Francine. "He will have to go with us!"

"Mr. Feldworth is owner of the *Maldah*," returned the captain. "I cannot force him to leave the ship. But the rest of you will obey my command. I shall use force, if necessary."

"Be calm, Francine," insisted Feldworth, swaying toward the girl's chair. "From the shore, you can inform the coast guards. They may bring us aid. With our wireless out of commission, we shall need assistance of that sort."

"Your uncle is right, Francine," stated Hadlow, quietly. "We shall take to the lifeboat. What about it, Jalway?"

"I should prefer to remain aboard," returned the promoter, still wearing his fixed smile. "But the captain has ordered otherwise. He must be obeyed. Moreover, Francine"—he turned to the girl—"I cannot forget your safety."

"You are ready, Professor?" inquired Hadlow.

Professor Marcolm responded with a solemn nod of his white-haired head.

"Two crew members will go with you," declared the captain, deciding that the matter was settled. "You, Mr. Hadlow, and you, Mr. Jalway, are as capable as any man aboard this yacht. Four able-bodied men are all that the lifeboat will require.

"Bring most of your luggage to the deck. It will serve as ballast. The crew members—I am sending Hoskins and Dashler with you—have arranged provisions and firearms. Ten minutes."

With that, the officer swung about and went out through the door that he had entered. Hadlow arose; Jalway did the same. Together they aided Francine from her chair. The trio headed toward an inner door at the right of the oak paneling.

FRANCINE looked hopelessly toward her uncle. He smiled encouragingly. The girl departed with her companions. Professor Marcolm staggered to his feet. Gripping a corner of the inner doorway, he clung there and extended his hand to Kingdon Feldworth.

"A sorry ending to our cruise," observed the owner. "If we had left Havana a day sooner, Professor, we might have escaped this storm. I should like to go with you; but my place is here."

"The captain is right," declared the professor, in a crackly tone. "We must obey his order. Your niece will be safe, Mr. Feldworth. We shall take good care of her."

"I am counting on all of you, Professor," smiled Feldworth. "Cheer her up as much as possible. Keep assuring her that I am safe."

The professor turned and went through the inner door. Feldworth swayed across the cabin and found a chair. He was solemn as minutes passed. The outer door opened. Hoskins and Dashler entered. Both were brawny-looking fellows.

"The luggage, sir?" questioned Hoskins, speaking to the owner.

Before Feldworth could reply, Seth Hadlow appeared with two large suitcases. Then Francine arrived; behind the girl came Bram Jalway, staggering with the burden of a small but heavy steamer trunk.

As the sailors relieved him, Jalway went back and returned with a small valise. A moment later, Professor Marcolm arrived with his carpetbag and cylindrical oilskin bundle.

Donning slickers and overcoats, the passengers followed the sailors to the deck. Engines were pounding, holding the yacht in position for the launching of the lifeboat. Lanterns, held by crew members, threw a strange glow amid spray from sweeping waves.

No words were spoken. The howling of the gale made voices hopeless. The two sailors were in the lifeboat; others of the crew helped the four passengers aboard. Then came the creak of davits. The little boat lowered toward the teeming ocean.

The captain had gone to the bridge. Pounding engines were forcing the *Maldah* into the waves, bringing temporary shelter to the side where the boat was being launched. From a larger vessel, the lowering of the lifeboat might have been, disastrous. But the skipper had calculated upon the low build of the yacht.

NESTLED deep among bags and wraps, Francine Feldworth saw the white side of the yacht rise ghostlike in the wind-swept darkness. For an instant, the girl shrank back, fearing that the lifeboat would crash against that threatening wall of steel. Then the swell ended. The tiny boat twisted away.

The yacht dipped downward. The funnel loomed, distinguished by the wraith-like cloud of smoke that eddied in the wind. A wave hoisted the lifeboat like a cockleshell, hurling it clear of the disabled *Maldah*.

The menace of the launching was ended. The

lifeboat, clear away, was dipping deep into the valley of the waves. It was heading toward the darkness of the shore, leaving the *Maldah* as a row of fading lights that flickered and went out with every surge of the tumultuous sea.

Yet the hazards which the voyagers faced amid the waves were small compared to the strange menace that would lie beyond. Death was to strike amid the storm. It was fortunate that The Shadow had chosen to accompany the others to the shore.

CHAPTER V
STRANGE WELCOMES

BLACKNESS lay ahead as the lifeboat neared the shore. Four oarsmen were at work, timing their strokes as the little craft poised upon the crests of waves.

Francine had been stationed near the bow. One of the sailors had given her a flashlight. The girl was blinking the torch as a signal to those on land.

...a quick shot from the boat brought rescue from the foolhardy sailor. blade into

In response, she could see the wave of lanterns, moving toward the right along the beach.

Hadlow and Jalway were plying oars, along with the sailors. Professor Marcolm was at the stern, handling the helm. Francine could not see him through the darkness; nor could she turn the light in his direction, for its gleam would be lost to those ashore.

The girl knew that the professor was observing the lanterns from the beach. Plainly, they were signaling that safety lay to the right. The professor was handling the rudder to bear the lifeboat in that direction.

The roar of surf came from ahead. The climax of the danger would be found when the boat struck the crashing breakers. As they veered farther to the right, Francine noticed that the roar was dulling. The lights, however, were closer than before.

They were swinging a new signal, calling for

The man with the knife went staggering, just as he tried to plunge the Dashler's body.

the boat to cut in to shore. White breakers foamed in the darkness. All were to the left, the boat was escaping them. The professor was responding with the tiller. The pitch of the lifeboat lessened.

Sweeping strokes came from the oars as the craft entered the area of an even swell. Shining the light toward the water, Francine suddenly realized that they had been guided to a haven. Those signaling lights had drawn them past the end of a sandbar that must mark the entrance to a shallow inlet. They were safe from the surge of the surf.

The boat was circling the moving lights. The arrivals from the yacht passed inside the line of the beach. Hails came above the whistle of the wind. The men in the boat answered the calls from the shore.

Professor Marcolm swung the helm. The bow of the lifeboat was cutting toward the left. The boat scraped suddenly upon the sand of the bar. A slow, heaving swell drove it almost to land.

Dropping their oars, the two sailors sprang overboard, leaving the control of the boat to Hadlow and Jalway. Waist deep, they splashed past the bow, outlined by Francine's flashlight as they seized a rope to haul the boat up to the bar.

A few moments later, they were clear of the water. The bow of the boat jolted upward as Hadlow and Jalway plied the oars while the sailors pulled.

Lights were coming toward the boat. Dropping the oars, Hadlow and Jalway swung about, ready to aid in the landing. An electric lantern gleamed from among the men ashore. It showed one of the sailors—Hoskins—moving forward to meet the advancing throng.

THEN came a crackly cry of warning from the stern of the lifeboat. Professor Marcolm issued it. The others became rigid. From the group on shore, a man had sprung forward, leaping upon Hoskins. A knife blade glimmered in the light. The sailor staggered.

With that attack came spurts of flame from beside the electric lantern. Gunshots, puny in the whir of the wind, accompanied those bursts. Francine dropped into the boat as a bullet struck the gunwale. The rescuers on the shore were opening fire on the castaways from the yacht!

Dashler, the second sailor, was leaping forward squarely into the lantern's glare. Maddened when he saw Hoskins fall, Dashler was foolishly rushing to the side of his companion. He was heading into what would have been his own doom, but for the prompt action of the three men in the lifeboat.

The captain had placed loaded rifles aboard. Three guns were in the center of the boat. Hadlow, seizing two of the rifles, hurled one to the professor. Jalway, grabbing another, was the first man to open fire.

Hadlow's rifle spoke next; the professor, clutching the weapon thrown to him, also managed to join in the outburst.

As Dashler, unarmed, was suddenly pounced upon by the man who had murdered Hoskins, a quick shot from the boat brought rescue to the foolhardy sailor.

The man with the knife went staggering, just as he tried to plunge the blade into Dashler's body. The sailor tripped upon the beach as he sought to grab his crippled enemy. He formed an easy target for the fiends upon the shore. Death would have been his lot but for another timely shot from the lifeboat.

A rifle bullet found a perfect target: the electric lantern. Out went the light. All that remained were the bobbing glimmers that had been seen before. Hadlow, springing to the bow of the lifeboat, dashed the flashlight from Francine's hand. Again his rifle barked, to mingle with Jalway's fire. A flash came from the professor's gun.

Bobbing lanterns now were targets. Shots from the men on shore were wide; but the marksmen in the lifeboat were able to take aim. Lanterns went bounding to the sand as their holders threw away the telltale objects. Flashes from guns were receding. The enemy was in retreat.

In the darkness, Hadlow and Jalway each found the same idea. The two sprang overboard and floundered to the sandbar. When they reached it, they stared in vain for new flashes from the night. The enemy had fled.

The two men gave the lifeboat another drag. Francine came over the bow; Jalway carried her to the sandbar. The professor followed, gripping his rifle. He had fired only a few shots; he had ceased when the foe had fled. Dashler came stumbling back through the darkness.

"Got another gun?" queried the sailor, gruffly.

"How many were there?" demanded Jalway, in the darkness.

"Three, I think," recalled Dashler.

"Then there's no more," put in Hadlow. "What about ammunition? We've emptied our rifles."

"I don't think there's any extra cartridges," returned the sailor.

"There's some here," crackled the professor, thrusting his rifle into Dashler's hands. "I only fired three shots."

DRIZZLY wind beat upon the castaways as they realized their plight. It was lucky for them that the opposition had ended. The gun now held by Dashler was the only rifle that could be used. Huddled in a group, they waited, almost ready to return to the lifeboat. The mercy of the storm seemed better than the fierce welcome of the fiends who had awaited them.

As minutes passed, eyes strained through the darkness. Discarded lanterns had been extinguished by the wind and rain. There was no indication that the attackers intended to return. Staring seaward, the castaways saw no sign of the *Maldah*. The yacht had hoisted anchor to drive out into the storm.

A flashlight clicked. Jalway had produced it. The promoter glimmered the rays upon the lifeboat. Wading into the water, he began to bring out luggage. Hadlow aided him. Professor Marcolm remained with Francine while Dashler stood guard with the rifle.

Dragging and carrying their possessions, the little group advanced. Jalway, leading with the flashlight, came upon the body of Hoskins. The sailor was dead. Blood from his knife wound stained the dark, water-soaked sand.

The castaways moved forward. Jalway's light revealed no sign of any attackers. Evidently the fleeing men had taken their wounded along with them. Slowly, the little group neared the wide stretch of the long beach. Crossing it, they came suddenly to a fringe of trees.

They were on the edge of a thick Georgia woods, almost tropical in its density. Trees above were creaking as the wind sighed through heavy branches. Below, where the people stood, the shelter produced a lull. Voices could be understood without shouting.

Jalway threw his flashlight about the group. Francine had slumped upon the little steamer trunk; Hadlow had dragged it along from the sand bar. The professor was beside her, his hand upon the girl's shoulder.

Hadlow was extracting a cigarette from beneath his slicker, while Dashler was standing amid a cluster of luggage. The sailor had his rifle in readiness. He had brought along the two emptied weapons. They were lying on the fringe of the sand.

"These woods are our best refuge," informed Jalway, in a voice that was steady in the lull. "If we can find some sort of opening among them, we can make camp for the night. You hold the flashlight, Professor. Francine can remain with you while we scout about."

Professor Marcolm received the flashlight. He extinguished it as the other men moved off through the darkness. Then he flashed it with intermittent blinks. Five minutes passed. Suddenly Hadlow returned.

"Wave the light, Professor," he ordered. "Bring in the others. I've found something."

"A path?" questioned Francine.

"Better than that," replied Hadlow. "A house. I saw the lights in the woods."

JALWAY and Dashler arrived while Hadlow was pointing out the direction in which he had investigated. The professor's waving of the flashlight brought them in. The sailor offered an objection when he heard Hadlow's plan to proceed to the house.

"Maybe that's their hangout," he insisted. "They might get us like they got Hoskins. I'd like to get square with the fellows that killed my matey; but it ain't policy to walk into their camp."

"The rogues fled along the beach," reminded Hadlow. "This house is in the direction of the inlet. In my opinion, it offers safety rather than danger."

"That sounds likely," put in Jalway. "What is your opinion, Professor?"

"The same as Hadlow's," crackled Marcolm. "Come, my friends. Let us fare toward this habitation."

Leaving the luggage, the group followed Hadlow's lead. Using the flashlight, the sportsman picked out a path at the entrance to the woods. The glare showed a narrow but clean-cut passage. Hadlow turned out the light and spoke.

"There's the glimmer." His voice was solemn beneath the shelter of the swaying, creaking oaks. "Unquestionably a house. Suppose that Jalway and I go in advance. You follow, Professor, with Francine."

"What about me?" asked Dashler.

"Stay in the background," ordered Hadlow. "Cover with your rifle. If we run into trouble, you can open fire to protect us."

SHOULDER to shoulder, Hadlow and Jalway advanced. They came to a clearing where the white tabby walls of an old building showed its spectral bulk among the trees. The lighted windows had been at the side. Here, only the whiteness of the house was visible. Reaching a stout oak door, Hadlow knocked.

A long pause. The wind sighed heavily through the trees, then whistled eerily as its angry gusts rose violently in the night. Hadlow rapped again. The drawing of bolts followed. The door opened.

Just within the threshold stood a huge, big-fisted man whose face was fierce and challenging. Light from the hall showed the water-soaked visitors. The big man eyed them with a glare that was not pleasant.

Close by the trees, Marcolm and Francine could see the man's face plainly. So could Dashler. The sailor shifted his rifle. The professor stretched out a hand to withhold him. Listening, they could hear the growled challenge of the man within the door.

"What you want here?"

The voice was thick and uncouth. Hadlow's reply was a quiet one that the listeners could not hear; but they caught snatches of Jalway's steady tone. The castaways were explaining their plight. Their story brought results. The big man stepped back and motioned them to enter.

Jalway turned and signaled. Professor Marcolm led the others to the house. They followed Hadlow and Jalway into a lighted hallway. The big guardian eyed Dashler's rifle in suspicious fashion, then closed the door and bolted it. He departed through the hallway, leaving the little group talking in puzzled whispers.

A few minutes passed. Then the big man returned from the rear of the hallway. He opened a door on the right, turned on a light and ushered the arrivals into a living room. Francine gasped in amazement. The others looked around in surprise.

They had expected to find small comfort in this island home. Instead, they discovered a living room that was almost sumptuous. Comfortable chairs and lounges stood upon handsome Oriental rugs. Heavy oak bookcases were filled with volumes; these stood upon either side of a fireplace.

EACH viewer studied a different portion of the room, admiring its contents. One pair of eyes, however, found a focal spot that others scarcely noticed. Those eyes were The Shadow's. Still maintaining his guise of a castaway, the master sleuth gave no expression that anyone could have detected.

The Shadow was looking toward a mantelpiece above the fireplace; he was viewing an object that hung from the wall over the mantel. To others, it was but an ornament—tasteful and inconspicuous. To The Shadow, it was a symbol that marked the end of an important quest which he had not yet undertaken.

The Shadow had left the *Maldah* knowing that all was safe on board. He had wanted to reach shore, that he might fare forth in search of George Dalavan, the murderer whom he had encountered near Miami; through finding Dalavan, The Shadow had hoped to uncover the supercrook whom the murderer served.

There had been murderers on this shore; but even to The Shadow, their presence had not signified a link to the coming quest. Until he viewed this living room, The Shadow had gained no inkling of connected crime. He had it here, the link he wanted. Above the mahogany plaque; upon its square surface was a design done in bronze.

The plaque represented a shield, supported on each side by a gryphon. The design was a perfect match for the embossing imprinted upon the sheet of paper that The Shadow had found in the dead hand of James Tolwig.

This house on the Georgia coast was the headquarters of the supercrook who controlled dozens of rogues like Dalavan; the man who managed a ring that dealt in international theft, wholesale smuggling, and open murder.

A voice spoke from the doorway of the room. With the others, The Shadow turned about to meet the owner of the house. Playing his role of a chance castaway, The Shadow was face to face with the master crook whom he had not expected to meet for a long while to come.

CHAPTER VI
THE UNSEEN GUEST

THE man in the doorway did not look the part of a master criminal. His appearance was quite the opposite; it ended any apprehensions held by The Shadow's companions. Pleasant of voice, friendly in attitude, the master of the lonely house was one who knew how to make his guests feel at home.

He was portly and bald-headed; his face was wreathed in a smile. He was attired in a green silk dressing gown; in his hand he held a meerschaum pipe that he had been smoking. There was nothing to connect him with the fray on the beach; but The Shadow knew that this genial individual was certainly responsible for all crime that might strike upon the isle.

"Good evening." The portly man spoke in a half-chuckled tone. "My name is Purvis Elger. It is not often that I am honored with unexpected guests. Allow me to welcome you to my humble abode."

Another servant stepped up behind Elger. He was tall and cadaverous—a contrast to the huge, big-fisted fellow who had been at the door. Elger ordered the pair to bring in the luggage that the castaways had carried with them. Bowing, shaking hands, Elger himself ushered the guests to their individual rooms. He suggested that they change their attire, then join him in the living room.

Soon afterward, the group assembled, wearing dry clothes. Puffing at his meerschaum, Elger listened to their story, then spoke.

"The yacht should come safely to harbor," he declared. "There are many inlets along this coast. The *Maldah* will find haven. As for the strange attack that took place upon the beach, it is something that can be definitely explained."

PAUSING, Elger puffed his meerschaum. He

PURVIS ELGER —master crook whom The Shadow is seeking

studied Bram Jalway, who was languid and half smiling; ready, apparently, to believe what his host might have to say. Elger noted Professor Marcolm; he saw an absentminded look upon the savant's features. Eyeing Seth Hadlow, Elger observed a serious countenance. He felt sure that he could convince the sportsman with the coming explanation.

"This isle," announced Elger, "is but one of many that line the Georgia coast. It is called Timour Isle; it once formed a colonial plantation. The manor house was in the center of the isle. This building was a lookout house, almost a fortress. The slave quarters were on the opposite side of the isle.

"All was ruin when I came here. Jungle had overgrown the remains of the other buildings. But the tabby walls of this lookout house were partly standing. Though built of shell, sand and lime, they survived the elements; and their proximity to the beach prevented overgrowth. I restored the building; I am still enlarging it. Meanwhile, I have lived here, devoting myself to study."

Elger nudged toward the hallway with his meerschaum pipe.

"My den," he added, "is at the back of the house. I spend most of my time there. I have two servants. Golga, the one who admitted you, stays on duty at night. Royne serves as cook and does day duty. The windows"—Elger gave a sweep of his hand—"are barred. The reason for such protection is because outlaws sometimes visit this isle and those that adjoin it."

"The men on the beach!" exclaimed Francine. "They were outlaws?"

Elger nodded.

"I speak of them as outlaws," he declared. "Some are fugitives from justice. Others are merely treasure seekers; but of a disreputable sort. The fugitives come here because the marshland between the isles and the mainland are an obstacle to searchers. As for the treasure hunters, they count on the fact that such pirates as Abraham and Blackbeard once used these islands as headquarters."

"Famous pirates, those," put in Jalway. "Do you think that Abraham and Blackbeard actually buried treasure here?"

"Possibly," returned Elger. "There is also a chance that colonial inhabitants of these isles buried their own valuables to keep pirates from finding them. Anyway, the treasure hunters come here; and they often fight with other groups who have the same quest.

"Those murderers whom you encountered were either outlaws who decided that you might be bringing valuables ashore; or they were members of a treasure-seeking band who looked upon you as rivals. In either case, they probably did not expect that you would be armed."

"Isn't it dangerous, living here?" queried Francine. "Those outlaws might attack this house at any time!"

"No," stated Elger, "they are skulkers. Real criminals who hide out along this coast do not come in bands. They would be too few to make an attack. The riff-raff come in numbers, to dig about for buried wealth. They would pillage an empty house, if they found one. But they are too fearful of the law to attempt an actual attack.

"They saw a chance to prey upon persons whom they thought would be helpless. Probably they have fled to the other end of the island, to take a boat that they have hidden in the marsh. But there is always the danger of encountering individual prowlers hereabouts. While you are my guests, I must insist that you remain indoors after dark."

SOMETHING in Elger's final sentence made Francine look about in wonderment. Bram Jalway understood the girl's expression. He smiled slightly as he spoke.

"Mr. Elger has informed us," said Jalway, "that communication with the mainland is impossible and will be for some days to come. The storm is rising to hurricane intensity. Even the back channels might prove difficult to navigate."

"And the roads on the mainland," added Elger, "will be impossible. It would be futile for any of you to leave here. While you are my guests"—his pleasant smile broadened—"this house will be yours. We are well stocked with provisions. There are plenty of books to read. Only one thing is lacking."

"A radio?" questioned Francine, looking about the room.

"You have guessed it," laughed Elger. "I ordered one; but its shipment was delayed. A little boat comes over from the mainland, once or twice a week; but we cannot expect it to arrive until after the storm has subsided. So we shall have no radio."

"I don't mind," declared the girl, with a smile. "To me, Mr. Elger, this is the most wonderful house that I have ever seen. Fancy finding it in this lonely spot. I was merely worried about my uncle. That was all. I had hoped that we could notify the coast guards that the *Maldah* is in distress."

Golga and Royne appeared just as the girl finished speaking. The big servant spoke to Elger while the cadaverous man stood by. Elger turned solemnly to his guests

"They have brought in the sailor's body," said Elger. "It is locked in the construction house, with the tools that the workmen left here. I suggest that we leave the body there until we can inform the authorities. Is that agreeable?"

He was looking from one man to another, not knowing which one to accept as the leader of the group. Catching nods from all concerned, Elger spoke to Golga. The servant handed his master a bunch of keys.

Royne had already left the living room. As conversation resumed, the cadaverous servant returned bringing a large tray laden with coffee and sandwiches. Elger waved his hand toward the refreshments.

"Help yourselves," he said. "Make yourselves entirely at home. You have your rooms. Retire when you please. In the meantime, I shall ask you to excuse me. I have been working tonight on problems in non-Euclidean geometry, and I should like to resume my studies."

THE castaways did justice to the coffee and sandwiches. The constant whistling of the increasing gale seemed remote in this secluded spot. Refreshments ended, the group relaxed. Professor Marcolm arose and smiled.

"I have studies of my own," he remarked, "but I shall forego them tonight. I am going to bed. Good night."

"Not a bad idea," grunted Dashler as the professor departed. The sailor had been sitting silently in a corner. "I've got a bunk and I'm going to use it."

The others chatted for a short while after Dashler had left. Then they, too, decided to retire. Hadlow and Jalway had been given rooms on opposite sides of the hall, while Francine's room was across from the professor's.

Royne, the cadaverous servant, had disappeared. It was Golga who came into the living room after the guests had all retired. The big servant began to gather up cups and plates. That task completed, he turned out the light and carried the tray along the hall toward the kitchen, which was at the rear of the long, low building.

Only the rear hall was lighted. It formed a dim corridor past the doorways of rooms where the guests were stationed. While creepy, whistling winds wailed unrelenting about the secluded house, a cloaked figure emerged from the blackness of the front hall. It was The Shadow; ghostlike in his glide, he moved along the rear hallway.

A light glimmered beneath a door. With noiseless stride, The Shadow reached the doorway. His gloved hand moved forward; it gripped the doorknob and moved the door inward, inch by inch. The Shadow peered into the room that Purvis Elger had termed his "den."

To the others from the *Maldah*, that abode was merely the private quarters of a man who chose the life of a recluse. To The Shadow, this den was the lair of a cunning supercrook, identified by the gryphon plaque upon the living room wall.

The den looked like a study. A desk was piled high with books. Other volumes lay upon a lounge. The walls of the room were lined with bookcases, which held more volumes than the shelves that The Shadow had seen in the living room.

The den was empty; but a light from a half-opened door indicated an inner bedroom. Elger had gone there. Taking advantage of the supercrook's absence, The Shadow entered the den and closed the door from the hall.

A heavy bookcase ended near a corner. The space formed a niche against the wall. The Shadow glided in that direction; he became a tall shape of motionless black, as he took to the improvised hiding place. From here, The Shadow could peer straight toward the half-closed door of the bedroom.

The barrier opened as he watched. Elger came out and went to the desk. He began to consult an opened book that lay there. He was interrupted by a knock at the door from the hall.

Elger spoke. The door opened. Golga entered. The servant's face wore a cunning gleam. Elger noted it and smiled.

"They have all retired?" he questioned, softly.

"Yes," growled Golga.

"Turn in then," ordered Elger. "I shall talk with you in the morning."

Golga departed. As soon as the servant was gone, Elger arose and went to the door. He locked it, then extinguished the light. He crossed the den and entered the bedroom, leaving the door partly opened.

THE SHADOW moved from his hiding place. Stealthy in the darkness, he followed Elger's course. He peered into the bedroom. Elger had removed his dressing gown; he was donning coat and vest, all that he required to be fully clad.

Besides a bureau and a bed, this room boasted

a bookcase in an obscure corner. These shelves appeared to be stocked with the overflow of volumes from the den; but The Shadow noted that the books were lined in perfect order. That indicated some other purpose; for Elger, if he used those books, would probably have allowed them to reach a stage of disarray.

The real purpose of the bookcase became apparent as Elger approached that corner of the room. Removing one volume, the portly man pressed a hidden spring. The bookcase swung outward, like a hinged door. Beyond it loomed a blackened passage.

Elger entered. His bald head moved downward. The man was descending steep steps. Hardly had he disappeared before the bookcase closed automatically. At the same instant, the light went out in the bedroom.

A soft laugh in the darkness. The Shadow's cloak *swished* slightly as his form moved forward. A tiny flashlight glimmered. A gloved hand found the book that Elger had removed. The Shadow drew the volume forth, then probed the space where it had been.

A *click*. The Shadow stepped back as the bookcase opened. Musty, dampened air issued forth from the staircase in the wall. Moments passed; then that atmosphere ended. The bookcase had closed. The room was silent.

The Shadow, alert upon the trail, was following the course that Purvis Elger had taken. He was on his way to learn the secret that lay beneath this house on Timour Isle.

CHAPTER VII
CAVERNS OF WEALTH

A TINY flashlight glimmered amid inky blackness. A soft laugh came from hidden lips. The light went out. Stealthily, The Shadow swished forward through a passage that was low and long beneath the ground.

The Shadow had reached the bottom of the hidden stairway. Waiting there, he listened to the sound of fading footfalls from ahead. Positive that Purvis Elger had left this dank corridor, the black-garbed investigator was again taking up the trail.

At intervals the flashlight blinked, its small circle directed toward the rough stone floor of the passage. Though hidden traps seemed unlikely, The Shadow was taking no chances in his pursuit.

As he proceeded, however, he became confident that the only secret of this corridor was its hidden entrance. Oozing spaces between the stones showed that the moist ground offered no possibilities of a hidden pitfall.

The passage ended one hundred yards from the house. The Shadow encountered a stone wall in the darkness. Instead of using his flashlight, The Shadow waited in the gloom; then he sensed a slight draught from the right. That indicated another corridor. Groping, The Shadow found the passage.

A few rods brought him to another barrier. This was a door, sheathed with metal. Cautiously, The Shadow opened it. Dim light greeted his keen eyes. The Shadow was in a square-walled cavern, which was hazily illuminated by the glow from an opening beyond.

Dim shapes stood by the wall. Burnished surfaces reflected the dim glow. Eyeing these figures, The Shadow discerned that they were suits of armor, standing like rigid sentinels. They were not the only objects in the cavern.

Large chests were stacked along the wall. Upon them rested several vases that gleamed dully in the light. In a corner stood a group of metal cylinders. The Shadow could guess the nature of their contents: rolled-up paintings, stowed in these tubes to prevent injury from dampness.

Passing the metal sentinels, The Shadow reached the opening beyond. From darkness, he gazed into a second, smaller cavern. This room contained a few odd chests; beyond it was the opening to a larger, darkened room.

MOST important, however, were the living occupants of the middle room. Two men were seated upon chests; the glow of a lantern showed their faces. One was Purvis Elger; the other was a hard-faced, roughly clad fellow, with bristly, unshaven cheeks.

The Shadow had seen that countenance before. Elger's companion was a New York mob-leader, known as "Ruff" Turney. He had disappeared from Manhattan some months ago. Rumor had it that Ruff had been slain in a wholesale mob killing.

Blended with the darkness of the room that he had crossed, The Shadow waited, listening. He had caught the sound of voices during his advance; now he could distinguish the words that passed between the men whom he had uncovered. Purvis Elger was talking in a testy tone.

"You knew my orders, Ruff," announced the portly man. "There was no excuse for that attack on the lifeboat. You should have given the word to scatter."

"That's what I did," growled Ruff. "But it was too late. We got fooled, chief. It wasn't until the sailor came running up that we knew those mugs weren't from the *Dalmatia*."

"You should not have been on the beach at all. I told you that the *Dalmatia* would anchor off the lower inlet."

"We saw the lights from there, chief. Then the ship anchored farther up. We figured the captain had missed his bearings. That's why we went out to the beach and sent up our rockets."

"I told you that the *Dalmatia* was a tramp steamer, like the others that have anchored off here."

"I know that. That's what we thought the ship was. We saw a line of lights, coming up and down with the waves."

"A low line?"

"Sure. Kind of low, but the way they went up and down, it was hard to figure them. Say—what was the boat, anyway?"

"A yacht. The *Maldah*, owned by a shoe manufacturer named Kingdon Feldworth. And you and your outfit mistook it for a tramp steamer!"

ELGER ended his utterance with a contemptuous snort. Ruff Turney's bristly face showed a sour expression. The mob-leader stroked his chin; then grunted an excuse.

"If you'd been out on the beach, chief," he said, "maybe you'd have been fooled, too. We couldn't figure how far out the ship was. Just lights—that's all. Looked like a hundred-to-one shot on it being the *Dalmatia*."

"That part is excusable," decided Elger. "In fact, everything was all right up to the time of the attack. But that was the big mistake. You started too much trouble."

"I didn't start it, chief. The outfit thought it was coast guards, when the sailor came running up. Nicky yanked a knife before I could stop him. He stabbed the sailor."

"And after that?"

"The rest of the mob began to fire. At the boat. But those birds were sharpshooters. They dropped Nicky. They plugged our searchlight. They clipped Hungry when we started to beat it. We brought Nicky and Hungry along with us."

"Seriously injured?"

Ruff scowled as he heard Elger's question.

"Dead," informed the mob-leader. "Both of 'em. That cuts the crew down to four. I left 'em over in the cabin of the boat."

"Anchored in the swamp?"

"Sure. Back of the old ruins where the slave houses used to be. I came in alone through the big passage. Don't worry, chief. Nobody's going to spot that boat of ours."

"There is no occasion to worry," declared Elger. "The people from the lifeboat found my house; so I welcomed them. Golga and Royne brought the sailor's body into the construction house."

"Want us to snatch it out of there?" inquired Ruff. "There won't be any evidence if we do."

"No evidence," snorted Elger, "except the testimony of five persons who saw the sailor die. We shall keep the body where it is, Ruff; later, I shall inform the law of what occurred on the beach. My position is a perfect one. I am a respectable citizen who had chosen the life of a recluse.

"No one knows that my lookout house has a passage that leads to these caverns, under the ruins of the leveled mansion. Nor do they know that these caverns are also connected with the ruins of the old slave buildings."

"It's a great setup, chief."

"It is. But its worth depends upon a complete separation between myself and your band. Should the law come here, I can state that questionable characters have been about. In doing so, I can divert search from your actual hiding place.

"As an emergency measure, you and your men could abandon the boat and hide out in these caverns. But it is best to create the impression that nothing is wrong on Timour Isle. Unfortunately, your crew injured that situation tonight."

Ruff grunted, then put a suggestion.

"We bumped off the sailor," he growled. "Why not rub out the crowd? Then there'd be nobody left to talk."

"That would be unwise," returned Elger, dryly. "At least, for the present. The yacht managed to steam out to sea. If it comes to safety, those aboard will institute a search for those who came ashore. The captain will give the exact location of this isle. If the castaways are found alive, my position will be strengthened.

"Should the *Maldah* flounder, as I hope it will, the news will reach us. We can then dispose of our unwelcome guests. The world will believe that they went down with the yacht. In either event, we shall have several days to wait. The hurricane has not abated."

AS Elger paused, a ticking sound came from a box at the rear of the cavern. It was a telegraph sounder. Elger read the clicks, then turned to Ruff, whose blank look showed that he was unacquainted with telegraph codes.

"From the shack on the mainland," stated Elger. "Tully says he has picked up a wireless from the *Dalmatia*. The ship is putting into Charleston. It will probably stay there until the hurricane is over."

Approaching the box, Elger busied himself with a telegraph key. He notified Tully that he had received the message. That done, the bald-headed crook turned about with a complacent smile.

"Tully will keep us posted," he stated. "Since the *Dalmatia* is bound for Tampico, Mexico, it will unload no freight in Charleston. It will not come under inspection. The *Dalmatia* will bring us our last cargo. We shall hold our trophies here, then ship them ashore after construction begins at my house. Loaded boxes will go to the mainland on the construction barges."

"It may be tough, chief," interposed Ruff, "unloading all this swag. Dalavan got into trouble down in Miami."

"That was an exceptional case," retorted Elger. "Dalavan is safe in New York. Once he arrives here, he and I can arrange to dispose of treasures wholesale. Dalavan can line up plenty of other men like himself."

"Dalavan is a smooth guy, chief."

Elger sat thoughtful; suddenly he chuckled.

"Since the *Dalmatia* is in Charleston," he remarked, "I shall have Dalavan board the tramp steamer there and accompany the final shipment when it comes ashore at Timour Isle."

With that decision, Elger began to puff his meerschaum, eyeing Ruff Turney. A crafty look came into Elger's gaze; The Shadow could see the glint of the supercrook's eyes. Elger had decided that he had talked enough. He waved his hand as a dismissal to Ruff Turney. As Ruff arose to depart, Elger added final words:

"Lay low with the crew, Ruff. Report here as usual. I shall contact you personally, or through Golga or Royne. I shall hold my guests until after the *Dalmatia* has unloaded. Meanwhile, Tully will learn the fate of the *Maldah*. The lives of my guests will depend upon what happens to the yacht."

AS Ruff departed, Purvis Elger indulged in a smug smile. The master crook was pleased. In this cavern, surrounded by millions of dollars' worth of stolen, imported wealth, Elger felt an absolute security. He was unperturbed because his house had gained unwelcome guests. Elger was confident that he could handle any opposition.

During his conversation with Ruff, Elger had heard the hardened crew leader mention trouble that Dalavan had encountered in Miami. Apparently that news had been flashed through from Tully some time ago; and Elger considered it of little consequence, even though it had involved The Shadow. Evidently, Dalavan had reported a perfect getaway, stating that his identity was unknown to The Shadow.

Yet The Shadow had learned the name of George Dalavan; he had gained it here, in the very headquarters of the master crook whom Dalavan served. Purvis Elger, with all his confidence, would have been overwhelmed with astoundment had he realized that he, himself, was under the keen observation of The Shadow.

It would be a while, however, before Elger would guess that The Shadow was present on Timour Isle. Elger had decided to play a waiting game. Learning that fact, The Shadow had chosen to adopt a similar policy.

There was much to learn, here on Timour Isle. There would be loose threads to gather, before the final stroke. The more that Elger planned, the better it would please The Shadow.

CHAPTER VIII
THE SHADOW ACTS

NONE of Purvis Elger's detailed methods had escaped The Shadow. While he remained on vigil, the master sleuth summarized new facts that he had learned; and added them to those that he had previously gained.

For some time, Europe had been stirred by robberies in England and the continent. Rare paintings had been filched from museums, priceless treasures stolen from palaces. Relics such as archeological trophies and suits of armor had disappeared. Many other items of immense value were gone.

Those items could not have been fenced in Europe, but it was possible to dispose of them in America, to private collectors who would say nothing. It was also a simple matter to ship them to South America and the Orient, for disposal there; but that could only be done from the United States.

The real game had been to get the treasures to America. The Shadow had known that when he had heard of the Lamballe tiara, mentioned by chance while he was in Havana. He had immediately surmised that James Tolwig, the intended purchaser, would be approached by a member of the thieving, smuggling ring. George Dalavan had been such an agent.

How had the goods come to America?

The Shadow had suspected the answer; at last he had found it. Tramp steamers, putting out from

European ports, had carried the stolen goods in their cargoes. The European authorities had counted on all ships being inspected at receiving ports; hence, they had not supposed that the stolen treasures would be aboard such vessels.

Elger had managed the shipments by having the ships pass this isolated section of the Georgia coast. There, they had unloaded the swag; Ruff Turney and his crew had received it and brought each shipment ashore in their small boat. One more cargo would complete the job; it would come by the *Dalmatia*.

ANOTHER point impressed The Shadow. Long ago, Elger must have done some treasure hunting of his own. On Timour Isle, he had uncovered the ruins of the old manor house; he had discovered the secret vaults and passages. The caverns and their underground routes dated from colonial days, when they had been used in case of pirate raids.

Naturally, the manor house had been the focal point, with passages leading to the slave quarters and the lookout house. Elger had simply changed the arrangement. He kept the look-out as his own abode; he had Ruff and the receiving crew back in the swamp, near the site of the vanished slave quarters.

The caverns were doubly protected; either Elger or Ruff could come to them. Far apart, there seemed no connection between the two groups of inhabitants on Timour Isle.

Elger had already fenced some swag through Dalavan, as a "feeler" for the future. That meant a contact; and Elger had one. A telegraph cable led through the swamp to the mainland. Near some town was Tully, the telegrapher, ready to relay messages anywhere. Tully also had a receiving station for wireless messages; thus he had learned about the *Dalmatia* and would gain facts regarding the *Maldah*.

While The Shadow watched Elger, the portly crook finished his reverie. He carefully dumped the ashes from his meerschaum and placed the pipe in his pocket. That done, Elger turned to the telegraph key and tapped a message with his pudgy hand. The Shadow read the clicks, which were sent in Morse.

Elger gave the names of the persons who had arrived on Timour Isle. He stated that they would remain as his guests for the present. He instructed Tully to gain information regarding the yacht *Maldah*. Elger added orders that concerned George Dalavan.

The taps of the key told Tully to send a letter to New York by the night mail, instructing Dalavan to come to Timour Isle. Elger forwarded the suggestion that Dalavan travel to Charleston and board the *Dalmatia* there. He added, however, that such procedure would be optional. Should Dalavan prefer, he could come to the isle by the usual route.

Elger did not specify details regarding the "usual route." It probably meant that Dalavan had formerly come to some town in Georgia, perhaps the one where Tully was located, and from there had reached Timour Isle by a small boat.

Through such expeditions, Dalavan had doubtlessly received the Lamballe tiara and other valuable items, which he had taken along to peddle to close-mouthed curio collectors. It was evident to The Shadow that Dalavan had been confident that he had left no trail from Miami; otherwise, the murderer would have headed for the safety of Timour Isle. Unquestionably, Dalavan had discounted the importance of the sheet of paper that he had been forced to leave at James Tolwig's.

In suggesting that Dalavan come by the *Dalmatia*, Elger was making allowance for the hurricane. There would be a chance that the usual route would be closed for some days after the storm, as Georgia roads are frequently flooded after heavy rains.

His orders completed, Elger arose and turned directly toward the cavern where The Shadow stood. As he stepped forward, the crook did not spy the tall form of the onlooker.

The Shadow faded away before Elger arrived. He chose a darkened spot behind the suits of armor; there, The Shadow waited while Elger went through the cavern and chose the passage back to the lookout house.

DARKNESS followed Elger's departure, for the crook took the lantern with him. Soon, The Shadow's flashlight carved the blackness. Entering the central cavern, The Shadow focused the gleam upon the telegraph key.

A low laugh whispered through the musty air. Gloved fingers pressed the telegraph key. It clicked; then came a pause. Again, The Shadow tapped. There was a response from the other end. The Shadow began to send a message. His taps were a perfect copy of Elger's leisurely style.

"Add in letter to Dalavan," ordered The Shadow. "Obtain information regarding preferred stock Argentum Silver Mines. Learn if any is available at nineteen.

"Also inquire about Eastern Zinc, Incorporated. Selling at twelve and one quarter. Make inquiries through Rutledge Mann, investment broker, Badger Building, New York.

"Ask for information on Consolidated

Securities; send immediate report on same. Tell Dalavan to approach Mann as a possible client who has learned of these investments."

The Shadow waited while Tully's reply ticked back. The man on the mainland was repeating the message. He had taken it as a bonafide order from Elger.

The tiny flashlight cut a line of illumination across the central vault as The Shadow made his way toward the exit that Ruff had taken. Passing into the next cavern, the investigator discovered another store of valuables.

Here were other chests. The Shadow lifted one and judged from its weight that it contained metal, probably gold or silver plate. Upon a box in the corner of the room stood a cluster of bronze and silver statuettes. Against another wall was an upright mummy case.

Apparently, Purvis Elger had used many connections with continental thieves in order to acquire this hoard of valuables. Recalling the rogue's conversation with Ruff, The Shadow estimated that at least a dozen shipments must have been taken ashore at Timour Isle.

A DOOR led from this cavern. It was locked, to close the path that Ruff had taken. The flashlight's gleam focused upon a keyhole. A gloved hand moved forward, carrying a blackened metal pick. The Shadow probed the lock.

The door yielded. The Shadow stepped through and locked it from the other side. His flashlight glimmered to show a passage wider than the one that led to Elger's house. This had evidently been used—years ago—for the removal of valuables to the safety of the swamp.

This passage was also longer than the other. When The Shadow reached the end of it, he found himself in a low cellar. His light showed a flight of steps in the corner. Moving upward, The Shadow encountered a heavy trapdoor. He raised it and emerged into the night.

Winds whistled fiercely through the trees that sheltered this spot. Moist, matted underbrush settled soggily in place as The Shadow lowered the trap. He had come from one of the cellars in the old slave quarters. The entrance was hidden by clustered jungle weeds that rested on it.

A glimmer of the flashlight showed a tangle of cypress roots that formed a higher level. In darkness, The Shadow stepped upward, then paused abruptly. From close by, he heard a squdgy sound; indication of a footstep in swampy ground. The Shadow waited; the next token was a scrape against a cypress root. The Shadow wheeled; shot both hands into the darkness.

The move was timely. A bulky figure hurtled upon The Shadow. A snarl came from the attacker's lips as The Shadow grappled. It was not Ruff Turney's tone. This fighter was an underling, like "Nicky" and "Hungry," the two who had been slain on the beach. The fellow had merely chanced upon The Shadow.

Luck served the attacker. Twisting away, The Shadow backed against a cypress; lost his footing and came to one knee. Hamlike hands clutched for his throat; The Shadow gave a gasp that brought a pleased snarl from his antagonist. The thug choked harder, ignoring the clutch of The Shadow's hands upon his arms.

That was all The Shadow needed. His grip tightened; he shot his body upward like a trip hammer. His shoulders hoisted backward; the attacker was propelled headlong by the sudden jujitsu thrust.

It came so forcefully that the thug lost his finger grip upon The Shadow's throat. A surprised snarl sounded as the crook took his six-foot dive; there was a crackling of underbrush, followed by a dull crash some distance below.

Crawling down beside the cypress roots, The Shadow used his flashlight to discover an opening in the junglelike growth. The gleam displayed a pit, eight feet deep; at the bottom lay a twisted figure, back upward, but with goggle-eyed face turned full about.

The thug had plunged through a third layer of overgrowth into a forgotten cellar. His head had struck the stone floor; his neck had been broken in the crash. It was plain that his death had been instant.

THE SHADOW extinguished his light. He took to the marshy ground; changed course to seek a higher level. Picking a direction through vines and brambles, he reached a spot where the howling winds increased; and the roar of surf came with crashing tumult.

The Shadow had gained the beach, above the lower inlet. He took a course beneath the fringing trees. Shrouded beneath the overhanging branches of oaks, the weird prowler moved toward the lookout house. Reaching the building, The Shadow skirted the tabby walls to arrive at a side window of the living room.

There, he found outside bars, set in a frame held by heavy screws. The Shadow produced a small combination tool that served as screwdriver. He loosened the framework and removed it.

The Shadow had anticipated this easy entry. He knew that Elger had no need for barred windows; these frames were a mere pretense, to build up Elger's claim that he was a recluse who feared prowlers.

A bulky figure hurtled upon The Shadow.... Hamlike hands clutched for his throat.

The Shadow opened the clamped window sash by means of a thin metal wedge. Entering the house, he replaced the barred frame; then clamped the window. He blended with the blackness of the living room.

Soon, motion ceased within the silent house.

Only the banshee-like wail of the hurricane remained. Howling winds seemed angered as they twisted among mighty trees that thwarted their wrath. Those winds alone carried the secret of The Shadow's presence on Timour Isle.

Tomorrow, Ruff Turney would find his crew another man short. Discovery of the body would not indicate a fray. It would look as though the dead thug had stumbled over the cypress roots in the darkness, to accidentally plunge into the pit.

One man more or less did not concern The Shadow. Though he was stranded on this lonely isle, like the other castaways, he had accomplished much. He had listened in on Elger's schemes; he had seen the wealth that the master crook had hidden; he had learned the identity of George Dalavan.

Most important, however, was the fact that The Shadow, like Purvis Elger, had gained contact with the outside world. The supercrook could move distant men into action; and he had done so. The Shadow, by his added message, had accomplished the same.

In New York, The Shadow had agents of his own. He had sent them information through Elger's own outlet.

The carrier of The Shadow's message would be none other than George Dalavan!

CHAPTER IX
THE NEXT NIGHT

A NEW evening had arrived on Timour Isle. The castaways were gathered in Elger's living room. Seth Hadlow and Bram Jalway were chatting while they smoked. Francine Feldworth was curled up on a couch reading a volume from a bookshelf. Professor Marcolm was at a desk in the corner, working problems on a chessboard, while Dashler was playing solitaire upon the window seat.

Ceaseless winds were wailing; tonight their intensity seemed greater than before. The captain of the *Maldah* had spoken wisely when he had predicted that the storm would increase. Purvis Elger's statement that it would be impossible to reach the mainland was borne out by the added fury of the tempest.

Elger had dined with his guests. After that, he had retired to his study. At intervals he dropped into the living room, always puffing at his meerschaum. Golga, too, was occasionally about.

"I'm turning in early," remarked Jalway to Hadlow. "This storm is endless. The only way to forget it is to sleep."

"Unless you're in the middle of it," returned Hadlow. "I'll wager that it's doubly bad out on the beach tonight. We're lucky that we came ashore when we did."

"One satisfaction," reminded Jalway. "It will be a tough night for those rogues who attacked us. I doubt that they will venture on the beach tonight."

"The trees are sheltering, though," said Hadlow. "It would be no trick at all to move about the island if one kept to the fringe of the woods."

A clatter came from the writing desk. Professor Marcolm was putting the chessmen away in their box. Rising, the white-haired castaway closed his board. He crossed the room, paused to mumble a good night, then continued on through the hall.

"The professor must have gained my copyright idea," remarked Jalway, with a slight smile. "I'm sure he didn't hear me say that sleep was the best procedure on a night like this. Well, I'm copying his example. Good night, all."

Jalway arose and departed. Hadlow finished a cigarette, then arose, stretched his long arms and spoke to the others. Francine looked up from her book; seeing that three of the castaways had decided to turn in, the girl tucked her book under one arm and followed shortly after Hadlow.

Dashler finished his game of solitaire. He looked about and shrugged his shoulders. The sailor felt the room chilling and oppressive with his companions gone. Gathering up the playing cards, he went to his room.

A DOZEN minutes passed. Golga entered the lighted room and looked about. Finding that all had retired, the big servant extinguished the light and went to the back hall. There he entered a room of his own and seated himself stolidly in a chair.

Half an hour passed. It was Golga's job, apparently, to maintain this vigil, unless otherwise directed by Elger. The servant did not seem to mind it. But when the clock on his table was pointing to the hour of eleven, Golga arose as though by plan. He went back into the rear hall. There, he noted a light from beneath the door of Elger's study. Golga kept on to the front.

There, the servant noted another light from beneath the door of Francine's room. He recalled that the girl had been reading a book. Probably she had stayed up after the others had gone to bed. Golga kept on past silent doorways. Suddenly, he paused. A slight, whistling noise came to his ears.

Golga entered the living room. He turned on the light. He heard the same noise again; from the rear corner. Advancing there, the servant made a prompt discovery. The corner window was unlocked; more than that, it was slightly raised.

Wind, whining about the tabby walls despite the shelter of the trees, had caused that whistling. Golga could feel the puffs of outside air. As he reached the window, he noted also that the outer bars had been removed.

Golga paused abruptly. He turned, quickly went back across the living room and extinguished the light. He crept along the front hall, stopping at every door. First, Seth Hadlow's. There, by chance, Golga heard a motion from within, as of the occupant turning in his bed. He also caught a slight sound that sounded like a cough.

Stopping outside of Bram Jalway's door, Golga heard no sound at all. He rested his hand upon the knob, and then changed his mind. He moved farther along the hall and stopped at the professor's door.

No sound from within. Carefully, Golga turned the knob. He opened the door and entered. He could see the professor's form in the bed; he also spied the whiteness of the man's hair upon the pillows. The professor stirred. Golga backed out and quietly closed the door behind him.

He looked toward Francine's door. The light still shone from beneath it. As Golga watched, the light clicked out. Francine had finished reading. Golga knew that the girl was in her room.

The big servant paused only for a moment when he reached Dashler's door. The sound of the sailor's snores were sufficient evidence that Dashler was there. Returning frontward, Golga listened, but heard no sound. Boldly, he opened Jalway's door and flicked a flashlight upon the bed.

No one there. The room was empty. Golga extinguished his light, promptly closed the door and crept creaking back toward Elger's study, anxious to report to his master. Reaching his objective, the servant knocked at Elger's door. There was no response. Golga rapped louder.

A SOUND from within. Elger was coming from the inner bedroom. He opened the door and admitted the servant. Golga's face bore an expression that proved he had a message of importance. Elger closed the door without a word.

The rear hall remained gloomy and silent for a full minute. Then came a *swish* from the front. Blackness took on a tall, living shape. The Shadow advanced toward the door of Elger's den. He paused to listen outside the barrier. His gloved hand gripped the knob and opened the door a fraction of an inch. Voices came to The Shadow's ears.

"Within the last half an hour?" Elger was demanding. "You're sure of that, Golga?"

A growled affirmative from the servant.

"You looked in Jalway's room," came Elger's next remark. "Well, that proves he was out. But are you sure that all the others were where they belonged?"

"The girl turned out her light," informed Golga, gruffly. "I could hear the sailor snoring; and I saw the professor in his bed."

"What about Hadlow?"

"I thought I heard him, at first. I can't be sure about it, like the others. But I would have looked in there if I hadn't found Jalway missing."

"Leave the windows as they are," decided Elger. "Keep watch in the living room and let me know when Jalway returns. We can let him think that his trip has not been discovered. Maybe we can find out what he is up to, Golga."

Pausing for a few moments of reflection, Elger finally added:

"Ruff lost another man last night. The fellow dropped through into one of those old cellars at the slave quarters. It was an accident, though. I don't think that Jalway could have been at large last night."

The door closed imperceptibly. The Shadow faded into the darkness of the front hall. Half a minute later, Golga appeared and went forward. When he reached the living room, the servant heard no whistling from the corner.

Bringing out his flashlight, he found the window bars back in place; the window sash had also been closed. The screws of the bar frame were loose, however. They had been hurriedly replaced.

Returning to the front hall, Golga paused between the first doors. He heard a distinct cough from Hadlow's room. Stopping at Jalway's door, Golga listened intently. He heard someone moving about within the room. Golga crept onward, to report to Elger.

Again, a blackened shape appeared as soon as the servant had entered the den. Once more The Shadow approached and performed his motion at the door. Listening, he caught Golga's new report. He heard Elger grumble.

"Jalway, all right," came Elger's opinion. "Well, we'll keep a watch on him. So long as he snoops around outside, there's no reason to worry. But it proves that we've got to look out for him.

"Smart, choosing a window in the living room. He figures that if we noticed it was open, we wouldn't know who did it. Well, Golga, we've got Mr. Jalway's number. We'll keep it.

"Turn in for the night. I'm not going below until tomorrow evening. I'll be up a while, and I'll take a look in that front hall myself before I go to bed. After this, we'll check on Jalway. But we'll make no move so long as he does his prowling outside."

The Shadow faded from the door. His laugh came as a sibilant whisper as he reached the darkness of the front door. No echo remained when Golga reappeared from the den. The servant went to his own room.

BACK in the den, Purvis Elger sat puffing at his meerschaum. His right hand steadied the pipe, while his left drummed softly upon the desk. A slow, crafty smile wreathed itself upon the schemer's lips.

Purvis Elger had learned that one of his guests was a prowler. He had decided that the fellow was playing a lone game. That, to Elger, was proof that there would be but one to watch: Bram Jalway.

Cunningly, Elger was planning a way to bring Jalway's prowls to an end, should occasion make that course advisable. He was satisfied that the fellow could cause no damage to affairs here on Timour Isle.

There was reason for Elger's smile. The shrewd crook was basing his opinions on Golga's report. Golga was vigilant. He had learned that one guest was missing. Elger was confident that the servant could keep tabs on whatever might happen in this house.

But Elger's smile would have faded had the crook realized how little Golga had actually discovered. Master, like servant, held to the impression that these castaways—Bram Jalway included—were all ordinary persons.

Not for an instant had either suspected that among the group was one who moved with the stealth of night itself. They did not know that this house of crime was harboring the secret presence of The Shadow!

CHAPTER X
THE SHADOW'S MESSAGE

THE next morning brought a letdown of the high winds that swept the Georgia coast. The center of the storm had passed, but mountainous waves still beat upon the shore of Timour Isle.

The hurricane, reduced to a gale intensity, had gone northward, along the Atlantic seaboard. Ships had scurried to the shelter of the Chesapeake capes. New Jersey beach resorts were suffering damage from heavy waves.

In New York, strong winds were screaming fiercely among towering skyscrapers. A chilly drizzle was driving down into the canyons formed by Manhattan streets. New Yorkers were gaining a taste of the tempest that had paralyzed shipping along the coast.

High in one of those Manhattan towers sat a placid, round-faced man who seemed oblivious to the sights outside. He was busy at a desk in his private office, studying lists of stocks and bonds. He was Rutledge Mann, a quiet, methodical investment broker.

A stenographer announced a visitor. Mann studied a card that bore the name of George Dalavan. The visitor was unknown to Mann; nevertheless, the investment broker ordered the girl to show Mr. Dalavan into the private office.

Dalavan entered. His lips held a slight smile beneath his clipped mustache. In every deal that he made, Dalavan liked to meet men who looked easy to handle. Mann belonged in that category, according to Dalavan's estimate.

It was Dalavan's belief that Purvis Elger had gained information regarding certain securities through the guests on Timour Isle, for they were people of wealth. Dalavan had wondered why Elger had sent word to negotiate through one particular broker; and upon seeing Mann, Dalavan thought he had the answer.

The transactions probably required a broker who would not suspect that a big deal was underway. Mann appeared too dull a person to catch on to any smooth work.

"I came to talk about investments," informed Dalavan. "I was told that you might know about them. What facts can you give me about Argentum Silver?"

A SLIGHT flicker of surprise appeared upon Mann's rounded features. It ended as the investment broker smiled and leaned beck in his chair. Mann's answer was so complacent that it finished the slight suspicion that flashed through Dalavan's mind.

"Argentum Silver," announced Mann, "was a

freak issue that has disappeared from sale. At what price were you advised to buy it?"

"At nineteen."

"No wonder your friend recommended it. Argentum Silver was snapped up at twenty-seven. It cannot be had at nineteen."

Dalavan looked disappointed; then he stated:

"I was also advised to purchase Eastern Zinc, Incorporated, at twelve and one quarter."

"That could have been done," returned Mann. "Eastern Zinc was a good buy at that figure. However, the stock is off the market. Eastern Zinc was recently absorbed."

"What about Consolidated Securities?"

Mann nodded as he heard Dalavan's question. The investment broker seemed pleased by his customer's interest in that stock.

"Consolidated Securities is as yet unlisted," stated Mann. "I understand that all has been subscribed; but there are option holders who would sell small blocks at a reasonable profit. It is something of a speculative offer; but I can advise you definitely when I have obtained a late report on the stock. Where could I reach you later today?"

"At my hotel," replied Dalavan. "I am stopping at the Bonzell. Room 1214."

Mann made a notation on a desk pad.

"You will hear from me by five o'clock," he told Dalavan. He glanced at his watch. "I shall go downstairs with you, Mr. Dalavan, as it is my lunch hour. I expect to meet some brokers during lunch and will make initial inquires when I talk with them."

The two left the office and descended to the street. Dalavan headed toward Times Square; Mann took the opposite direction. As soon as he was out of Dalavan's sight, Mann hailed a cab.

SHORTLY afterward, Mann reached a modest apartment house. He rang a bell that bore the name Slade Farrow. He was admitted promptly to an apartment; there, he shook hands with a keen-faced, middle-aged man whose eyes showed a gleam of interest when they spied Mann. It was plain that Farrow saw something unusual in this visit.

"Mr. Farrow," stated Mann, in a careful tone, "I have come here on a matter which concerns The Shadow. Both of us have served him. Posing as an investment broker, I work for The Shadow. Your part has been a different one. As a criminologist, you have knowledge of the underworld. In times of emergency, you have supplied able workers to The Shadow. Men who were once crooks, but who have gone straight."

"They are always ready when The Shadow needs them."

"He requires them at present."

Farrow's eyes gleamed with interest at Mann's statement. He waited while the investment broker paused, then listened intently as Mann resumed.

"A few weeks ago," declared Mann, in a confidential tone, "The Shadow left New York. You will be surprised to learn that he had no motive in doing so other than to enjoy a needed rest. Crime seemed in abeyance, here in New York. It was a logical time for The Shadow to take a vacation."

Farrow nodded in agreement.

"The Shadow informed me," resumed Mann, "that he intended to cruise aboard the yacht *Maldah*, as a guest of the owner, Kingdon Feldworth."

"The *Maldah*!" exclaimed Farrow. "That yacht has been reported missing. You mean The Shadow is aboard?"

"The Shadow *was* aboard," replied Mann. "But it is apparent that he has come safely ashore from the yacht. I received a message from him today."

"Through whom?"

"Through a man whom I must class as an enemy, until I learn more about him."

SLADE FARROW was dumfounded by the investment broker's statement. Word received through an enemy. It passed belief. Incredible though The Shadow's methods were, this startling revelation surpassed all that Farrow had known in the past.

"A short while ago," explained Mann, "a suave visitor named George Dalavan came into my office and inquired regarding stock issued by the Argentum Silver Mines. No such stock exists. The mention of it means that Dalavan is to be watched. He is a criminal."

"His identity is known to The Shadow?" inquired Farrow.

"Perhaps," returned Mann. "Perhaps not. I merely know that Argentum Silver Mines is the key to check upon the man who made the inquiry. But that was only part of the information that Dalavan unwittingly brought me.

"He also mentioned a stock called Eastern Zinc, Incorporated. He quoted two figures: nineteen and twelve and one quarter. Those do not fit in with any prearranged code with the exception that Zinc signifies The Shadow.

"It seems logical that under the circumstances, The Shadow is anxious to communicate his location. Furthermore, Dalavan referred to an unknown stock called Consolidated Securities. The term Consolidated refers to The Shadow's agents, with whom I have contact. Evidently he requires their aid."

Slade Farrow smiled in meditative fashion.

Eyeing the criminologist, Mann caught what was in Farrow's mind.

"The Shadow relies upon you in cases of emergency," asserted the investment broker. "I have previously been instructed to call upon you in time of perplexity. Evidently, The Shadow resorted to some device to convey an additional message. One that he believes you can solve."

Farrow arose and paced across the room. He was considering all that Mann had told him. At length the criminologist paused to face the investment broker.

"Mann," declared Farrow, "I am working on the assumption which you have gained: namely, that The Shadow is subtly trying to tell us where he is. It is obvious that he has landed from the crippled yacht. He might be anywhere between here and the Florida Keys.

"Assuming that he knows his own location, the first information that he would give might be the name of the State where he has come ashore. As I recall it"—Farrow paused as he plucked an almanac from the desk and thumbed the pages—"the nineteenth State in point of size is Georgia. Yes"—again a pause—"that is correct. Georgia is the nineteenth. That is where The Shadow is."

"Somewhere on the Georgia coast!"

"Exactly." Farrow was bringing out an atlas. "His reference to Eastern Zinc is probably a reminder of that fact. By use of the word Eastern, he emphasized that point. So from the number twelve and one quarter we must learn his exact location."

FARROW opened the atlas to a map of Georgia. He ran his finger along the coastline. Mann looked on, a trifle glum, for he could not see how the criminologist could manage to locate the right spot. Farrow's chuckle, however, showed that the man had an idea.

"Obviously," declared Farrow, "The Shadow has consulted a map of his own. Since there is no way that we could guess the exact scale of that map, his only course would be to give us a percentage scale."

"I don't quite understand," put in Mann.

"Simply this." Farrow laid a ruler along the map. "Consider the north to south distance of Georgia in terms of one hundred units or segments, reading upward, in the manner of latitude. That scale"—Farrow was marking it off with a pencil—"would apply to any map, large or small.

"Here is twelve. One quarter more puts us on this spot. See that tiny island, Mann? The one that has no name? That is the spot from which The Shadow sent his message."

Leaving the atlas, Farrow went to a filing cabinet and brought out some larger maps. He found one that showed a portion of Georgia, on a large scale. He compared it with the map in the atlas.

"Here we are," declared Farrow. "This map names the island. It is called Timour Isle. Not much more than a mile in length. Thick marshes between it and the mainland."

"That must be the location," decided Mann. "I shall send agents there at once."

"Perhaps," put in Farrow, "it would be better to check on Dalavan first. I presume you arranged to meet him later?"

"I am to call him at the Hotel Bonzell. Room 1214."

"Why not send Hawkeye over there?"

The query brought a prompt nod from Mann. There was every reason why he should approve. "Hawkeye" was a protégé of Farrow's, who had enlisted in The Shadow's service. Hawkeye was a clever trail finder; at that art, he had encountered only one who was superior: The Shadow.

Mann picked up Farrow's telephone. He dialed a number; a quiet voice responded. Mann held a short conversation; he was talking to Burbank, The Shadow's hidden contact man. Not only did Mann request that Burbank assign Hawkeye to the required task; he also urged that other agents—active ones—be ready to leave for Georgia.

A FEW hours later, George Dalavan strolled from his room in the Hotel Bonzell. As he passed the door of Room 1212, Dalavan failed to notice that it was ajar. A small, wizened-faced man was in that room; the man was Hawkeye. Craftily, he had made an entry to the room that adjoined Dalavan's.

Noting that Dalavan was not wearing hat and coat, Hawkeye decided that he was merely going to the lobby. Hurriedly, Hawkeye crossed the room and worked on a connecting door that led into Room 1214. There was sufficient space for him to get at the bolt on the other side; and Hawkeye managed the task, although he was no expert with locks.

Hawkeye had originally planned to crawl out the window and reach the sill of Dalavan's room; but this route, through the connecting door, was preferable.

Once in Dalavan's room, Hawkeye put in a prompt telephone call to Burbank. In a hotel the size of the Bonzell, the operator naturally thought that the caller was either the occupant of 1214, or a friend.

A brief report given, Hawkeye started a search of Dalavan's suitcase. He came upon a letter that the man had received that day. In it, Hawkeye read the details of what had occurred on Timour Isle, as transmitted from Elger to Tully.

The letter suggested that Dalavan go aboard the *Dalmatia* at Charleston, unless he should prefer to come by the usual route. Included in the letter was the mention of the stocks that Dalavan had discussed with Mann.

Hardly had Hawkeye slipped the letter back into its envelope before there was a sound outside the door of Room 1214. Quickly, Hawkeye scurried across the room and reached the connecting door. He slid beyond it; but had no time to close the barrier. Dalavan stepped into 1214, strolled across the room and began to pack his suitcase.

He had not seen the opened door to 1212. Hawkeye wanted to shut it; but feared that the stir might catch Dalavan's attention. Cautiously, the little spotter waited, staking everything on a break that he expected. The break came.

Dalavan's telephone rang. The mustached man turned about to answer it. Hawkeye closed the connecting door. As he started to turn the knob, he heard Dalavan talking to Rutledge Mann.

"Hello, Mr. Mann..." greeted Dalavan. "Yes... Thirty-six shares of Consolidated Securities... Price quoted twenty-two and one half... You can arrange the purchase..."

HANGING UP, Dalavan turned suddenly. He thought that he had heard a sound from the connecting door. He eyed it suspiciously; then, with a long stride, he walked across and tried the door. He found it unbolted.

Thrusting a hand into his pocket, Dalavan yanked the door open; looked into the next room. He saw no one. Hawkeye had made a quick sneak out into the hall.

Stepping back into his own room, Dalavan entered a closet; from a high shelf, in a spot hidden from view, he brought out the square-shaped suitcase that he had brought from Florida. He opened it, viewed the Lamballe tiara, the money, and other items. With a smile, Dalavan set the case upon the floor.

Relieved to find that the swag was untouched, he decided that any intruder could not have managed to search the room.

Nevertheless, Dalavan's subsequent actions showed that he was worried because of the incident which had occurred. The murderer brought out a carbon copy of a brief note that he had typed to Tully; he shook his head as he burned this duplicate of a letter already sent.

From his pocket, Dalavan produced a ticket and Pullman reservation, both to Charleston, South Carolina. Again, he shook his head. It was plain that Dalavan intended to go to Timour Isle by the old route; not aboard the *Dalmatia*.

Packing up, Dalavan left the hotel room; he checked out of the Bonzell, carrying his case of swag with him. He took a cab to the Grand Central Station; there, he switched to another taxi and rode to the Pennsylvania Station. When he reached that destination, Dalavan indulged in a smile. He was confident that his trick with the cabs had thrown any followers off his trail.

DALAVAN was correct in his conjecture. Nevertheless, the reason why he had escaped pursuit was different than he supposed. The answer came early that evening, when Rutledge Mann again called upon Slade Farrow. Together, these men who served The Shadow went over a series of newspaper clippings that Mann had brought along.

The newspaper accounts mentioned the *Dalmatia*. The tramp steamer was in Charleston; but it had reported several crew members lost during the hurricane. It was on that fact that Mann and Farrow depended for results, as their conversation proved.

"If Hawkeye leaves on the 9:30 train," declared Farrow, "he will arrive in Charleston soon enough. Hawkeye is crafty; he will be smart enough to arrange a berth for himself aboard the *Dalmatia*. He can pass himself as an able-bodied seaman."

"Vincent and Marsland will leave later," announced Mann. "Their train will get to Charleston by tomorrow afternoon. If Hawkeye does manage to place himself aboard the *Dalmatia* as a crew member, he should be able to work them aboard with him."

Farrow nodded. He knew Harry Vincent and Cliff Marsland, as competent aides of The Shadow. Teamed with Hawkeye, they would make a useful trio. Dalavan had never seen any of them; if he should be aboard the *Dalmatia*, he would not recognize the three as agents of The Shadow.

"If Hawkeye fails," added Mann, "he can wire Richmond. Vincent will pick up the telegram there. In that case, he and Marsland will have to find their own route to Timour Isle."

Mann and Farrow parted. Their work was done. They had received The Shadow's message; they had put active agents on the job. The Shadow had relied upon such cooperation and he had gained it. Affairs were tightening on Timour Isle. Crooks were converging to that focal point. Soon, Purvis Elger would be prepared to deliver murder.

Yet The Shadow had countered, despite his isolated situation. Through Elger's own ace, Dalavan, The Shadow had arranged for aid of his own; The Shadow's men had chosen their route to Timour Isle. The Shadow could depend upon his agents to offset the reserves whom Elger soon would gain.

CHAPTER XI
THE NEXT NIGHT

LATE the next afternoon, sunshine came to Timour Isle. Scudding clouds had cleared. The fury of the storm had ended. Purvis Elger, smiling when he entered the living room, had suggested that his guests might like to stroll abroad.

All had accepted the suggestion with the exception of Professor Marcolm. The white-haired savant had brought several manuscripts from his bedroom. He was busily engaged in the translation of an Arabian epic. He seemed pleased that the other guests were going out. It offered him a chance to work undisturbed.

Elger invited the old man into his study. Marcolm accepted. He found it a better place to work; and occupied himself at a corner table while Elger, at the desk, delved into mathematical problems. It was nearly dinner time when the two scholars ended their work.

Entering the living room, they found Bram Jalway pacing about, puffing at an empty pipe. Elger was smoking his meerschaum; he smilingly proffered his pouch. Jalway filled his briar and lighted up.

"Where are the others?" queried Elger.

"Somewhere close by," replied Jalway, "walking about under the trees near the beach. Looking at the Spanish moss, I guess. Funny how that stuff clings to the branches. Even the hurricane didn't seem to loosen it."

"How long ago did you come in?" inquired Elger.

"About half an hour ago," responded Jalway, puffing at his pipe. "I couldn't see much use in strolling about a deserted beach."

The front door opened a moment later. Seth Hadlow and Francine Feldworth entered, followed by Dashler. As the arrivals began to chat with Elger, Royne entered to announce that dinner was served.

The dining room was located in a rear extension of the house, near the kitchen. As usual, the guests enjoyed their meal; for Royne had proven himself a capable cook. While they were finishing their dessert, Elger spoke to Royne. The servant went from the dining room.

"I've sent Royne to look for some of my special tobacco," said Elger to Jalway. "A blend that I had put away for unusual occasions. You seem to be enjoying your briar pipe. Keep it ready for this new smoke. In the meantime, suppose we adjourn to the living room."

They moved to the front of the house. There, Royne reappeared, to state that he had not been able to find the tobacco. Elger excused himself. He was gone for several minutes.

He returned with a tin of the missing blend. He offered it to Jalway who filled his briar. Elger followed by putting a pipe load in his meerschaum.

THERE had been nothing suspicious about the procedure. Yet it fitted with something that The Shadow had learned on a preceding night. Elger had said that he would send Royne to contact with Ruff Turney; to learn what Ruff's man had discovered.

Royne's futile hunt for the tobacco had been a cover for that contact. His claim that he could not find the tobacco had given him a chance to report to Elger.

Whatever the crook's plans might have been, Elger kept them from his guests. In fact, he reversed his usual procedure. Instead of retiring to the seclusion of his study, he remained in the living room and chatted pleasantly.

Conversation turned to the matter of the *Maldah*. Francine began to express anxiety concerning her uncle. Her companions tried to reassure her. It was Elger who delivered the most comforting announcement.

"The storm has abated," he declared. "Within a day or two we should have contact with the mainland. I would not be surprised if a boat should come here shortly."

"We have the lifeboat," remarked Hadlow. "It is high on the beach, undamaged by the waves."

"It would not be suitable for the back passages," returned Elger. "A power boat is needed for those channels. Moreover, most of them are blind entrances into the marshes. Only a pilot familiar with the channels can pick his way through them."

"You are sure that people will come here soon?" questioned Francine.

"Positively," replied Elger. "A boat would have come yesterday but for the storm. Be patient, Miss Feldworth. There will not be long to wait."

A slight pause while Elger puffed at his meerschaum. Then the master of Timour Isle turned to another subject.

"There may still be danger on this isle," he remarked, in a cautious tone. "Those vandals who attacked you on the beach may have found themselves stranded by the hurricane. There is a chance that they are still about.

"Therefore, I would suggest that all continue to remain indoors after dark. If those rogues were lying low during the storm, they might approach this house now that the weather has abated. For that reason, I intend to keep my servants on guard."

Troubled looks appeared upon the faces of the listeners. Elger dismissed them with a casual wave of his hand.

"No occasion for worry," he assured. "This house is a miniature fortress. But to be ready in case of trouble, I shall have Golga stay on duty here in the living room. Royne will guard the back of the house."

That ended the subject. Elger had played his part well. He had made it appear that he was taking the precaution purely to avoid an invasion; at the same time he had definitely made it plain that the living room window would not be a possible exit for anyone who might wish to prowl from the house.

Puffing steadily at his briar pipe, Bram Jalway suggested a game of bridge. He, Hadlow, Francine and Elger made up a table. Professor Marcolm took his manuscripts to his bedroom. Elger offered him the use of the study; but the white-haired man declined, stating that he would retire early.

Dashler played solitaire on the window seat; finally the sailor decided to turn in; and a short while later, the bridge game came to an end. The last three guests went to their rooms; Elger called Golga, then retired to his study, leaving the servant on duty in the living room.

IN the seclusion of his study, Elger indulged in a smile. He had subtly blocked the prowling game tonight. His guests had retired; it was time to keep a rendezvous with Ruff Turney. For tonight, Elger knew, there would be return news from New York.

Pocketing his meerschaum, Elger extinguished the study light. He went into the bedroom, opened the big bookcase and descended by the secret stairway. The bedroom light went out. Hardly had blackness come before the outer door of the study opened. The Shadow glided into the empty room.

Elger's new plan of action had worked perfectly for The Shadow. Golga, stationed in the living room, would have no need to search the rooms that the guests occupied, for he was blocking the outlet that had been used before. Thus The Shadow had a perfect opportunity to spy upon Elger himself within the house.

Crossing the study, The Shadow entered the bedroom, opened the bookcase and descended. He reached the lower passage and kept on through until he arrived in the first cavern. The sound of voices from the central room told him that Elger and Ruff were already holding conference.

"Tully's been trying to click something through to you," stated Ruff. "I've heard his taps while I've been waiting. Better get in touch with him, chief."

Elger moved over to the telegraph outfit and began to tap for Tully. A response came. The receiver clicked a message. The code was plain to The Shadow, listening from the outer cavern. But it meant nothing to Ruff Turney, until Elger gave his explanation.

"Dalavan started south last night," stated Elger. "He is going to board the *Dalmatia* at Charleston. He will come ashore with the shipment."

"How soon?" inquired Ruff.

"The *Dalmatia* sails late tomorrow," replied Elger. "Tully picked up a radioed shipping report to that effect. That means she'll be off the coast during the night. You'll meet her."

"And bring in the swag?"

"Part of it. The rest will come in by one of the boats from the *Dalmatia*. Hexler and his outfit will handle it. They'll join up and take orders from you. This is the last job, remember."

"I get it. No need for them to go back aboard."

"None at all. The captain of the *Dalmatia* has been paid to keep mum. He doesn't know what he's unloading. Thinks it's liquor on which the duty is too high for shipment through the customs."

"He must be a sap."

"He probably is, or he would not be the skipper of a hopeless tub like the *Dalmatia*. Here's something else important. The *Maldah* has been sighted, stranded in shoal water by Hamplin's Inlet."

"That's only twenty miles from here. Who sighted her?"

"A coast guard cutter. It couldn't get through; and the *Maldah* has signaled that she needs no aid."

"No radio report?"

"None. The *Maldah* has apparently been unable to repair the wireless equipment. So nobody knows yet that some of the passengers came ashore."

"Why do you think Feldworth is stalling them off? His ship's aground."

"He probably doesn't want to pay salvage on the yacht. I can't see why, though. He has plenty of money. It works to our advantage, however. There won't be any search for these castaways until after we unload the *Dalmatia*."

Tick—tick—tick—

THE SHADOW listened. A new message was coming from Tully. Elger was back at the key, acknowledging. Clicked words followed. An exclamation came from Elger's lips. The Shadow knew the reason. He had heard the message also. He lingered to hear Elger's comments to Ruff.

"Tully just got a phone call from Dalavan," announced Elger, in a harsh tone. "Dalavan's in Georgia. Got off a train at the station near Tully's shack."

"He isn't going to Charleston, then?" quizzed Ruff.

"No," Elger spoke, grimly. "Somebody spotted him in New York at the Hotel Bonzell. It may have been The Shadow."

"Dalavan took it on the lam?"

"Yes. With the evidence that would have made trouble. That's all Tully knows. He's going to bring Dalavan here. He's bringing Chunk along, too. They'll pull in by boat at the upper inlet and wait there while Dalavan comes up to the house."

"To report to you?"

"Yes. He can pose as a chance visitor. I'll introduce him to the other guests in the morning. We'll say that he sent the boat back, not knowing that I wanted to make contact with the mainland. But the boat will stay here."

Elger paused, then glanced at notations he had made while receiving Tully's message. A puzzled frown appeared upon his countenance.

"Here's something I can't figure out," he remarked. "Dalavan told Tully that he can purchase thirty-six shares of Consolidated Securities at twenty-two and one half. Says they are on order."

"Some stock you ordered, chief?" inquired Ruff.

"No," returned Elger, still puzzled.

"I never heard of the stock before. I'll ask Dalavan about it when he comes."

A MOTION beyond the door of the cavern; The Shadow was moving further back into the darkness. Since Elger did not intend to question Tully regarding Dalavan's mention of securities, there was no reason for The Shadow to remain. The Shadow had learned facts that strengthened his position.

Elger believed that The Shadow was in New York; that it was he who had tried to spot Dalavan. This proved conclusively that Elger did not have even the mildest suspicion that The Shadow was one of his guests on Timour Isle.

More important, however, was the quotation of figures that Tully had given over the wire. Rutledge Mann had purposely named thirty-six shares of Consolidated Securities as the number available; and there was a reason why he had stated the price as twenty-two and one half.

Even without a map at hand, The Shadow knew that South Carolina was the thirty-sixth State in size; and that Charleston was located at point twenty-two and one half, according to The Shadow's system of measurement.

The Shadow knew that Mann had discovered the meaning of the message that had come through Dalavan. Mann had sent an answer back through the same channel. Since The Shadow wanted agents here, Mann's message naturally signified the route that they had chosen. They would board the *Dalmatia* at Charleston; The Shadow was sure that they would find a way to come ashore with the swag, when the tramp steamer neared Timour Isle.

Under the circumstances, the fact that Dalavan suspected he was followed and had chosen to come by the usual route was all for the better. Edging away in darkness, The Shadow caught a last statement from Elger to Ruff.

"I'm going to tell Golga to be ready for Dalavan," informed Elger. "I shall come back here, to arrange the treasures for later shipment to the mainland. When Dalavan arrives, Golga can show him into the den. Dalavan can wait for me there. It will be a few hours before he arrives."

Elger turned toward the outer cavern that led to the secret passage to his house. He encountered vacated darkness. The Shadow had departed. Moving noiselessly through the gloom ahead, The Shadow was en route to the look-out house.

The Shadow was gone from Elger's den when the master crook arrived there.

CHAPTER XII
THE SHADOW'S CHALLENGE

MIDNIGHT had passed. All was quiet in the house on Timour Isle. Golga, seated in the darkness of the living room, was listening intently. He was under orders from Purvis Elger.

Hours ago, his chief had stolen in here to announce that George Dalavan was due to arrive tonight. Then Elger had departed. Golga had waited stolidly, until the time for Dalavan's arrival had neared. The big servant had become restless.

Pacing to the door of the living room, Golga listened. All silent in the hall. The guests were asleep. Outside winds were scarcely audible tonight. There were no disturbing sounds to cover noises that might occur within the house.

A scratching tap from the front door. Golga moved cautiously in that direction. Slowly, he drew back the bolts. He opened the door a few inches. Pallid moonlight showed a mustached countenance beyond. It was George Dalavan.

Stepping back, Golga admitted the arrival. He closed the door and bolted it, drew Dalavan into the living room. Cautiously, the servant whispered Elger's instructions. Dalavan nodded his understanding. He tiptoed out into the hall, back toward Elger's den.

Golga listened from the door of the living room. The servant wanted to be sure that none of the guests had heard Dalavan's entry. No sound disturbed the silence of the hallway. Golga moved back into the living room.

It was then that darkness stirred. From a doorway

in the hall, blackness came to life. A shrouded form blocked the slight light that came from the rear hall. That shape became the figure of The Shadow, moving stealthily, unheard by Golga, toward the goal that Dalavan had chosen.

George Dalavan had entered, carrying his square-shaped suitcase. When he reached the den, he found the room deserted. Placing the case upon the desk, he opened it and removed four objects. The first was the Lamballe tiara; the second, the envelope containing Tolwig's fifty thousand dollars; the third was the sheaf of shorthand notations compiled by the dead investigator Bagland; the fourth, the receipt that Dalavan had signed.

With a suave grin, Dalavan spread these exhibits upon the desk. He looked toward the door of the bedroom, expecting Elger to appear. Seeing no sign of his chief, Dalavan lighted a cigarette and strolled about the study, glancing at books that were strewn there.

The door from the hall was opening, inch by inch. Keen eyes were peering inward. The door moved more swiftly. Blackness edged into the room. The Shadow, cloaked being of vengeance, closed the door behind him and stared steadily at Dalavan.

The murderer heard the slight click of the door. He turned about, expecting to see Golga. Dalavan's face showed sudden horror; the cigarette dropped from his trembling fingers. Once again, Dalavan was staring into the looming mouth of an automatic, gripped by an avenger in black.

DALAVAN froze, exactly as he had done at Tolwig's bungalow near Miami. He had discounted The Shadow's prowess; for his safe flight had given him confidence. Moreover, the New York episode had made Dalavan believe that he could shake The Shadow from his trail. Thus The Shadow's unexpected appearance, in Elger's own den, was a complete blow to Dalavan. The murderer quailed.

"I—I killed Tolwig," gasped Dalavan. "But it—it was in self-defense. It was Lovett who—who started it—"

Dalavan paused, incoherent. He could see no mercy in the gleam of The Shadow's eyes. However, as he stared helplessly, Dalavan saw something that The Shadow did not observe. The door from the hall was opening; its *click* had been drowned out by Dalavan's words.

With momentary rally, Dalavan steadied, hoping to hold The Shadow's attention. There was a further motion at the door; Dalavan saw Golga, crouching forward. The servant had a long-bladed knife. A few seconds more and Golga could spring upon The Shadow.

In those seconds, however, Dalavan overplayed. His lips compressed beneath his mustache. His eyes showed shrewdness. The Shadow saw that they were looking beyond.

The Shadow jabbed his .45 warningly toward Dalavan. As the crook quailed instinctively, The Shadow spun about. Instantly, he whirled toward the door.

Golga was already springing inward. The big menial's blade flashed from his driving hand. Despite Dalavan's unconscious betrayal, Golga, through quick action had gained the edge on The Shadow. An instant's pause for perfect aim might have been fatal to the black-cloaked warrior.

The Shadow fired at the hand that held the knife. Hard upon the automatic's spurt came a cry from Golga as the bullet clipped the servant's wrist. The down-coming hand seemed to jolt as its fingers opened. The long knife skimmed past The

As the crook quailed instinctively, The Shadow spun about. Instantly, he whirled toward the door. Golga was already springing inward.

Shadow's shoulder, and clattered against the wall beside Dalavan.

The timely shot would have eliminated an ordinary foeman. But Golga was a vicious, deadly fighter. The man scarcely halted in his lunge. Shooting his free left hand forward, he hurled himself upon The Shadow and drove the avenger back against the wall.

Flaying arms gripped The Shadow in a furious grapple. Twisting, the cloaked fighter tried to wrestle free. He partially succeeded, then drove his left fist squarely to Golga's chin. The servant lost his hold. Clearing him, The Shadow swung toward Dalavan.

The cowered crook had become a fiend. During the momentary struggle, Dalavan had yanked a revolver from his pocket. Wielding the snub-nosed .32, he was leaping forward to clip The Shadow at close range. That advance was to prove his undoing.

DALAVAN had the bead on The Shadow. His aim would have served at a dozen feet as well as five. But Dalavan, in his maddened effort, had chosen the closer range. He was still surging forward as he pressed the trigger of his gun.

The Shadow's left arm was swinging as his right hand aimed. His gloved fist struck Dalavan's wrist just as the fellow fired.

The crook's hand jolted up; the bullet whistled through the brim of The Shadow's slouch hat. Dalavan, bringing his arm down in cudgel-like fashion, sought to loose a second slug.

The Shadow's automatic roared. Dalavan's surging body bounded in the air. With a frantic cry, the crook came jouncing upon his half-crouched foe. It was a death plunge; for The Shadow's bullet had found the murderer's heart. Yet, dying, Dalavan was a man of fury.

The Shadow rolled sidewise beneath the writhing form that hit him. Dalavan's gun went clicking to the floor. The Shadow, twisting, freed himself from the murderer's body. Then, of a sudden, he dived sidewise on the floor.

Golga, seizing his knife with his left hand, had pounced back into the fray. His driving stroke was on its way even as The Shadow made his voluntary sprawl. The blade went wide, plunging on The Shadow. Golga poised for another stroke with the knife. A roar sounded from the floor.

The Shadow had delivered a backhand shot. Golga's body wavered; his left hand wobbled back and forth. Balanced on one knee, Golga stared straight ahead, while a sickly expression dominated his evil face.

The Shadow, rolling clear, watched the strange result. Golga was like a rocking statue. The knife loosed from his shaking hand. It dropped, blade foremost, onto the floor. Then the servant's body crumpled. A fierce death gasp came from ugly lips as Golga's arms sprawled outward on the floor.

Lunges—shots—the knife strokes—all had followed with quick succession. In less than two dozen seconds, The Shadow had accounted for this pair of would-be slayers. Already the cloaked victor was at the desk. Unscathed, The Shadow was sweeping tiara, cash and notes into the case that Dalavan had brought.

With a fierce, mirthless laugh, The Shadow sprang to the door of the den and gained the rear hall. Quickly he crossed that space and merged with the front darkness.

A MOMENT later, Dashler's door banged open. The sailor came out into the hall.

"What's up?" was Dashler's growled query. "Did I hear shots?"

A voice answered from the rear hall. Hearing footsteps, Dashler moved in that direction, to encounter Royne. The cadaverous servant reached the door of the study.

"Look!" cried Royne, pointing to the bodies on the floor. Then, seeing that Elger was not in the room: "Stay back. Go and call the others."

As Dashler obeyed, Royne hurried into the bedroom. He saw that this apartment was empty; he knew that Elger must be below. While Royne hesitated, the bookcase swung open. Elger himself appeared.

Royne pointed to the study. Elger quickly closed the bookcase. With the servant, he entered the study to look at the bodies. He picked up Dalavan's gun and held it in readiness as footsteps came from the hall.

Dashler was back. Following him was Professor Marcolm, clad in a dressing gown, his white hair unkempt. The two stopped on the threshold. As Dashler reported to Elger, Marcolm stared with wide eyes at the bodies.

"I knocked at the other doors," stated Dashler. "I told Miss Feldworth to stay where she was. I called to the others to come."

Seth Hadlow appeared as Dashler finished speaking. The sportsman's face was solemn. He eyed the bodies half curiously; then, in mechanical fashion he reached in the pocket of the dressing gown that he was wearing. Methodically, Hadlow produced a cigarette and placed it between his lips. But he did not light it.

"Where is Jalway?" demanded Elger.

"I called him," responded Dashler.

"Go find him," ordered Elger.

The sailor turned. Before he had gone a dozen steps, he encountered Jalway coming from the front hall. The promoter was fully dressed, except for his necktie. He spoke to Dashler as he advanced.

"What's up?" was Jalway's query. "Did you say something about shots?"

DASHLER motioned toward the den. Jalway stopped on the threshold. His eyes opened. The sight of the two dead men seemed to astonish him. His expression carried inquiry.

"What has happened here," declared Elger, solemnly, "is this. I expected a visitor. Mr. George Dalavan, whom you see dead before you. I did not know when Mr. Dalavan would arrive."

"Quite naturally not," interposed Hadlow, "since you had no communication with the mainland."

"Exactly," emphasized Elger. "But it appears that Mr. Dalavan arrived tonight. Golga must have admitted him and sent him into the den. I was asleep in the adjoining bedroom"—he pointed to the door that he had come from—"and my door was closed."

"Did you hear shots, sir?" asked Dashler.

"Yes," replied Elger, "but I had no idea they were so close at hand. I arose; I heard commotion here. I entered to find Royne beside the bodies. Tell me: can anyone supply evidence regarding what occurred?"

Headshakes were the only answers.

"We must assume then," decided Elger, "that someone came in with Dalavan. He must have sought to kill Dalavan, and Golga intervened. Both are dead. The killer has escaped. Let us examine the front door."

Elger led the way. The group followed. They found the front door bolted. Elger stepped into the living room and turned on the light. He looked at the windows. One was closed but not locked.

Elger opened it. He noted that the barred frame had been removed. Flicking a flashlight to the ground outside, Elger saw the frame there. A smile appeared upon his lips—an expression which no one observed. Elger turned in from the window.

"The assailant," stated Elger, "must have effected an entry by this route. He has escaped by the same outlet. Royne"—he turned to the servant—"take Dashler and go to the upper inlet. See if, by any chance, there are men there with a boat. The ones who brought Dalavan from the mainland."

Royne and Dashler departed. At that moment, Francine appeared in the living room. The girl's face was pale as she looked about inquiringly. Elger, as spokesman, told Francine what had occurred.

Royne and Dashler returned, bringing two roughly clad men who looked like natives from the mainland marshes. This pair was Tully and "Chunk"; men known to Elger. But he gave no sign that he recognized them. He took the two into the den, leaving the guests in the living room.

WHEN Elger returned alone, he made a brief announcement. He stated that he had hired the two men to remain on guard for the night. The bodies had been removed by these new hirelings.

"The men tell me that the trip was difficult," stated Elger. "They do not want to attempt a return journey for another day, at least. The regular channels of the marshes have been altered by the severe winds.

"These men are armed and have identified themselves as reliable parties. With Royne and Dashler, they can guard the place tonight. There are no cartridges suitable for the rifles that you people brought; so I am giving Dashler my own revolver."

This frank arrangement pleased the guests. The inclusion of Dashler among the watchers gave an added security. The castaways retired; so did Elger. The four pickets went on duty. It was taken for granted that some outsider must have entered to battle with Dalavan and Golga; and that the intruder must have fled the house.

In his den, Elger indulged in a dry smile. With three of his own men on guard, he felt that the field was safe. Tomorrow, he would take steps to avenge the deaths of Dalavan and Golga.

The Shadow had challenged Purvis Elger's henchmen. In that challenge, The Shadow had dealt death. He had gained wealth and evidence that George Dalavan had brought to Timour Isle. Yet Elger, though he knew the import of this evening's battle, was still unperturbed.

With guards on duty, with the majority of his guests lulled to a sense of false security, this crafty master of crime was playing a waiting game in answer to The Shadow's challenge.

CHAPTER XIII
THE TRAP IS LAID

ANOTHER day had passed at Timour Isle. Subsiding winds had left only a heavy, heaving swell with odd chunks of wreckage along the beach. Purvis Elger's guests had gone out to view the flotsam and jetsam strewn by the tide. They had found nothing that could have come from the yacht *Maldah*.

That fact was mentioned during the evening meal. It brought a reassuring comment from Elger, who was presiding at the head of the table.

"I believe the *Maldah* is safe," stated the portly host. "We shall know positively by tomorrow night. Thanks to the two men from the mainland."

"Tully and Chunk?" inquired Jalway, using the nicknames by which the men had introduced themselves.

"Yes," nodded Elger. "When morning comes, they are going to set out for the mainland. The channels should certainly be clear by then. I shall have them notify the authorities regarding the deaths that have occurred here.

"They will bring back sheriff and coroner. When those officials arrive, I feel sure that we shall gain news concerning the outside world. That should include a report of the *Maldah*."

FRANCINE appeared relieved by Elger's statements. The portly man arose and made another announcement.

"I am going to my den," he said, "to make a full detailed report of all that has occurred since your arrival on Timour Isle. I shall send that report ashore with Tully and Chunk.

"This evening, I shall rely on your cooperation in guarding the house. I have instructed Royne to give revolvers to the three who are unarmed. You, Mr. Jalway; you, Mr. Hadlow; and you, Professor Marcolm.

"If any of you care to fare forth, you are welcome to do so. I believe that the best way to deal with the cowardly assassins who are near this isle is to let them know that we are prepared. But I advise any who choose to go out to use the utmost discretion. We want no more deaths."

With this statement, Elger excused himself. He left the dining room and went into his den. He locked the door behind him on this particular occasion. Immediately afterward, Tully, who was lounging in the hall, took up a casual position near the door.

From the den, Elger entered the bedroom. He opened the bookcase and descended into the secret passage. He moved along to the caverns. A light was burning when he arrived. Ruff Turney was waiting for his chief.

Tonight there were no spying eyes as the two conferred. The Shadow had found no opportunity to trail Elger to his lair. But The Shadow, incidentally, had no reason to look in on tonight's conference. He already knew the plans that the crooks had made.

AS conversation moved between Elger and Ruff, it became apparent that the two were plotting on a side scheme that they had not as yet discussed. Elger was explaining how he had duped his guests; and with it, he was mentioning certain consequences that might develop.

"I've bluffed them, Ruff," boasted Elger, as he faced his tough lieutenant. "I told them that I figured somebody from outside had killed Dalavan and Golga."

"They fell for it?" queried Ruff.

"Absolutely," replied Elger. "And it was all for the benefit of one person present: Jalway."

Ruff nodded. Elger puffed at his big pipe.

"Golga was capable," mused Elger, reflectively. "He planted it cold upon Jalway. That one man is the troublemaker in my house. He's playing a lone hand.

"Unquestionably he planned to go out last night. But he knew Golga was in the living room. When he heard Dalavan come through the hall, he decided it might be Golga, going to the den. So he went there."

"And encountered Dalavan?"

"Yes. Killed him in a fight. Golga pitched in and Jalway finished him, too. Then he ran for it. Got to the window in the living room."

"Then turned yellow?"

"Hardly yellow, Ruff. He decided it would be better to stage a bluff. He came back. He looked as surprised as the others. He tried a bluff of his own; so I countered with mine. I went to the living room and found the window unbarred. I decided—for Jalway's benefit—that an outsider had done the dirty work."

Another pause. Then Elger chuckled.

"Dalavan had a box with him," declared the master crook. "I can guess what was in it. That Lamballe tiara and maybe Tolwig's dough. Dalavan talked a little to Tully and Chunk. They told me so when I got them alone last night."

"Did he tell them much?"

"Unfortunately, no. He assured them that all was well; and he mentioned that he had valuables with him."

"If Jalway's got the box now, why don't you make a search for it?"

"He may have chucked it somewhere outside the house, or he may have planted it inside, in some place that would make it impossible to pin the goods on him. No, Ruff, I have a better way to deal with Mr. Bram Jalway.

"I'm giving him rope"—Elger paused for a few furious puffs of pipe smoke—"and it will be enough to hang him. I suggested that my guests look about tonight. Leave the house, if they wished to do so. But I added that they should be careful."

"I get it. Then if Jalway goes out, we can grab the others—"

"No, no, Ruff." Elger was impatient in his interruption. "Those others are our alibi. Don't you get it? If they looked upon Jalway as their protector, the game would be difficult. But Jalway, thinking himself a fox, is playing a lone hand. That gives me the chance to step in as the real protector.

"I've given guns to all of them. I have warned them to be careful. If anyone goes out, it will be his own funeral if he gets hurt. And I believe"—Elger's tone was crafty—"that Mr. Jalway is going to walk into trouble."

"You mean we're to watch him?"

"Exactly. You and the men that you still have. Cover the house, Ruff. Capture Jalway if he appears. Bring him here, through the entrance from the marsh."

"What if he puts up a fight?"

"Don't kill him—unless you have to do so. We'll make him talk. We're going to find out what he did with the swag."

"What about the others, chief?"

"Later we shall form a searching party. Tomorrow—after the shipment has come ashore from the *Dalmatia*. We shall look for Jalway's body. We shall find it. Riddled with bullets, somewhere in a swamp. You and your crew will be gone."

"In the boat?"

"A few of you. Others, including those from the *Dalmatia*, may be in hiding in these caverns. I shall decide about that later."

"But when the others find Jalway, then—"

"They will be reminded of my admonition that all should be careful. They will stand by me when I testify to the law that Jalway disobeyed my orders. That sailor, Hoskins; Dalavan; Golga; and finally Jalway—all will be classed as victims of outlaws who have terrorized Timour Isle."

RUFF TURNEY nodded. He could see the merits of this scheme. Purvis Elger had run into difficulties of late; but the master schemer was figuring the best way out. The elimination of Bram Jalway was an absolute necessity to the culmination of his schemes.

"Personally," remarked Elger, in a cold tone, "I should like to eliminate all these castaways. But the fact that those aboard the *Maldah* may begin a search is something that I cannot ignore.

"There is no telling how much Jalway may have learned. He is a menace. We must finish him, and we must regain the articles that he stole. That is the course we shall take; and through it I shall strengthen—not weaken—my position with the other unwanted guests."

With an imperious gesture, Elger pointed to the opposite exit. Ruff nodded as he arose. It was time for him to start out and assemble the band for the capture of Bram Jalway.

"I shall see you later, Ruff," reminded Elger, as he arose and stalked toward his own passage. "I feel positive that Jalway will go out tonight. I shall allow half an hour for his capture. So I shall come here at the end of that period, starting my time with Jalway's departure from the house."

The two crooks took their opposite courses. When Elger reached his study, he filled his meerschaum from a tobacco jar and donned a smoking jacket. Puffing his pipe in leisurely fashion, he strolled out to the living room.

All of the guests were present. Francine Feldworth was curled in a large chair, reading a book. Seth Hadlow was seated in a corner, quietly smoking a cigarette. Professor Marcolm was busy with his manuscripts; but the gray-haired guest looked weary and irritable.

Bram Jalway was strolling about the room. He showed signs of curbed restlessness. Elger gave him a cheery greeting, then sat down to talk to Hadlow. The conversation, though quietly conducted, became disturbing to Professor Marcolm. The white-haired man looked about.

"We are bothering you, Professor?" inquired Elger. "If you wish, you may use my den for your work. It is quiet and secluded there."

"I shall go to my own room," returned the professor, politely. "A little more work, then to bed. I am quite nervous, Mr. Elger. Quite nervous."

HE began to gather up the manuscript pages. Jalway stopped his pacing and turned to Elger.

"I'm going out a while," announced the promoter.

"To the beach?" inquired Elger.

"Yes," said Jalway. "I want to look about. To see what it is like at night. There is mystery on this isle."

"Too much mystery," inserted Hadlow.

"I should not advise you to go out alone," reminded Elger, concentrating on Jalway. "If you wish, I can send Royne with you."

"He may be needed here," returned Jalway. "I shall not go far from the house. I am armed"—he produced the revolver that he had received from Royne—"and I can take care of myself."

Abruptly, Jalway turned on his heel and strolled to the front door. Chunk, on guard there, drew back the bolts and allowed Jalway's passage. Elger resumed conversation with Hadlow.

Professor Marcolm finished gathering his papers and left for his room. Fifteen minutes later, Francine yawned and announced that she intended to retire. The girl departed. Another quarter of an hour elapsed. Conversation lulled between Hadlow and Elger. The latter arose.

"I must bid you good night," he said to Hadlow. "Since Professor Marcolm is not using my den, I can engage in some important research there."

"And I'll read a while and then turn in," stated Hadlow, with a quiet smile. "Good night, Elger."

Leaving the living room, Purvis Elger headed directly for the den. Arriving in that room, he locked the door behind him. The fiendish leer that appeared upon his pudgy face was one of anticipation.

For Purvis Elger was confident that his plan had gained success. He was sure that on his coming visit to the rendezvous, he would find Bram Jalway a captive in the hands of Ruff Turney.

CHAPTER XIV
THE PRISONER TALKS

BRAM JALWAY, when he left the tabby-walled house, had acted in direct opposite to his announced plan. He had said that he would keep close to the shelter of the house. Instead, he took a rapid and immediate course toward the beach.

Keeping along the fringe of oak trees, Jalway formed an obscure figure. At times he was completely lost beneath the thick streamers of Spanish moss that hung from long, low boughs. At other moments, the moonlight broke through to show him clearly in its glow.

At such intervals, Jalway quickened his pace and moved closer to the woods. At last his course cut through the underbrush. Jalway wallowed knee-deep through gnarled roots, as he passed the ruins of the old mansion in the center of the isle.

Followers were on his trail. In this jungle it was difficult for one to note lurkers who were familiar with the terrain. Moving away from the house, Jalway skirted a bit of marshy land and came out near the lower inlet.

Here were sand dunes, ghostlike in the filtered

moonlight. Passing one, Jalway came to the edge of a swamp that lay between parallel dunes. This was a typical Georgia slough; called a "hammock," in the Southern parlance.

It stretched into the end of the isle and as Jalway sought the higher ground, he came beneath the shelter of huge pines and cedars that vied with the oaks for dominance.

Swamp lay beyond. That was where Jalway was heading. All the while, he was circling farther from the house that he had left. He was cutting deeper into the terrain that harbored Ruff Turney's band.

Unwittingly, Jalway was making the trap easier. He had escaped attack, for he was going in the very direction that his stalkers wanted. He paused on the verge of swampy land where trees formed a veritable jungle. Seeing nothing through the blackness, Jalway began to retrace his steps.

The course that he took was directly toward the ruins of the old slave buildings. Stumbling through mushy soil, finding foothold upon spots of thicker ground, this investigator came almost to the spot where the hidden entrance to the lower passage was located.

Wrenching free from tangling brambles, Jalway seemed undecided concerning his next move. As he paused, he heard movement close behind him. He turned in that direction, drew his gun and suddenly flicked a flashlight from his left hand. The glare revealed a dodging figure. Jalway aimed.

At that instant, two men pounced upon him from in back. Struggling, Jalway sprawled in the thicket. His arms were gripped. Ruff Turney's growl ordered him to make no trouble. For a moment, Jalway persisted in the struggle. Then his gun was gone; two more men had fallen upon him. Thongs were wrapped about his arms and legs. A gag was jammed between his teeth.

More growls. The captors hoisted their prisoner. Ruff's light blinked. A dozen paces brought the band to the brush-covered trapdoor. Ruff raised the entrance. The others dragged Jalway down the steps. Ruff took the lead through the passage.

PURVIS ELGER was awaiting their arrival. Puffing impatiently at his meerschaum, the portly crook indulged in a venomous smile when the prisoner was lugged into view. He had the captors lay Jalway back against the box that housed the telegraph outfit. Ruff dismissed his men. Elger and the lieutenant alone remained with the prisoner.

"Cut the gag, Ruff," ordered Elger.

Ruff complied. Jalway moved his jaws, then studied Elger with a look almost of contempt.

"Surprised, eh?" quizzed Elger, in a sarcastic tone.

"Yes," admitted Jalway, hoarsely. "I was looking for a bunch of thugs. But I didn't expect to find you in with them. I suppose you've got a passage of your own, leading to this hangout."

"An excellent guess," chuckled Elger, puffing at his meerschaum. "Well, Jalway, your goose is cooked. You might as well talk. What did you do with the box you took from Dalavan?"

"The box I took from Dalavan?"

"Why stall, Jalway? We know you killed Dalavan and Golga. We've been checking on you right along."

Jalway smiled sourly and shook his head.

"You must be smoking opium in that big pipe of yours," he parried. "If you think I bumped those fellows, you're all wrong. I never saw Dalavan in my life before I joined you in your study and saw him dead upon the floor."

"Want me to make him talk, chief?" inquired Ruff, in a vicious tone. "I've got a few ways of doing it, you know."

"Not necessary, Ruff," replied Elger. "Jalway is too sensible to force us to resort to torture methods. Come, Jalway"—he eyed the prisoner coldly—"you're through. Why not admit the point?"

"I can't admit what I don't know," challenged Jalway. "I figured you bumped that fellow Dalavan yourself, Elger. I thought he must have killed Golga and you shot him to get even. I didn't blame you for covering up."

"Let us return to your own case," suggested Elger. He drew over a chest and sat upon it. "One night, Golga reported that you had made an exit from the house by way of the living room window. Do you admit that you were out?"

"Sure," replied Jalway. "Why not? I wanted to look around, like I was doing tonight."

ELGER eyed Jalway coldly. Ruff showed impatience; the lieutenant wanted to give the prisoner the heat. Elger, however, had smoother methods. He decided to talk further; to lull Jalway and thereby induce the prisoner to commit himself by some unguarded statement.

"Look about you," suggested Elger, suavely. "This is your opportunity, Jalway, to see the actual state of affairs on Timour Isle. Here you see millions in treasures stolen from Europe. My business is the importation of such rarities.

"Tonight, a final shipment is coming from a tramp steamer called the *Dalmatia*. Ruff and his men mistook the *Maldah* for that ship, the night you landed. This telegraph line makes contact with the mainland.

"Until tonight, Tully was in charge at the other end. He informed me, by the way, that the

Maldah is twenty miles up the coast. The yacht is stranded; and refusing offers of salvage."

A curious gleam came into Jalway's eyes. They showed eagerness, which Jalway quickly restrained. Elger was puzzled by the expression; but he decided to press his final point.

"Tonight," declared the master crook, "Dalavan brought me spoils from New York. He had a suitcase with him. It contained a tiara and the sum of fifty thousand dollars. The case is gone. You, Jalway, are the man whom I hold responsible."

Elger waited for the effect upon Jalway. He noted a return of the prisoner's eager expression—a look that gave Jalway the air of a schemer. Jalway spoke; but he did not refer to the main theme. Instead, he took up a subject that Elger had merely chanced to mention.

"Since the *Maldah* is safe," remarked Jalway, "a search will eventually begin for the passengers who came ashore here. You will have to produce them, Elger."

"Some of them," returned Elger dryly. "For an alibi."

Jalway grimaced. He knew that he would not be included among the rescued. It was obvious that Elger would attribute his death to outlaws. Jalway changed his tone.

"Regarding Dalavan's suitcase," he said. "Suppose you learn that I did not take it? What will you do then? Eliminate the other survivors until you find the right one?"

Elger nodded, while he puffed his pipe.

"The less the number of survivors," reasoned Jalway, "the better your position, Elger, provided that you kept just one, who would support any statements that you might make. Such a survivor could help you dispose of the others. He could state later that all were lost in the overturn of the lifeboat. He would say nothing about the deaths of Dalavan and Golga. In brief, Elger, you would be greatly helped by an ally as crooked as yourself."

"Not a bad idea, Jalway," approved Elger. "You would like to be that one survivor. I am willing to make the deal, if you turn over the goods you took from Dalavan."

"I can't do that." Jalway shook his head wearily. "I swear I'm not the man who took the stuff. All I can do is help you regain it by aiding in the elimination of the others who came from the *Maldah*."

"I'm a crook," snarled Elger, "and I like to deal with crooks! If you could deliver the stuff, that would prove you worthy! Since you can't—"

"I can help you get it," interjected Jalway. His face was as fierce as Elger's. "As proof of my worth, I can show you the way to a clean-up that is right along your alley. I can give you the low-down on Kingdon Feldworth. Why he's refusing offers of aid for the *Maldah*. Why he doesn't want the yacht salvaged—"

"Hold it!" Elger spoke with a tone of conviction. He had caught the channel of Jalway's talk. "Cut him loose, Ruff."

DUMFOUNDED, the lieutenant cut the thongs that held Jalway. Elger, meanwhile, produced a tobacco pouch from his pocket. As Jalway struggled to his feet, Elger proffered the pouch.

"Got your briar with you?" he asked.

Jalway nodded, grinning.

"Fill it and smoke up," ordered Elger with a chuckle. "We'll talk as crook to crook. I've seen the light. You know something that's worth while—something that will make our deal a real one.

"Sit back, Ruff, and listen." Elger shook his head as he observed the lieutenant drawing a revolver to cover Jalway. "Put away that rod. You won't need it. This man has convinced me. Spill it, Jalway. I'm listening."

Jalway rubbed his chafed wrists. He produced his briar and filled it with Elger's tobacco. Elger extended a lighted match. Jalway puffed away and seated himself on a chest opposite Elger's.

Aromas of briar and meerschaum mingled while Jalway began to talk. Elger, listening, inserted comments of his own. Schemers both, the two were in accord, while Ruff Turney sat astounded as he heard the game that the crafty pair developed.

CHAPTER XV
THE NEW GAME

"WHEN I went aboard the *Maldah*, in New York," stated Jalway in a candid tone, "I did so with the intention of building up a reputation with Kingdon Feldworth. I figured that he was wealthy enough to be due for a trimming at some future date."

"I take it that swindling is your game," observed Elger.

"It is," admitted Jalway. "But I've kept it nicely undercover. When I fleece saps like Feldworth, I do it indirectly. Stock deals in which I appear to be a dupe also."

"Did you ever handle a stock called Consolidated Securities?" inquired Elger.

"Never heard of it," returned Jalway. "It sounds like a flimflam. Where did you hear about it?"

"Through a friend." Elger was eyeing Jalway carefully. "Forget it. Go on with your story."

"In Havana," resumed Jalway, "we all went

ashore. Hadlow took Francine about the city; the old professor went to a museum. Only the captain and Feldworth were aboard the yacht when I returned unexpectedly.

"A flock of Cuban stevedores were loading some boxes aboard the *Maldah*. They took them into the cabin, then came out and went away. I saw the captain come from the cabin. Figuring that Feldworth was in, I strolled up and rapped at the door. Feldworth admitted me. He thought I was the captain coming back. The boxes were gone."

"Where were they?" asked Elger.

"I'm coming to that," explained Jalway. "I must have looked about in rather curious fashion, because Feldworth guessed that I had seen the boxes. He shut the cabin door and took me into his confidence."

"Regarding the contents of the boxes?"

"Yes. It appears that Feldworth had met a wealthy Cuban in New York. One of those fellows who had to scamper from Havana after the revolution. The Cuban had left a million dollars' worth of rare curios buried in Havana. He was hard up; he sold the lot to Feldworth for two hundred grand. But Feldworth had to get the stuff."

"He managed it without trouble?"

"Yes. The Cuban had told him where the stuff was buried. He also gave Feldworth the names of certain loyalists in Havana. Those chaps were the stevedores—fake ones, of course—and they delivered the goods aboard the yacht. Went after the stuff pronto when Feldworth told them where it was stowed."

"Where did Feldworth put the boxes?"

"In a secret compartment at the end of his cabin. He opened it and gave me a look into one of the boxes. I had a flash of some rare stuff. Jeweled hangings—cloth of gold—enough to tell me that the million dollar talk was true."

"So that," mused Elger, "is why Kingdon Feldworth prefers not to abandon his stranded yacht."

"Absolutely," stated Jalway. "You know the laws of salvage. A claim on the cargo as well as the ship itself. It isn't the *Maldah* that Feldworth cares about. He wants to get that stuff ashore. That's why he's sticking to the ship."

ELGER nodded. Exhaling pipe smoke, he studied Jalway closely, expecting some suggestion. It came.

"Suppose," said Jalway, "that raiders went after that yacht? They could massacre the crew, get the stuff ashore, and take for cover. This cavern would be as good a hideout for Feldworth's stuff as it is for the swag you've already got."

"It would," agreed Elger, "and there would be no trouble in disposing of the goods."

"You're getting it," said Jalway. "The only fellow who might blab would be the Cuban. And he'd keep quiet. He's gotten his dough."

Elger nodded. Ruff eyed his chief. The lieutenant, too, was seeing possibilities. He expressed them.

"With that mob from the *Dalmatia*," put in Ruff, "we'd have a cinch, chief! This looks like a pipe—"

"Restrain your enthusiasm, Ruff," interposed Elger. Then, to Jalway: "Continue with your story. Tell me about your actions here on Timour Isle."

"That's easy," stated Jalway. "Now that you know the inside of the game. When the lifeboat hit the beach, we encountered opposition. Then we came to your house. You welcomed us and told us that there were desperate characters hereabout. You fooled me. Perfectly."

"Yet you decided to look about the island—"

"Certainly. Because I figured that the *Maldah* would get stranded somewhere. I was going to go out through the window of my bedroom; then I figured that might be bad if found out. So I picked the living room window instead."

"And your purpose was to hunt up the outlaws?"

"You've guessed it. I figured if they were tough enough to bump Hoskins, they'd be good enough to form a pirate party and go after the *Maldah*. I wanted to make contact with the outlaws. I felt sure they must be at the lower end of the island."

Elger was almost convinced by Jalway's story. The portly supercrook held to one lone, lurking suspicion. He decided to settle it by a final quiz.

"Where were you last night?" demanded Elger. "At the time when the shots were fired?"

"Outside again," returned Jalway promptly. "I still wanted to contact the outlaws. Golga was in the living room, blocking me; but when I heard him go back to your den, I hurried to the living room. I loosened the frame and scrambled through."

"After the shots were fired in the den?"

"I didn't hear any shots. I was starting to close the window when I heard Dashler rousing every one from the front hall. I thought it best to come in; but I left the frame as it was. When you discovered it and sprang your theory regarding an outsider, I thought you were trying to cover up the fact that you bumped Dalavan."

"Evidently," chuckled Elger, "we each gave the other undue credit. I suppose you thought that I was still trying to play innocent tonight?"

"I did," rejoined Jalway. "That's why I chanced

a bold stroll on the beach. I still wanted to meet up with the outlaws."

ELGER pulled a penciled sheet from his pocket. He studied the notations then spoke to Jalway.

"The night when Golga learned that you were out," declared Elger, "he saw a light beneath Francine Feldworth's door and also heard the girl moving about. He entered the professor's room and saw the old man asleep in his bed. He heard Dashler snoring, when he stopped outside the sailor's door. He thought that he heard Seth Hadlow cough."

"What has that night to do with it?" queried Jalway. "I have already admitted that I was out of the house."

"One of those four people," declared Elger, "was responsible for the deaths of Dalavan and Golga. That is why I am trying to check on all of them."

"Last night is all that counts," persisted Jalway. "Just the same, I see your point. Golga wasn't sure about Hadlow."

"That's it," acknowledged Elger. "I have an idea that Hadlow was looking about from the start. If so, he is the man who encountered Dalavan; and finished Golga as a sequel. Hadlow is the man that we must watch. He may know too much."

Elger pocketed his notes and turned to Ruff Turney.

"Ruff," said Elger, "when you go out to the *Dalmatia*, tell the captain to stand by. Tell him that you are bringing out some boxes loaded with junk for him to heave overboard."

Ruff looked about in surprise. He nudged his thumb toward the treasure chests, then queried:

"Which of the stuff is fake?"

"None of it," chuckled Elger while Jalway smiled. "We are simply going to murder our unwelcome guests and put their bodies into weighted boxes. We shall require four such caskets."

"Why bump the girl?" queried Jalway. "If this is staged like a raid, she will think it's on the up and up. I've sort of had my eye on Francine, even though she's more partial to Seth Hadlow—"

"I understand," interrupted Elger. "If you managed to save her, she would be all for you. We can make a bargain, Jalway. If Francine listens to reason, she can live. If not, she will die like the others—"

"Agreed."

THAT settled, Elger remembered another item. He spoke to Ruff, telling him to arrange for three extra boxes to carry the bodies of Dalavan, Golga and Hoskins. That done, Elger gestured toward the farther cavern, indicating that both Ruff and Jalway should use that exit, while he went back through the regular passage to his house.

"Prepare to contact the *Dalmatia*, Ruff," ordered Elger. "I shall rely upon Tully and Chunk to work with Jalway and myself. Your course, Jalway, is to complete your stroll and circle back to the house. I shall be there, wondering about your safety. Remember: we must dupe Seth Hadlow. The old professor and the sailor will cut no figure."

Pocketing his big meerschaum, the arch-crook started for his own passage while Ruff and Jalway went in the opposite direction. Ruff carried the lantern that had provided illumination for the conference. En route to the house, Purvis Elger indulged in an insidious chuckle.

The arch-crook felt that he had bargained well with Bram Jalway. Fully convinced by the promoter's story, keyed with hope of further swag through a piratical attack upon the crippled *Maldah*, Elger looked forward to a profitable alliance.

Since George Dalavan was dead. Elger would need a new man to organize a crew of smooth agents who could unload the European spoils. Bram Jalway was just the sort to fill the bill. He would simply come in for Dalavan's share of the proceeds from the loot.

An excellent arrangement, since Jalway had revealed that there was a million dollars in additional booty aboard the *Maldah*. In fact, Elger was glad that Dalavan had died to make the replacement possible. As for the tiara and the money that Dalavan had brought, Elger felt confident that they would be regained.

Once the four victims were eliminated, the lost items could be found; for Elger felt sure that Hadlow must have hidden them somewhere inside the house. The sooner the climax, the better, in Elger's estimation; for Hadlow would have no time to bury the tiara and the cash in some outside hiding spot.

With Bram Jalway as an ally, the game seemed ironclad to Purvis Elger. Though he counted Seth Hadlow as a capable foeman, Elger had no inkling that the hand of The Shadow was involved. Therefore, the master crook felt no insecurity regarding the grim game in which Bram Jalway had promised to cooperate.

CHAPTER XVI
THE SHADOW WAITS

WHEN Purvis Elger regained his study, he immediately went out into the hall and strolled in the direction of the living room. A frown furrowed his wide forehead as he heard the sound of voices, Francine's among them.

Entering the living room, Elger found the girl and Dashler talking with Tully and Chunk. Royne was standing in the background. The cadaverous servant's face was troubled; it cleared as the man saw Elger.

"What is the matter?" inquired Elger. He looked about in his usual friendly fashion. "Where are the others? Hadlow—Jalway—the professor?"

"Jalway is still out," responded Dashler. "Hadlow has gone out to look for him. Neither has returned. I have just been talking about making a search."

"I said we should wait for you, sir," put in Royne. "That's why I rapped at your door, Mr. Elger."

"I thought I heard someone knocking," said Elger. "I was in the bedroom, dozing, with the door closed. So Hadlow went out to look for Jalway. How long ago?"

"About fifteen minutes back," replied Dashler. "I was in my room, or I'd have gone out with him."

"I couldn't sleep," added Francine. "I came out to learn if anyone happened to be up; when I learned that Mr. Hadlow had gone out to search, I called for Dashler."

"Well, well," mused Elger. "I had no idea that this complication would occur the moment that I told my guests they could fare forth. What were you two doing?" The question was to Tully and Chunk. "Why did you let Hadlow go out alone?"

"Your orders, Mr. Elger," reminded Tully, in an uneasy tone. "You let Mr. Jalway go out. We didn't stop Mr. Hadlow."

"They will probably return shortly," decided Elger. "If they do not, we shall begin a search. By the way, where is Professor Marcolm? I hope he managed to desist from a stroll along the beach."

"The professor is asleep," stated Francine. "I knocked at the door of his room and he answered. But he was so drowsy that I hesitated to disturb him. I called Dashler instead."

"I warned Jalway," remarked Elger, filling his pipe from the ever-ready pouch. "I told him—and Hadlow heard me—that this milder weather might mean new danger on Timour Isle. But both these chaps are armed. I believe that they can take care of themselves. Suppose"—he glanced at his watch—"that we allow them ten minutes to return."

The others nodded in agreement. They sat down about the room. Elger lighted his meerschaum and paced back and forth. He was more troubled than he cared to reveal. Hadlow's trip outside was something that he had not foreseen.

WHILE the little group remained in the living room, the island outside the house was gloomy beneath the faint rays of a cloud-enveloped moon. Giant oaks still swayed in response to fitful winds. The steady roar of the surf beat up hollow echoes from the beach.

Far out to sea, a line of lights was moving to the south. Vanishing, then reappearing beyond the long swells, that slow streak of illumination indicated the presence of a ship.

From beneath the shelter of moss-laden boughs, keen eyes were watching the lights at sea. The ship was anchoring off Timour Isle. Those same eyes spied another light. From the south of the island, beyond the sand dunes, a small boat was putting out to sea.

Ruff Turney and his squad were on their way to contact with the *Dalmatia*. A soft laugh whispered from the gloom. It was the strange mirth of The Shadow—a tone of suppressed mockery that echoed weirdly in the wafting breeze.

Then came silence. The author of the laugh had moved away. Silently, beneath the fringe of trees, The Shadow was returning to the house. No sign marked his passage toward the clearing that surrounded the white tabby walls.

Ever mysterious, even when uncloaked, The Shadow had become a part of the night itself. No human eye could have discerned his approach to the old lookout house.

FIVE minutes passed, while the vague lights from the living room windows shone unblinkingly along the tabby walls. Then from the pathway to the house, a figure stepped suddenly into view. A strolling person advanced toward the door.

The arrival turned suddenly, as though hearing a sound close by. He spied another person coming from the edge of the clearing. The man by the door spoke.

"Who's there?" he challenged.

"Hadlow," came the quiet response. "Is that you, Jalway?"

"Yes." Jalway laughed slightly. "Rather spooky, the way you stepped into sight."

"I was looking about for you," returned the sportsman. "I thought maybe you had circled the house. Where have you been, old chap?"

"Down to the end of the island. Come. Let's enter. They may be worrying about us."

Jalway rapped on the door. It opened promptly. As the two men entered, Francine Feldworth sprang from the living room to greet them. Concern still showed on the girl's face. It was plain that she was glad that the men had returned.

Purvis Elger, stepping from the living room, gave a cheery welcome. At the same time, the portly man was observant. He noted that Francine's greeting to Hadlow was more spontaneous than her welcome of Jalway. This fitted with the rivalry that Jalway had mentioned during the conference in the cavern.

Professor Marcolm's door came open. The white-haired guest had heard the commotion in the hall. Attired in a dressing gown, he blinked sleepily as he crackled a question regarding the disturbance. Francine turned to explain concerning the absence of Jalway and Hadlow.

"I heard you knock some time ago," recalled Marcolm, in a wheezy tone. "I was on the point of rising then; but I went back to sleep almost unconsciously. This new noise, however, completely awakened me."

"Stay up and have a cup of coffee," suggested Elger. "I'm sending Royne to get some refreshments."

"That would mean staying up all night," smiled the professor. "With me, a sound sleep is the only sleep, and coffee disturbs it. I miss those lulling winds that marked our first nights here. But I believe"—he paused to scratch his tousled mop of hair—"that I can sleep again if I remain undisturbed."

His tone almost reproachful, the professor returned to his room and closed the door behind him. The others went into the living room.

In casual manner, Elger questioned Jalway regarding his stroll on the beach. He asked him if he had seen any sign of prowlers. Jalway shook his head to give a negative reply. Hadlow remarked that he had also found the beach quiet. He added that he had looked for Jalway along the upper inlet.

ROYNE appeared, pushing a tea wagon from the kitchen. The cadaverous servant had prepared sandwiches as well as coffee. Host and guests welcomed the refreshments and began to devour them with gusto. All were chatty, except Francine.

The girl had a sense of impending danger. She tried to attribute it to the worry that she had felt during Seth Hadlow's absence. Nevertheless, the foreboding remained. Francine noted that Purvis Elger was more than unusually jolly. She saw Bram Jalway smiling in his natural fashion. Seth Hadlow seemed less solemn than usual. Dashler, finishing his second cup of coffee, showed no sign of worry.

Francine could not understand why she felt those qualms. Yet she had cause for foreboding, though she did not know the reason. Doom was hovering over Timour Isle tonight. New schemes had been concocted by Purvis Elger, the master crook who posed in friendly guise.

Those lights at sea; the moving light beyond the sand dune—both were proof that men of crime had gathered to perform service for an evil chief. They were offset only by the fact that watching eyes had seen those symbols of lurking crime. The Shadow had spied the moves that were being made.

The Shadow's plans—like Elger's—were settled for this night. Before the crook's schemes reached their culmination, The Shadow would enter into the game. For the present, however, he was playing a waiting part, within the very building that sheltered an evil master and a group of intended victims.

When The Shadow's turn arrived, he would surely introduce an element of surprise that had not been discussed by Purvis Elger and Bram Jalway during their conference within the caverns of stolen wealth.

CHAPTER XVII
ABOARD THE *DALMATIA*

THREE men were grouped in a grimy, bunk-lined compartment. The dingy glow of oil lanterns illuminated their faces. One was a crafty-eyed little fellow. The others were keen-visaged young men whose countenances showed determination.

The little man was Hawkeye. His companions were Harry Vincent and Cliff Marsland. Hawkeye, first in Charleston, had gained his berth aboard the *Dalmatia*. More than that, he had found places for Harry and Cliff.

Like Hawkeye, the other agents of The Shadow had shipped aboard as able-bodied seamen to replace members of the crew swept overboard while the *Dalmatia* had been fleeing the hurricane.

The rest of the crew were up on deck. The ship was anchored off Timour Isle. One occupant alone remained in the forecastle with The Shadow's agents. That was a snoring man who lay sprawled in a lower bunk, rolling back and forth with every long sway of the ship.

"I've talked with Hexler," whispered Hawkeye, "and he's slated me to go ashore with the landing crew, to take the place of this fellow, Lopey"—he paused, indicated the dead head in the bunk—"so that puts me in the game. But Hexler don't want more than one."

"That's tough," remarked Harry, grimly.

"You bet it is," acknowledged Hawkeye. "But it's lucky that I'm in on the deal. I worked my head off getting Lopey loaded up with that grog we found in the hold. Say—it would be tough if Hexler found out I handed Lopey the booze."

"Lopey passed out before Hexler had a chance to question him," said Harry. "Cliff and I lugged

Lopey down here. He could hardly talk when Hexler found him up near the bow. What's he going to do with Lopey?"

"He's taking him ashore," replied Hawkeye. "Just to have him later on. But he's supposed to bring six men with him. All in good shape. That's why he gave me the chance.

"It's tough that those poor guys who went overboard weren't part of Hexler's outfit. Then there'd be jobs for you two fellows, too. But as it is, you're slated to stick with the ship until she reaches Tampico."

"But we're going ashore tonight," put in Harry

"That's the ticket," agreed Hawkeye. "But how're you going to make it?"

"I'll tell you how." It was Cliff who spoke. "We'll lug Lopey up on the deck. If the captain wonders where we are, tell him what we're doing."

"And then?" prompted Hawkeye.

"Then," stated Cliff, "the stuff will be on its way up from the hold. We'll start down to help. But instead, we'll cut back to the stern. We'll lower one of the small boats on the port side."

"You'll have a tough time in this swell—"

"Maybe. It would be easier on the starboard side, but the unloading will be done in the lee of the ship; so we'll have to risk the outside. We'll clear the stern and head for the upper end of the island."

HARRY nodded his accord with Cliff's plan. Before further discussion could begin, footsteps clattered at the head of the forecastle stairs.

"Hey, you, below there!"

"Aye, aye, sir!" responded Hawkeye. The little man scampered to the steps. "Coming right up."

"Who else is down there?" growled the man at the top, as Hawkeye reappeared. The Shadow's agent recognized the second mate.

"Two seamen," returned Hawkeye, "bringing up Lopey. He's got to go ashore."

"Hurry it up!" bawled the mate, leaning toward the forecastle.

With the mate following, Hawkeye headed toward the starboard side of the ship. Reaching the rail, he saw a small cabin boat moored below. A man was coming up the rope ladder that the *Dalmatia* had lowered.

Hawkeye stared as he saw the hard face beneath the lantern light. He knew this fellow from days gone by. Ruff Turney, missing mob-leader from Manhattan. Hawkeye shrank back behind the rail, then shrugged his shoulders.

He had been small fry when Ruff was a swaggering mob-leader. He realized that Ruff would not remember him, even if they came face to face.

Boldly, Hawkeye edged forward to join Hexler. This man—leader of the minions on the *Dalmatia*—was a brawny, rough-faced fellow who looked like a seaman.

"Where's Lopey?" growled Hexler.

"Coming up," responded Hawkeye.

He turned away as Ruff joined Hexler. Hatches were off the hold; boxes were being raised by the crew. Other men were lowering a boat on the lee side of the *Dalmatia*. Harry and Cliff, coming from the forecastle, were bringing "Lopey" toward the side.

They dropped the sodden mass of humanity upon the deck, then turned and moved away. The second mate, challenged them.

"Where you going?"

"Down to the hold, sir," replied Cliff, "to help with the boxes."

"Get a move on then," growled the mate.

Hawkeye noted Ruff observing Lopey's prostate form. The mob-leader grunted, then turned angrily to Hexler.

"What's the matter with this dope?" he demanded.

"Drunk," informed Hexler. "Got hold of some grog that was aboard. First thing I knew, he'd gone blotto."

"Making you one man short?"

"I've got this mug"—Hexler turned to indicate Hawkeye—"and he'll fill in for Lopey. Says he can handle a gat."

"Can you?" demanded Ruff.

"Sure," acknowledged Hawkeye.

"He shipped aboard at Charleston," explained Hexler. "He's not one of the regular bohunks in the crew. This is a guy we can use."

"Looks all right," admitted Ruff. "But that doesn't help. We're still short-handed."

"How come? I've got six—"

"The chief wants more. Two, anyway. But coming out here, I began to figure it would be tough to get them. We can't yank off the regular members of the crew. The captain would put up a squawk—"

"Say"—Hexler had an idea—"There were two other birds came on at Charleston. Buddies of this guy. What about 'em, Ruff?"

"What are they like?"

"Tough eggs."

HAWKEYE put in a clincher of his own.

"We was hiding out in Charleston," he confided to Ruff. "The three of us. We ain't seamen; we just bluffed it. We used to be with Cozy Doman's mob."

"Yeah?" quizzed Ruff, in surprise. "A bunch of bank workers."

"Sure," acknowledged Hawkeye, with a nod. "We cut loose from Cozy after he pulled that job in Wilmington, North Carolina. It was getting too hot. That's why we was laying low."

"Go get your pals," ordered Ruff.

Hawkeye turned and hastened off, as though heading for the hold. But he changed direction as soon as he was out of sight. Running to the stern, he came upon a boat that was hanging loose from the davits.

"Cliff!" whispered Hawkeye, hoarsely. "Harry!"

The two agents popped into view. They had ducked into a companionway at the sound of Hawkeye's footsteps. Quickly, Hawkeye gave them the news.

"Duck down into the hold," he suggested. "I'll tell Hexler you're coming up."

Returning, Hawkeye found Hexler impatiently awaiting him. Ruff had gone away to confer with the captain. What he was doing was arranging for the *Dalmatia* to stand by until a cargo came from shore.

"Where are the other guys?" demanded Hexler.

"Coming up," replied Hawkeye. "You'll see 'em in a minute."

THE last of the boxes had come from the hold. Immediately following came Cliff and Harry, up through the open hatchway. They slouched over as Hawkeye beckoned. Hexler studied the new recruits. He had not noticed Harry and Cliff carefully before. Now he nodded, convinced that they would measure up to Ruff's requirements.

Boxes were being lowered into the boats; some into Ruff's cabin launch; others into the boat that the *Dalmatia* had dropped. Ruff's crew was exchanging greetings with the men in the *Dalmatia*'s boat. These outfits had met before.

Ruff came back from his confab with the captain. He eyed Harry and Cliff, then nodded approvingly to indicate that they were satisfactory.

"We're coming out again," he told Hexler. "Bringing back the boat to the ship here and loading some stuff aboard. We'll arrange all that later. Let's go."

Cargoes were loaded. Hexler motioned to the rope ladder. Harry and Cliff descended; then Hawkeye followed. The little man got snarled in the rope. That seemed to please Ruff.

"That bird's no seaman," chuckled the mob-leader, speaking to Hexler. "You can tell it from the way he tangled. You hit a ten strike, getting these three bimboes. They're just the ones we'll need."

"More work ahead?"

"Plenty. You'll get the dope later."

Ruff leaned over and motioned Hawkeye into the *Dalmatia*'s boat, separating him from Harry and Cliff. Hexler descended, stepped aboard Ruff's boat and shifted over into the other boat as Hawkeye had done. Ruff was the last to come down the ladder.

The two boats pushed off from the heaving side of the *Dalmatia*. Ruff's boat began to chug toward the island, its motor throttled low. The *Dalmatia*'s boat followed, propelled by the strokes of brawny oarsmen.

Combined crews of crime were on their way to accomplish evil. Timour Isle was threatened with armed invasion as the first step toward a fiendish purpose. But with those invaders were coming men prepared to strive for right.

Though outnumbered by their dangerous companions, The Shadow's agents were grimly prepared to play their part when the time of conflict came.

CHAPTER XVIII
THE ATTACK

THE powerboat was the first to meet the lower inlet. Passing the sand dunes, the craft veered toward a channel which Ruff, at the tiller, picked with accuracy. The boat came to a stop with its prow wedged in a muddy landing place.

Ruff ordered all ashore. Harry and Cliff followed the other members of the crew. Ruff led the way through heavy underbrush, while his men brought the boxes from the boat.

Stacking the spoils, Ruff ordered his crew toward the beach. They skirted a sand dune, then waited on a little point. Ruff swung a lantern; an answering glimmer came from the inlet. The boat from the *Dalmatia* was heaving toward this portion of the shore.

Hexler and his henchmen landed. Ruff ordered his own men to take the boxes that had come from this second boat. The shore crew lugged their burdens off through the darkness, toward the spot where they had left the first load.

Cliff and Harry remained with Hexler's crew. Ruff held confab with Hexler. Nods of agreement were exchanged beneath the dull moonlight. Ruff turned and took the path along which his burden carriers had gone.

HAWKEYE sidled over beside Cliff and Harry. The Shadow's three agents were again united. Yet the situation was not entirely to their liking. Though they exchanged no comments, all held the same idea.

They knew that danger was abroad. Two crews of thugs were ready to deliver an attack somewhere. If Hexler's crew should strike, The

Shadow's agents would be in the proper place. But if Ruff's outfit intended trouble on its own, that mob could move unmolested.

One thought alone was saving. Ruff's outfit had a definite task; to store the boxes that had been brought from the *Dalmatia*. That signified that the criminal work would probably be shifted to Hexler and his outfit. As members of that band, The Shadow's agents might find opportunity to counteract trouble.

There were eight men besides Hexler. Lopey had been left in the boat, which was drawn high on the shore. Thus The Shadow's agents were outnumbered two to one. But such odds did not trouble them. Like the rest of the crew, they were armed. They felt capable of tendering a good account should the pinch arise.

"We're going up the island." Hexler growled this information as he joined his men. "Don't worry about those other fellows. This is our job. We're heading for a house at the upper inlet!"

Harry nudged Cliff. This was the kind of news they had been waiting for. It meant that Hexler, not Ruff, was scheduled to attack some place on Timour Isle.

"The house is in a clearing," continued Hexler. "When we get there, plant yourselves on the edges. Ready for a rush when I give the word."

Affirmative growls from the band. The Shadow's agents joined in the comment. Hexler was about to start the march when a thick voice called from the shore. "Lopey," a trifle unsteady, was coming to rejoin the invaders.

"Get back in the boat!" ordered Hexler, in a rasping tone. "Stay there until we get back!"

"I'm all right," growled Lopey, rubbing his forehead. "The air's got me braced. Comin' in from the ship brought me to. Say, I was groggy—"

"Join up with us then," snapped Hexler, "and keep your trap shut!"

"All right," agreed Lopey. "But listen, Hexler—it wasn't my fault, gettin' plastered that way. There was a guy on the ship—"

"Lay off the chatter," broke in the leader, "or you'll go back in the boat with a cracked konk! Get me?"

"All right," responded Lopey. "But if I get that lousy guy—"

Hexler handed the big fellow a jab in the ribs. Lopey doubled up, regained his footing and trailed in at the rear of the mob.

Hawkeye, up ahead, whispered to Cliff:

"I'm not letting Lopey lamp me. If he wises that I'm with the outfit, he may spill something to Hexler. Lopey thinks I'm with the crew on the *Dalmatia*."

"I get it," responded Cliff, in an undertone. "Keep ahead of us, Hawkeye. When we get to the house, pick a spot where Lopey won't see you."

OTHER members of the band were closing in. Trudging northward, the complete crew skirted the edges of the forest strip. They straggled into little groups as they marched along. This gave The Shadow's agents a chance for further comment.

"The job is ours," whispered Harry. "This shore outfit is busy storing those boxes. Maybe they'll join us later."

"We'll work quick when we get the chance," put in Cliff. "We don't know what we're going into; but if we can get the jump on Hexler and his bunch, we ought to come through clean."

"Maybe he'll spill more when we get there," added Hawkeye.

Others were overtaking the trio. They trudged along in silence, veering left as the coastline took a slight curve. All was peaceful on this isle, where the steady roar of the surf was lulling in its monotony. Men of crime seemed strangely out of place in the setting.

They were coming close to the upper inlet. Hexler, apparently, had gained complete directions from Ruff; for the leader moved forward to slow his band. He pointed out an opening between the trees. Leading, he took the path toward the house.

Dull lights glimmered from white walls as the invaders reached the clearing. Here Hexler halted the crew and delivered an order for deployment.

"Spread out all around," he instructed. "I'm going up to the house. I'll rap; they'll let me in. There'll be talk at the front door.

"Then I'll come out again. Watch for a move of my left arm. Up and down: that'll mean to close in. Do it in a hurry. But there's one point more. If I start things quick, I'll signal with a shot. That'll mean to rush the place."

A pause. The invaders were ready to spread. Hexler picked out two men from the crew. He called them by name: Jake and "Curry." He pointed toward the house.

"Sneak up there," he ordered, "you two. One on each side of the door. Well out of sight. Then when you get the signal, I'll have the two of you close by."

Jake and Curry sneaked forward across the clearing. Hexler gave a final injunction to the remainder of the band: one that was most important.

"We've got friends inside there," he informed, "so keep your rods steady. Any guy that tries quick shooting will answer to me later. Maybe we won't have to fire a single shot.

"But if there's trouble, use your noodles. Aim

for the guys that aim for you. Leave the others alone. That's simple enough. Remember: hold it for the pinch. Not before."

He motioned with his right hand. The invaders spread along the edge of the clearing, Cliff and Harry moving to the right. Hawkeye sneaked past his fellow agents and took a spot on the flank.

Hexler moved cautiously forward. He beckoned to Jake and Curry. They closed in from the wall and listened while their leader whispered the same instructions that he had given to the balance of the mob.

WATCHING, the deployed invaders saw Jake and Curry resume their positions on the sides of the door. Then they watched Hexler walk boldly up to the portal. The leader had his left hand in his pocket. It was plain that he was left-handed, that his hidden fist was gripping a ready revolver.

Harry, between Hawkeye and Cliff, was tense and alert. He knew that his fellow agents were the same. This was the time for which they had been waiting long. They had reached Timour Isle, headquarters of The Shadow.

Yet they had gained no contact with their hidden chief. They knew only that word had gone to him that they were coming. Had The Shadow received that word? Was he ready, waiting, relying on his men? Or had The Shadow encountered danger here alone—had he met with some adversity that had already placed him in the hands of foemen?

The next minutes would tell. To these aides of The Shadow, the immediate future hovered in the form of Hexler's tight fist, raised to tap upon the door. For with Hexler's knock, the tide of invasion would be ready for its surge.

CHAPTER XIX
STROKE AND COUNTERSTROKE

INSIDE the house, Tully and Chunk were still keeping the semblance of weary guard duty. One man was slouching in the hall; the other was standing by a window of the living room.

Purvis Elger was lounging in a chair, smoking his pipe. Jalway was across the room, leaning against the bookcase, while Hadlow was standing at the entrance to the hall, his hands in his coat pockets.

Francine had gone to bed. The tenseness had wearied the girl. That same feeling of uneasiness had extended to the others. Elger was affable; Jalway appeared matter-of-fact; and Hadlow looked calm and unperturbed. Yet every one of the three possessed a peculiar alertness that had not previously been evident.

A knock from the door. Hadlow started, then smiled quietly. Jalway looked curiously toward Elger. The portly crook lowered his meerschaum from his lips and called to Tully.

"Was that a knock at the door?" he inquired.

"Sounded like it," returned Tully.

"Did Royne go out?" inquired Elger.

"No, sir." The reply came from Royne himself as the servant appeared from the hall. "Did you want me, Mr. Elger?"

"There was a knock at the door"—Elger paused as the rap came again—"yes, I was sure of it. Probably someone has come in from the mainland. Suppose you answer it, Royne."

As he spoke, Elger arose from his chair. He walked past Hadlow and joined Royne. Tully was standing with arms akimbo, ready to draw a gun if so commanded.

"All right, Dashler!"

These words came as a sudden order, from the lips of Seth Hadlow. The sailor, who had been at his solitaire on the window ledge, came suddenly to his feet, swinging a revolver with which he covered Chunk, by the inner window.

At the same instant, Hadlow brought his hands from his pockets. In each was a revolver. Stepping to the center of the living room, he held the guns so that they kept a sweeping level upon Elger, Royne and Tully.

"Stand where you are!" ordered Hadlow. "Don't answer that door!"

TRAPPED men obeyed. They were all in the hall—the three whom Hadlow covered—and the sportsman moved leisurely out in their direction. His new step cornered them between himself and the front door. Elger and his henchmen formed an astonished trio, all with their hands half raised.

Bram Jalway remained motionless, his briar pipe poised in his right hand. His position at the bookcase placed him almost in line with Dashler's gun. The sailor was not covering Jalway; but Elger, looking past the corner of the doorway, saw that the promoter was trapped.

Jalway's only part was to play innocent. It was apparent that Hadlow had not included him among the enemies whom the sportsman had so suddenly decided to control.

Elger, master at bluff, began to sputter a protest. Facing Hadlow, he met the sportsman's determined gaze and demanded an explanation.

"What—what is this?" questioned Elger. "Have you gone mad, Hadlow? Are you afraid of enemies outside this house?"

"I am concerned with those within," announced Hadlow, steadily. "You, Elger, and your associates, of whom there are too many. No one is going to answer that door—until I give the word."

He motioned with one gun. The gesture was for Elger and Tully. The two men backed into the living room, toward the corner where Chunk was standing. A louder rapping came from the front door. Hadlow ignored it.

"There has been murder on this isle," denounced Hadlow, in a steady voice. "I have seen evidence of it; and I suspect those responsible. You, Elger, have deliberately attempted to forestall justice. I have suspected you of planning new crime. I have anticipated it."

"This is preposterous!" protested Elger. "What do you say to it, Jalway?"

"It puzzles me," declared Jalway, eyeing Hadlow, who was using one gun to cover the living room, while he kept the other on Royne, at the front door. "Off hand, I would say that our friend Hadlow is deluded; and yet"—he paused to light his pipe—"there may be merit in what he tells us."

Pounding at the front door. Still Hadlow remained firm. He added one more statement to his accusation.

"You are a smug crook, Elger." Hadlow said it in a positive tone. Then, to Jalway: "I would have called upon your aid had you not gone out tonight, Jalway. The only person to whom I could appeal was Professor Marcolm. I told him that I sensed danger.

"He gave me his revolver. This second weapon which I hold. I managed to instruct Dashler to aid me. I was afraid, Jalway, that you would not return. Danger lurks on Timour Isle. But you are here; and I am counting on you to aid me in this emergency. Have you your revolver ready?"

Jalway nodded. He drew the weapon.

"Cover those men in the corner," ordered Hadlow.

JALWAY did so, an even smile upon his lips. He backed toward the front of the room and motioned Dashler to stand beside him. The sailor obeyed. At that moment, Francine came into the hall. The girl gasped as she saw Hadlow with his pointed guns.

"Step into the living room, Francine," ordered Hadlow, promptly. "Stand behind Jalway and Dashler. You will be safe there."

Mechanically the girl obeyed. She had caught only the last of Hadlow's accusations. As yet, she could not grasp the understanding that Purvis Elger was a crook. Jalway motioned Francine to the safety of a corner.

A final, emphatic pounding came from the front door. Hadlow, seeing that Jalway and Dashler held the men in the living room at bay, was ready to concentrate upon this new point. His smile tightened.

"You are the master of this isle, Elger," he commented. "Tully and Chunk are evidently members of your evil band. But there are others. Those who now crave admittance. Let them come. I am ready."

Leveling both revolvers toward Royne at the front door, Hadlow issued a stern command:

"Unbolt the door!"

Royne started to obey, half trembling as he reached for the upper bolt. The grating must have been heard from the other side, for the pounding ceased.

Framed in the door of the living room, Hadlow was concentrated on delivering a surprise to those outside the house. He was not ready for the attack that came from another quarter.

A SWIFT figure came pounding from the hall. A pair of brawny hands caught Hadlow's wrists from behind and tried to wrest the guns from the sportsman's hands. Before Hadlow could manage to twist a weapon free, two others were upon him. Then a fourth.

At the same instant, Jalway performed an unexpected move. Shooting out his left hand, the promoter caught Dashler's wrist and snapped it upward; at the same instant, he jabbed his revolver into the sailor's ribs.

Seth Hadlow had been overpowered by Ruff Turney and his crew. The mob-leader and the shore band had pulled the unexpected. They had come through the passage from the caverns where they had left the swag. Entering through Elger's study, they had been ready to cut off the retreat of any fugitives.

Creeping forward, Ruff had seen Hadlow in the front hall. He had passed the word to his underlings. Their creeping attack had culminated in a perfect finish. Hadlow, disarmed, was in their power. Ruff, rising from the floor, was ready with a revolver, to join an attack on Dashler.

That was unnecessary. Elger, Tully and Chunk had given Jalway aid. Bounding across the room, they had downed Dashler. Tully was rising with the sailor's gun; Chunk was seated on the fellow's chest.

Francine Feldworth had tried to aid Dashler. Seeing Jalway's treachery, she had grabbed at the promoter's arms. But the girl had been too late. Jalway had wrested free from her grasp. His revolver was now pointed in the girl's direction. Francine was subsiding in the corner.

Triumphant, Purvis Elger was standing in the center of the room, his glaring eyes on Seth Hadlow, who sat, dejected in the grip of Ruff Turney's men.

Sarcastically, Purvis Elger leered at the helpless sportsman. Then the master crook turned toward the door, where pounding had come anew.

"Open the door, Royne," ordered Elger. "Let us see who our new guest may be."

CHAPTER XX
MEN MARKED FOR DEATH

PURVIS ELGER was back in his living room. Ranged with their chief were Tully, Chunk and Royne. Ruff and his henchmen were in the hall; with them a newcomer. Hexler had entered to take his stand beside the land lieutenant.

Three prisoners were bunched in a corner of the living room. Seth Hadlow pale and dejected, was backed against the wall. With him was Dashler, glum but stolid. The third in the group was Francine Feldworth.

The final occupant of the room was Bram Jalway. Calm and unruffled, the traitor seemed almost neutral in his attitude. He appeared to be waiting for Purvis Elger to speak. Yet he seemed to lack animus toward the prisoners.

"I have been branded as a crook," sneered Elger. "You, my friend"—he was looking straight at Hadlow—"are the one who made the denunciation. Very well. I am a crook.

"I have ruled this island unmolested—until you and your companions appeared. Your presence is a menace to my safety. Therefore, you shall be eliminated. All of you."

"You intend to murder us?" queried Hadlow, in a strained tone.

"I intend to dispose of you," corrected Elger. "This man"—he indicated Hexler—"has come ashore from a ship called the *Dalmatia* which is anchored off Timour Island. The captain of the Dalmatia is a useful man; but a stupid one.

"He was kind enough to unload smuggled goods tonight; and he used one of his boats to aid in bringing boxes ashore. We are sending the boat back to him. With it, a few heavy boxes that will be of no use to us. Those boxes will be dropped overboard. Miles at sea."

"Our coffins," declared Hadlow, solemnly.

"Precisely," nodded Elger. "And there will be caskets, too, for the corpses that now lie in the construction house out back."

A PAUSE. Elger chuckled, then puffed at his pipe.

"You are a fiend," said Hadlow, slowly. "A murderous fiend. There is no use to cry to you for pity. Dashler and I are willing to receive the death that you offer.

"But you can have no purpose in slaying Francine Feldworth. Let the girl go free. She has not harmed you."

"I can provide for that, Hadlow," put in Jalway. "Tonight, I made a deal with Elger. Francine will be allowed to live. At my request."

"At the request of a traitor?" demanded Francine. The girl's face was scornful. She turned to Hadlow. "Why ask for any mercy from men like these? I would sooner die with you, Seth."

"That would be foolish, Francine," said Hadlow, placing his arm on the girl's shoulder. "I could stand death if I knew that you were safe. I can't believe that Jalway is a traitor. I believe that he was forced into this."

A smile showed on Jalway's lips. Hadlow was aiding his cause. Smugly, Jalway took up the suggestion.

"I had no other alternative, Francine," he declared. "I can assure you of safety. Elger has promised me your life. With one condition only; that you never tell of the events that have occurred here."

"What!" exclaimed Francine. "You expect me to live, carrying such a secret? Knowing that you were a party to the murder of the man"—she looked toward Hadlow—"of the man I loved?"

Hadlow tried to soothe the girl. It was useless. Her denunciation begun, Francine persisted.

"I do not want the life you promise," she told Jalway. "As long as I live—if I should live—I shall seek vengeance for the crimes in which you have had a part. If you let me live, I shall try to denounce you, whenever opportunity comes. I shall have no part in your schemes."

"It is useless, Jalway," remarked Elger, in a tone of feigned sorrow. "The girl will make trouble for us. She must die. With the others."

Jalway looked perturbed. His keen eyes met Francine's in an almost hypnotic stare. But the girl remained steady.

"I can save you, Francine," began Jalway, slowly. "Remember, I can save—"

"Only if you save the others also," broke in the girl. "If Seth Hadlow dies, you will be his murderer."

Jalway remained staring for a moment. Then he turned away. He looked toward Elger and shook his head.

"You are right," he admitted coldly. "It is useless. The girl must die. Call on the executioner."

ELGER turned to Hexler. The brawny man from the boat was merciless in expression. He seemed to have no qualms concerning the slaughter of innocent victims.

"We will bind and gag them here," stated Elger; "then you and your crew can carry them to the lower inlet. Riddle them with bullets among the sand dunes. Make the execution a prompt one.

"Ruff and his men will go back by the route they used to come here. They will bring empty boxes, weighted. Also the bodies from the construction house. Ruff has the key.

"Load the new corpses with the old. Place two competent men aboard the *Dalmatia*, to see that the boxes are dropped when the ship is well out to sea. We do not want anyone aboard the tramp steamer to learn what the boxes contain."

Elger turned, to deliver an order to Royne. The tall servant departed. His purpose: to get ropes and strips of cloth. Elger had a reason for wanting the victims bound and gagged. He feared that pleas for mercy particularly from Francine—might cause a weakening among Hexler's crew.

The man from the *Dalmatia* grasped that thought. His lips formed an ugly leer. He nudged his thumb toward the open front door.

"Don't worry about those huskies of mine," he growled. "They'd massacre a whole town if they were paid for it. Ruff tells me you'll want them later."

"I shall," Elger chuckled. He spoke clearly, that Francine and the other prisoners might hear. "We have located the yacht *Maldah*. It is aground in an inlet, twenty miles north.

"Kingdon Feldworth has hidden treasure aboard. New swag, as attractive as that which we have already gained. We are turning pirates, Hexler. Long enough to sink the yacht, after we have gained new spoils."

A cry from Francine. The girl spoke pleading, incoherent words. She was thinking of her uncle's safety. Begging, she manage to gasp to Jalway.

"I shall keep quiet," the girl promised, "even—even if you do slay Seth! If only—if only my uncle can be spared!"

"Our plans are made," declared Elger, coldly, speaking for Jalway. "Your uncle will die like the rest. No one who was aboard the *Maldah* will survive!"

"Which reminds me of the professor," added Jalway, apparently deaf to Francine's pleas. "He is fond of sleep. By foregoing his coffee, he has managed to slumber through this commotion. Perhaps, Elger, it would be best to eliminate him while he is still in repose. Turn a short sleep into a long one—"

As he spoke, Jalway stepped toward the door. He was almost to the hall when Elger stopped him. Royne had returned with the gags and ropes.

"We'll save the shooting for outside," decided Elger. "Put away your revolver, Jalway"—he motioned toward the gun that the promoter had drawn—"and leave the job to Hexler.

"Ruff—you and one of your men get the professor from his room. Drag him out, and tap that white head of his if he starts to jabber. Make it quick. There is no more time for delay. We must capture the *Maldah* before dawn."

RUFF nodded. He stepped from the room, with a man behind him. Royne pointed out the professor's door. Jestingly, Ruff tapped. A crackly voice responded.

"Come out a minute, Professor," called Ruff, in a disguised tone. "Mr. Elger wants to speak to you."

Ruff stepped back with a grin, holding his revolver at his side. His companion made the same move. Elger, puffing at his meerschaum, was standing in the doorway of the living room, smiling in anticipation of the doomed man's surprise.

The door swung open. But the professor did not appear. Ruff motioned his companion back, so the old man would not see them until he actually reached the hall. All were watching for the stoop-shouldered, white-haired figure. He did not arrive.

Instead, a whirling form swept suddenly into view. A strange, amazing shape that twisted from the room with a rapidity that was astounding. With that surprise arrival came a startling, eerie laugh—a chilling tone that rang out in strident mirth through this house of doom.

A figure in black that swung to a sudden stop. Glaring eyes that burned from beneath the brim of a felt hat. Gloved fists that projected from the folds of a black cloak, with looming automatics unlimbered for prompt action.

Professor Thaddeus Marcolm existed no longer. His guise had been discarded by the occupant of that secluded room. In the professor's place was a master fighter bent on bringing an end to crime.

The Shadow!

CHAPTER XXI
FIGHTERS OF THE NIGHT

LONG had The Shadow delayed this revelation. Well had he timed his plans for battle. Tonight, he had gone out by the window of his room; its bars were as easily removable as those in the living room.

He had seen the lights of the *Dalmatia*. He had watched the little boat going out to meet it. More than that, he had ventured forth again, to hear the approach of the landing party.

The Shadow had counted on the presence of

his agents. Yet he was taking a chance that they were not there. Listening from the door of his room, he had learned enough to know that victims were marked for deaths. Now was the time to save them. He had waited, knowing that he would be summoned.

In his quick arrival, The Shadow gave his enemies no chance to recover from their surprise. Instant death was all that these murderers deserved. The delivery of quick punishment, moreover, was The Shadow's one hope of conquering overwhelming odds.

Automatics roared through the darkened hall. Point-blank, The Shadow downed Ruff and his henchmen as the two were raising their guns. As Purvis Elger dived for cover of the living room, The Shadow loosed another pair of bullets.

These slugs were meant for Ruff's other henchmen. They found their targets. The mobsters swayed, then toppled, losing their revolvers when they fell.

Royne was leaping for The Shadow. The advancing fighter wheeled. He stopped the servant's body as a quick bulwark; he flung the fellow forward just as Hexler fired. The sea lieutenant's bullet clipped the staggering form of Royne. The Shadow's left-hand automatic barked.

Wounded by a quick shot, Hexler went diving through the doorway, out to the safety that his band would bring. The Shadow, leaping over Royne's prostrate form, was in quick pursuit. But he stopped short at the living room.

TULLY and Chunk were driving out to get him. Revolvers barked with hasty aim. Bullets zipped past The Shadow. One shot skimmed the master fighter's shoulder. The automatic roared new fury to the echoes. Tongues of flame were pointers to the hearts of Tully and Chunk. The villains sprawled simultaneously.

Swiftly, from close range, The Shadow had burrowed straight through the startled enemies who had sought to block him. Each pair of foemen had been beaten in quick struggle. Ruff and his companion had gone first. The second brace of mobsters had been clipped while aiming guns at their formidable antagonist.

The interlude with Royne and Hexler had given Tully and Chunk their chance to enter the fray. These men from the mainland had fired. But The Shadow, more accurate than they, remained unscathed save for a trifling flesh wound, while his foemen had come to grief.

In this brief but terrific thrust, The Shadow reached a vital, strategic point; the door to the living room. He had two alternatives: one, to deal with Purvis Elger and Bram Jalway; the other, to follow Hexler. Both were essential to triumph. His problem was which to tackle first.

In his well-calculated drive, The Shadow had counted upon possible aid. Hadlow and Dashler had not yet been bound. Those two could assist in fighting Elger and Jalway.

Outside, there was the chance that agents were along with Hexler's band. The Shadow had counted upon that possibility. But it was plain that the source of greater danger might come from those outside raiders.

Nevertheless, The Shadow, here to save innocent lives, cast caution aside as he deliberately chose Elger and Jalway as his first adversaries. Those two had been sheltered by the protecting cordon of lesser henchmen—the cohorts whom The Shadow had shattered.

Jalway was covering Hadlow, Dashler and Francine, holding his fire only because he thought the struggle in the hall would be short-lived and in favor of the crooks. But Elger, who had seen The Shadow come from Professor Marcolm's room, was ready in reserve to meet that avenging foe.

As Tully and Chunk sprawled to the floor, Elger gave a maddened shout. Leaping toward the front end of the room, he cried to Jalway for aid. The two were directly in front of the amazed prisoners. Should The Shadow fire wild, his shots would strike the persons whom he had come to aid.

Jalway swung at Elger's cry. Together, they aimed for the elusive, blackened figure that came whirling from the hall. A chilling, sardonic laugh resounded through the room as The Shadow swung the muzzles of his automatics toward these two fiendish foes.

That laugh was calculated. It made Elger and Jalway forget all but The Shadow. It inspired two other men to prompt and efficient action. Hadlow and Dashler leaped from Francine's side. Hadlow took Elger; Dashler bore down on Jalway.

Gripped by formidable antagonists, the two crooks writhed. The Shadow, seeing the instant success of his ruse, wheeled toward the outer door, ready for the attack of Hexler's mob.

OUTSIDE, waiting attackers had been startled by the suddenness of the conflict in the house. Hexler's henchmen, lulled by the interval that had followed their leader's entrance, were totally bewildered by the unexpected outburst.

Shots were the emergency signal. Yet the mob had remained latent during the opening moments of the fray. It was not until Hexler came staggering from the doorway that they decided upon action.

Roaring like a wounded bull, Hexler had swung about the moment that he was in the clearing. Free from The Shadow's fire, he turned and began to pump hot lead back into the empty hall.

As he blazed with his revolver, using his good left hand, the lieutenant shouted for the charge. Jake and Curry sprang from their positions beside the door, ready to join with their leader when he drove to the new attack. At the same instant, seven men from the edge of the clearing came leaping into view.

Shots burst from ready guns; Cliff, Harry and Hawkeye were firing toward the house. A bullet sizzed by Hexler's ear. Wheeling, the lieutenant saw Hawkeye pausing to take aim. Hexler roared a command.

Curry, too, had barely escaped a long-range shot. He swung about, with a cry to Jake. The three men coming from the other side of the clearing stopped short to aim at The Shadow's agents.

Cliff shouted to his companions. The three dropped flat upon the edge of the clearing. Cliff swung his gun across to deal with the reserves. Harry and Hawkeye did likewise. It was a well-timed move.

For Cliff knew that The Shadow would be coming from the beleaguered house. With Hexler, Jake and Curry turned about, the cloaked fighter would get the trio unaware. The danger lay from the four advancers across the clearing. Those men, if unhindered, would come up to find The Shadow as a target, should the black-garbed warrior appear.

It was a reverse of the expected. A clipping of the reserves. A dependence upon The Shadow, to which all his agents were trained. But Hexler, having fled from the formidable foe, understood the move the moment that The Shadow's agents quit their shooting toward the house.

He and the two beside him were at long range from The Shadow's agents. Counting upon that, Hexler snapped a command to Jake and Curry. With his cry, Hexler went hurtling squarely into the open house door, his two men at his heels.

"Get them!" barked Cliff, to Harry and Hawkeye.

THE SHADOW'S agents came to their feet. They forgot the men across the clearing. Two of those reserves had toppled to the ground. A third, wounded, was aiming unsteadily. The fourth, not yet clipped by The Shadow's agents, opened a wild fire. A chance shot dropped Hawkeye. The little man fell wounded, a bullet in the thigh.

Shots from within the house, The Shadow had swung from the living room at the crucial moment. His automatics loosed their thunder straight against the three men who were making a massed attack: Hexler, Jake and Curry.

Hexler uttered a hoarse cry as he sought to fire. Then the big rogue shot forward on the floor, striking squarely on head and shoulders. His revolver went clattering to The Shadow's feet. Jake and Curry stopped short, aiming.

Hexler's plunge had cleared the way. Straight came The Shadow's shots. Tongues of flame, bursting from the blackness of a shifty, wavering figure that bobbed elusively as puny revolver shots barked in return.

Jake tottered. Curry staggered back, wounded, then dived for the door, momentarily protected by Jake's wavering body. The Shadow came sweeping forward. Jake, slumping, snarled and aimed point-blank for the swift shape that was bearing down upon him.

The Shadow's left arm swung. Automatic drove hard against revolver. Jake's weapon clattered from his trigger-squeezing grasp. It cracked against the wall before the man could fire. Weaponless, the dying thug sank to the floor. The Shadow's shots had been mortal ones.

Curry was vicious as he hurtled from the house. In flight, he thought of other foes. Leaping from the door, he aimed straight for two figures that he saw beneath the clearing moonlight—those of Harry and Cliff.

Harry had swung to the left, because of Hawkeye's fall. But Cliff was aiming for the door. Shots roared through the clearing. Quick, rapid fire, accompanied by sizzling slugs that whistled from flaming gun muzzles.

Cliff and Harry were the focal point of a simultaneous attack that came from separate angles. Curry, like the man across the clearing, was aiming to kill. But these rogues were dealing with capable marksmen.

Curry toppled with a groan, as Cliff clipped him with a timely shot. An instant later—before Cliff could turn to aid—Harry delivered a perfect shot toward the crook across the clearing.

The ruffian twisted about, went rolling crazily upon the sward. Echoes rattled back from the tabby walls of the look-out house. Then came silence. The Shadow, his form grotesque in the moonlight by the front door, had arrived to see his agents triumph.

Cliff and Harry turned to Hawkeye. They raised the wounded man; as they did, Hawkeye's gun came up in his right hand. With a sharp cry, the little fighter aimed across the clearing; steadying himself against Cliff's shoulder.

One crook had been wounded over there. He was the fellow who had faltered in his aim. But now he was steady on one knee, pointing a gun straight for the door of the look-out house. He had seen The Shadow. He was aiming to kill.

SHOTS soared from three spots. From the crouching crook; from Hawkeye's spot; from the doorway where The Shadow stood. Those bursts seemed simultaneous; yet fractions of seconds separated them.

The Shadow's shot was first, straight for the gun hand of the aiming crook. It clipped the fellow's knuckle just as his finger pressed the trigger. Diverted, the crook's bullet plastered itself against the tabby wall beside The Shadow's shoulder.

The crook's altered shot was the second and Hawkeye's burst was almost with it. Seeking to save The Shadow, the wounded agent had delivered quick but perfect aim. The crouching crook toppled forward, a bullet through his heart, while his smoking gun dropped from his broken fingers.

An ominous lull came hard upon fleeting echoes. Then from within the house burst the sound of another gun. Elger and Jalway, arch-crooks of the lot, had found a chance to fight. That shot betokened trouble.

Whirling, The Shadow disappeared into the blackness of the hall. Victor against hordes of crime, the master fighter was heading in to deal with the most dangerous of the lot.

CHAPTER XXII
THE LAST STROKE

THE shot that The Shadow had heard had been a random one. It had come from the revolver gripped by Bram Jalway as the crook still writhed in Dashler's grasp. Gun pointed upward, Jalway had found no other target than the ceiling. Yet his shot turned an overwhelming tide.

Seth Hadlow had already subdued Purvis Elger and was holding the portly crook against the wall. But at the sound of Jalway's shot, Hadlow turned instinctively. Elger wrestled free and dived to the floor.

His gun was lying there, where he had dropped it in the struggle. Regaining the weapon, Elger twisted away from Hadlow and made an upward stroke. His gun muzzle delivered a glancing blow to Hadlow's chin. The sportsman went down with a thump.

Dashler, seeing this, made a valiant effort to grab Jalway's gun. It was a mistaken attempt. Jalway, copying Elger's motion in reverse, drove his weapon downward. Dashler's gripping arm partially absorbed the shock; but a glancing stroke struck his skull. The sailor sagged.

Hadlow and Dashler were prey for the crooks. But a spontaneous cry from Francine gave warning to both Elger and Jalway. Staring hopelessly toward the door, the girl had seen a new figure arrive. The Shadow had returned for battle.

Entering, The Shadow had dropped his brace of automatics. He had emptied those weapons in his previous fray. His gloved hands were whipping a new pair of weapons from beneath his cloak.

With Elger and Jalway taking time to fire at the senseless forms of Hadlow and Dashler, The Shadow would have had perfect opportunity to clip the crooks. But Francine's cry had placed him at a disadvantage.

ELGER and Jalway wheeled toward the door as one. Separated by a dozen feet, they offered a dual problem to The Shadow as he yanked his guns to view. Marvelous marksman though he was, the position placed him so that he would have to pick one foe an instant before the other.

Both men were desperate. Both were killers. It might have been an equal choice to an ordinary fighter. But The Shadow, instantaneous in his decision, took immediate preference. His eyes swung to the left, where Elger stood alone. His left-hand automatic flashed its flame.

Elger staggered. He tried to hold his gun; but he failed. The portly crook lost the weapon and went sagging to the floor, clutching his chest, coughing from the mortal wound.

The Shadow's quick gaze had shifted toward Jalway, who had stepped in front of Francine. It was Jalway's position that had made The Shadow allow him the momentary chance to aim. For The Shadow had counted on a break. It came.

Francine, by her cry of gladness, had brought grim menace to The Shadow. But it was that very reaction of the girl that had caused The Shadow to fire first at Elger. He was relying upon Francine's spontaneous promptness. The Shadow had decided well.

As Jalway's finger pressed the trigger for a death shot, Francine was already leaping forward. The girl's frail hands caught at the man's wrist. The effort was sufficient; it diverted Jalway's aim.

A bullet boomed from the crook's gun. The shot went wide by half a dozen inches. It missed the turning form of The Shadow. But Jalway, with a furious oath, leaped to another measure.

Twisting, he grabbed the girl's body with his left arm and swung Francine as a barrier against The Shadow's shot. His revolver leveled, he tried to turn it toward the evasive foe at the doorway.

The Shadow swept into the room, ahead of Jalway's swing. Jalway fired one shot—another—but his turning aim, handicapped by Francine's struggle, was too late on both occasions.

As Jalway's finger pressed the trigger for a death shot, Francine was already leaping forward.

Then, suddenly, The Shadow stopped short. He fired one shot as Jalway, swinging his arm wide, gave him a momentary target. The bullet burned Jalway's forearm. With a cry, the crook let Francine fall away. Still holding his gun, he tried to press the trigger. His shot was never fired.

The room roared with a mingled burst that sounded like an artillery barrage. Cliff and Harry had dashed into the house. They fired simultaneously with The Shadow. Three bullets spun Jalway to the floor. The crook was motionless before the echoes ended.

Purvis Elger, crumpled by the bookcase, was staring with glassy eyes. The arch-crook could not reach his gun. He tried to fume incoherent words; his strength ebbed with the gasps.

Half rising with a final effort, Elger buckled and sprawled dead. His hand clutched at the bookcase as he fell; loosened volumes tumbled and thudded the floor beside the master crook's prone form.

COMPANIONS in crime had received just doom. Bram Jalway, whom The Shadow had suspected of criminal intent aboard the *Maldah*; Purvis Elger, whom The Shadow had identified as an evil rogue, even before he had met the master of Timour Isle. Above the mantel over the fireplace, burnished bronze reflected the room's light. That gryphon shield would no longer be the symbol of a supercriminal.

From beneath his cloak, The Shadow brought forth a sheet of paper; he let it flutter to the floor, where it fell beside Elger's body. The side that came upward showed the same symbol as the bronze above the fireplace.

The Shadow had returned the piece of evidence that he had acquired on the night when George Dalavan had murdered James Tolwig. That scrap of paper had come from Purvis Elger; The Shadow had given it back to its dead owner.

Seth Hadlow was reviving, with Francine beside him. Dashler, after a momentary sway, was regaining his senses. The Shadow turned to his agents. He gave a hissed order. Cliff and Harry turned about and headed for the front door.

The Shadow glided toward the hallway. For a moment he stood there, barely discernible, blackness against a gloomy background. Then he whirled. The crimson lining of his sable cloak flashed momentarily in the glow from the living room.

Then The Shadow, too, was gone, the only token of his parting a hissed, sardonic laugh that left strange, ghoulish echoes quivering through this room where men of crime had died.

CHAPTER XXIII
NEW DAWN

THE pink light of a new day was breaking along the Georgia coast. The stretched expanse of rose-tinted ocean was heaving with long, restless swells. The power of the waves had ended. These heavy rises and falls were but a reminder of the storm that had spent its fury.

The glow from the horizon revealed a small powerboat chugging northward, past islands where stretches of sand ended in strips of towering, blackened trees. This was the little cabin boat that Ruff Turney had kept hidden in the swamp below Timour Isle.

Dashler was at the tiller; as the sailor nonchalantly guided the boat, two others talked of events that were past. Seth Hadlow was seated beside Francine Feldworth, while they discussed the episode on Timour Isle.

"The professor gets the credit," acknowledged Hadlow, in a solemn tone. "If it hadn't been for him, we'd be boxed up deep beneath the ocean."

"The captain of that tramp steamer was a dupe," said Francine. "He thought that Purvis Elger intended to get rid of useless curios by dropping them at sea."

"But he didn't stay around to wait," added Hadlow. "He must have hauled up anchor and sailed hours ago. Probably he was afraid that coast guard cutters might be off the shore."

A PAUSE followed. Francine, nestling close to Hadlow, sighed pleasantly as she looked toward the brightening sky. This day was dawning with perfection.

"The professor didn't miss a trick," commented Hadlow. "That case in his room—with the tiara, the fifty thousand dollars and the stenographic evidence. It showed that fellow Dalavan for a crook as bad as the others."

"And the note we found," said Francine. "The one that told us to follow the passage to the caverns; then on to the old slave quarters and the spot where this boat was run ashore. It gave us all we needed."

"Full proof of Elger's crimes; and Jalway was working with the rogue."

"It will enable us to inform the law. Those treasures will be reclaimed intact."

"To go back to their true owners."

Another brief pause; then Hadlow spoke speculatively.

"Who was Professor Marcolm?" he inquired. "Where did your uncle meet him?"

"In New York," replied Francine. "The professor had heard that uncle was going on a cruise. He wanted to come along; to check on charts of the Atlantic coast."

"Those were the things he brought ashore? His maps? I wondered what he had with him?"

"He took his belongings after he saved us from death. He must have had his black attire with them, also those huge guns that he carried."

Hadlow recalled another matter after Francine had spoken. He expressed his recollection.

"The night we landed on Timour Isle," he said, slowly, "I fired blindly with my rifle; and I am sure that Jalway did the same. We were confused; yet we seemed to get results. The reason was that the professor fired also. I remember that his three shots punched in between ours with peculiar precision."

"Do you mean," questioned Francine, "that the professor—or whoever he was—saved us that night?"

"I do," affirmed Hadlow, soberly. "His shots were timed to perfection. He dropped the thug who attacked Dashler. He smashed the bull's-eye lantern. He clipped another enemy, by the fellow's gunfire, which served as a target. In addition, he saved some cartridges while we wasted all of ours."

The powerboat was turning. Looking from the side, Hadlow and Francine saw that Dashler was guiding the craft into an inlet. The sailor pointed.

"There's the *Maldah*," informed Dashler. "Dead ahead. It looks like they're maneuvering her off the bar. We'll be aboard soon."

Coming to their feet, Hadlow and Francine looked over the little cabin. They saw the yacht, white smoke pouring from its funnel.

"There's your uncle on the deck," declared Hadlow. "He has seen us."

"He looks happy," laughed Francine. "And he'll be happier when he learns how fortunate we have been."

"And finds out what he was saved from," added Hadlow. "Those villains on Timour Isle would have made short work of the *Maldah*."

"But they never got their start," chimed in Dashler, from the stern.

The cabin boat pulled up beside the yacht. Soon the castaways were pouring out their story to Kingdon Feldworth and the captain. The owner turned to the skipper.

"The radio working?" he inquired.

"Just repaired," informed the captain. "And we'll be off this bar in half an hour."

"Send word to the coast guards," ordered Feldworth. "When we're clear, head for Timour Isle. We'll meet the cutters there."

WHILE the reunion and its aftermath were taking place aboard the *Maldah*, another group of voyagers was faring north from Timour Isle. Their vessel was the small motor boat in which Tully and Chunk had come from the mainland. But their course was not outside the string of islands that fringed the Georgia coast.

The little boat was chugging through an inner channel. Clear of the marshes, it was traveling beneath the shelter of an inner shore. The tiny craft was almost shrouded in a setting that dawn had not yet reached.

Gliding beneath huge overhanging boughs that streamed with beards of Spanish moss, the voyagers were nearing the end of their trip to the mainland. In the center of the boat were Harry Vincent and Cliff Marsland; between them, Hawkeye, chipper despite his wound.

Shrouded at the rear of the boat sat a black-cloaked figure, a silent pilot who guided the craft with unerring skill. Picking channels that he did not know, The Shadow had weaved a remarkable course in from Timour Isle.

Far from that isolated spot where he had waged war against crime, The Shadow was bringing his agents to security. From the mainland they could transfer Hawkeye and take him north by train.

The boat had entered the channel of a sluggish creek. Moss hung almost to the surface of the water as The Shadow swung the tiller. The prow dug deep into thick soil. The shrouded pilot had found a landing place.

The motor ceased its throbs. Solemn silence hovered as strange aftermath to the events that had gone before. The howl of the hurricane; the thunder of avenging guns—those sounds seemed part of a far, distant past.

Yet as the boat lingered, with its occupants motionless, there came a manifestation that woke echoes of the past. It was the first utterance from that weird pilot at the stern; the first sound that The Shadow had given since the departure from Timour Isle.

A laugh that quivered from hidden lips. A burst of mockery that rose through the thick air of the sylvan glade. A haunting cry that rose to a fierce crescendo, then broke into a shuddering tone that faded with uncanny suddenness.

Chilling echoes answered The Shadow's triumphant laugh. Phantom tongues gave weird but mirthless reply; then they, too, dwindled into nothingness.

Silence, strange and unfathomable, again clung to this lonely landing place upon the Georgia shore. Crime had been conquered by The Shadow and his aides. New day had led them forth on further quests.

THE END

INTERLUDE by Will Murray

This volume of The Shadow is set in a part of the nation not normally associated with the Dark Avenger—the sunny South.

Terror Island has a curious backstory. Walter Gibson turned it in on May 18, 1934 under the provisional title of "Death Island." At that point, Walter was a solid year ahead of schedule, and this novel should have hit print early in 1935.

Instead, it broke in the August 15, 1936 issue—over two years after Gibson turned it in! It's not clear why the manuscript sat dormant for so long. Just two months previously, Gibson had written *The Plot Master,* which was set on the imaginary Death Island. Maybe editor John L. Nanovic saw a conflict between the two story locales and shelved "Death Island" for a while, then lost track of it. For several years, he had a manuscript safe whose combination no one could remember. Perhaps it held overflow inventory, and this tale was one of its hostages.

One thing is certain, *Terror Island* is no dog. Opening in Miami, the narrative takes place largely on an isle off the coast of Georgia, which is a very unusual locale for a Shadow story.

"I liked to do stories in real places," Gibson once explained, "mainly Florida, the Carolinas, New England.... I preferred Shadow locales I was familiar with, though others were well researched."

Although imaginary, with its plantation-and-pirate history, the barrier isle Gibson called Timour Island smacks of solid research and reality. No doubt Walter visited a similar spot—such as colorful St. Simons Island—and modeled his own after its rich background.

Criminologist Slade Farrow makes another of his rare appearances in this tale. Just months before *Terror Island* was written, he had helped The Shadow recruit a number of new agents to the Master Avenger's cause, including Hawkeye, Tapper and others. That story was told in *The Chinese Disks.* In this tale, Hawkeye is still nominally under Farrow's control—an arrangement which had changed by the time *Terror Island* actually saw print. Shadow readers may or may not have noticed this continuity glitch back in 1936. But this is the tale where Hawkeye is formally handed off to the Master of Darkness.

Our other selection, *City of Ghosts,* comes from 1939. Street & Smith paid for it on May 11th, and released it in the November 15, 1939 issue. It's set in the imaginary Pomelo City, in central Florida, a locale Walter Gibson knew well.

"I knew all this stuff from living down there," he once related. "My father in law at the time owned an orange grove. People don't seem to realize that. They think I was spending my time down in the Village, or doing some other crazy thing."

In fact, in the mid 1930s Walter began dividing his time between New York, Orlando, Florida and his summer retreat in Gray, Maine.

"I would go into the office in New York and set up as many as three or four stories ahead—get the plots all okayed by the editor," he reminisced. "Well, I'd get four ahead and then I could take off for Florida. I didn't have to worry for two months because I had my plots right with me. Even then, I didn't have to go back to New York. I could send them in. Then I would go up to Maine on the summer, where I had a camp, and bang them out up there."

In 1935, he arrived in Orlando only to read a *Sunday Sentinel-Star* report of his own demise, dated October 5. Years later, Gibson recalled the unsettling event:

> The same applies to [Harry] Charlot, who is credited with the early radio scripts for the *Detective Story Magazine* program, in which he called the announcer "The Shadow." We had never heard of him either, until around 1936, when he died suddenly in New York. I was in Orlando, Florida, working on a Shadow novel when I saw a headline saying that the author of The Shadow was dead. By then, the magazine had been going for five years and I don't think the real Shadow program, based on the magazine, had begun. I called S & S by long distance and found they were as baffled as I was. They corrected the story in N.Y., and I went to the Orlando newspaper with a half-finished Shadow MS in one hand and the check for the previous story (which had just come in) in my other hand. That convinced them that the Shadow author was still alive.

Charlot had died on the third of October, apparently the victim of self-poisoning. That novel in progress was *The Broken Napoleons.*

Gibson told the *Sunday Star-Sentinel,* "I wrote the first Shadow story nearly five years ago. It was printed in *The Shadow Magazine,* which immediately became a regular publication; and which now appears twice a month. Since all of the Shadow stories have been of my origination, I felt that this statement should be made. No other author has been connected with this work; and The Shadow, as a character, has been developed through my stories."

With Gibson out of town, the unexpected news rocked Street & Smith. Nanovic quickly alerted *Doc Savage*'s Lester Dent of the true situation:

> You probably wondered what happened to Gibson, if the papers there carried it, which they

> probably did. However, Gibson is safe. The other fellow might have had something to do with the radio program, but not with the stories. Although it took us plenty of time to get the story straight—and then it wasn't printed right, so we still have trouble answering queries.

Before the truth was fully known, the magazine *Writer's Review* gave some space to the impact of Charlot's death:

> There has been much discussion concerning the strange actions and death of the author who created the famous *Shadow* character of crime stories. He was found dead of poison in a cheap flophouse on the Bowery having disappeared from his comfortable home a few days previously. Before that, he had been under medical care for mental disorder.
>
> Haters of pulp writing blamed it all on his pulp crime stories. But what about the hundreds of other writers of bloody crime fiction? As a rule they are all pretty normal. One well known editor when asked for his opinion said: "That's merely a coincidence. You can't blame it on pulp, all writers are more or less nuts anyway. I've seen just as many nuts among slick writers as I have among pulpiteers."

One wonders if that anonymous editor was John Nanovic.

The Shadow Magazine ran a correction in its December 1, 1935 issue. It read:

> Recent newspaper articles reporting the death of Harry E. Charlot have credited him with creating the character of The Shadow and writing the Shadow stories for Street & Smith. We wish to say that The Shadow was created for our readers by Maxwell Grant, and that every Shadow story printed has come from the pen of Mr. Grant as the exclusive author of The Shadow's exploits, and that he will continue to produce them for *The Shadow Magazine* alone. Any other statements are erroneous....

Of course, S&S wasn't about to publicize Walter B. Gibson. Maxwell Grant's true identity was still unknown to the general public. It would be months before another writer would be assigned a Shadow novel. Eventually, the confusion died down. And inevitably, Walter's name was revealed in print.

City of Ghosts was the first Shadow exploit set in Central Florida. At that time, Walter was married to his second wife, Jule, known familiarly as Jewel. Her father F. J. Martin owned the orange grove mentioned earlier.

Gibson began to winter in Florida in 1935. He usually headed south by train after Christmas, shipping his car by rail as well. He rented a Pullman car, which allowed him to write en route. He was living high during a harsh period.

"The Depression was a beautiful time to live in Florida if you had a few bucks," he once recalled. "I had the money and really enjoyed myself."

As it happened, Walter hit Orlando the same month the horrific Labor Day hurricane of 1935 swept the Florida Keys and tore up parts of south Florida. It's unclear if Gibson had arrived in Florida prior to the storm making landfall, or not.

Interviewed at various times, Walter sang the praises of the Sunshine State.

"When I went South, Florida was just great from a writer's standpoint," Gibson recounted. "I really enjoyed my years there. They were some of the best of my life.

"My wife and I rented a bungalow out near Maitland on a citrus estate for $15 a week. We had a sleeping porch, two more bedrooms, living room, dining room, refrigerator, wood for the fireplace, all the orange and grapefruit we could pick, plus the use of a boat on the lake.

"I liked Florida. It was a good place for me on plot ideas. My writing also went well there. I spent ten winters in that state and enjoyed every one of them. I stayed because I got sand in my shoes and couldn't get away."

Gibson was not alone in that sentiment. Street & Smith scribes Lester Dent, Laurence Donovan, Paul Ernst, Theodore Tinsley and *Bill Barnes*' Charles Spain Verral also frequently fled the northeast for Florida at different times in the year.

Walter Gibson

Jule Gibson

Pulp writer William R. Cox once recalled, "I met Gibson at Ted Tinsley's rented place on Anna Maria [Island] in the early '40s. Ted was the 'part time Shadow' you know, relieving Walt when he was weary. Walt was a great amateur magician."

City of Ghosts' Pomelo City is based in the ghost town of Interocean City, which was built between Tampa and Daytona, but abandoned while only half-completed. Its name derives from the fact that it was midway between the Atlantic Ocean and the Gulf of Mexico, in the Orlando metro area. Gibson's coinage comes from the original name for a grapefruit, pomelo.

"I saw a lot of ghost towns in Florida in the 1930s," Gibson once recalled. "These communities were created by the boom of the 1920s, then just died out in the following Depression.

"Florida was like a sleeping giant in the '30s. Just waiting to be awakened. Local residents mistakenly thought people would come here to live. They didn't realize the potential of the tourist trade."

Long before Orlando became a major theme park center, Walter envisioned an amusement park as a solution to the area's need to attract visitors from the colder parts of the country.

"Florida evolved into what I expected," he remarked. "That included a flood of tourists from the North and the creation of major attractions like Disney World."

In subsequent years, Intersession City sprang up in place of the abandoned Interocean City.

The Pomelo Hotel which figures prominently in this story was lifted from a similar ten-story edifice that once existed near Haines City. It sat isolated about 40 miles west of Orlando, apart from any large community.

Kewanee Springs is no doubt based on a real locality too.

"There were springs galore in Florida," Gibson reminisced. "Silver Springs was advertised a lot, but several others were just as big, including Waculla Springs near Tallahassee. I utilized some of these springs in the stories I set in Florida, and they added important local color."

A keen student of history, Gibson often recalled that the roots of the Great Depression lay in the Florida land speculation boom of the 1920s.

It was a time when new cities were springing up in the Everglades and the sky seemed the limit for land prices. The bubble began straining in 1925, when press reports suggested that buyers were in short supply and prices had been grossly inflated. Then came the devastating September 1926 hurricane which swept across Miami and into the interior of the state. That popped it.

When that bubble burst, it presaged the economic collapse of the 1930s. Walter often said that if one wanted to know when the next depression was due, just look for a real estate boom and bust. The jury is still out on whether or not our most recent speculative bubble will lead to a greater depression.

That's just one of the themes visited in *City of Ghosts*. Here's how John Nanovic previewed it:

> What's coming up in the next issue? Well, the novel, for instance, is "City of Ghosts," and it's such a bang-up yarn that in the course of the excitement, The Shadow comes as close to being a real ghost as he has ever come! It's a story about Florida; something about the boom times there, and something about the aftereffects of these boom times. Also things that will probably be new to you: for instance, that Florida is good ranch country; just as good as any out West. We are so used to thinking of Florida just as a winter playground that other information about this state just slips by.
>
> Maxwell Grant has spent many winters in Florida, and is well acquainted with all parts of the state.

In 1977, Gibson returned to Orlando for the first time in 40 years to attend a convention. There he met a librarian who remembered him well. She had seen Walter give a magic show when she was six!

Despite its Sunshine State locale, *City of Ghosts* was actually written in Maine! It's amusing to think of Walter Gibson, chain-smoking over his Smith-Corona typewriter, writing a story set in faraway Florida from his woodsy retreat in the Pine Tree State. •

A Complete Book-length Novel from the Private Annals of The Shadow, as told to

MAXWELL GRANT

CHAPTER I
THE CITY THAT DIED

THE passengers aboard the *Silver Bullet* stared from the windows in surprise, when the sleek streamliner glided to a stop at Pomelo Junction. Except for a dilapidated station, there was no sign of human habitation.

As for the branch line that connected there, its track was nothing but a double streak of rust curving off to nowhere through the Florida pinewoods.

Its pause no more than momentary, the *Silver Bullet* was moving south again. Persons at the observation window glimpsed the tall passenger who had alighted, standing with his bags beside him. Then he, like the station, was gone from sight, as the streamliner whirled past a main-line bend.

Back on the weatherbeaten platform, Lamont Cranston smiled as a rattly touring car jounced up to the station. Its driver, beefy-faced and shirt-sleeved, clambered out to meet the arrival. He took a look at the bags and the hawk-faced gentleman who owned them, then queried:

"You're Mr. Cranston?"

Cranston's reply was a quiet acknowledgment.

The beefy-faced man introduced himself as Seth Woodley, and gestured toward his rattletrap car. Cranston saw the word "Taxi" on a printed label that was stuck to the windshield.

"I'm from Leesville, the county seat," vouchsafed Woodley. "That's where they sent your telegram. They said you were fixing to get off at Pomelo Junction and would need a taxi."

"Quite right," returned Cranston. Then, as Woodley was putting the bags in the car: "How long will it take you to drive me to Pomelo City?"

A satchel dropped from Woodley's hand as the fellow turned about. His eyes squinted in the late afternoon sun. The same glow brought a glisten from the gold fillings in his back teeth, so wide was his gape.

"You're fixing to go to Pomelo City?"

"I am, if you can take me there," replied Cranston, calmly. "Since the branch line has been abandoned"—he was looking toward the rusted track—"I presume that the highway is the only route to Pomelo City."

Woodley's jaw clicked shut. Grimly, he gestured Cranston into the car; then took the wheel. They rattled off along a well-paved highway, with Woodley driving in silence.

CRANSTON'S eyes were taking in the scenery. The ground differed somewhat from other areas of Florida, for this was a "hammock" region, the term derived from small ridges, or hammocks. The slopes were well wooded with pine, while gullies showed clusters of cypress, indicating swampland.

In fact, as the scene progressed, it improved. The car rolled past fenced-off orange groves, with sprinklings of other citrus trees. Fertile slopes showed rows of young tuna trees, promising future profits to their owners.

It was not until Woodley slowed his car to take a side road, that the reason for the fellow's grimness became apparent.

Then Cranston saw a battered sign pointing to Pomelo City, the name scarcely legible. He observed the road ahead—a single lane highway of red brick. The road, itself, was proof that something was wrong with Pomelo City.

Brick highways dated years back. Built in single lanes, they forced passing cars to turn out along the sand shoulders. When traffic warranted, they were widened, by concrete strips on either side.

This road had not rated such improvement. On the contrary, it had been allowed to deteriorate. Grass was sprouting up among the bricks; in some cases, there were gaps in the wobbly, irregular surface.

Woodley took those bumps as a matter of course, even though they shook the chassis of his ancient car. There were times, though, when he yanked the wheel frantically, to avoid an actual catastrophe. Those were the times when he spied bricks that were upended in the paving.

Along the fringes of that grass-sprouting road, Cranston soon spied scenes of true desolation. One slope showed a pitiful array of withered stalks that had once been promising tuna trees. A level field displayed sawed-off stumps that represented a former citrus grove.

"The Medfly got those trees," spoke Woodley, gloomily. "They had to chop 'em down. A funny thing, the Medfly. No more trouble from it anywhere in Florida, except around Pomelo City."

They were approaching a bend where the tilted, broken roof of a farmhouse poked up from the ground level. Woodley nudged his thumb in the direction of the new exhibit.

"A sinkhole," he said. "Lots of 'em start around here, but the ground don't usually cave right underneath a house, like it did there. That only happens near Pomelo City."

Cranston's gaze was fixed toward the ruin, as if he wanted to observe the sinkhole itself. Woodley gave a chuckle, slowed the car as they completed the curve.

"Here's a real sinkhole for you, Mr. Cranston!" he said. "Plumb in the middle of the road. That's one reason why nobody drives over here anymore."

He was taking a sandy detour that skirted the sinkhole. Cranston saw the hollow from the brink. The sinkhole looked like the shallow crater of an extinct volcano. Measuring a hundred feet across, it showed ground that had sunk twenty feet.

The cavity was lined with sand, except where gaunt stretches of broken limestone showed a miniature cliff formation. Mixed with the sand at the bottom of the sinkhole were trunks of small trees and chunks of paving.

"When the rainy season comes," announced Woodley, as he swung from the detour, back to the brick road, "that sinkhole will fill up. Right now, we're having a drought, and it's been harder on Pomelo City than anywhere else. See that grapefruit grove?"

Cranston saw the grove, but needed Woodley's statement to recognize that the trees had ever borne grapefruit. The grove was barren; like the fruit, all leaves were gone. The trees, themselves, seemed wilted.

"They tried to save it," said Woodley, glumly, "by pumping water from the lake. Only, the lake went dry. Yes, sir, the bottom dropped plumb out of it, like it has with Pomelo City!"

THE lake came into sight. It was nothing but a pitiful expanse of caked clay, that gave off the odor of rotted fish. Cracks in the clay denoted limestone cavities, that had opened when the water level sank. Those gaps had sucked the lake dry.

Beyond a thinned woods appeared Florida's symbol of a town: a large water tank set on three tall legs. That tower, with its conical roof, was Cranston's first view of Pomelo City.

At a distant view, it was quite the same as many other man-made reservoirs that Cranston had seen while a passenger upon the streamliner. It was different though, when the car came closer.

Then, the rust of the supporting tripod was visible. The scarred tank showed its lack of paint. Gaps could be seen in the cone that topped it. Odd blackish splotches showed near the uppermost point. Woodley pressed in the clutch pedal, raced the old motor to a roar.

Immediately, the blotches took to wing. They were buzzards. Frightened by the noise of the approaching car, the huge birds circled away from the water tank. Their actions showed that they intended to return to their roost when the car had passed.

"You can't fool a buzzard," declared Woodley. "They know when anything has died. They know that Pomelo City is dead, even though people are staying there because they won't believe it! You'll see for yourself, Mr. Cranston."

The car struck the short main street. It jolted over broken layers of concrete, which were matched by the remnants of shattered cement sidewalk that lined the ruined thoroughfare. On either side were crumpling buildings that had once been stores.

Some had boarded-up fronts, as weather-beaten as the station platform at the junction. Others simply displayed gaps, instead of show windows. Between the sidewalks and the crumbled curbs were frowsy brown-leaved palm trees that looked on the verge of collapse.

Passing a ruin that had once been a theater, Woodley drew up in front of a stucco-walled building that looked like a three-story blockhouse. Above the entrance was a sign proclaiming the place to be the Pomelo Hotel.

Alighting, Woodley carried the bags into a lobby that was furnished with tumbledown wicker chairs. While the taxi driver was shouting for the proprietor, Cranston eyed the hotel register.

It bore the proprietor's name, Martin Welf, at the top; otherwise, the page was blank, indicating that the hotel had no guests.

Welf arrived at Woodley's shouts. The proprietor was a portly, baldish man, who stuttered in bewildered fashion when he learned that Lamont Cranston intended to become a guest.

When Cranston had registered, Welf picked up the bags and started toward the stairway. He was obviously a one-man staff: clerk and bellboy, as well as hotel owner.

Woodley grunted thanks, when Cranston handed him a ten-dollar bill as taxi fare and said that change would not be necessary. Plucking his passenger's sleeve, Woodley confided:

"Maybe you won't like it here, Mr. Cranston. I'll tell you what I'm fixing to do. Sheriff Harley has allowed that he ought to come over here some night on account of talk he's heard, about some folks starting trouble. I'll offer to make the trip this evening."

Welf was calling wheezily from the second floor: "Right this way, Mr. Cranston!"

"So if it ain't to your liking," added Woodley, quickly, "you can go back to Leesville with me, later tonight, Mr. Cranston."

Nodding his thanks, Cranston turned toward the stairway, wearing a smile that Woodley did not see. At the top of the stairs, Welf was waiting at the open door of a front room. He announced, apologetically, that the hotel chef had left, but that he could supply sandwiches and coffee if Cranston wanted dinner.

"I dined on the train," Cranston told him. "I hope, however, that the cook will soon return. I intend to stay in Pomelo City a long while, Mr. Welf."

HIS eyes wide with amazement, Welf backed from the room. Cranston locked the door and strolled to the front window. He saw Woodley's old car go bouncing away, watched it take the winding road from town.

Buzzards flapped up from the water tower as the car went past. Circling against the darkening sky, they returned to their roost. By then, Woodley's car had dwindled into the dusk. Cranston's last contact with the outer world was gone.

As Cranston watched the street below, feeble streetlights flickered into being. They were pitifully dim, those lights, as they glowed through the dried clumps of leaves that hung from the drooping branches of the dead palm trees. They looked weak enough for a puff of wind to extinguish them.

Turning from the window, Cranston stepped to a chair, where Welf had placed a satchel. Opening the bag, he drew out a black cloak and slid it over his shoulders.

With that action, Lamont Cranston seemed to disappear, except for his hawkish face, which remained, like a floating mask, above the chair.

Next came a slouch hat. When he had clamped it on his head, Cranston's face was also gone. His hands merged with the gloom, like the rest of him, for he was encasing them in thin black gloves. Blended with the semidarkness, Lamont Cranston had become The Shadow.

A strange being that belonged to blackness, The Shadow had begun the mission that had brought him to Pomelo City. He had become a living ghost in a city that had died!

CHAPTER II
GHOSTS IN THE NIGHT

A TINY flashlight glimmered in the darkness. Its rays fell upon a batch of newspaper clippings spread upon a bureau so shaky that it wobbled at the slightest touch. In the increasing darkness of his hotel room, The Shadow was reviewing the facts that accounted for his visit to Pomelo City.

News of the town's plight had filtered to the outside world, but in such small and occasional dribbles that no one, other than The Shadow, had sensed the full import of what had happened to the place.

Singly, the clippings meant very little. They mentioned things that The Shadow had seen firsthand, today: the scourge of the Mediterranean fruit fly; the appearance of some sinkholes; the drying up of a lake.

Besides these were accounts of a cattle epidemic, which had fortunately faded out; a reappearance of the supposedly extinct black wolf, which had once roamed wild in Florida; finally, reports of accidents that constituted a common sort—hunters shot by mistake, and automobiles wrecked through chance collisions.

Added up, these facts produced a definite total. Hundreds of people had found absolute reason to move from the vicinity of Pomelo City. Citrus growers, farmers, even the native "crackers" of the backwoods, had met with circumstances that deprived them of livelihood and security.

Their exodus had caused townspeople to depart. Dependent upon the trade of the surrounding territory, Pomelo City had no longer been a prosperous place. The abandonment of the branch railroad, the collapse of the highway that linked the town to the world, were added occurrences dooming Pomelo City to oblivion.

Threaded through that change of circumstances lay a more insidious factor: that of tragedy. Over a year or more, the toll of life had been heavy. Curiously, the toll had been on the increase, as the total population dwindled. Hunting accidents, automobile crashes, had occurred in recent months.

Beneath all this, The Shadow saw the operation of an evil hand, one not content to let Pomelo City linger toward its finish. Harder, and repeated strokes had been delivered. Because of them, Pomelo City could aptly be termed dead.

The tiny flashlight went black. Stepping to the window, The Shadow gazed upon the street below, where night had fully encroached upon scrawny palms, until the feeble lights were merely flickery twinkles in the midst of thick darkness.

With death, the town had become a city of ghosts. That term applied to The Shadow, the only stranger present. It also fitted Pomelo City's few remaining inhabitants.

Martin Welf, the hotel proprietor, was one. In the face of adversity, he was carrying on with a business that was little short of hopeless.

Whether it had guests or not, the Pomelo Hotel actually required a fair-sized personnel, merely to keep up appearances. Alone, Welf was handling a dozen jobs, in the place of employees who had deserted him.

ACROSS the street, The Shadow saw two building fronts that flanked an abandoned arcade. Both places had lighted windows. One was a real estate office, that bore the name of "Chester Tilyon, Realtor."

At a desk visible through the window sat a haggard man with gray-streaked hair, who kept looking toward the street, as if dreaming of long-past days when people actually bought houses and rented property in Pomelo City.

The other building was a department store. What stock it still had, mostly cheap clothes and farming implements, was confined to the show windows on the ground floor. Inside, a few lights showed barren counters.

Standing in the doorway was the man whose name appeared above: "Louis Bayne." His clothes were no advertisement for the wares he sold, for his attire was shabby, and too large for him. From the drawn appearance of Bayne's face, The Shadow decided that the man was half starved.

In hope of selling the new clothes that he still had in stock, Bayne was wearing his old ones. Worry, as well as poverty, had caused him to shrink from a man of bulk to a creature that could pass as a living skeleton.

Two cars were on the street. Both were of expensive makes, but very old. Tilyon's car, parked near the real estate office, appeared to be in fair condition; but Bayne's antiquated sedan was scarcely more than a wreck. One fender was gone; the radiator shell was badly bashed. Moreover, the car bore added scars, such as a dented door, that denoted a recent accident.

The sheer shabbiness of the desolate scene made it seem that nothing could stir up action. Remembering the buzzards on the water tower, The Shadow could picture the huge birds watching Tilyon and Bayne, hoping that one or the other would soon die on his feet. Both men seemed to be waiting for something that could never happen, either in their favor, or against it.

Then a motor's rumble announced the unexpected. An old touring car rambled into sight along the main street, scraped against a leaning palm tree, and disgorged four rough-dressed men. Visitors had come to Pomelo City.

They were men from the backwoods, the sort who came to town on Saturday night. Two of them approached Bayne's store and began to look at the show windows, while the proprietor eyed them anxiously. These men weren't customers; that became apparent when they turned their attention to Bayne's car.

The Shadow saw Tilyon get up from the desk in the real estate office, to see what was going on. A moment later, Welf appeared at the front of the hotel.

There was a challenge in the air: something that indicated ill feeling between the local business men and the crackers who had come to town. Each group seemed completely concerned with the other; perhaps with special design.

For The Shadow, watching from the window higher up, saw something that the men below did not notice; a thing, perhaps, which one faction might have chosen that the others should not observe.

A car had pulled into the rear street beyond the abandoned arcade. The Shadow caught the glimmer of its lights, just before they were extinguished. The very fact that the unheralded arrivals had chosen to come by a deserted back street, aroused The Shadow's immediate interest.

LEAVING his room, The Shadow moved rapidly toward the red light that denoted exit onto a fire escape. Descending, he arrived in a little courtyard at the side of the hotel, next to the old theater. Gliding through a narrow archway, he reached the front sidewalk.

Crossing the street was no problem to The Shadow. The dry-leaved palm trees threw shrouding darkness that offset the flickering streetlights. It was simply a case of choosing the swiftest route to the desired destination.

Taking a wide route to circle the buildings opposite, The Shadow was a living ghost, blanketed in darkness. He rapidly reached the street in back of the arcade.

Darkness was thick, but by zigzagging along the narrow rear street, The Shadow expected to find the car that had pulled up behind the arcade. Instead, he reached a corner beyond Bayne's store without encountering anything. The fact meant that the car must have crept ahead without lights.

Feeling for the building wall, The Shadow retraced his steps, using his flashlight guardedly.

He came upon evidence at the back of Bayne's store: a door with a broken padlock. Though cheap, the padlock was a new one; it had probably been smashed within the past few minutes. Whoever had done the deed had entered the store, and should certainly still be inside.

Easing the door inward, The Shadow entered. He did not have to worry about the opening door betraying him. His flashlight was extinguished, and he had a background of perfect darkness. But the men who had already entered were less fortunately placed.

By the dim light from the front of the store, The Shadow could see them; three in number. They were crouched figures, creeping about among the unused counters, sprinkling something on the floor. The odor of kerosene was only too evident. Incendiaries were at work here, while Bayne, the storekeeper, was occupied out front.

Using creeping tactics of his own, The Shadow reached beneath his cloak and plucked an automatic from a holster that he had worn even before reaching Pomelo City. Whatever dirty work this tribe was up to, they were due for a surprise before they finished it.

As they were skirting back toward the rear door, The Shadow came into their very midst.

The unknown men had him surrounded without knowing it, which was exactly what The Shadow wanted.

With counters forming an excellent shelter, The Shadow set finger upon the button of his flashlight. He was ready to press it, to throw a sweeping ray of thin, sharp light about the group. His lips prepared to voice a sinister laugh, The Shadow intended to take these antagonists unawares.

If they wanted battle, he was in the right position to return it; to their sorrow, not his own. The Shadow was entrenched among the counters, and he had a clear path of fire toward the rear door, should the marauders seek it when they fled.

A sound made The Shadow pause. It was a creak of that very door; the one that he, too, had entered. None of the prowling men could have reached it; evidently, a fourth man had arrived.

Whispers sounded in the darkness, but they were wordless. The newcomer had simply passed a signal for the others to join him.

At that moment, it seemed policy to wait, since the actions of the prowlers were deliberate. The whispered signal had sounded like a mere preliminary to something more to come. So it was; but the coming action was the climax.

An object swished through the darkness, straight for The Shadow's head. Chucked blindly from the doorway, it almost found a target that the thrower did not know existed. With an action as rapid as it was instinctive, The Shadow flattened among the counters to escape the unseen missile.

The thing struck the floor beside a counter which, fortunately, sheltered The Shadow. As it landed, the object exploded with a forceful puff that shook the floor of Bayne's dilapidated store and made the counters quiver.

Though the blast was not heavy, the consequences were. The bursting bomb spurted liquid fire in every direction. The flames encountered pools of kerosene, licked up the inflammable liquid in one mighty gulp.

In a single instant, the whole rear of the store was lighted like a furious inferno, a mass that was rising ceiling high, with The Shadow trapped in its very midst!

CHAPTER III
BROKEN BATTLE

THE same instinct which had saved The Shadow from the bomb, was the factor that preserved him from the flames. Had he risen at the moment when the furious hell broke loose, he would have been ignited like a human torch.

Instead, he sprawled on the floor, his cloak sleeve drawn across his eyes. The lash of the roaring flame whipped above him, finding other tinder instead. The intervening counters took the blaze, leaving an air pocket in between them.

Though the seconds were few, they seemed interminable. During those moments, The Shadow could actually see the flame through his closed eyelids. He held his breath, for he could feel the scorch of the blistering fire that swept above him. Then, as his ears detected a louder crackle, he knew that his brief opportunity had come.

Liquid flame had spent itself. The counters and other woodwork were taking fire. Coming to his feet, The Shadow saw licking tongues of red; but the circle was incomplete. There were gaps between the counter ends, that offered temporary paths clear to the rear doorway.

Lurching, The Shadow started an amazing, twisty course. The flames had found new fuel, but they were too late to stop him. Their glare revealed the cloaked figure that was escaping them; but otherwise, they did not harm The Shadow as he zigzagged toward the rear door. Yet, in disclosing The Shadow's presence, the flames did damage enough.

Bayne, faced toward the rear of the store, saw The Shadow. So did the astonished crackers who stood out front. They yelled to their companions, who came running with shotguns, just as Bayne whipped out a revolver, to aim in The Shadow's direction.

Beyond the flames, The Shadow was lost from Bayne's sight before the shrunken storekeeper could fire. But the men at the rear door were quick enough to recognize The Shadow as a foe. Themselves fleeing from the renewed blaze, they considered it a good place for The Shadow to stay. Fortunately, the shots that they fired were too hasty to score a hit.

Then The Shadow's drawn gun was busy, and the men at the rear were in new flight. Responding to their leader's yell, they dashed along the backstreet, diving for their car. Guns across their shoulders, they blasted at The Shadow as he lurched out through the exit.

As guns barked, The Shadow took a long sprawl. Landing shoulder first, he rolled across the street, beyond the area of light that came from the opened door. His foeman thought they had dropped him. Their guess was wrong.

The Shadow's dive was calculated. He wanted a spot where blackness would protect him from the shots that he knew would come. The next token that disclosed The Shadow's presence was a spurt from his own automatic. On hands and knees, he was answering the gunfire in swift, effective style.

A howl told that one foeman had fallen. Quick-witted pals yanked the fellow around the building corner. Another must have been clipped during the process, for there was every indication of delay while The Shadow was coming to his feet. Making for the corner, the cloaked fighter flattened against the wall, poked his gun past the building edge.

The wall was hot. Flames were roaring through the roof of Bayne's doomed store. The rising light was sufficient for The Shadow to pick out human targets, had there been any. But despite their delay with wounded comrades, his foemen had reached their car.

All that The Shadow had to shoot at was a tail-light, as it whisked between two buildings on the other side of the narrow cross street. Speeding to the space in question, The Shadow caught another fleeting flash of the fleeing car as it whipped around a turn.

Pursuit of the firebrands was useless, but battle still offered. Shots were sounding from the front street. Speeding beside the outer wall of Bayne's burning store, The Shadow arrived at the front corner just in time to witness a sad tragedy.

Bayne, an emptied revolver in his hand, was wavering on the sidewalk in front of his blazing building. The men with the shotguns were spread among the palm trees; their shots had found the shrunken storekeeper.

IT was the hope of saving Bayne that caused The Shadow to swing into sight. One of the armed men spotted him and shouted. Instantly, all were driving for The Shadow, firing the few shells that they still had left.

Wheeling for cover, The Shadow escaped the hasty shots, but he knew that his heroic effort had not succeeded.

As he swung back around the corner, The Shadow caught a last glimpse of Bayne, diving forward to the sidewalk. The shotguns had finished him.

Circumstances still called for the unexpected, and The Shadow provided it. As his new assailants rounded the corner, they were startled by the sudden attack that the black-cloaked fighter provided. Hurling himself into the midst of them, The Shadow began cross slashes with his automatic, using his free arm to ward off the clubbing blows of shotguns.

Fully supposing that The Shadow would be in flight, the crackers were taken totally off guard. Their shotguns were bashed from their hands; stooping, The Shadow snatched up one of the lost weapons, used it to swing wide, sweeping blows that covered a wide range.

Welf and Tilyon, stooped above Bayne's body, were amazed when they saw four men come staggering around the corner, warding off imaginary blows. Neither Welf nor Tilyon spied The Shadow. His opponents in flight, the cloaked fighter was taking off to darkness, carrying a bundle of shotguns with him.

Two cars were rolling in along the main street. The driver of one saw the men who staggered from the corner; he drove ahead, intending to find what lay beyond. The men in the second car piled out to see what could be done about the blazing building.

By that time, The Shadow was gone. Picking a roundabout route, he crossed the street a half block from the burning store. The men who were looking for him had gone in the opposite direction; a quick path back to the hotel seemed a simple matter, and would have been, if another carload of backwoods residents had not bowled in from a side street.

Caught between the background of the conflagration and a pair of flickering headlights, The Shadow was again human game for another batch of misguided natives who carried shotguns; but this time, the weapons were fully loaded. As before, his only course was close range action, and he took it.

Wheeling aside before the car could run him down, The Shadow flattened and rolled beneath the car step. He came up, seemingly from nowhere, as men were piling out to look for him.

This time, shotguns talked, but they did nothing but split the air. The Shadow was slashing at his adversaries with a heavy automatic and plucking away the shotguns that he warded off.

Even more astonishing was the way in which he disarmed these newcomers. There were only three of them, and they weren't as ready as the previous crowd. They were relying, too, on gunshots instead of clubbing tactics. Tilting up those unwieldy barrels was mere routine for The Shadow.

Three dazed men were fumbling about, wondering where their guns had gone. The Shadow was around in back of the car, strewing the shotguns as he went. Vanished from the midst of his blundering opponents, he left them with the final impression that they had battled with other than a human foe.

They found their guns, when they looked for them; but discovered no trace of The Shadow. He had vanished, so they thought, through the blank side wall of an old garage. Their curious belief was inspired by the fact that the shotguns lay near that wall.

They didn't realize that The Shadow had reversed his course during their bewilderment. Across the street, he was fading into blackness behind the Pomelo Hotel.

REACHING his room, The Shadow discarded his black garb, while he watched the finish of the structures opposite. The flames had gutted Bayne's store; gobbling the wooden arcade, the fire was taking hold of the adjacent building where Tilyon's real estate office was located.

Men were busy getting papers and furniture out of Tilyon's place. Among them, The Shadow saw Woodley, the Leesville taxi driver. Woodley's car and another had come from Leesville, and the

Astonishing was the way in which The Shadow disarmed these newcomers.

second automobile evidently belonged to Sheriff Harley, for the man who stood beside it could have been no one else.

Tall, lanky, and long-jawed, the sheriff was shouting for men to forget the fire; good advice, since there was no way to stop the blaze. Not a breeze was stirring, and there was no chance that the flames could spread beyond the two buildings that they were consuming. The sooner it burned itself out, the better.

Carrying Tilyon's office equipment, men were crossing the street toward the hotel. Rapidly, The Shadow stepped out into the hallway, locking the door behind him. Descending to the lobby, he was waiting there when the carriers entered. With the group came Welf, followed by the sheriff.

Stopping short, Welf blinked. The hotel proprietor had forgotten that he housed a guest. Then, assuming that Cranston had witnessed the whole scene from the lobby, Welf introduced him to the sheriff. Taking the same thing for granted, Sheriff Harley proffered a hearty handshake.

By the time the rest had entered, The Shadow was in conference with Harley and Welf. Among the latecomers were the out-of-towners from the backwoods. Those who had riddled Bayne with shotguns looked very regretful. Solemnly, they laid their weapons in a corner.

They observed Cranston suspiciously at first; then, as his eyes calmly met their gaze, their doubts faded. They were convinced of one thing: that this leisurely mannered, well-dressed stranger could not have been the foe that they and their belated friends had battled around the streets of Pomelo City.

His guise of Cranston serving him in perfect stead, The Shadow was soon to hear strange testimony regarding his own amazing prowess. Testimony to which he, as Cranston, could add details as a chance and impartial witness!

CHAPTER IV
THE SHADOW STAYS

SHERIFF HARLEY proved himself very versatile. He had taken over duty as police chief and fire marshal of Pomelo City; with those tasks settled, he showed new ability. The sheriff became coroner, judge, and jury, in investigating the causes of Bayne's death and the fire that swept the dead man's store.

Harley questioned the crackers first. He knew them all, and called them by their first names when he demanded to know why they had come to town this evening. A rangy, solemn-faced fellow named Jim Fenn decided to act as spokesman for the rest.

"We warn't fixing to start no trouble, sheriff," drawled Fenn. "We just allowed we ought to take another look at Bayne's car. Some folks don't appear satisfied about how it was smashed up."

"Bayne ran that car into a sinkhole," returned the sheriff, coldly.

"We ain't disputing you, sheriff," argued Fenn. "Only, we allow that Bayne might have bunged up his car first. He hit that sinkhole the same night that Joe Betterly was run off the road and killed, along with a couple of his kinfolk."

Fenn's companions murmured assent. It explained the feud between Bayne and the backwoods populace. The Shadow remembered one of the clippings in his collection, a small item culled from a Jacksonville newspaper.

A week ago, Joe Betterly, a local farmer, had been found dead with two companions, in a badly wrecked car, near Pomelo City. The crash had been attributed to a hit-and-run driver, though Bayne had not been mentioned. Such suspicion was obviously a local matter, confined to the backwoods dwellers.

Looking at Welf and Tilyon, The Shadow could tell by their expressions that neither held Bayne to blame. They seemed angered by Fenn's charges.

Sheriff Harley handled the tense situation admirably. Silencing mutters from both factions, he asserted:

"There's no harm in wanting to look at a man's car. Go ahead, Fenn. What happened next?"

"The fire started," declared Fenn. "All of a sudden, like somebody throwed a match into a tank of gasoline. First thing we knowed, Bayne had a revolver out and was shooting.

"Into the store?"

"Yeah. Leastwise, until we was coming over to see what was up. We was fixing to give Bayne a help, only he forgot the trouble inside the place and turned on us."

"Still shooting?"

"Plenty, sheriff! Yelling he was going to kill the pack of us. We didn't like to use our guns, sheriff, but we was out in the open, and we hadn't no choice. I don't allow that we could do different than we did."

The sheriff turned to Welf and Tilyon. Despite their loyalty to Bayne, they had to agree that Fenn's testimony was correct.

"Bayne lost his head," conceded Welf. "I'll say this for these men"—he gestured toward Fenn and the other crackers—"that they used their shotguns in self-defense. I'd like to know, though, if friends of theirs set off that blaze in Bayne's store."

"We'll get to that, Welf."

For the next five minutes, Sheriff Harley grilled the crackers in first-class style. They had one story and they stuck to it: Neither they, nor any of their friends, could have had a part in starting the fire.

"All right," spoke the sheriff, suddenly. "If none of you fellows had a hand in it, who did?"

Men shifted uneasily. They looked to their spokesman, Fenn. He muttered something; his companions gave him nods.

"There was somebody in that store, sheriff," said Fenn, slowly. "It was him that Bayne fired at. I seen him, sheriff"—Fenn drew a long breath—"and he looked mighty like a ghost!"

SHERIFF HARLEY did not laugh. Instead, he drew a toothpick from his pocket and began to chew on it. After weighing the statement long and seriously, he questioned:

"Did he act like a ghost, too?"

Fenn nodded. He stabbed his finger toward the floor, made a wide circle with his arms.

"He was like that, sheriff," said Fenn. "In the middle of the fire. No human could have got out of there alive. He was all in black, except when the flames lit him up redlike. I don't allow he was the devil"—Fenn shook his head begrudgingly—"but he might have been Satan's twin brother."

Fenn's pals supplied emphatic nods.

"We run into him later," continued Fenn. He was pointing from the lobby toward Bayne's store, where flames had dwindled, "when he was right yonder, by the corner. I'm saying this, sheriff: nobody but a ghost, and an ornery one, could have tooken the shotguns out of our hands the way he did!"

Doubt flickered on the sheriff's face, until he caught looks from Welf and Tilyon. They remembered a surprising battle that they had witnessed.

"Fenn and his friends were fighting somebody," stated Welf. "But we didn't see who it was. The way they bounced back after they went around the corner, they might have run into a brick wall!"

"That's what the ghost did!"

The man who hoarsed the statement was one of the three who had come in the last car. He and his two companions began to chatter the details of their fray with The Shadow. They described their adversary as a mammoth batlike ghost.

"Plumb into a brick wall, sheriff! That's where the ghost went. And he cut through it without leaving a mark! Unless"—the speaker hesitated, inspired by a fresh theory—"unless he flew clear over it, like a buzzard!"

The sheriff's own men remembered the excitement at the corner. They were sure that an unknown fighter had been on the ground when they arrived. The speed of his disappearance inclined them to the ghost theory. Veering to that viewpoint himself, the sheriff finally turned to The Shadow and questioned:

"Did you see any of this, Mr. Cranston?"

"I was in my room," came Cranston's calm-toned reply, "shortly before the trouble started. I am positive that I saw the lights of an automobile on the street in back of the arcade. That is the only new evidence that I can offer."

The sheriff looked relieved. The report of a mystery car indicated human hands, not ghostly ones.

"In the case of Betterly and his kinfolk," decided the sheriff, "we came to a verdict of death caused by persons unknown. Bayne was exonerated, and that finding stands.

"This fire tonight was set by persons unknown. The same parties, maybe, that ran Betterly's car off the road. As for Bayne's death"—the sheriff pocketed his toothpick—"he just got excited. Your plea stands, Fenn: self-defense."

Strolling over to the corner of the lobby, where Chester Tilyon had placed the desks and filing cabinets from his real estate office, Sheriff Harley remarked approvingly:

"A good idea, Tilyon, setting up your business here. Pomelo City never was much of a town, but you and Welf are all that's left of it. It's safer for the two of you to stick together."

FENN and the other crackers were moving from the lobby, deciding that they had been dismissed. The sheriff had dropped the ghost theory, but they still clung to it.

Catching their mutters, The Shadow heard one man argue that it might have been Betterly's ghost. The others didn't agree. Feeling badly about Bayne, they decided that their feud was a mistaken one. It was Fenn who suggested another possibility.

"I seen ghost lights t'other night," he voiced, in a low, confident drawl. "In that empty filling station on the abandoned road. Nobody but a ghost would be hanging around a place like that, the way it's like to fall into the sinkhole under it."

Fenn's idea carried weight, judging from the nods that his companions gave as they left the hotel. Looking toward Tilyon and the sheriff, The Shadow observed them still engaged in conversation. Neither had heard what Fenn said.

But Welf, standing behind the desk, was close enough to hear. Welf's elbows were propped up; his chin was resting in his hands, while his eyes were half closed in a sleepy fashion. His pose, as The Shadow analyzed it, could be a pretense.

Sounds of departing cars came from outdoors.

Fenn and his backwoods friends were leaving town. Judging from the direction that the cars took, none was going toward the abandoned road that Fenn had mentioned. Joining Tilyon and the sheriff, The Shadow gave a sidelong look toward Welf.

A sly smile showed itself on Welf's lips. Then, shaking himself from his pretended drowse, he came over and joined the others. His expression became poker-faced, as he listened to Sheriff Harley.

"There's been strangers roaming this territory," the sheriff was telling Tilyon. "I heard that from Graham Clenwick, when I was over to his ranch. He thinks they're cattle thieves, but maybe they're worse than that. Beginning tomorrow, I'm going to search every shack in this county.

"I'm suspicious of strangers. That don't apply to you, Mr. Cranston"—Harley smiled toward The Shadow—"because any man who comes out into the open is to be trusted. I mean strangers that stay in abandoned farmhouses. We've found traces of them."

Starting toward the door, the sheriff was met by Woodley, the taxi driver, who whispered something to him. The sheriff nodded; turning about, he said:

"Maybe you're fixing to go to Leesville, Mr. Cranston. If you are, we'll wait until you get packed."

"No, thank you, sheriff," replied The Shadow, calmly. "I prefer the quiet of Pomelo City. I take it that tonight's commotion was something out of the ordinary."

Grunting a good night, the sheriff left, accompanied by the astonished Woodley. Turning to Welf and Tilyon, The Shadow added, in his same even tone:

"I like your hotel, Mr. Welf. You can count upon me as a steady guest. I am also glad to see that you are in business, Mr. Tilyon. Tomorrow, I would like to talk about buying some real estate."

WHILE both men stood speechless, The Shadow strolled toward the stairs. Welf and Tilyon, the last of the diehards doing business in Pomelo City, had met a person more remarkable than a ghost. They had found a customer.

As for The Shadow, his disguised lips voiced a whispered laugh as he reached his darkened room. Reaching for cloak and hat, he resumed the black garments that he had so recently discarded. They, like his guns, would be needed for another venture, to begin very soon.

The Shadow intended to visit the forgotten filling station where Fenn had seen the "ghost lights." Perhaps it was the present habitation of the "persons unknown" responsible for the death of Louis Bayne. He was in no hurry, however, to begin his expedition. There was something else that he expected first.

Listening at his partly opened door, The Shadow could hear sounds from the lobby below. He was checking on Welf and Tilyon. He heard a good night, spoken in Welf's voice; then footsteps on the stairs. Oddly, the sounds dwindled as they reached the second floor; but The Shadow knew why.

Welf, having lulled Tilyon, was advancing on tiptoe, to listen at the door of his lone guest, Cranston.

Silently closing the door, The Shadow heard Welf's sneaky approach. Soon satisfied that his guest had retired, Welf stole away. The Shadow moved toward the window; outside, feeble street-lamps had been extinguished, but the scene glowed dimly from the embers of burned buildings across the way.

Swinging out through the window, The Shadow lowered himself beside the wall. A clinging thing of darkness against the grimy old building, he remained unnoticeable until he dropped. Even then, his cloaked shape showed but fleetingly.

Peering through the corner of a window, The Shadow saw Tilyon in the lobby. The real estate man was seated at a desk, busy with papers that he was taking from an open filing cabinet. Tilyon was too occupied to notice what was going on behind him.

Martin Welf was stealing down the stairway from the second floor in a fashion remarkably catlike, considering his portly build. Past Tilyon, Welf eased toward a doorway to the kitchen, threw back a pleased grin when he reached his goal without detection. From the kitchen, Welf could easily get outdoors and go his own way without Tilyon's knowledge.

There was only one plausible answer as to Welf's destination. He was going to the abandoned filling station that he had heard Fenn mention. Welf knew that the dwellers there were human—not ghosts, as Fenn supposed. Whether Welf regarded them as friends or foemen was a question yet unanswered.

But Martin Welf would not be the only visitor to that forgotten spot, nor the first. Already, another figure was on the move, starting swiftly for the same goal, to be there ahead of Welf.

He was one who, more than any other, could claim the title as the ghost of Pomelo City, for he had been mistaken for a weird specter this very night.

The Shadow!

CHAPTER V
THE BURIED GHOST

TWO slanted sentinels reared themselves in darkness. They were the battered, paintless gasoline standards that fronted the abandoned filling station on the forgotten road just outside of Pomelo City.

Like the tilted standards, the building itself was askew. It was another evidence of the ill luck that had dogged all enterprise in the neighborhood of Pomelo City. The owner of the filling station had been unfortunate enough to build the structure over a future sinkhole.

Gradually, honeycombed rock had given way, until the owner had considered the place unsafe. With business gone, he had left these parts, abandoning the building to a fate that was gradually overtaking it.

The oddity was that the filling station had not already collapsed. Even in darkness, its walls gave the appearance of a strain too great for further support.

Shrouding a tiny flashlight in the folds of his cloak, The Shadow found the reason for the building's survival, as he approached the side wall. Attached to the filling station was a sort of shed that served as a garage and workshop. Planted on solid ground, the shed served as a prop against the canted building.

Evidently the filling station proprietor had been up to date, for the shed had a grease pit, a thing uncommon in rural Florida.

Perhaps the digging of the pit and the installation of large gasoline tanks had aided the progress of a hidden sinkhole. The pit, however, was still intact, except that its concrete lining was badly cracked.

The shed had no door, but its rear wall was complete, serving as a lopsided wedge against the weight of the leaning service station. How long it would last was a question; but any severe test, such as a heavy rain or a strong wind, would undoubtedly dispose of the last prop and complete the building's doom.

There was a door leading from the shed into the filling station proper. Trying it guardedly, The Shadow found that it was bolted from the other side. Leaving the shed, he circled the structure. Reaching the far side, he saw the "ghost lights" that Fenn had mentioned.

They were eerie, those lights, strange streaks of glow that would appear spooky from a distance, but which were very simply explained by closer observation. They came from cracks in the wall, and a dim space above showed that the roof widened into a large fissure.

Reaching the roof was an easy task for The Shadow. He returned to the back of the shed, used the outside of the rear wall to reach the lower roof. Then, getting a clutch between spread boards beneath the torn tar paper, he worked his way to the gap that he had observed.

THE interior of the service station, viewed from above, was nothing but a large, bare one-room shack. It had two doors—one at the front, the other at the side leading into the shed.

Its windows were boarded over and the present occupants had stuffed the crevices with newspaper, something which they had failed to do with cracks high up the wall and along the roof.

At present, there were two occupants. They made a thuggish-looking pair, with their ratlike faces. Guns bulged from their hips; their conversation came in snarls.

Their talk began when one reached for a bottle of liquor that stood on a big empty carton which served them as a table. The other stopped him, with the comment:

"Lay off, Skate! Tony wouldn't like it."

"O.K., Dingbat," returned Skate. "What Tony says goes. Only, it's been a long time since we've talked to Tony Belgo."

The name was familiar to The Shadow. Tony Belgo was a big-shot New York crook whose disrepute equaled his misdeeds. It was unusual, however, to encounter Belgo's outposts in a remote section such as this.

"We've hung around here long enough," asserted Skate, as if to excuse his desire for the bottle. "The way we've been sneaking from one farmhouse to another, the yaps will be thinking we put the jinx on this burg."

"Let 'em think it," snapped Dingbat. "Tony told us to stick with Enwald, didn't he?"

"Yeah, but what's it getting us?"

"We'll know when Enwald gets back. He's about due."

The statement was correct. From his vantage point on the roof, The Shadow could observe something unknown to Skate and Dingbat. A car with dim lights was creeping along the abandoned road, obviously heading for this filling station.

It couldn't be Welf. If the hotel man had used a car, he would have been here long ago. Obviously, it must be the man called Enwald.

While The Shadow watched, the car purred up to the station and nosed into the shed that housed the grease pit. Dingbat caught the throbs of the motor when it arrived. He unbolted the door in answer to a rapped signal.

The man who entered was sallow and peak-faced. His expression was a glum one, and the first thing he did was shoulder Dingbat aside in order to reach the bottle. After a long drink, Enwald squatted in a rickety chair and stared at his two pals.

"Well?" demanded Dingbat. "What about it? Going into town?"

"Not tonight," returned Enwald in a smooth but dejected tone. "Hell busted loose there! It wouldn't be smart, showing up right after the sheriff was on deck investigating a fire that burned half the town."

Dingbat and Skate showed interest. They wanted to know who started the blaze.

"The crackers, I guess," declared Enwald. "Nobody would be starting fires to collect insurance money. The companies wouldn't pay on anything in a burg like Pomelo City."

He reached for the bottle again. Dingbat offered no objection, as he had with Skate. He simply inserted a reminder, which he voiced with a significant growl.

"Tony's waiting to hear from you, Enwald," said Dingbat. "You sold him on the proposition of going after this guy Clenwick, who owns the big ranch. Better not forget it."

"I'm not forgetting it." Enwald's tone carried its easy purr. "There's something you fellows want to remember, too. Tony is leaving the whole thing up to me. If I say the job looks good, Tony will go ahead with it. If I say to lay off, he'll listen."

"That's all right by me. Only, Tony will be sore if he don't hear one way or the other."

"He can wait a day or two more. Right now, I'm going to have another drink. Then we'll clear out of this dump and pick a better place to stay, tonight."

THE only break to the ensuing silence was the gurgle of liquid pouring into a glass. Passing moments, however, brought recollections to The Shadow. He was piecing past facts to the present, summing up the existing factors in and around Pomelo City.

First, there were the residents of the jinx town itself: Welf, Tilyon, and formerly Bayne. Next, the backwoods faction, as represented by Fenn and the other natives. Both of those groups had suffered, apparently, from the hoodoo that dominated this territory.

Third in the list was a rancher named Clenwick, mentioned earlier by the sheriff, later by Enwald. That brought The Shadow's thoughts to the fourth faction, at present on actual display: Enwald and the two thugs supplied him by a crook named Tony Belgo.

Enwald had come here to make trouble for Clenwick. Behind such trouble lay crime. All that could have a bearing on events in Pomelo City earlier this evening. It could date back farther, to the time when a hoodoo had first struck this region.

The fact that Dingbat and Skate knew nothing about the fire until Enwald told them, merely indicated greater depth to the plot. There might be other groups of thugs posted elsewhere, all under Enwald's control.

He was a smooth-looking person, this Enwald; his very manner marked him as something of an enigma. He was the sort who could be working on his own, while pulling a deal with Tony Belgo.

Was Enwald linked with Martin Welf?

As The Shadow pondered on that question, slow, crunching footsteps sounded from the gravel in front of the filling station. A flashlight blinked, then darkened. Enwald must have caught the sound, or spotted a gleam through some crack in the wall, for he spoke hastily to his companions.

"Douse the glim," undertoned Enwald. "Somebody is out front. Get to the shed. I'll join you."

Dingbat blew out the oil lantern that illuminated the bare room. Footsteps moved about; The Shadow could hear the drawing of a bolt. Then came silence, long and painfully slow. Stretching toward the spot where the roof crevice widened, The Shadow worked his legs through and downward.

He was dangling in darkness, above a space where all was silent. The only sounds were from the shed. Whether Enwald had joined the thugs at the car did not matter. If the sallow man still remained, The Shadow would be able to handle him alone. Hanging by his hands from the gap in the roof, The Shadow prepared for the drop, then let go.

With a surprisingly slight thump, a black shape landed in blackness. A gloved hand was drawing an automatic, the instant that The Shadow reached the floor. With a soundless whirl, The Shadow was away from the landing spot, toward the door that led to the shed. Had Enwald been on hand to spring at the arrived intruder, he would have found nothingness.

But Enwald was gone. The Shadow heard his voice from the car. A moment more, The Shadow would have been on his way to the shed, to trail the crooks, leaving the empty nest to Welf; but an interruption ruined the move.

The door of the shack flung inward, a flashlight bored the darkness. There was a sharp, elated cry from the front of the place—a tone that The Shadow recognized as Welf's. Though incoherent, it told all.

Welf had found the ghost!

The Shadow was directly in the path of the burning flashlight. He looked like a ghost, but he was human and Welf knew it. Ghosts didn't carry guns, whereas The Shadow did.

IT was Welf who stood in danger; not The Shadow. The thing to do was drive Welf back before Enwald and the thugs came after him. To accomplish that, The Shadow wheeled to the

The Shadow looked like a ghost, but he was human and the intruder knew it.

depth of the room, shoving his gun threateningly toward Welf. Instead of quailing, Welf opened fire.

His first shots were hasty; therefore, wide. Knowing that Welf would try to trap him in the nearer corner, The Shadow did the unexpected. He reversed his course, toward the door to the shed that served as garage. There, he could meet incoming thugs, slug them back with a surprise attack, and save Welf from death. A perfect plan, had Enwald decided to return.

But Enwald had a different idea. As The Shadow reached the door to the shed and yanked it open, a motor roared beyond. With a lurch, the car left it's parking spot above the grease pit. Carrying Enwald and his pals as passengers, it smashed through the rear wall of the shed!

Enwald had done more than make a getaway. He had broken the prop that saved the filling station from ruin. The rumble that followed the motor's roar was a sound far more formidable. Welf's wild shots sounded puny in comparison with the splintering crashes that thundered from every wall.

The flashlight found The Shadow at the doorway to the shed. Welf aimed, accurately for once, and pressed the trigger, but his shot was too late to drill the figure that he mistook for a ghost. The Shadow was no longer there when Welf fired.

The Shadow was gone with the dropping floor, into engulfing blackness. The frantic dive he took was long, but downward, smothered beneath the caving mass of walls and roof. With one huge shudder, the doomed building had collapsed, carrying The Shadow into the lurking sinkhole beneath.

From a living fighter, The Shadow had become a buried ghost!

CHAPTER VI
TWO MEN HOPE

WHATEVER his own fate, The Shadow had certainly saved the life of Martin Welf. So suddenly had things happened that Welf was unable to realize the result until it was all over. His gun emptied, he was still tugging the trigger, and holding his flashlight out, when he saw that he no longer had a target.

That wasn't all. Everything else was gone—the car, the shed, as well as the filling station. Welf stared, unbelieving, then lowered his flashlight. Beyond a spot that had once marked the doorway to a dilapidated building, lay a sea of débris.

A sinkhole, shaped like an inverted cone, had swallowed the remnants of the collapsed building. Rubbish lay like waves, half a dozen feet below; probably the pile of shattered planking extended to a depth of twenty feet.

Welf's foot slipped on the edge; he dropped the flashlight as he caught his footing. The torch clattered down into the loose junk and disappeared. Staggering back, Welf gripped one of the tilted gasoline standards, clutched it to make sure that he was on solid ground.

Off in the distance, the astonished man saw the dwindle of dim lights. He realized that a car had shaken itself clear from the falling wreckage and carried away some occupants.

Who they were, or how many, Welf could not guess. But he knew that one being—a ghost, perhaps—had remained, to be buried beneath the collapsing building.

Welf shuddered. He remembered The Shadow's gun, the thing that had made him think the black-clad figure to be human. But he recalled that the gun had not answered his revolver shots. Nor had Welf's shots seemed to take any effect whatever upon that specter in black.

It must have been a ghost—the ghost of a man with a gun. Perhaps it was the embodiment of the jinx that had ruined Pomelo City, for the collapse of the old filling station simply represented another disaster to the town.

With that thought, Welf turned about, began a groping, stumbling course back toward the town itself. He had the urge to travel fast, but couldn't. Not only did he lack a flashlight to pick his way along the miserable road, but his knees shook so badly that they could scarcely support his portly frame.

Not once did Welf look back toward the ruin. He wanted to forget it, fearing that the ghost would manage somehow to emerge from its tomb. Such a thing seemed possible to Welf's strained imagination.

It *was* possible. It happened!

EVEN while Welf's stumbly footfalls still sounded from the poor paving, there was a stir amid the wreckage in the sinkhole. A gloved hand slid upward, tested a shattered crossbeam, pressed it to one side. Boards slipped downward, missed a slouch-hatted head that promptly shifted aside.

The Shadow was playing a grim game of jackstraws. In the midst of crisscrossed beams and planks. He had made one amazing escape from destruction; a swift one. Now, he was engaged in a slow-motion effort to get back to solid ground, with every move threatening doom.

At times, boards slipped endways; their slide made the whole mass settle deeper. Yet The Shadow, fairly close to the surface when he began his trip, managed always to gain a new grip and a solid foothold. Head and shoulders up from the debris, he caught a long strip of metal, gave an upward pull.

There was a clatter as he came free. Boards rattled downward as he wrenched past them, but their fall was not a long one. They filled the actual space that The Shadow had left, and the sudden way in which they choked the gap was an explanation of The Shadow's self-preservation.

When the ground had given under the smash of the collapsing building, the near wall of the grease pit had crumpled with it. But The Shadow, diving in that very direction, had found a clear path to what remained of the pit.

There, flattened beneath a half wall of concrete, he had lain in a protecting pocket, while timbers had slid into the sinkhole itself.

Chunks of wood, mostly the ruins of the shed, had imprisoned him, but when settled, they had not formed a serious barrier. Fortunately, the building was of somewhat flimsy construction, whereas the concrete was strong.

The metal strip that The Shadow had gripped was the ledge along the remaining side of the pit. Firmly fixed in the concrete, it gave the very sort of hold he needed to come back to the surface. It was well, though, that he emerged when he did.

Rumblings sounded from below, as the sinkhole made new inroads. As he came to his feet, some distance from the pit, The Shadow heard a crackle that marked the yielding of concrete. Those crackles were followed by the dull thump of disintegrated stone, finding its way downward in chunks.

WHEN Martin Welf reached the hotel, he was too shaky to attempt a stealthy entry. He stumbled in through the front door, and his arrival brought a startled outcry from Chester Tilyon, who was still busy at his desk.

Sagged in a chair, Welf related the details of his journey. He told Tilyon how he had overheard Fenn talking about ghost lights out at the old filling station.

"I was afraid the sheriff would make another blunder," explained Welf. "It seemed better to go out there on my own and take a look around. But it seems"—Welf shook his head ruefully—"that I did some blundering myself."

"You certainly let some troublemakers get away," declared Tilyon. "But what about this ghost you saw?"

"I don't know," returned Welf, slowly. "Maybe there wasn't one, Chester. Whoever went away in the car certainly would not have left anyone behind."

"Probably not," agreed Tilyon. "But suppose that someone else was looking around there, just as you were?"

The question made Welf stare at Tilyon. Both were so concentrated on the subject at hand that neither saw the moving blackness entering the lobby from the kitchen doorway. It had crossed to the stairway and blended shadowlike into the upper darkness, when Welf suddenly gulped:

"You mean—Cranston?"

Tilyon nodded solemnly. Welf came to his feet and started shakily upstairs. Tilyon followed; stood by when Welf knocked at Cranston's door. At last, a sleepy voice responded.

Welf gave a grateful sigh. He didn't know what to say, so Tilyon did the talking for him.

"Sorry, Mr. Cranston," said Tilyon. "We thought you were still awake. We're having coffee downstairs, in case you would like to join us."

Hearing Cranston accept the invitation, Tilyon motioned to Welf. They went downstairs and hurriedly began to get the coffee ready before Cranston arrived. When they heard his footsteps descending, Tilyon undertoned to Welf:

"Don't mention your trip tonight. Let's boost the town, the way we intended. It's our only chance for a comeback, Martin. Cranston may be interested."

Tilyon did the boosting, while the three drank their coffee in the lobby. Pomelo City wasn't a bad place at all, the way the real estate man described it. He laid a map upon his desk and indicated a large red circle, with Pomelo City in the center.

"This is a pomelo area," stated Tilyon. "As you probably know, the term 'pomelo' is the correct name for grapefruit. When growers first came here, they specialized in grapefruit, so the town was later called Pomelo City.

"We had our boom days. The town grew, like the groves. Finally, we settled back to normal, an overbuilt town; but we had a population of several hundred, and the place offered a real future. Growers were raising oranges, as well as grapefruit; slopes were planted with tuna trees, to meet the rising demand for lacquer.

"Farmers occupied the sparser lands; what was left was bought by Graham Clenwick, a very wealthy rancher, who began to improve the local cattle. Then"—Tilyon gave a depreciating shrug—"well, we just ran into a jinx, that was all."

Cranston's eyes were steady, questioning. Tilyon finally decided to admit all facts. He mentioned the Medfly, sinkholes, drying lakes, the appearance of the black wolf, unreported elsewhere in Florida. People had become fearful; chance accidents had caused others to migrate.

"Those things could hardly have been designed,"

1
GAS
3
OIL
2
1. Overhearing in Pomelo City a rumor about a ghost in an abandoned filling station outside the town, The Shadow decides to investigate, thinking it may furnish a lead to a recent murder. In the dead of night he approaches the . . .
2. . . . filling station and by means of a shed attached to the main building, climbs to the roof. There, through a . . .
3. . . . crack in the roofing boards, he listens to a conversation among crooks, about a well-known New York mobster whom they are expecting. Thus does The Shadow get on the trail of crime!

argued Tilyon. "At least, not all of them. It's been slow panic, encouraged by superstition. Business went dead as a result. But Welf and I have stayed, and so has Clenwick.

"He's had his troubles. He had to slaughter his first herd of cattle, because of some disease that ruined it. But Clenwick is banking on the future. He knows that Florida is the future land for cattle raising. There are large ranches throughout the state, and Clenwick intends to make his as good as the best."

TALK of Clenwick interested The Shadow, since he knew that the wealthy rancher was the cause of Enwald's presence in this vicinity. Casually, he encouraged Tilyon to mention Clenwick further. Welf put in an impatient interruption.

"Let's talk about Kewanee Springs," he said to Tilyon. "That will interest Mr. Cranston more than anything else he could hear about."

"In just a moment," smiled Tilyon. "I'll finish the Clenwick story first."

Tilyon ran his finger along the map, indicated a road that ended in a tiny black square.

"This is Clenwick's present residence," he said. "It's the old Severn mansion. The place is owned by Laura Severn and her brother Roger, who's an invalid. The house was built a hundred years ago, and it's belonged to the Severns ever since. They are right nice people.

"The trouble is, they had to sell most of their property, this generation did. All they have left is the house and the grounds around it. That would have gone, too, if Graham Clenwick hadn't helped them out. He bought up the mortgage so they wouldn't be evicted, and he's living there at the house, paying them enough rent to carry the interest charges."

Tilyon might have kept on talking about Laura Severn and her brother, if Welf had not reminded him that the discussion concerned Kewanee Springs, as its principal theme. Tilyon promptly moved his finger to the right of the road that showed on the map.

"The Springs are over here," he said. "They form the main source of the Kewanee River. Like a lot of other large springs in Florida, they give so large a flow that the river is navigable right up to the source.

"There's millions of gallons of water flowing from those Springs, everyday. Those millions of gallons may mean millions of dollars, Mr. Cranston! Not just from Kewanee Springs, but from what the place could do to bring back Pomelo City. Kewanee, when developed, ought to bring a hundred thousand tourists here every year.

"We've got the town, all waiting for them. They'd fill it, Mr. Cranston. We wouldn't have to worry about citrus groves, tuna trees, and ranches. As the only gateway to Kewanee Springs, Pomelo City would make the boom days look like child's play!"

Tilyon's enthusiasm was real. He began a description of Kewanee Springs, terming the place as "Nature's Wonderland." He was talking in terms of golden grottoes, crystal waters, and unspoiled jungle, when Cranston intervened with the practical question:

"Who owns Kewanee Springs?"

"We do," inserted Welf. "Tilyon and I. If you'll back the development, Mr. Cranston, we'll give you a one-third interest, with certain costs deductible. We can talk such terms later—but first, you ought to see the Springs."

"I believe that I have heard of Kewanee Springs before," recalled The Shadow. "There is an Indian legend in reference to the place, is there not?"

Tilyon gave an uneasy laugh.

"Yes," he admitted. "Some story about a devil that used to drive the Seminole Indians away from these parts. There are people who still believe it. The legend has had its part in causing superstitious people to leave here.

"But this jinx stuff can't go on. Intelligent people laugh at talk of ghosts. In fact, it's the type of thing that ought to bring them here. My idea is to meet the situation head-on: play up the Seminole devil, and make him work for us!"

THOUGH Tilyon was no longer trying to make a sales talk, he was actually succeeding with one. His theory of how to beat the Seminole devil was better than his description of Kewanee Springs. Welf was observant; he saw that Cranston was interested. When Tilyon paused to take a breath, Welf inserted the suggestion that they start for Kewanee Springs in the morning.

That ended the discussion for the night. Back in his room, The Shadow gazed out into darkness and whispered a soft-toned laugh. Clenwick, the ranch owner, and his friends, the Severns, could wait until tomorrow night.

Then, The Shadow would find a way to look in on them, as he had with Enwald and the thugs furnished by Tony Belgo. The Shadow was confident that future adventures after nightfall could be handled with less dire consequences than those which had attended his recent foray.

Meanwhile, in Kewanee Springs, with its legend of the Seminole devil, The Shadow might find some new clue to the strange hoodoo that had turned Pomelo City into a forgotten city of ghosts!

CHAPTER VII
DEATH BY THE BRINK

MORNING looked peaceful in Pomelo City. Charred ruins opposite the old hotel had improved the scene, if anything. Bayne's store and Tilyon's real estate office had been as scarred and ramshackly as most of the structures that still remained, while the obliterated arcade could have been termed the town's outstanding eyesore.

Discounting the ugly buildings, the dead palm trees and the battered paving, The Shadow found the outlook pleasant. The horizon showed pine woods and distant cypress clumps, while the ground had green patches of luxuriant palmetto.

Except for the buzzards that roosted on the battered water tower, the distant view was typical of Florida. To all appearances, this territory had a future. Two men, at least, believed in it: Welf and Tilyon.

Those two were waiting breakfast, when their new friend, Cranston, joined them. Welf had appointed himself cook and had handled the job well, as the bacon and eggs proved. During the meal, the three chatted about outside matters, avoiding all discussion of Pomelo City.

The first indication that local subjects were still troublesome came when a car pulled up in front of the hotel. A voice shouted through the doorway; Welf hurried to the sidewalk, Cranston and Tilyon following.

Beside the car stood a man who was mopping his forehead with a grimy handkerchief. He pointed to the rear seat. There lay another man, his sightless eyes staring from a swollen purplish face.

"Bit by a coral snake," said the man by the car. "Too late to take him to the Leesville Hospital. My nerve was getting me, so I stopped here."

Welf looked at the body in the car. He gave a solemn nod, as he pronounced the one word:

"Dead!"

The man on the curb pocketed his handkerchief and climbed back into the car. He seemed somewhat relieved at learning the exact status of the victim.

"Guess I'll drive to the Leesville morgue," he said. "Good-bye. I won't be seeing you fellows again."

The car pulled away. Welf watched it pass the water tower. He looked relieved, too, because the buzzards did not swoop down. Evidently the big birds were overfed.

"There go the last two orange growers," remarked Welf, glumly. "The live one says he won't be back. I don't blame him for—"

Welf stopped at a warning glance from Tilyon. Both looked at Cranston, who appeared quite unperturbed. Tilyon suggested that they get started for Kewanee Springs.

Ten minutes later, the three were riding from Pomelo City in Tilyon's car. From the sand road that they traveled, the scene was lifeless, except for the thin smoke of distant brush fires, a common sight in Florida, where natives frequently burn out the underbrush from wooded patches.

Ahead lay a thick stretch of vivid green, which took on a truly tropical appearance as they reached it. Parking the car at the entrance to the Springs, the visitors followed a footpath beneath huge live oaks, where great beards of Spanish moss hung from massive boughs.

The woodland had a cavernous effect; a profound silence gripped the setting. Sunlight was dwindled by the mossy branches, producing a cool, comfortable effect. A limpid pool came into sight, completing the picture of a natural paradise.

KEWANEE SPRINGS occupied a great limestone chalice, its brim fringed with palmetto. Above were pines and oaks; off in the distance were the tufted tops of tall cabbage palms.

The pool itself was of perfect blue, an absolute reflection of the sky. At spots where trees bent above the brim, the blue hue faded. There, every detail of the bank was mirrored by crystalline water.

A few hundred feet across, the pool showed a gap in the farther bank. That was the beginning of the Kewanee River, perpetually supplied by its unfailing source. Clusters of floating hyacinths added a touch of colorful splendor to the pool's outlet.

The squat hulk of a flat-bottomed boat was drawn up beside the shore. Posts set in the gunwales supported a weatherbeaten canopy. A pair of battered oars lay in the stern. When they reached the boat, Tilyon pointed to its interior.

An oblong well ran from bow to stern. It was built on the principle of a centerboard well; high-walled, so that no water would come up through it. The bottom of the well consisted of framed sheets of glass.

Tilyon explained, unnecessarily, that the canopy cut off the sunlight, thus rendering objects visible through the glass bottom. He took the oars, while Cranston and Welf sat on either side of the oblong well, laying their coats on the seat beside them.

Shoving the boat out from the shore, Tilyon propelled it across a shallow stretch of eel grass. He reached a deeper space, where the grass parted to display a limestone hollow. He announced the depth as thirty feet, though it seemed that the bottom was within a hand's reach.

Fat, big-horned catfish were lolling in the cavity; among them, a smaller species: striped fish called breame. Large turtles flapped idly beneath the plate glass, poked their noses upward and seemed to wonder at the substance that they struck.

Drifting from that spot, the boat reached another fissure in the rock, where the limestone had a yellowish glisten.

Tilyon called the spot the golden grotto, and pointed out long, slinky fish, curiously spotted. They were the leopard gar, creatures of prey, like their namesakes.

Crossing another patch of eel grass, the boat reached an immense cavity. Looking up at the bank, The Shadow saw a high rock, its exterior broken in steplike fashion. Its angles continued down beneath the water, to form a ledge twenty feet below the surface.

Those twenty feet, however, did not constitute the entire depth of this cavity. Below the ledge was a sheer drop, which Tilyon estimated as sixty feet in total depth.

"The Devil's Rock," he said, pointing to the shore. "They call the shelf below the surface the 'Devil's Ledge.' Under the shelf is the dwelling place of a great warrior's spirit.

"Ages ago, according to the legend, this pool was shallow and dry. A drought settled on the land, and when pleas to the rain god brought no result, a Seminole chief mounted the forbidden Devil's Rock and offered himself as sacrifice to the evil spirit dwelling in the earth.

"Immediately, the solid limestone split below him and a vast river of water gushed into life. In keeping with his promise, the chief hurled himself into the new-formed pool, and was swallowed beneath the broken ledge. There, he dwells with the earth devils, but at times his ghost appears upon the Devil's Rock.

"Seminoles claim to have seen him standing there; but at any sign of a human presence, he plunges into the pool, vanishes beneath the ledge, and does not return until his next appointed hour."

THE SHADOW was listening carefully to Tilyon's version of the legend. In all such stories, there was usually a basic truth. Looking into the depths of the huge spring, The Shadow analyzed the possible facts that might have produced the Indian tale.

Having recounted the legend, Tilyon was producing statistics. The great spring, he declared, was actually a subterranean river, fed by other underground streams. Its volume of water varied from twenty to thirty million gallons daily, according to the season.

Enough water to supply the city of Miami, if anyone wanted to pipe it there. At present, the water went to Jacksonville, but not by pipeline. The Kewanee flowed into the Oklawaha, which in turn flowed into the St. John's River, on which Jacksonville was the principal port.

"I'm not thinking of this place as a reservoir, though," declared Tilyon, seriously, as he slowly rowed the boat from the great spring. "A trip like this is worth a dollar of anybody's money. We'll have a lot of new boats built, and equipped with electric motors.

"During the winter season, Kewanee should attract a thousand customers a day. We can add the feature of a jungle cruise down the river. They've done it other places, so Kewanee won't be unique. But the other springs look civilized. We'll keep Kewanee primitive."

He was pushing the boat toward the outlet, pointing out more limestone fissures as the boat passed across them. The Shadow noted that they differed in hue; some were blue, others chalkish in their whiteness. New varieties of underwater plants appeared as the boat progressed.

"If this scow doesn't hit a rock or an alligator, I'll show you the lower spring," promised Tilyon. "It's right around the bend, and you never saw a prettier woodland glade! Every time I look at it, I expect to see a flock of dryads or nymphs come dancing out from the palmettos. That one spot, alone, is worth more than—"

Tilyon went voiceless. The boat had swung the bend. Staring straight ahead, he held the oars motionless above the water. The Shadow looked in the direction of Tilyon's gaze, and Welf did the same.

Near a small rock at the fringe of the promised sylvan pool was a girl who rivaled the forest nymphs that Tilyon talked about. Her slender, graceful figure was accentuated by the thin silken garment that adorned it.

Startled by the splash of a dropping oar, the girl raised her head and looked toward the boat. Her blue eyes opened wide; her lips parted in a soundless gasp. Alarm brought perfection to a face that was beautiful against a background of fluffy golden hair.

Behind the girl lay a bathing suit, with clothes that she had already discarded. Not expecting intruders in this isolated spot, the girl had approached the pool while she was undressing for a swim. At sight of the approaching boat, she drew folds of flimsy silk up toward her shoulders, gave a quick glance toward her other garments.

Then, realizing the scantiness of her costume, she acted upon a sudden impulse. Seeking quick escape from her plight, the girl twisted toward the pool, flung her arms ahead of her as she made a quick dive into the water.

At that moment, a log stirred from the bank. Only The Shadow saw it come to life. His casual eyes, alone, were taking in the entire scene, while his companions had their attention centered on the girl. The Shadow recognized the thing from the bank, just as it began to move.

It wasn't a log; it was an alligator. From ugly nose to tapered tail tip, it measured a full sixteen feet. Large enough to be a man-eater, the reptile was heading after human prey. The splash of the girl's dive told that she was in the water, straight across the alligator's path.

NEITHER Tilyon nor Welf saw the sudden speed that their new friend, Cranston, displayed.

With his left hand, The Shadow gripped one of the half-rotted posts that supported the boat's frayed canopy. His right, whipping into the folds of his discarded coat, snatched something that he had buried out of sight.

Just as the girl's golden-haired head bobbed up from the water, The Shadow went overboard in a sideward dive. He was still gripping the canopy post, and his sheer weight ripped it loose. Clutching the broken chunk of wood, The Shadow landed flat, his left side striking the water first.

Neither Tilyon nor Welf heard the ripping of the wood, nor did they notice the shiver of the boat. They were chilled by the scream that the girl uttered, as she saw the alligator's snout loom through the water, mere yards away. Frantically, she twisted about and tried to swim for shore, too late.

Big jaws had opened. The whip of the reptile's tail spurted the creature forward. Another second, and the cavernous mouth would have gulped for its helpless prey.

But the alligator never reached that golden-haired head, and the sleek shoulder just beneath it.

Into that wide-open mouth was thrust another head, along with a pair of ready hands. Daring the coming *click* of the creature's fangish teeth, The Shadow thrust in his left hand, with the stout cudgel that it bore. His right fist, too, was swinging into action, bearing an object that he had carried high and dry: a .45-caliber automatic.

The Shadow had brought rescue to the girl, only to dare the same fate that she had escaped. Death was due upon the brink of the tropical pool. Whether the human fighter would survive, or his reptilian foe gain victory, was a question that the next dozen seconds would decide!

CHAPTER VIII
THE BROKEN JINX

STARING from the drifting boat, Tilyon and Welf thought that they were witnessing the finish of their new friend, Cranston. They knew the dangers of battling a bull alligator in its native habitat. Not only had Cranston taken on the largest 'gator that either of the witnesses had ever seen, but he was giving the creature all the odds.

Wrestling an alligator was one thing; an expert human might survive such combat. But to thrust head and arms into a 'gator's open jaws was a quick route to suicide. Unfortunately, Cranston had been unable to take another choice. His measure was the only method that could have saved the girl.

Raps from the stick that Cranston held would trouble the 'gator less than fleabites. As for the .45 in his other fist, its slugs could dent the reptilian's scales and nothing more.

Tilyon was grabbing an oar, lifting it, to take a blow at the 'gator's back. As he made that move, the oarsman realized its futility. Like Cranston, he was trying to combat a mammoth menace that was nothing short of a floating ironclad.

Neither Tilyon nor Welf had seen The Shadow in action the night before. Hence, they did not guess that the fighter they knew as Cranston was capable of special measures in every struggle he undertook. Therefore, what they saw amazed them.

The 'gator's big jaws started shut as The Shadow thrust himself between them, but the teeth did not close upon a victim. Instead, the jaws stopped, retaining a yawn that was scarcely less than complete. The Shadow had used his first weapon more rapidly than the 'gator could bite.

The weapon was the stanchion from the boat. With a twist of his left wrist, The Shadow had turned the stout stick upward in the 'gator's mouth. A veritable wedge, the piece of wood was holding the big jaws wide.

Had the stick been barbed, the measure would have proven more than temporary. But the ends were blunt; the alligator did not mind them. The creature waggled its broad jaw from side to side, threatening to dispose of the restraining stick. Only the power of The Shadow's clutch prevented it.

The Shadow's head was withdrawn from the 'gator's mouth, but his left arm was necessarily within it. Welf was shouting for Cranston to release the stick and swim away, but that wouldn't help.

The fierce "yonk-yonk" that issued from the 'gator's throat proved that the aquatic beast was fully enraged. The reptile had already proven itself a faster swimmer than the lithe girl who had escaped it. Only by fighting the creature to the death could The Shadow hope to assure his own survival.

Instead of loosing his hold upon the stick, he brought his other hand into action. From the sweep of his arm, the witnesses thought that he was going to club the 'gator's snout with his heavy automatic; but he stopped short of that mark.

The Shadow was simply keeping the gun above

Whether the human fighter would survive, or his reptilian foe gain victory, was a question that the next dozen seconds would decide.

water. From the level of the reptile's nostrils, he dipped his fist and shoved the gun into the reptilian's wide-wedged mouth.

THE dart of a shirtsleeved arm in front of its eyes caused the alligator to take measures of its own. The creature gave a wide lash with its tail; shoving its head down into the water, it carried its human foeman with it.

Tilyon was busy thwacking with his oar, hoping to divert attack toward the boat; but Welf saw the 'gator's head, watched the creature's eyes take a long, outward bulge.

They were extending like miniature periscopes, those eyes, proving that the 'gator intended an underwater swim. It was starting the usual procedure that all alligators used when land prey proved too tough: that of keeping below the water's surface until its victim drowned.

With those extended eyes, the 'gator could pick its own path through the pool. It "yonked" again as it dipped its open jaws. Cranston's head dipped completely from sight. Only his right arm was visible through the side of the 'gator's open face.

The next "yonk" was suppressed by a muffled roar. The observers saw a flash within the alligator's mouth. The flash was repeated thrice, in rapid succession, each time with an accompanying roar. Those bursts came from The Shadow's gun.

He wasn't wasting shots from the .45 upon the reptile's scaly, bulletproof hide. With his right fist thrust far into the jagged mouth The Shadow was pumping bullets down the alligator's gullet!

Smoke was curling from the side of those big-toothed jaws, as the 'gator's head went beneath the water, except for its periscopic eyes. Glinting sunlight made it difficult for the men in the boat to see what happened to Cranston. The alligator's tail was lashing the water furiously.

Out of that lashing, the creature took a sideward roll. Its head swung above the surface. Big jaws waggled, then clamped shut. The upright stick was no longer between them. It had disappeared.

So had The Shadow.

For a moment, Welf was crazy enough to think that the alligator had swallowed Cranston entire. Then he heard a shout from Tilyon, who was pointing to the stern of the boat. Cranston's head had come into sight, twenty feet away from the stricken alligator. He still had his gun, but he had released the helpful stick. It was floating downstream.

The girl had reached the shore. Kneeling on the bank, she stared toward the pool, saw the alligator's lashing roll and watched its whitish belly come into sight. She knew that the creature was in its death throes, but she could not spy The Shadow. He was beyond the intervening boat.

Blood was marring the crystal water; it made an ugly, oily blotch that drifted with the writhing alligator. The girl mistook the crimson stain for the lifeblood of her rescuer. Coming to her feet, she stood on tiptoe, forgetful of her meager garb.

Water-soaked silk was clinging askew, as the girl poised her lithe body, ready for another dive into the pool; her purpose, this time, to aid her rescuer, if such were possible.

A rattle from the boat ended the girl's tableau. She saw Cranston's face come over the stern of the boat. Tilyon and Welf were helping him on board. He let the gun drop from his right fist, extended his hand to receive the congratulating clasps that his companions offered him.

The girl relaxed. Conscious of herself again, she turned about, gathered up a bundle of clothes and scampered into the palmettos. Gazing from the boat, The Shadow saw the green foliage close behind the girl's pink-clad form.

Tilyon pushed the boat to shore. The girl reappeared, wearing a dress that she had slipped over her shoulders; her feet were encased in sandals that she hadn't taken time to buckle. Brushing back the damp hair that strewed her forehead, she proffered her hand to Cranston, while her lips spoke heartfelt thanks.

Both Welf and Tilyon had met the girl before. She was Laura Severn, who lived in the old mansion where Graham Clenwick was a resident guest. They introduced Laura to Cranston.

"I WAS just a startled fool!" exclaimed Laura, in self-reproach. "I always look for 'gators when I'm ready for a swim. But today I wasn't quite ready when you all came along.

"I've never stayed when I've seen that big 'gator here. He's been watching for me, and he'd have gotten me this time"—she emphasized the statement with a lovely shudder—"if you hadn't come along, Mr. Cranston."

Calmly, The Shadow claimed the blame as his own, stating that it was the boat's sudden arrival that had caused Laura to so hurriedly seek the pool where danger lurked. His rescue, as he expressed it, was merely an effort to amend an error.

"It's mighty sweet of you," said Laura, "to look at it that way. But I still owe you thanks, Mr. Cranston, and my brother will feel the same. We'd be delighted, sir, if you would accept our hospitality while you are hereabouts."

Welf remarked that Cranston was a guest at the Pomelo Hotel. Laura smiled sympathetically; she knew that Welf needed guests, and would prefer that Cranston should not move to the mansion.

With true Southern courtesy, the girl made her invitation definite, at the same time allowing for Welf's interests.

"If you could have dinner with us this evening," Laura told The Shadow, "I'm sure that Mr. Welf could arrange to bring you to our house and call for you later."

When Welf agreed that he could, The Shadow accepted the invitation. Laura shook hands again, gave a parting smile and left for the palmettos, to gather up the rest of her clothes and take the path home.

As the three men rowed back to the upper Springs, Tilyon kept vaunting the merits of Kewanee. He was still talking about the place when they reached his car and began the drive back to Pomelo City.

"We'll get that big 'gator and have him stuffed," decided Tilyon. "What an exhibit he will make! There'll be a story to go with it, too. Your story, Cranston: how you rescued the beauty from the beast.

"The Indian legend will do for the upper Springs. Maybe people won't believe it, but they'll like to look at Devil's Rock. They'll believe the story of the alligator fight, though, when they get to the lower Springs.

Glancing sidewise as he drove the car, Tilyon saw Cranston nod, and was pleased. He felt sure that this wealthy stranger from New York would aid in the development of Kewanee Springs and give Pomelo City its real chance for a comeback.

The Shadow's thoughts went farther than Tilyon supposed. The Shadow foresaw that Pomelo City would automatically regain life, when the menace that enshrouded it was gone. Whatever that mysterious menace, it accounted for the ceaseless jinx that had brought death and mystery to these parts.

The jinx was broken. By his rescue of Laura, The Shadow had ended the long line of certain tragedies that had thinned the inhabitants of this region. More than that, The Shadow had gained an opportunity he wanted.

This evening, as Lamont Cranston, he would be a guest at the Severn mansion. There, he would meet Graham Clenwick—another man who, like Tilyon and Welf, was staying on the ground despite the existing hoodoo.

From Tilyon and Welf, The Shadow had learned much; but it was all that they could offer. He was confident that Clenwick could supply more facts of value. The Shadow was making progress in his campaign to restore Pomelo City.

Sooner or later, he would have the answer to the riddle that had made the place a city of ghosts!

CHAPTER IX
AT THE MANSION

IT was Tilyon who drove Cranston to the Severn mansion, at five that afternoon. They took a long way around, so that Tilyon could point out some features of the extensive area that constituted Clenwick's cattle domain.

In Florida, straggly towns like Pomelo City were often termed cities, though they had never boasted more than a few hundred inhabitants. It seemed, therefore, that talk of ranches would also be exaggerated. Such was not the case.

Florida cattle ranges were huge, rivaling many in the West. In recent years, they had risen to vast proportions, bringing many cowboys to the state. Dude ranches, too, had been established in sections of Florida, as The Shadow had learned from wealthy friends.

Clenwick's ranch was a big-time enterprise. After passing a desolate stretch where wavering brush fires burned, Tilyon pointed out grazing cattle in a thinned area of timberland.

"Good-looking beasts," he observed. "Not scrawny, like the kind the crackers raise. There's no buzzards hovering around here, waiting for cows to drop dead. But those are stock that Clenwick sold to some native. The crackers let their cattle roam the open range. Clenwick's property is all fenced in."

They reached the fenced area. The Shadow saw more cattle, among them Brahman steers, imported from Texas.

A mounted cowboy, evidently one of Clenwick's cattle hands, was riding through the woods. He tilted back his ten-gallon hat, to observe the car more closely. Recognizing it as Tilyon's car, he waved a cheery salute.

"Clenwick is keeping the place policed," said Tilyon, approvingly. "What Sheriff Harley said is true. There have been suspicious persons in this neighborhood."

Taking a shortcut along a sand road, Tilyon drove in the direction of Kewanee Springs, until he struck the road that led to the mansion. Following that road, they rode through a massive old gate and came upon a sight that only old Florida could have offered.

Time must have stopped when the mansion house was built. The old colonial structure stood beyond a perfect carpet of green lawn, shaded by the finest specimens of live oak anywhere in Florida.

As at Kewanee Springs, the trees gave a cavernous effect, the streamers of Spanish moss resembling stalactites dipping from the ceiling of a grotto. But the space was vaster, and through the open spaces The Shadow could see the white of magnolia trees in full blossom.

The air was sweetly scented with the odors of many flowers. The whistling chirp of the mockingbird brought melody to the surroundings.

Alighting from the car, The Shadow turned to view the scene, while Tilyon drove away. When the sputter of the motor had faded in the distance, the visitor was impressed by the almost mystic silence that pervaded this century-old setting.

Even the mockingbirds had quieted. Dreamy laziness held sway. The Shadow's own thoughts were drifting into the past, when a welcoming voice spoke from the mansion doorway:

"Good evening, Mr. Cranston!"

LAURA SEVERN was standing on the veranda. Smiling in greeting, the girl added new charm to the scene. She was attired in a simple frock, which harmonized with the surroundings. Her hair was fluffed again, and daylight, filtering through the lofty trees, gave it the hue of old gold.

In gracious fashion, she ushered the visitor into the mansion. From the quiet central hallway, she pointed out the spacious library and the ancient dining room. Then, conducting Cranston through a rear door that led out beside the long wing of the house, the girl suggested:

"Suppose we visit my brother Roger. Mr. Clenwick has not yet returned from the ranch, so you can meet him later. But it isn't far to where Roger is. He's down near the Seminole Punch Bowl."

The Shadow was quite willing to meet Roger. He was also intrigued to learn more about the Seminole Punch Bowl, whatever it was. Laura led the way along a rustic path that followed a quick-rippling brook. A quarter mile brought them to a tiny lawn in the center of thick circling pines.

A man was stretched out in a wheelchair. Hands clasped behind his head, he was staring upward between his shirtsleeved elbows. He wore a scowl on his pasty face; the contortions of his lips indicated ugly mutters.

Laura gave an anxious glance toward Cranston, then called softly:

"Roger!"

Instantly, the man's manner changed. Coming around in his wheelchair, Roger's face was all smile. With a friendly greeting, he extended a warm hand to the visitor.

"Accept my thanks, Mr. Cranston," said Roger, "for rescuing my sister. Laura told me everything that happened, and I agree that the fault was hers, not yours."

During the next half hour, Roger Severn kept up a lively conversation. He talked about places where he had been, but always his statements were dated. They referred to things of five years ago, or more, before Roger had become the victim of a spinal ailment.

Roger's chat was gay, but it masked bitterness with the world. He was wearing out his strength in conversation. Noting it, Laura told her brother to rest while she showed Cranston the Seminole Punch Bowl, on the other side of the tiny glen.

The bowl was a shallow pit of packed stones that received the little brook. Swirling water formed a whirlpool that slackened as it filled. Then, under pressure, the water was sucked down through the stones.

Filling again, the bowl repeated its action at half-minute intervals. In its small way, the vanishing brook that ran into the Seminole Punch Bowl was as interesting a phenomenon as the great subterranean river that issued from beneath the Devil's Ledge at Kewanee Springs.

It was time to return to the mansion. With a weary smile, Roger decided that he would rather remain at the glen and have his meal brought there. The Shadow walked back to the house with Laura; as they entered the rear door, they heard the clatter of hoofs from the front.

A man dismounted from a horse, handed it to another horseman, and entered the house. A servant had turned on the hallway lights; in the glow, The Shadow saw a tall, heavily built man advancing with long, sure strides.

Seeing Laura, the newcomer swept his rancher's hat from his head. His face was broad, square-jawed, beneath his high-bridged nose. Fixing keen eyes upon Cranston, he finally turned back to Laura, expecting her to introduce the visitor, which she did.

THE man was Graham Clenwick. He hadn't heard the story of Laura's escape from the alligator. The girl told it in vivid detail; Clenwick's face becoming solemn as he listened. He didn't treat the adventure humorously, as Roger had.

When Laura had finished, Clenwick laid his left arm around the girl's shoulders in a protective, fatherly gesture. He extended his right hand to The Shadow in a forceful grip. His thanks were voluble; he gave them in a booming voice.

"There have been too many tragedies around here," announced Clenwick, soberly. "Fortunately, none have fallen upon this household, but I am fearful that they might. You must promise me, Laura, that you will stay away from that dangerous Springs."

Giving a halfway promise, Laura departed for the kitchen, to see about dinner. Clenwick turned to Cranston.

"This is a remarkable country," declared the rancher, "but a very fearful one. Nature has made strange freaks in this terrain, particularly the sinkholes. I heard today that a new one caved through, carrying an abandoned filling station with it."

Casually, The Shadow asked about the sinkholes, inquiring about such matters as their width and depth.

"Most of them are small and shallow," declared Clenwick, "but apparently they enlarge with years. Take the Giant Sinkhole, for example. Picture a rounded cavity a hundred feet across, withered trees leaning over its brink, dead brush clinging to its precipitous walls. At the bottom, a stagnant pool, so deep that no one has ever measured it.

"When I came here, the Giant Sinkhole was the worst of all local hazards. Cattle wandered into the pit, because the clay brink gave under their weight. For all we know, human beings may have blundered into that fearful trap."

Pacing the floor with a heavy stride, Clenwick gradually lost his solemn expression. He brightened, as he stated:

"I ended the menace of the Giant Sinkhole by fencing it with barbed wire. I have done the same with other sinkholes on my property. I have won the friendship of the natives hereabouts, by supplying them with wire for the same purpose. Every time a new menace appears, I try to counteract it."

Laura entered, to announce that dinner was ready. During the course of the meal, Clenwick began to talk about the jinx that hung over Pomelo City. Like Welf and Tilyon, he argued that it was purely local superstition; but he proposed a different remedy.

"We've got to forget Pomelo City," he boomed. "A difficult step for Welf and Tilyon, but it's better than their plan of rotting with the town. Look at what happened to poor Bayne! I tell you, that town is a city of ghosts!

"Having seen Pomelo City, Mr. Cranston, I know that you will agree that it is little better than a cemetery. Soon, Welf and Tilyon will be legends, like the Indian ghost of Kewanee Springs. I understand they want to develop the Springs. Have they approached you on the subject?"

The Shadow nodded.

"A good investment," decided Clenwick. "One that I would take up, except for my sole interest in ranching. But first, they should forget Pomelo City. The right step is to abandon that forsaken town and make Kewanee Springs an attraction in its own right."

Clenwick's proposition had soundness. As they retired to the library, he was stating how a lodge and cabins could be built at Kewanee Springs, bringing tourists directly to the place.

"A fresh start is the only way," said Clenwick. "My experience proves it. My ranch, which adjoins this mansion, is building steadily. When ticks and other plagues injured the weaker cattle; I brought in Brahmans.

"I've helped the local cattle raisers, poor fellows, by taking over mortgages that the banks wouldn't handle. I supplied them with stock when their own cattle died. I'll turn this whole area into the best grazing land in Florida—"

CLENWICK paused, head tilted, a cigar raised halfway to his mouth. A car had rolled in through the driveway; its smooth hum marked it as a strange one, since most of the local automobiles were rattletraps.

Though Clenwick couldn't place the car by the sound of the motor, The Shadow recognized it. He had heard that same smooth hum the night before, when a car had rolled into the shed beside the abandoned filling station.

The coming of that car promised an early answer to a pressing riddle. Clenwick's visitor was to be the sallow man named Enwald, the smooth crook who was leagued with the Manhattan racketeer, Tony Belgo!

As Lamont Cranston, The Shadow was perfectly placed to learn facts that might pertain to future crime, as well as gaining clues to a mystery of the past—the jinx that hovered above Pomelo City!

CHAPTER X
CRIME'S MISSION

USHERED into the library by a servant, the sallow-faced visitor introduced himself by his full name: Roy Enwald. Smooth-mannered and presentable, Enwald looked like anything but a crook. Perhaps it was his lack of company like Dingbat and Skate that gave Enwald gloss on this occasion.

Nevertheless, the shrewdness of his peaked features showed that Enwald might be a schemer in his own right. An odd contrast, his voice had a tone of real sincerity, as he purred:

"I'm a friend of Terry Knight."

Clenwick clapped Enwald on the shoulder.

"You're welcome, then!" boomed the rancher. "Any of Terry's friends are friends of mine!"

Smiling, Enwald lighted a cigar that Clenwick tendered him. Introduced to Cranston, Enwald shook hands very cordially, then looked around the room.

"I expected to find Terry here," said the sallow man, smoothly. "This is the last place where I heard from him."

"Terry has the wanderlust," returned Clenwick, with a broad smile. "He never stays anywhere more than a few months."

"He stayed in Texas a long while."

"Because he was looking for oil. When he found the fields too crowded, he became a rancher. That's how I happened to meet him. My business is raising cattle."

Enwald nodded at Clenwick's statement.

"So I learned in Pomelo City," he said. Then, turning to The Shadow: "Like yourself, Mr. Cranston, I am a guest at the Pomelo Hotel. Which reminds me that I have a message for you. Mr. Tilyon says that he will call for you at half past ten."

The message delivered, Enwald returned to the former subject. He wanted to know if Clenwick had heard from Knight after his friend had left Florida. Clenwick shook his head.

"Soon after I came here," he explained, "I had a letter from Terry, stating that he was out of a job. So I wrote him to come to Florida. He was enthused, for a while, over the ranch that I had started; then he lost interest.

"He was on his feet again, and had enough money to head for Mexico. So he left, claiming that he could make a place for himself in the oil fields that the Mexican government was taking over. I wasn't surprised that he wanted to go. Terry never did care much for cattle raising."

Enwald nodded. Then: "Do you think that everything is all right with Terry?"

"It must be," replied Clenwick, warmly. "Otherwise, I would have heard from him. Terry never writes"—Clenwick gave a deep chuckle—"except when he's down and out!"

A VOICE was calling from the rear hall: Laura's. Since the others were busy, The Shadow strolled out to learn what the girl wanted. Laura greeted him with a winsome smile.

"Here's your chance to help both members of the Severn family," she said. "I just wheeled Roger in from the glen, but I can't manage to bring the chair up the back steps. Could you handle it for me, Mr. Cranston?"

The Shadow agreed that he could. Out back, he found Roger slumped in the wheel chair. Laura's brother was too tired to disguise his impatient mood. He pointed to the car lights that he saw in front of the house, and demanded:

"Who's the new visitor?"

"A chap named Enwald" was Cranston's reply. "He says that he is a friend of Terry knight."

"That lout!" snapped Roger. "What a time he gave us! Clumping into the house at all hours of the night, messing everything with his grimy boots. He was always behind on his pay for board and lodging, too."

"How long was he here?"

"Two months or more. It was ghastly! But he did us two good turns. He brought Clenwick here, by informing him that this was good cattle land; and after that, Knight went away, to Mexico. Clenwick hasn't heard from him since, and I term it good riddance."

The Shadow had swung the chair into the house. From the rear of the hall, Roger caught his first glimpse of Roy Enwald. Clenwick had introduced the visitor to Laura. Enwald was talking to the girl. Clenwick had gone into the library.

As The Shadow pushed the wheelchair closer, Clenwick came into sight. Enwald gave a sallow-lipped smile, muttered a good night and turned suddenly on his heel. He left the house rapidly; they heard his car drive away.

"What was that fellow saying?" demanded Roger, as the chair reached Laura. "Why did he leave so suddenly?"

"He was just talking about Terry Knight," replied Laura. "I told him that when Terry was our only boarder, he used to tramp everywhere, night and day. I said that Terry liked the country round here, until he tired of it."

"And then?"

"Mr. Enwald said that he had heard of some very lovely places hereabouts—"

Roger raised his scrawny fists in interruption, shook them toward the door. His temper broke.

"But Enwald meant Kewanee Springs!" stormed Roger. "I could tell by his smirk that he was jesting at your expense, Laura, because of what happened there this morning. If I had strength, I'd go after that cad and choke him!"

Roger's hands were writhing furiously. It was Clenwick who finally managed to soothe the invalid. When Roger sank back into the chair, Clenwick undertoned:

"I'll get him upstairs. After that, I'll turn in myself. It's been a hard day at the ranch. Good night, Cranston. Laura will chat with you until Tilyon comes."

When Clenwick had worked the wheelchair up the stairs, Laura turned, to see Cranston glancing at his watch. Noting that it was only half past nine, The Shadow questioned:

"You have a car of your own, Miss Severn?"

Laura nodded.

"Could I borrow it until tomorrow? I don't like to bring Tilyon all the way out here."

Conducting The Shadow to a barn that served as a garage for several cars, Laura gave him the keys to her coupé, and waited to close the door when he had left. The car rolled from the barn;

Laura spoke earnestly through the window.

"Really, Mr. Cranston," said the girl, "Roger was hopelessly bewildered tonight. He didn't mean the threats that he made against Enwald; Roger always finds fault with something, or someone, after a tiring day."

"I understand."

WITH that quiet statement, The Shadow drove away. His words, however, had more significance than Laura knew. The Shadow understood why Enwald had talked to the girl; why the sallow man had left so suddenly.

Roy Enwald formed a curious link between the missing adventurer, Terry Knight, and the New York racketeer, Tony Belgo. Enwald had come here to find out something, and had learned it. Because of that, Enwald had resolved upon a future course, a drastic one.

The Shadow intended to reach the hotel, to confront Enwald and learn more facts from the sallow man's own lips. That accomplished, The Shadow would have more links to the riddle of Pomelo City, town of ghosts!

Parking the car some distance from the hotel, The Shadow approached a fire escape that would take him to the second floor. Enwald was already in his room, as a light showed. But, as The Shadow reached the fire escape, sounds from above told that other visitors had arrived ahead of him.

Reaching the second floor, The Shadow stopped at his own room, to don garments of black. After that, he approached a door where a crack of light showed beneath. Using a special pick, he probed the lock. Easing the door inward as silently as he had unlocked it, he saw Enwald in conference with Skate and Dingbat.

Lowering a glass from his lips, Enwald thumped it on the bureau, reached for a bottle to pour himself another drink. His expression showed an ugliness that he had managed to restrain while at the mansion. His tone was raspy, when he stated:

"We're going through with it. The thing's a setup! Clenwick lives at the old house. The only other people there are a girl and her crippled brother, except for servants, who don't count. The flunkies are quartered in old buildings out back."

Skate put a question: "What about the hired hands?"

"You mean the *rancheros*?" Enwald's purr had returned. "They live over with the cattle, where they belong. We'll wait until the rest of our crew shows up. I'll tell them to go ahead; because if the mob moves in there quiet, it will be a cinch to snatch Clenwick without anybody knowing it."

Skate and Dingbat conferred, while Enwald went back to his bottle. The sallow man wasn't interested in the conference; he had told his story. He caught mutters, though, and understood them.

The thugs were agreed that they should kidnap Clenwick tonight, as soon as the mob arrived, and take him as a trophy to the big shot, Tony Belgo. From their comments, it was plain that Belgo was a high-powered crook who was taking up kidnapping as a new specialty.

"If the job goes sour tonight," remarked Skate, "we can make it look like we were after cattle. If we lam, Tony can dope out the next move."

"That makes sense," agreed Dingbat. "All that worries me is whether Clenwick is worth a couple of million bucks, like Enwald says."

Enwald finished his drink and gave a nod. His purred tone became a raucous pitch.

"He's worth plenty," declared Enwald, "and he'll pay up; Tony Belgo will know how to put the heat on him. I told Tony how to handle it, and I was right. But Tony won't begin until I'm miles away—"

MILES suddenly lacked interest to Enwald. He was thinking in terms of a few feet—the distance between himself and the door. Bleary-eyed, he fancied that he had seen the door ease shut, though it was supposed to be locked.

From somewhere outside came the rumble of a car motor; its sound ended abruptly. Dingbat forgot Enwald, sprang to the window and beckoned to Skate.

"It's the mob, all right," informed Dingbat, in a whisper. "They knew that Enwald would be here at the hotel. This is where Tony told them to come."

At that moment, Enwald was thinking in terms other than the mob and Tony Belgo. He had even forgotten Dingbat and Skate. Springing from beside the bureau, Enwald pounced to the door, grabbed the knob and gave it a quick turn.

He yanked. The door flew inward, sprawling the sallow man back upon the floor. Skate and Dingbat heard the noise and wheeled about, tugging guns from their hips. Their throats voice hoarse shouts.

A tall figure occupied the doorway. He was a being cloaked in black. Burning eyes peered above the gloved hand that had discarded its tiny lock-picking instrument for a more formidable object. The muzzle of a .45 automatic waggled back and forth between Skate and Dingbat, holding the two crooks motionless.

The thugs knew that this black-cloaked challenger was no ghost. Well versed in crime, they recognized a superfoe long noted for his skill at tracking down men of evil.

The Shadow!

How crime's most deadly enemy had traced them to this forgotten town in Florida they couldn't guess. Vaguely, they connected his arrival with a prowler who had come to the abandoned filling station the night before; but they thought that they had settled that foolhardy wayfarer.

The thugs were loosening their grip, ready to drop their guns, when intervention came in their behalf. Enwald supplied it, for the sallow man, influenced by drink and local legend, actually believed that he was viewing a ghost.

With a crazed shriek, Enwald grabbed a chair; from hands and knees, he threw it madly, defiantly, and with surprising accuracy.

Twisting, The Shadow threw up a warding arm. The chair glanced from his shoulder, but his shift, the duck of his head, gave the illusion that he was staggered.

Momentarily, he had lost his aim toward Dingbat and Skate. Inspired by Enwald's mistaken bravado, the two surged through the doorway, to grapple with the fighter in black in the hallway. Revolvers spoke, but The Shadow jerked Skate's gun hand upward, clashed Dingbat's weapon with his heavy automatic.

Crooks were joined by another fighter, more furious than they. It was Enwald, reeling into the fray, armed with an empty bottle. One against three, The Shadow was engaged in battle that offered a serious problem even if he won it.

Victory would not suffice unless The Shadow kept his presence in Pomelo City undiscovered. Otherwise, The Shadow's coming campaign would come to naught before he started it.

The Shadow knew—too well!

CHAPTER XI
DEATH BELOW

LOCKED with two thugs like Skate and Dingbat, The Shadow held advantages that his antagonists did not suspect. He had long ago trained himself to battles of this sort; and in actual experience, he had frequently utilized the many tricks he knew.

Thuggish fighters were all alike. Given odds in their favor, they used them recklessly. In certain ways, The Shadow preferred to handle two such foemen, rather than one. A pair would always behave true to form.

Skate and Dingbat were doing just that. Each was trying to clutch The Shadow with a free hand, and get a gun fist into play. The Shadow, both hands in sweeping action, was actually equalizing the struggle.

He had hauled a second automatic from beneath his cloak, and the way he sledged those big guns was a sight to be remembered. Back against the wall, he was slashing past the hands that grabbed for him, striking the gun fists of his foemen.

Guns blasted. Their shots were wide, including the ones The Shadow loosed. But the whine of bullets past their ears did not please the brawling mobbies. Stirred to new frenzy, they tried to batter past The Shadow's guns. That was when he grappled.

Whirling, he spun the two men about with him. On the outside of the circle, they were flung hard along the farther wall, as the reeling trio ricocheted against it.

Jolted, they lost their grip upon The Shadow. They came back for more, but not as promptly as they had at first. This time, one or the other seemed due for a blow from one of The Shadow's descending guns.

It was Enwald who spoiled the picture.

Wielding the bottle, Enwald had been trying to swing it over the heads of his pals to reach The Shadow. That was one reason why the cloaked fighter had wheeled away from the far wall. Enwald's swings had come too close.

There was no calculating the fellow's strokes. Enwald wasn't of the thug type; he was a fighter who had an individual style. His drinks had handicapped his accuracy; but with that loss, he had gained an eccentric touch that was highly dangerous.

His blows might come in from anywhere, when least expected. The Shadow had to keep away from Enwald, for the present.

The sallow man was driving in again, before The Shadow could settle either Skate or Dingbat. Grappling with one thug, The Shadow reeled him against the other, who also came to grips. Again, the three were in a spin, The Shadow the center of it, before Enwald could smash home a blow.

Opportunity came The Shadow's way.

Close to that spinning path was the broken chair that Enwald had flung into the hallway. Stopping short, The Shadow hooked one foot against it. Past the glaring faces of Skate and Dingbat, The Shadow saw Enwald lunging forward with the bottle. A hard kick, a sideward shove—the thing was done.

The Shadow and his two adversaries were gone from Enwald's path but the chair was there. The sallow man tripped over it. The bottle went clattering along the hallway like a bouncing tenpin. Enwald went headlong after it, in the fashion of an overbalanced bowler.

Again, The Shadow's feet were busy, tripping the legs about him. He went to the floor with the two struggling thugs, snapping a shot as they fell.

The bullet found Dingbat's left shoulder, as a frenzied snarl told. Viciously, Dingbat shoved his gun for The Shadow, pressed the muzzle home.

This time, The Shadow failed to shove the

The muzzle of a .45 automatic waggled back and forth ... holding the two crooks motionless.

revolver aside. Dingbat pressed the trigger. An agonized shriek sounded through the hallway. The gun muzzle wasn't poking The Shadow's ribs. Skate's body was the obstacle. Dingbat had blasted his own pal with a mortal shot.

PUTTING an elbow clamp on the arm above Dingbat's gun hand, The Shadow hoisted the wounded crook to his feet. Shoving the fellow farther along the hall, The Shadow gave a sideward twist to meet Enwald's return. The sallow man was coming back again. He had reclaimed the big quart bottle and was gripping it by the neck, swinging the thing like a bludgeon.

In fact, Enwald's hand was already sledging downward when The Shadow saw him. Nothing could have stopped the bottle's descent for The Shadow's head; not even a warding lift of The Shadow's right arm, for it was held too low.

Nor could Enwald be stopped. His drive, his swing, had become matters of momentum that were beyond control. But the bottle was a different matter. The Shadow's right hand tilted its gun straight upward, in a fraction of the time required for a full lift of his arm. The Shadow fired.

There wasn't any bottle when Enwald's descending hand slashed inches away from The Shadow's face. Chunks of glass were flying, some bouncing from the brim of The Shadow's slouch hat. Enwald was gripping the jagged-edged bottle neck; nothing more.

The Shadow's bull's-eye had been a whiskey label, and he scored a hit. The bullet from the .45 burst the bottle like a soap bubble, a half yard from The Shadow's head.

Enwald's follow-through carried him at an angle past The Shadow. Half sprawled to the floor, the sallow man was wondering what had become of the bottle.

That didn't bother Dingbat. He was concerned with matters of his own. Twisting his one good arm, the thug managed to release it from The Shadow's grip. Dingbat lost his revolver in the effort, for he couldn't tug it past The Shadow's elbow. When the gun hit the floor, the crook didn't stop to snatch it up.

They were close by the stairway leading down into the lobby. Knowing that The Shadow would be after him, Dingbat made a headlong flight down the stairs, shouting incoherently as he went. He was hoping that arriving mobbies had entered by the lobby. They had.

As Dingbat took a long, hard tumble to the tiled floor of the lobby, The Shadow saw Tilyon and Welf darting into the kitchen. They were away in time to avoid an entering mobster crew, five strong.

The crooks heard Dingbat's howls, saw him sprawl. From below, they glimpsed the vague outline of The Shadow at the top of the stairs.

Revolvers barked, too hastily for accuracy. Down from the stair top stabbed answering tongues of flame. The Shadow's shots clipped the first two of the incoming mob; after that, his bullets were digging chunks out of the lobby floor, for the others had turned about.

Guns spoke outdoors. Descending a half dozen steps, The Shadow saw Sheriff Harley and a few other men alighting from a car. The law had arrived to take its part in the fray. It wouldn't do to let crooks stay barricaded in the lobby.

That was why The Shadow lashed bullets to the full. He wasn't out for hits, for the mobbies were beyond the angle of his range. His purpose was to drive the whole band out into the street, where the sheriff's squad could round them up. The Shadow did not stop his barrage until his guns were empty.

THE system worked. Unwounded crooks were gone, preferring battle in the open spaces to The Shadow's flaying fire. Their crippled pals, ignored by The Shadow, were staggering after them.

Stumbling in the rear was Dingbat. The fellow caved in as he went through the doorway.

Dingbat was through. His wound, plus the skull-cracking fall upon the lobby floor, indicated that he would not long survive his dead pal, Skate.

The Shadow had not forgotten Enwald.

Others were mere mobsters in the employ of a big shot, Tony Belgo. Roy Enwald was different. He was a man with a plan—a schemer who had been living in this territory, giving orders to a pair of aides that Belgo had furnished.

More than a mere "finger man" working with Belgo's snatch racket, Enwald knew a lot more than he had told the thugs who worked with him. He was a schemer in his own right, Enwald, and his alliance with Belgo could well be a mere side issue, to further purposes of Enwald's own.

Most important was the fact that Enwald's presence in this area had been coincident with recent tragedies which had the definite earmarks of crime. Enwald, under proper questioning, could certainly tell a lot. Deprived of the protecting thugs, he should be an easy man to capture.

Turning toward the second floor, The Shadow made a quick drop to the steps, poking a gun over the top one. The move was timely. Enwald had found Dingbat's lost revolver, and was looking for The Shadow. Sight of a looming gun muzzle across the step edge was enough for Enwald.

He had nothing to shoot at, except the pair of blazing eyes beneath the brim of the slouch hat.

Afraid to trust his hurried aim against the point-blank fire of The Shadow, Enwald fled along the hall toward the fire escape.

The Shadow did not fire. He sprang up from the steps and took up the pursuit. Reaching the fire escape, Enwald turned about, too late. The Shadow was upon him.

One gun cloaked, the intrepid fighter in black was using his free hand to grab for Enwald's revolver. In his other fist, The Shadow swung a heavy automatic that was a permanent bludgeon; not something that could be shattered, like Enwald's vanished bottle.

Struggling as The Shadow enveloped him, Enwald threw his weight against the iron rail of the fire escape. Rusted metal gave; the thing flapped like a hinged gate. Over the edge they went, Enwald screeching from the folds of the black cloak that covered him like a pair of closing bat wings.

How Enwald managed a midair twist remained a matter unanswered. Usually, The Shadow performed such an action when diving along with a foe. By rights, Enwald should have taken the full brunt of that fall, but he managed to fling sideward and give half the shock to The Shadow.

Fortunately, the courtyard was no longer cement. It had filled, some time ago, with thick mud, now turned to powdery clay. The grapplers rolled apart when they struck the two-inch layer of soil. Neither was out of combat.

The jar, however, produced opposite effects. It drove some sense back into Enwald's drink-befuddled brain, whereas The Shadow found himself in a temporary daze.

AS he crawled for shelter beside the pitch-black wall, The Shadow couldn't quite remember where he was.

He fancied that he was in dark, watery depths awaiting the jaws of a powerful alligator. Memory of his battle at Kewanee Springs brought back kaleidoscopic pictures of Laura Severn.

The Shadow visioned her on the pool brink; then in the water. Next, he saw her in the glen—chatting with her brother; finally, he placed her in the mansion talking with Roy Enwald.

That thought jerked The Shadow to the present. It wasn't an alligator that he had to battle; it was Enwald. The fellow was somewhere in the darkness, with a gun.

Through his thin glove, The Shadow felt the cold metal of an automatic. The .45 was close beside his knee. Lifting the gun, he crawled along the wall toward the open but pitch-black rear space of the courtyard.

Even the handicap of carrying a lifted gun did not prevent The Shadow from making a soundless trip. The thing that betrayed him was a loose chunk of stucco, that dislodged from the wall as his cloaked shoulder brushed it.

Slight though the clatter was, it brought a response from the front of the court.

A figure rose against the grimy yellow stucco that formed part of the archway to the street. The form was made obscurely visible by the glimmer of a feeble street lamp flickering beyond. Raising himself against the rear wall, The Shadow tried to steady his gun, in case his position should be exactly guessed.

The man by the archway shifted. Without realizing it, he shoved his head and shoulders into the glow. He twisted his face back and forth and The Shadow saw the sallow features of Roy Enwald, though they seemed oddly blurred.

There was a flash of the man's teeth as Enwald gave an ugly leer. It was matched by the glitter of his revolver, when he lifted the gun to chin level. There were no more sounds of battle from the front street. Enwald's voice came in grated tone, no longer an oily purr:

"I'll get you!" rasped Enwald. "Whoever you are—wherever you are—"

He was waggling the gun somewhat in The Shadow's direction. Hearing no further sound, Enwald began to shoot. Spattering bullets chinked the stucco, one shot close to The Shadow's shoulder. In the midst of a dizzy sway, The Shadow pressed his own gun trigger.

Enwald heard the shot that blasted from the darkness. Clapping his hand to his chest, the sallow man staggered. Dropping the revolver, he clutched at the archway, lost his hold and rolled to the clay.

The Shadow did not see that fall. He had performed a soundless slump of his own, but not from the effect of Enwald's bullets, for none had struck him. Sheer effort to shake his daze had been too much for The Shadow's giddy senses.

Echoes faded from the courtyard. All was silent in that blackened square. Quiet had come anew to the city of ghosts. Of all spots in Pomelo City, the tiny courtyard between the decrepit hotel and the abandoned theater seemed the proper residence of departed spirits!

CHAPTER XII
AGAIN, THE GHOST

MINUTES passed before a whisper stirred the courtyard. It was a sibilant tone, one that carried a spectral touch. It came from the archway where Enwald's body lay. In the darkness, it actually seemed that voice could have come from the dead man's ghost.

Then, like a wraith from darkness, the whispering being appeared. The Shadow had come out of his daze; he had groped to the archway to look at Enwald's body.

The single shot had killed the sallow man. It had been a question of Enwald's life or The Shadow's. Despite the frequency of Enwald's fire, The Shadow had survived. The gaping bullet hole in Enwald's body told why.

There was no hope of hearing more from Enwald. From the fragmentary statements that the man had made, The Shadow would have to piece together the rest of crime's story. He could hope to do so, now that he had covered the matter of his presence on the scene.

Catercornered across the street, some distance beyond the short row of flickery lights, was the place where The Shadow had left Laura Severn's car. Steady again, the black-cloaked fighter glided out from the archway. Keeping to the shelter of the brownish palm trees, he picked a blackened stretch and blended with it as he crossed the street.

Once in the coupé, The Shadow rolled his cloak and hat beneath the seat. Loading his emptied automatics, he tucked them into the holsters that he wore beneath his coat.

Starting the motor with a quick press of the starter pedal, The Shadow drove the car up to the hotel. He alighted in the guise of Cranston, a quizzical expression on his face as he saw Welf and Tilyon peering from the lobby. The two hurried out to meet their friend.

Another car swung the corner; it was a large, high-powered roadster. Before Welf or Tilyon could take to cover, a voice stopped them. Another friend was clambering from the roadster: Graham Clenwick.

The broad-faced man wanted to know all that had happened; so, for that matter, did Cranston. It was Tilyon who gave the details.

"It started soon after the new guest came back here," related Tilyon. "In my opinion, that chap Enwald had a lot to do with it. The shooting began upstairs, probably in his room. While Welf and I were wondering what to do about it, a whole crew of hoodlums invaded the place.

"We ran for the kitchen. We saw the crooks go dashing out. The sheriff arrived at about that moment, but he and his men couldn't stop the mob from getting to their car. The last we saw of them, they were speeding away with the sheriff after them."

The Shadow inserted a dry comment, in Cranston's tone. He remarked that Laura had offered him her car, that he had taken time coming back to town. This was one occasion when he had been too late to help take care of trouble.

Clenwick expressed the same sentiments.

"I was surprised that you left so early, Cranston," he said. "When I came downstairs, I found that Laura had gone to bed. I called up to her; she said that you had taken her car. Having no one to chat with, I strolled over to the ranch.

"I learned that the sheriff had stopped there. He'd seen suspicious parties in the neighborhood, so some of my men had gone out in a car to help him look for them. I came back to the house, took the roadster and drove in here."

CLENWICK didn't realize that his account showed a great flaw in Cranston's. It left a half-hour gap, at least. Laura certainly couldn't have returned to the house, turned out all the lights, then managed to undress and go to bed in any time short of ten minutes.

The walking distance from the mansion to the ranch was at least ten minutes more, which meant twenty for the round trip that Clenwick mentioned. All of which made it very curious that Cranston, even if he had driven very slowly, should have arrived at the hotel only a few minutes ahead of Clenwick.

There was a point, though, that pleased The Shadow. Clenwick had no way of really knowing just when Cranston had reached town; not unless Welf or Tilyon told him. They, in their turn, were too stirred over other matters to bother about driving times or distances.

Actually, The Shadow had made a very rapid trip in from the mansion, making the journey in about the shortest possible time. A glance at his watch told him that he had spent another fifteen minutes in Pomelo City, from the time when he looked in on Enwald's conference until he saw the fellow dead beneath the archway.

It was important to let that quarter hour be forgotten. Changing the subject, The Shadow put anxiety into Cranston's tone, when he asked if crooks could have gotten into his own room.

Neither Welf nor Tilyon had thought of that possibility. They decided it would be wise to go upstairs, to see.

On the second floor, the four men found Skate's body, along with plenty of gunfire evidence, including Enwald's shattered bottle. They noted that Cranston's room was untouched; but Welf, peering along the hall, saw the dangling rail of the fire escape.

Using flashlights, they descended the fire escape and probed the courtyard. It was Tilyon who came across Enwald's body. Turning to Welf, Tilyon said:

"I guess Enwald was the one who fought off the mobsters. They must have gotten him in the finish."

Welf shook his head.

"There was more to it than that," he declared. "You know it, as well as I do. The ghost was back again! We saw him, didn't we?"

Tilyon was loath to acknowledge the fact; but finally, he did. Once committed, he was emphatic. Turning to Clenwick and Cranston, he asserted:

"Ghost or no ghost, he was there, at the top of the stairs. The same man the crackers talked about. He looked like a big black blot, except for the shooting he did. His guns were spouting like a turret of a battleship!"

Cranston's response was a smile, intimating that his friends had over-employed their imaginations. But Clenwick accepted the story seriously.

"It must have been the ghost," Clenwick argued, "because I'm sure that Enwald wasn't on the level. His talk about Terry Knight was a subterfuge. Maybe Enwald knew Terry once, but he was merely using the fact as an excuse to call on me. Don't you think so, Cranston?"

The Shadow nodded.

"Terry couldn't have sent Enwald here," added Clenwick. "Not a chance of it! A rough chap, Terry is, but always a square shooter. I'll write to friends of mine, to see if they have heard from Terry. If we can locate him, I know that he will give us the real facts regarding Enwald.

"From the looks of the fellow"—the rancher was gazing at Enwald's body—"I'd say that he came from the Southwest. But I would also venture that he belonged to some band of border outlaws, of the sort that used to trouble us in Texas. He looks like a thieving bird who joined a different flock."

CARS were rolling in along the main street. A great variety of men poured from them. The first car contained the sheriff and his deputies. The next held a quota of Clenwick's big-fisted ranch hands.

The rattletraps that followed were filled with natives of the sort who had invaded Pomelo City the night The Shadow arrived there. The crackers weren't wearing guilty looks on this occasion. They had done their share, along with the law.

"We nearly nabbed those mobsters," announced the sheriff, ruefully. "They finally slipped us, but they had to lighten their car by throwing some dead pals overboard. Bring out the bodies, men."

Deputies brought out the bodies, two of them. The Shadow recognized one as Dingbat. The other was a crook that The Shadow had wounded in the lobby. The thug's body showed other bullet holes, received during the running battle from which the crook-manned car had escaped.

"Your boys helped a lot," said the sheriff, to Clenwick. "It's lucky I talked to them this afternoon and told them to be posted. They came along just when the crooks almost had us ambushed."

The sheriff wanted details of the shooting at the hotel, for his arrival in Pomelo City had been a chance one at the time. Tilyon gave his previous account; this time, he included the ghost, simply terming him as "somebody upstairs."

That reference did not escape the natives. Shifting their shotguns, the men from the backwoods began a spreading murmur. The sheriff shouted for silence.

"What if the fellow is a ghost?" he demanded. "He's on our side, isn't he? If I ever meet him, I'll shake hands with him!"

The mumblings silenced, but it was evident that the muttering men weren't anxious to be members of the sheriff's welcoming committee. From the way they shifted their double-barreled shotguns and looked across the street, then up to the hotel, they had their own idea of a greeting for a ghost.

If they met him, they'd deliver a salute in the ghost's own direction. Observing their expressions, The Shadow was forewarned.

"You're going to Leesville, sheriff?" The Shadow quietly inquired.

Sheriff Harley grinned.

"I allow you'll be going along tonight, Mr. Cranston?"

"Not at all" was the calm response. "I'd simply like you to send a telegram for me, to my broker in New York. I'm finding Pomelo City a very interesting place, sheriff. I have resolved to extend my stay here."

Later, The Shadow gazed from the window of his hotel room upon the main street of the ghost town. Again deserted, the scene showed faintly under the glow of a rising half-moon. Softly, The Shadow's lips phrased an understanding laugh.

He had fitted the picture better than he hoped. He could see a curious, yet simple, answer to the menace overhanging Pomelo City. Some facts that looked large were small; other factors, mere trifles, were highly important.

The thing to do was to wait, but not for long. Should certain complications come—and they were likely—the issue would be forced. When that happened, The Shadow's turn would come.

CHAPTER XIII
COMING CRIME

DURING the next two days, a lazy lull lay over Pomelo City. Even the buzzards atop the water tower sat morose and listless. Things weren't dying around the ghost city, because there were so few creatures left to die.

True, sudden death had taken toll, but that hadn't helped the buzzards. The sheriff had promptly removed the bodies of dead crooks. No further threats had come to Pomelo City to disturb the local residents, Tilyon and Welf, or Cranston, the one out-of-towner.

There was life at Clenwick's ranch and the backwoods near it, where farmers and cattle ranchers were finding new opportunity under Clenwick's protection. Life, too, at the mansion where Lamont Cranston was a regular caller.

On his visits, The Shadow chatted often with Laura Severn and her brother Roger, but they talked very little concerning the strife that had occurred in Pomelo City.

The case of Roy Enwald was closed.

It was fully conceded that Enwald and the thugs accompanying him were responsible for certain troubles in this region. To them could be attributed the accident that had forced Betterly's car off the road, resulting in three deaths; also, the fire that had ruined Bayne's store, bringing another death in its wake.

The sheriff claimed that robbery had been Enwald's purpose, but that the fellow had picked the wrong town. Finding that Pomelo City had nothing to offer, Enwald had resolved to look over the Severn mansion. It didn't occur to the sheriff that there might be a deeper plot, backed by a certain big shot named Tony Belgo.

Only The Shadow knew that fact. He was acting upon it. His telegram to New York was actually a message to his secret agents, telling them to locate Tony Belgo.

However, Sheriff Harley was not idle. He was determined to make sure that nothing else happened in the Pomelo City area, and he adopted effective measures to prevent it. There were only a few roads leading into the terrain, and the sheriff had posted deputies on all of them.

Clenwick's crew of ranch men were taking moonlight rides on horseback. They weren't just looking for stray cattle, those Florida cowboys that Clenwick had imported from other regions. They were watching for stray crooks, chance left-overs from Enwald's band.

The natives, too, were on patrol, with shotguns, for ostensibly the same purpose. They were more anxious, though, to meet the black-garbed ghost that had worsted them in one fray at Pomelo City. In fact, the county was considerably stirred, and rumors of the Pomelo City trouble became news in all parts of Florida.

LATE that second afternoon, a group of men were seated in an eighth-story room of a Jacksonville hotel. Their faces were of a thuggish variety, but they were well groomed enough to pass muster. Jacksonville wasn't entirely unacquainted with hard characters from the Northland.

In fact, the city was a favorite stopping-off point for such gentry, when en route to Miami. Mobbies had a habit, sometimes, of staying in Jax until they learned how things were doing, farther South.

If their mugs didn't have too much of the rogues'-gallery look, and they behaved themselves, it wasn't difficult for them to stop at good hotels.

Tony Belgo never had any trouble putting up his crew. His face was thick, flat-nosed, with pudgy lips; but people seldom noticed it. Tony had a way of distracting their attention by flourishing a roll of bank notes big enough to choke any hotel clerk.

Tony never choked clerks, though. He simply let them faint when they saw the size of the figures on the bills that made up the big roll.

Tilted in a chair, his back toward the screened window that overlooked the St. John's River, Tony was summing up certain facts for the benefit of his supporting cast.

"See what this bladder says?" Tony flourished an evening paper that bore the Jacksonville imprint. "The hick sheriff is covering all the roads. What can he do? There's no State coppers here in Florida."

One of the mobbies began an objection. He had been in the crew of two nights ago. Things could be pretty hot around Pomelo City, he testified.

"We'll make them hotter," promised Tony. "Enwald found out the thing was a setup. That's what Dingbat told you, didn't he, before he croaked?"

"Yeah," came a reply, "and he was saying something about The Shadow, too."

Tony Belgo gave a leer.

"The Shadow's in New York," he said. "He popped in on some racketeers the other night, and scared 'em nearly cuckoo! He can do a lot, The Shadow, but he can't hop from Florida to New York inside a couple of hours."

Swinging from his chair, Tony stepped to a bureau and yanked open the drawer. He drew out a rolled map, spread it on the table.

"You know the dodge we've been working," he told his mob. "Bringing in aliens was a pretty sweet game, while it lasted. Only the G guys are wise to it. They're patrolling pretty heavy along the Indian River, just inside those islands along the coast.

"They've been looking over that cruiser that

we've been keeping at Fernandina. If we start off on a fishing trip, we'll have cutters tailing us. So I'm having the cruiser brought here to Jax. She'll show up tomorrow. When night comes, we'll start on a hundred-mile trip."

Crooks were anxious-eyed. They knew that cutters would be outside the port of Jacksonville. Tony saw their worry and gave a guffaw.

"We're not heading out to sea!" he chuckled. "We'll take a trip in the wrong direction. We're going inland!"

Tony traced the route along the map. He let his finger run southward, almost to Lake George, then marked the westward bends toward the headwaters of the Oklawaha. He came to the tiny line of the Kewanee River, traced it to its source.

"Nobody's watching the river," chortled Tony. "It lands us about a mile away from that house where Clenwick is staying, with no roads in between."

Rolling up the map, Tony tossed it back into the drawer. It wasn't necessary for him to add further details. Whether the scheme was his own, or purely a suggestion made by Enwald, it was a perfect one. A secret visit to the heart of a guarded district would assure the easy kidnapping of Graham Clenwick, for the rancher would be taken entirely unaware.

"Climb into your tuxedoes," Tony told his mobbies. "We'll make the rounds tonight and look over some of these night spots they've got here in Jax. You've got an hour to get dressed, because I'm going down to see about a place to dock the cruiser."

Tony Belgo wasn't the only person who went to the dock. He was trailed there, in another taxi, by a well-dressed young man who was also interested in mooring a boat.

The young man in question was Harry Vincent, a secret agent of The Shadow. He found out all he wanted.

WITH dusk, Lamont Cranston was ready to leave Pomelo City for another dinner at the home of Laura Severn. While he lingered, chatting with Tilyon, Woodley drove in from Leesville. The taxi driver brought a telegram from Cranston's broker.

Since the wire concerned business, Cranston took along a briefcase when he rode out to the mansion. He hired Woodley's taxi for the trip, and as they bumped along, The Shadow read the wire. It was the second coded message that he had received.

The first had stated that Harry Vincent had gone to Jacksonville because Tony Belgo was known to be there; it had also referred to a ruse staged by Cliff Marsland, another of The Shadow's agents.

Cliff had put on a black cloak and hat, to spring a surprise party on a few of Tony's racketeering friends in New York.

The Shadow had ordered that ruse, and it had worked. Not suspecting that The Shadow was in Florida, Tony Belgo was prepared to show his hand, according to the present telegram. He was bringing in a cabin cruiser from Fernandina to Jacksonville, by Harry's report.

Since the boat wouldn't be on hand until the next day, there was time for Cliff and other agents to join Harry in Jacksonville. From then on, they would be on their own. The Shadow could depend upon them to do whatever was required.

When dinner was ended at the mansion, Laura wheeled Roger out to the glen, where he liked to stay on moonlight evenings. Clenwick invited Cranston into the library; eyeing the visitor's brief case, the rancher asked:

"You've made a deal on Kewanee Springs?"

"Not yet," replied The Shadow. "Tilyon has been pressing me"—he opened the briefcase, to take out a thin sheaf of papers—"but I preferred to talk it over with you, first."

Chewing a cigar, Clenwick read over the papers that Cranston had brought. He sorted them as he went along, until they became two piles.

"I agree with these." Clenwick slapped one heap. "The Kewanee proposition is sound. But Tilyon is still too optimistic about reviving real estate in Pomelo City."

Opening a large map, Clenwick showed a penciled circle representing the Pomelo City area. The mansion was just within the circle; Clenwick's ranch was closer to the center. Clenwick began to tap large dots that were also within the area.

"These are the sinkholes," he said. "This is the Giant, the worst of the lot; but all of them are bad. The blue ones are the old; the red, the new."

The sinkholes made actual pockmarks on the map. Terming them a veritable plague, Clenwick moved his pencil to Pomelo City, which centered the circle.

"If a sinkhole shows up there," he predicted, "the town will drop through with it. This ground is no longer good, except for pastureland, because we can fence off the sinks, like I have done.

"Over here, though"—he moved his pencil to Kewanee Springs, outside the circle—"we get away from the high hammocks. I own land there that I'd exchange for property inside the circle. Good land, for anything but pasture."

The Shadow saw Clenwick's logic. The rancher pointed out another fact. Down the Kewanee River, on land that Clenwick owned, was an old steamboat wharf. Should the Springs be developed, rival persons might start cruises from that point, coming up to the headwaters.

"The Kewanee is a navigable river," reminded Clenwick. "I might be forced to let boats dock there. But Tilyon and Welf, operating craft of their own, could rule others off if they owned that lower wharf."

Turning away, Clenwick crossed the room to obtain a fresh box of cigars. Back turned about, he did not observe the new interest that Cranston had taken in the map. Temporarily, The Shadow had dropped all consideration of sinkholes, cattle lands, and other property.

His finger was at the extreme corner of the map, which showed the city of Jacksonville. From there, The Shadow was tracing the course upstream, from larger rivers into smaller. His finger stopped near the head of the Kewanee, at the little wharf on Clenwick's property.

The Shadow voiced no laugh. Even his lips were smileless. His eyes, alone, displayed a gleam; their flash was triumphant. The Shadow had traced the same course as Tony Belgo. He knew the course that coming crime would take!

CHAPTER XIV
THE NIGHT PATROL

TOMORROW night!

The Shadow had divined the time set by Tony Belgo for the coming raid. The finding was one of simple logic.

Belgo wouldn't have his boat until tomorrow. Once the cruiser was on hand, he would want to use it. Tony Belgo was not the sort who would delay when time meant cash.

Smoking a cigar that Clenwick handed him, The Shadow nodded further agreement to the rancher's plans of property exchange. All of Clenwick's suggestions were good ones, the sort that could be answered with a nod.

Actually, Lamont Cranston was not listening to Graham Clenwick at all. In a sense, he was no longer Cranston. He was The Shadow, except in guise. He was making mental calculations, not in terms of land and dollars, but in water and time.

A swift boat like Belgo's cruiser could leave Jacksonville at dusk, and be back at dawn, with a brief stop at the Kewanee River wharf. That was the way Tony would manage it. Therefore, the time of the big shot's arrival whittled down to a definite hour: the mid-point between dusk and dawn.

Tomorrow midnight.

What a perfect mesh the crook had spun for himself! This was one job that could be left to Sheriff Harley. The Shadow and his agents would remain in the background, while the local authorities laid their ambush.

Harley and his deputies knew the Florida terrain; Tony Belgo & Co. didn't. The peninsular jungle was quite different from the badlands of Manhattan. Crooks would have no chance when the law came on the job. A few might, but The Shadow and his agents could take care of them.

Orders to the agents; a tip-off to the sheriff. Such were The Shadow's prospective moves. He could send the orders early tomorrow, and give the tip-off later. Unless some intervening calamity prevented The Shadow from performing those simple duties, the case of Tony Belgo would be settled.

From considering the future, The Shadow snapped back to the present. There was much to be done before tomorrow. The trapping of a big-shot kidnapper would not clear the mystery that had jinxed Pomelo City. Facts were out of place; they needed to be readjusted. No longer was there time to wait. The Shadow's moves must come tonight.

A delicate task lay ahead—that of clearing up some local matters and keeping the facts from Tony Belgo, so the crook wouldn't know what might await him. It could all be maneuvered, though, before this night was ended.

Clenwick had finished with the papers and was handing them over. As The Shadow slid them into the briefcase, Clenwick reverted to the map. He was still talking about sinkholes, when he saw Cranston close the briefcase and rise with a smile.

"I think I understand the situation," affirmed The Shadow. "Good night, Clenwick. I'm going back to town, to talk with Tilyon."

"He isn't coming here for you?"

"No." The Shadow gave a leisurely gaze toward the window. "I told him that I would walk. The moonlight is ample tonight."

Clenwick wanted to go out to the barn and get his car, but Cranston resisted the offer. He didn't even care to leave his briefcase and call for it tomorrow. It was very light, he insisted, and held it at arm's length to prove the statement.

THE briefcase was much heavier than it looked. After walking a few hundred yards down the road from the mansion, The Shadow turned it over and opened a special compartment which formed an inverted V between the two sections that showed when the briefcase was open at the top.

From that hollow center, he removed his cloak, his hat, and a brace of automatics. Girded with that equipment, The Shadow added gloves, which he took from a pocket of the cloak. The briefcase found its way beneath a clump of palmettos.

Despite the moonlight, The Shadow was invisible. High foliage rendered a background against which he could easily blend. Taking a side path, the weird prowler became as much a creature of the night as any denizen of the Florida jungle.

Etched in The Shadow's memory were the salient features of Clenwick's map. All that he needed was direction, which he found with the aid of a flashlight and a tiny compass, which came from the end of the torch.

By occasional blinks, The Shadow picked a sloping route from the hammock region toward the Kewanee River.

Near the stream, he extinguished the light entirely. This was dangerous territory, as the night noises told. Strange cries of nightbirds, the calls of frogs that croaked with a bleat, were mild reminders of more formidable creatures that might be abroad.

Below a shelving bank, The Shadow passed a fringe of palmettos. In the moonlight, their curving stalks and bushy leaves gave the palmettos the appearance of an advancing army of mammoth snails.

A rattle came from that sector; The Shadow paused, then sidestepped. Past that danger spot, he again kept close to the palmetto bank.

Rattlesnakes gave warning; water moccasins didn't. Therefore, it was safer to stay by the palmettos than to step into the river edge. As for alligators, they were also present. Warning hisses sounded frequently as The Shadow followed the stream.

They weren't for his benefit, those sounds. The river jungle was so chock-full of animal life that every night produced the sounds of threatening conflict, when meddlesome jungle dwellers trespassed on each other's preserves.

It was strange, The Shadow thought, for men to claim ownership over property such as this, where they, the self-styled owners, wouldn't last a minute if they stepped in the wrong place.

MOONLIGHT revealed the river wharf, ahead. Working in through the brush, The Shadow kept his cloak tightly about him and pressed slowly ahead. Otherwise, the brambly twigs would have ripped the needed black garb from his shoulders. He struck the path he wanted, followed it to the wharf.

Warped, weather-beaten planking gleamed gray. Fish were splashing at the end of the battered pier. When The Shadow tore a cigarette apart and threw the pieces into the water, the hungry fish battled for the paper and tobacco.

An excellent attraction, Tilyon would call it. He would take to the idea of giving idle real estate in exchange for this usable landing place. It would be a sensible future: the Kewanee River under full development, with cattle grazing on grass that sprouted from the broken paving along the main street of Pomelo City.

But The Shadow was considering an earlier future. He was picturing this wharf as the chosen goal of Tony Belgo. It was an easy place to land; the next problem was the sheriff's ambush. Leaving the wharf, The Shadow started back along the path.

It led toward the mansion by a roundabout course. It was the only route that Tony and his mob could take, and it was ambush all the way. It had everything from rocks to palmettos, with little depressions that looked like budding sinkholes.

Having viewed tomorrow's probable battleground, The Shadow cut away from the path. He passed the temporary buildings of Clenwick's ranch and gave the squat cabins a wide berth. Away from the jungle, any ground was good. The Shadow set his course by the compass.

Trees loomed ahead; between them, The Shadow found a barbed-wire fence. He was at the Giant Sinkhole. His flashlight extinguished, he saw lanterns bobbing along the ground. They might mean some of the ranch hands; possibly, the lights were borne by natives on prowl.

The Shadow did not care to be mistaken for either a cattle thief or a ghost. But the choice he took to avoid either of those prospects was a far more hazardous one.

Flattening to the ground, he slid himself beneath the lowest strand of the barbed wire. Wriggling farther, he thrust his body over the very edge of the Giant Sinkhole!

Ground caved in, as Clenwick claimed it would. Like a beetle caught in a sand spider's trap, The Shadow was sliding into a one-sided vortex. His feet heeled the sand, sending it ahead; but there was no clutching the sheer limestone that scraped from beneath.

Arms flung wide, The Shadow managed to grip dried brush. Dead roots tugged loose under the strain; but by then The Shadow's hands were clutching for more. Some sapplings grew out from the steep wall; they stayed The Shadow's slide, until they bent too far.

It meant sure death to animals, that sinkhole, for they had no chance to seize the things that passed. For humans, too, it meant disaster, if the slide became too rapid. But The Shadow kept his downward skid under reasonable control.

He was barely sliding at the bottom, when he dipped into the slime that made a deep pool in the pit.

The stagnant ooze seemed rancid. Its greasy surface gave off bubbly sounds. Pulling himself from the muck, The Shadow clung to a chunk of projecting limestone and played his flashlight along the surface. Having studied the greenish pool, he turned off the light and rested.

LANTERNS glimmered above. A flashlight made a brief play down from the trees. Then, satisfied that no one would be foolhardy enough to venture a trip down into the Giant Sinkhole, patrollers went their way.

Inspecting the bank, The Shadow found projecting rocks that offered a chance to climb. He began the long trip upward, toward an irregular, inward curve that marred the rough circle of the brink. His flashlight aided his choice of bushes whenever he paused to rest; but his main guide was the moonlight.

At times, there were downward slips of several feet; but always, The Shadow knew where to reach for a solid hold. The hardest part was the sandy edge itself; the loose stuff crumbled away from whatever clutched it. The remedy was a long reach for the wire, which The Shadow caught between two barbs.

Resting by the trees, he gave a whispered laugh that joined with the breeze. It was welcome, that breeze, not because of its refreshing coolness but because it offered a chance for action tonight. The Shadow, through his meanderings, had come to one conclusion:

Stagnation was the cause of grief in this vicinity. Human affairs were in a scummy state, like the depths of the Giant Sinkhole. Only when stirred did men show life and an ability to understand. The battle with Enwald and the crooks had produced local alliances, but they hadn't proven enough.

Something was needed to straighten out present misconceptions; to clear the way for solid union among the right men. Deputies, natives, ranchers, all working individually, was not the proper system. They needed to know more about one another.

There was a way to bring about that result.

Leaving the sinkhole, The Shadow headed into the wind, which came from the direction of the river. He paced off the distance that he wanted, a matter of a few hundred yards. Stopping into the brush, he struck a match.

The flame licked all around The Shadow's fingers, scorching them through his dampened glove. He was applying the match to the brush; moving in a crosswise direction, he struck another match, then a third.

Flames were rising. Looking along the line, The Shadow saw quick lashes of fire streak into the dried brush, eating it like tinder. He was striking a fourth match as he listened to the crackle of the blaze.

Then into the increasing roar came another rising sound: a peal of insidious mirth. Weird mockery that momentarily drowned the fire's crackle, then faded like the darkness that was vanishing from about the flames.

The laugh of The Shadow!

CHAPTER XV
THE TRAPPED GHOST

WHATEVER fun or purpose The Shadow found in starting a first-class brush fire, he did not care to be connected with the deed. As he finished lighting a suitable line of blaze, he made for the path that led to the Severn mansion.

Following that sure but lengthy course, The Shadow neared the side lawn. He skirted the barn that garaged Laura's coupé and Clenwick's roadster, and finally reached the rear door that led into the main hall of the house.

Only the library was lighted, which meant that Clenwick was still up, though the others had probably retired. The Shadow wanted to talk to Clenwick; unfortunately, this was not a suitable time.

To return as Cranston would be difficult, for, in leaving, The Shadow had said that he intended to walk to town. To appear in the black garb of The Shadow was also inadvisable. Until the proper results had been produced, The Shadow intended to keep his presence unknown.

Therefore, he compromised by stealthily opening the back door and entering the hallway, where the gloom below the stairs offered an excellent place to wait. Great excitement was due, and news of it would be quick to reach the mansion.

It wasn't long before the clatter of hoofs came from the front drive. Clenwick heard the sound and strode out of the library. An excited ranch hand met him at the front door. In booming tone, Clenwick wanted to know the trouble.

"It's those fool crackers!" panted the man. "They've started another brush fire!"

"Another brush fire?" queried Clenwick. "What of it?" Then, his voice denoting sudden alarm: "Near enough to injure the ranch houses?"

"It's blowing that way," returned the man. "It hasn't got to the Giant Sinkhole yet, but it's pretty close."

Clenwick gave an angry exclamation.

"I've tried to educate those crackers," he asserted, "but they just can't get it through their heads that brush fires can spread after they've cleared a patch. Call out all hands and beat down that fire."

"They're working at it, Mr. Clenwick."

"What about getting some help from the crackers?"

"They're all over toward town. But some of the sheriff's men showed up. I think we've got the fire under control. Want me to ride over and get the crackers?"

Clenwick gave the suggestion a short consideration, then shook his head.

"I'll take your horse and find them," he said. "You run back to the fire. I'll tell those crackers what I think of them, and then send them over to help out."

THE two men left the house. From the rear door, The Shadow could see the glare of the fire, a flickering beacon. In a sense, that fire represented The Shadow's present hopes. He was expecting it to clear up more than mere brushwood.

Going through the hallway to the library, The Shadow began to look around. Always, he had been too busy chatting with Clenwick to really examine the place. Interested in maps and papers that he found, The Shadow gave little attention to the time that passed.

As he finished with a batch of loose papers, he glanced toward the rear window. The glare from the distance had faded, which meant that the brush fire might be out. Stepping from the library, The Shadow moved to the rear door and opened it.

For a moment, his cloaked figure was outlined against the hallway lights. A sharp cry greeted him; it was answered by another. Turning, The Shadow made for the front door. His arrival there was a signal for even louder whoops.

Clearing the steps, The Shadow made a quick return to the shelter of the veranda, just as shotguns ripped loose.

The crackers, heading toward the brush fire by way of the mansion, had found the missing ghost!

From a front room, Laura Severn heard the tumult and sprang from bed. Clad in a silk nightgown, she ventured to the window; there, she became the lone witness to a singular fray. The smooth, moonlit lawn was ringed by men with shotguns; others had come through the back of the house to reach the front door.

All of the natives were blasting away at something that they couldn't see. Gun stabs were answering them from thick flower beds along the veranda, but always from a different spot.

Confident of mowing down their prey, the crackers did not bother to reload. That fact brought the next act of the drama. Out from the cover of the veranda wheeled a black-clad figure, pumping bullets from a pair of big automatics. Foemen dived for the bushes, as the strange fighter crossed the lawn spurting bullets like a revolving turret.

The ghost!

Though the thought sprang to Laura's mind, she realized that this battler couldn't be a ghost. He was human, like herself, and he had become the prey of a motley crowd of half-crazed men whose superstition ruled them.

More crackers were coming up through the woods. They blocked The Shadow's route, caused him to make for the palmettos. The others, finding time to reload, were bellowing as they took up the trail. They were fifty against one, by Laura's estimate, until the girl halved those odds herself.

Digging her feet into a pair of slippers, Laura grabbed a dressing gown and flung it across her shoulders. Dashing downstairs, she sped out through the front door, shouting after The Shadow's pursuers. Though she carried no gun, Laura believed that she might call off some of the frenzied horde.

MEANWHILE, The Shadow was keeping up the most futile battle that he had ever experienced. Ducking through groves of tall pine, he deserted the needle-carpeted ground for a cluster of palmettos.

Twisting from that clump, he followed a path to a rough clearing that took him to a small swamp. Skirting the bad ground, he found another path and followed it.

All the while, he was keeping busy with his guns. Pausing between long dashes, he reloaded, trying to gauge his direction in the moonlight. Men with shotguns were as thick as mosquitoes, but they had a pleasant habit of blasting away at anything that looked black.

Constantly beyond their range, The Shadow saw them duck whenever he fired. They didn't know that it was unnecessary. The Shadow had no quarrel with these misguided men. Thinning their ranks wouldn't help him. He hadn't enough ammunition to down all the crackers in the county.

His one plan was to elude them; to let them believe that the ghost had staged another vanish. But there were too many on the job for The Shadow to complete his apparition act. Inexorably, it seemed, he was being boxed in the direction of Kewanee Springs, near the upper pool.

As he continued his zigzag retreat, The Shadow recognized that the natives had identified him with the ghost of the ancient Seminole chief. They were driving him toward the place where they believed he belonged: the Devil's Rock!

Such was apparent to Laura, also. Along every

path she saw converging men, heard the shouts they uttered. They were blocking The Shadow everywhere, and they wouldn't listen when she shouted.

Frantically, the girl decided that her only hope would be to reach the Springs ahead of them. Perhaps a few would heed her when she arrived.

Ignoring the paths, Laura took a straight course toward the Springs. She didn't care if rattlers and other hazards lay along the way. It was her job to stop murder, no matter what the cost. Her purpose was good, but her choice of routes a poor one.

As she stumbled through thick palmettos, she felt her dressing gown lashed from her shoulders. Past that clump, she ran into a quagmire that everyone else had avoided. Her slippers lost in the muck, Laura stumbled badly on rough ground, until she reached a thick mass of brush beyond which lay the pool.

She thought that her hair was streaming across her eyes, until she whipped it aside and found it to be Spanish moss that she had accumulated from low tree branches. Shouts were far away; so were the incessant blasts of shotguns.

Still intent upon her goal, Laura entered the last hazard, to find that it was the worst of all. She had to plunge through the low bushes with her arms across her eyes. Her nightgown was shredded by the brambly brush.

When the girl finally floundered through and fell breathless on soft ground, the moonlight showed an array of pink, silk patches fluttering from the brush behind her.

Beneath the shelter of a tropical foliage, Laura could here the murmur of Kewanee Springs. Crawling painfully forward, she spread aside the foliage and thrust her head through. She had reached a low, flat-slabbed bank at the edge of the upper pool.

WHAT Laura saw held her tense, totally forgetful of the ordeal that she had undergone. She had reached her goal too late; but, singularly, a lull had come before the climax.

Men were clustered in little groups about the large pool, but they no longer shouted. They were holding their shotguns at irregular angles, staring at something in the moonlight.

They were looking toward the Devil's Rock. On that high-jutting level stood the ghost that they had sought. Foemen flanked him, others were behind him, all waiting for the signal that no one gave.

He was a tall, thin shape—The Shadow. His cloak draped from his shoulders in truly spectral fashion. Beneath his down-turned hat brim his eyes alone caught the moonlight's gleam, to throw back a burning, challenging sparkle.

His gloved fists held weighty guns. Each .45 was a thing of threat. The Shadow's fifty foemen had heard those automatics talk steadily. All believed that many of their number must be lying dead along the paths.

With all their fusillades, they had not downed the ghost. Half a hundred strong, all wanted to make the final test, but none of the entire group cared to be the first. In this moment, The Shadow stood triumphant, but his glory could not last.

One move that marked him human would be his last. A single gunner, going berserk, would start the rest by delivering a shot. Well did The Shadow recognize the precarious condition of that lull. It could not last; therefore, he chose to be the one who ended it.

Lifting his head, The Shadow gave forth a burst of sardonic laughter; a taunt that seemed to voice his willingness to die—or live. It was victorious, that laugh, even though doom might be its sequel.

Such was The Shadow's challenge to the fates that had hitherto never failed in his behalf!

CHAPTER XVI
INTO THE PAST

AS strange-voiced echoes quivered above murmuring waters, men shifted uneasily all along the bank. Startled, they looked upward and about them. The trees, it seemed, were answering The Shadow's mirth.

Crouched in her hiding spot, Laura felt a shudder that tingled every inch of her. Chilled from head to foot, she felt that she was really gazing at a ghost. Yet reason told her that the being on the rock was human.

Too human. That challenge might be his last. She wanted to shout out, as she had intended, but she began to realize how very small and helpless she really was. Her cry, if she gave it, might become the death signal that fifty men awaited. If she came into sight, she might be mistaken for another ghost—a white one.

Under the light of the half moon, the whole scene was eerie, so unreal that Laura could hardly credit it. Yet she knew the place, and recognized the men who stood about. Their reality convinced her that The Shadow must be actual.

A mutter stirred the bank. The Shadow had moved. His hands went close to his cloak, then made a wide, outward sweep. Those hands were gunless; The Shadow had slid his automatics beneath his cloak.

Nevertheless, with open hands, he seemed even more formidable. His action indicated that weapons were unnecessary in the combat he could give.

The mutter, though, was restless. Men were tilting gun muzzles toward the Devil's Rock, each looking askance at his fellows. Given a few seconds longer, those guns would have been well aimed—and The Shadow knew it.

With a quick sweep of his arms, he clasped his hands above his head. He was falling forward as he made that sweep; his legs supplied a piston push. Almost before anyone realized it, The Shadow was off on a long dive into the depths of Kewanee Springs!

Guns blasted as The Shadow sliced the water. The first reports brought more. Flattening behind a tiny mound, Laura hoped that no shots would reach her. Fifty shotguns, each fired twice, made a cannonade that appalled her.

Echoes made those blasts sound like the saluting fire of an entire regiment. When she realized that no more shots would be forthcoming, Laura again spread the foliage and peered through. The men along the banks were staring at the water, waiting for The Shadow to reappear.

Nothing showed upon the water except a slouch hat, and it was floating, brim upward, like a tiny boat.

Remembering the contour of the pool, Laura wondered if The Shadow had struck the sunken Devil's Ledge. Then, recalling the length of his dive, she was sure that he had gone beyond it.

Enough shot had been discharged to weight a human body to the bottom of the Springs, had The Shadow received those slugs. But Laura could remember the slight splash of a straight-diving figure before the fusillade broke loose.

New mutters came from clustered men along the shore. They kept watching the water, counting off the minutes. They gave The Shadow five. When that time limit ended, they began to disperse, slowly at first, then quickly. From where she watched, Laura could hear wild scrambles as the last of the crackers left.

None had been desirous of beginning the gunfire at the black-garbed ghost upon the Devil's Rock. Similarly, none wanted to be the last to leave the roaming specter's haunt.

Very suddenly, Laura realized that she was alone upon the scene. Reaching the flat slab beside the bank, she crouched there, still fascinated by the pool and actually quite frightened.

Soft moonlight revealed a scene of strange solitude, wherein a sad and shivering girl kept gazing at a slowly drifting slouch hat.

LIFTING her eyes, Laura looked about. Her shudder ended, and she laughed. She tried to pretend that the whole thing was a dream; that she had merely left the house and stolen to the Springs on a moonlight escapade. The rest, she decided, could all be imagination.

Reality ended that mental journey. Laura's shoulder ached from a fall she had taken; her feet were bruised from the run across the rough ground. Her arms and thighs bore scratches from the brush, red streaks that she could count in the moonlight.

Looking toward the pool again, she saw the floating hat. It had drifted very close. Gingerly, Laura stretched from the brink and gripped the object.

At first, she was terrified to find it real. Then, sensing that it was the only proof of a tragedy, she arose, taking the hat with her.

Stumbling painfully, Laura found a path that led her home. All the way, she carried the hat pressed tightly beneath her arm. She wondered if it would vanish, like its owner; but it didn't.

Laura still had the hat, when she reached the soft lawn. She enjoyed the touch of the velvety grass as she stole across it toward the house. There were lights on the ground floor, but the doors were wide open. Convinced that no one was about, Laura entered and hurried upstairs, taking the hat with her.

As she dropped the hat on a chair, a sudden question gripped her. If The Shadow proved real, as the hat proclaimed—who could he be?

Certainly not a ghost. Therefore, he *was* human. A very brave human, who would risk anything—

With a sob, Laura sank beside the bed and buried her face in her hands. Only one man that she had ever met would have risked his life in a reckless plunge that promised no retreat. That man was Lamont Cranston, the rescuer who had saved her from the alligator.

Her sympathy toward The Shadow was immediately explained. Despite his black garb, she had recognized him. She had wanted to save him, but had failed.

Like the Seminole chief of the Indian legend, he had plunged from Devil's Rock, to be swallowed in depths from which he could not return. But the chief was legendary; Cranston was not. He could never live in an imaginary abode ruled by the spirits of earth.

Hoofs clattered outside the house. Laura heard Clenwick's voice. He was talking with other men; they were coming indoors. Checking her sobs, the girl reached for clothes that lay beside the bed and began to dress. The process completed, she stared at her reflection in the mirror.

Even the moonlight showed that her eyes were tear-brimmed, but Laura did not care. She didn't even notice the wisps of Spanish moss that still hung from her hair. Picking up the slouch hat, she went downstairs.

LAURA found Clenwick talking to the sheriff. The tone of Clenwick's voice was an amazed one.

"I still can't believe it!" he exclaimed. "Not on the testimony of five hundred men, let alone fifty!"

"They say they found the ghost here," insisted the sheriff, wiping the smudge of brush-fire ashes from his sweaty forehead. "When they chased him to the Springs, he went back to his home."

"Nonsense! I was here only a short while before. I saw no ghost. They had a ghost on their minds, those fools! When I came galloping up, they yelled out to ask if the ghost was after me."

"You must have come in a big hurry."

"I did," acknowledged Clenwick. "I didn't know that you chaps had the fire under control. I told the crackers to take the shortcut past the house and give a helping hand."

The sheriff shook his head. He was a man who accepted the testimony of witnesses only when their statements corresponded.

"I'd like to talk to someone reliable," asserted Clenwick, "who could swear on oath that some person, ghost or no ghost, dived into Kewanee Springs. I'd believe it, if such a witness could produce evidence to prove it!"

Laura stepped into the library. Solemnly, the girl spoke two words:

"I can!"

She extended the moist hat to Clenwick. His mouth half agape, the big man listened to Laura's story, while the sheriff drank in the tale with a similar expression. When Laura had finished, Clenwick offered the hat to Harley. The sheriff shook his head.

"Keep it here," he suggested. "I've got to go down to the Springs and look the scene over. Tell me, Miss Severn, could you identify the man who plunged into the pool?"

"I think," said Laura, slowly, "that he was Lamont Cranston."

Clenwick started to claim that such was impossible, then stopped himself.

"Cranston was here!" he exclaimed. "What's more, he started to walk back to town. But why would he have returned without telling me? And why should he have masqueraded in black, pretending to be a ghost?"

"Maybe he was fixing to surprise the crackers," returned the sheriff, soberly. "If he was, he did. Too well!"

The next hour was an anxious one for Laura. At the end of it the sheriff returned, bringing the unhappy news she feared. He had found no traces of a body at the Springs; in Pomelo City, he had learned from Welf and Tilyon that Cranston had not returned there.

Expressing the faint hope that Cranston had gone to Leesville in Woodley's taxi, the sheriff said that he would inquire when he reached the county seat.

When Harley had gone, Clenwick picked up The Shadow's hat, eyed it solemnly, and placed it upon the mantel above the library fireplace. As he turned to speak sympathetically to Laura, Clenwick heard the sound of a long-choked sob, then the clatter of heels upon the staircase.

Laura was seeking the solitude of her room.

While she undressed, the girl was sobbing. In bed, she actually wept herself to sleep. The sinking moon had almost faded when its beams showed Laura slumbering, her sad face streaked with tears.

The same gleam cast a dying silver upon the unrippling surface of Kewanee Springs, revealing the full depths of that crystalline pool. The water showed no traces of a black-garbed body.

Like the Seminole chieftain, The Shadow was a figure that had vanished into the past. A new legend that rivaled the old, he had taken the personality of Lamont Cranston with him.

CHAPTER XVII
BEFORE MIDNIGHT

THE next day was a gloomy, cloudy one, touched with a chilly atmosphere not uncommon in the Florida clime. In fact, the day itself seemed to represent the misery that Laura Severn felt when she thought of her vanished friend and rescuer, Lamont Cranston.

The missing man had not been seen in Leesville. Sheriff Harley brought that news, along with a telegram from Cranston's New York broker. Clouds were clearing when the sheriff called, for it was late in the afternoon. But Laura's own gloom only thickened.

Dinner was very late, and during the meal Roger Severn displayed an unruly mood. Graham Clenwick had come in from the ranch, and was talking sadly and sympathetically about Cranston.

Tiring of the topic, Roger leaned forward in his wheelchair and punched the table with a power that made the dishes rattle.

"It's always Cranston!" he snarled. "What if something did happen to the fellow? He liked risks, and took them. That was his privilege, and he paid for it!"

Laura arose from the table. Her dewy eyes and tight-set lips showed the sorrow that burdened her. The droop at the corners of her mouth gave her features a melancholy loveliness; but that wasn't what impressed Roger.

Laura was primly dressed in black jersey suit, long-sleeved, with a minimum of white trimmings at cuffs and collar. She had worn it because the day was cool and the sleeves hid the bramble scratches on her arms.

But Roger didn't take those facts into account. He grabbed his sister's arm as she passed, swung her full about.

"So you're in mourning, are you?" he sneered, eyeing the black attire and overlooking the trimmings. "Well, you'd better get over it. There's enough misery around here, without anyone making more!"

When Laura tried to wrench away, Roger showed that his arms had power, even though his legs were weak. He twisted the girl around in back of the wheelchair.

"Roll me down to the glen," he ordered. "It's warmer, and the moon is out. I'm tired of looking at a couple of gloomy faces!"

He threw an ugly glance at Clenwick, who smiled back patiently. Laura wheeled the chair from the dining room, out through the back door, and down toward the glen.

All during that quarter mile, Laura underwent torture because of Roger's tyranny. His head turned toward her, her brother kept up sneering comments over the back of the wheelchair.

They were almost at the glen, when Roger broke loose with a bitter outburst that proved a real index to his mood.

"Everybody lets me down," he grumbled. "Clenwick talked about sending me to a New York specialist, but he's been too busy to attend to it. Cranston handed me a lot of soft soap that I might have believed, if he hadn't shown himself a fool, last night.

"He said I'd forgotten how to walk; that if I made up my mind to it, I'd be on my feet again. He said if I couldn't do it on my own, he'd shock me into it. He argued that the strength of my arms proved that my legs were strong, too.

"So why should *you* have the weeps? Cranston didn't promise you anything, then let you down, Laura. But he did just that to me."

RETURNING alone to the mansion, Laura told Clenwick all that Roger had said. The rancher pondered; then:

"You don't think that Roger—" Catching himself, Clenwick shook his head.

"If Roger *could* walk," he said, "he *might* have walked without our knowing it. With those tempers of his, he might have done lots of things, even to starting a brush fire. But no. It's impossible!"

Laura agreed, but not through present regard for Roger. She reasoned that if Roger ever managed to walk, his enthusiasm would offset his ugly destructive moods.

Finding solace in a book, Laura temporarily put aside her woes, though the effort was difficult. She totally forgot the passage of time, until Clenwick reminded her of it.

"It's after eleven," he told her, "and Roger is still in the glen. I'm going over to the ranch, but I can wait to help you bring the wheelchair up the back steps."

"How long will you be gone?" asked Laura.

"Not more than half an hour," replied Clenwick. "I merely want to pick up the day's report."

"Roger can wait," decided Laura, "until you get back."

As soon as Clenwick left by the front door, Laura hurried out the back. She was going to repay Roger for his spite. If there was anything he hated, it was waiting at the bottom of those steps for someone stronger than Laura to haul him to the top.

Laura didn't intend to tell Roger that Clenwick had gone out. She would pretend innocence, while her brother learned the fact for himself. If Roger became nasty, Laura could go inside, coil in the big library chair and read her book while her brother chafed outside.

Eager to prolong that revenge, Laura actually ran to the glen. She saw the wheelchair, pounced upon the rear bar to spin the chair about, another thing that Roger did not like. The wheel chair whirled crazily, and Laura took a somersaulting tumble.

Laura found herself staring at the moon, her weight full on her shoulders, which were draped by her skirt. Straight above, her stockinged legs showed slender and black against a large gray tree trunk, while the tips of her trim slippers were pointing at an angle toward the moon.

Her breath gone, Laura was too astonished to move. Tilting her head clear back, the girl gave an upside-down look at the wheelchair. The view made her gasp. Rolling away from the tree, she clambered to her feet and stared again.

The wheelchair was empty!

FRANTICALLY, Laura looked for Roger. When she saw him, her gasp was happy. All animosity left her at the sight.

Roger was on the other side of the glen. Crouched, he was using his strong hands to steady his wobbly knees. With slow, half-creeping gait, he was moving forward on his feet!

As Laura dashed toward him, Roger took a

tumble, to land full length at the edge of the Seminole Punch Bowl. Writhing forward, he dipped his head and shoulders down into the tiny pool.

Fearing that Roger had hurt himself, Laura was shrieking as she reached him. But when she tried to draw him from the brink, he shook his head savagely. Gripping his sister's arm, Roger dragged the girl down beside him.

"Listen, Laura!" he gasped hoarsely. "It brought me here! The voice!"

Laura heard only the sighing gurgle of the disappearing pool. She fancied that Roger had fallen asleep and dreamed that the sound was a distant call. It was wonderful, though, that it should have stirred him into finding that his legs were good again. Laura tried to emphasize that point:

"You walked, Roger! You walked!"

Roger's hand tightened on Laura's arm. She listened, understanding that her cry had drowned a sound that Roger heard. Twice, the gurgle of the pool repeated; then, during the next interval, the voice came.

Up through the filtering stones drifted a vague, melancholy laugh—a tone that was eerie, yet real. To Roger, it had been a summoning call. To Laura, it was more: an echo, not just from depths, but from the buried past!

The laugh of The Shadow!

Laura was telling Roger that she had heard that same weird tone last night from the lips of the being in black atop the Devil's Rock. But Roger was too busy to listen. His arms in the Punch Bowl almost to his shoulders, he was hauling out the small stones in handfuls, shoving them to Laura.

Catching the idea, Laura flung stones on the ground as fast as Roger handed them to her. He was digging his way furiously down through the bottom of the pool.

The water level lowered while Roger worked; small stones began slipping through a cavity. Roger came to a large stone, the width of his body. It was wedged between two rocks.

His muscles bulging through his shirtsleeves, Roger strained upward. The large stone budged. Laura thrust her hands into the shallowed water and helped her brother with the stone.

Her strength, though frail compared to Roger's, added the needed poundage. They worked the stone away, managed to swing it to one side.

With the stone gone, the pool became a tiny waterfall. The trickle of the little brook took to a deep niche in one of the earth-rooted rocks. The open hole looked empty, but from it came a weary laugh, very close to the surface.

Turning his head to admit the moonlight, Roger caught the glint of eyes from darkness. A black-gloved hand arose, to paw at the slimy rock. Losing its clutch, the hand was slipping, when Roger grabbed the arm below it.

Again, Roger strained his shoulders. As he heaved upward, Laura clutched for the cloak folds that appeared. Another gloved hand wrapped itself across Roger's neck, to give him leverage. Two persons were tugging from above; the man below was aiding.

It was a hard drag through the rocky fissure. Roger and Laura might have failed, except for the cooperation that their burden gave them. Though his efforts were feeble, the cloaked being showed timely ability. Like a giant earthworm, he worked his body upward.

At last he was in the Bowl itself. His knees upon the stones near the side of the emptied pool, he clamped his hands upon the rock-rimmed edge. His face turned downward, the rescued being began a weary clamber. Hauling from either side, Roger and Laura turned that effort into a lurch.

Over the edge, the black-clad figure gave a forward stretch and settled on the soft, pine-needled soil, where his form relaxed, motionless. The faint laugh that trickled from his lips faded into a satisfied sigh.

The Shadow had fulfilled the famous legend. Following his plunge from the Devil's Rock, he had found the abode where fabled earth spirits were supposed to dwell. From that domain, like the Seminole chief of yore, The Shadow had returned!

CHAPTER XVIII
HOUR OF BATTLE

BROTHER and sister raised The Shadow from the ground. While Roger supported the black-cloaked shoulders, Laura gently tilted The Shadow's face into the moonlight. They recognized the face of a friend.

"You're right, Laura," said Roger, soberly. "It's Cranston! Bring the wheelchair. I'll get him into it."

In the chair, The Shadow lay motionless. Ready to wheel him to the mansion, Laura turned to Roger, who was standing near, leaning his weight against a tree.

"I'll come back later, Roger."

"You won't have to, Laura." Roger's smile was genuine. "I can walk!" He lifted his head proudly; then, remorse upon his sobering face, he added: "I'm truly sorry for anything I ever said."

Tears were streaking Laura's smiles by the time she reached the house. Brushing her eyes, she looked at the burden in the wheelchair. Cranston was heavier than Roger, and she had never managed to get her brother up the steps.

For a moment, she thought of waiting for Roger, who was plodding in easy stages along the path. Then, determination ruling her, Laura performed the formerly impossible. Step by step, with pauses, but no faltering, Laura worked the wheelchair and its occupant up into the house.

Rolling the chair into the library, she stopped it near the warmth of the fireplace, where embers were glowing in the grate.

As Laura tried to revive The Shadow, his eyes opened. A momentary glow told that he recognized her. He began to mutter words that were partly incoherent: something about a great grotto, long, endless passages, and waters that sighed.

Piecing that story, Laura understood. The Seminole legend was based on fact known to the Indians. Under the Devil's Ledge was some cavern where a brave once had swum, to bring back a true, but fantastic, story. Indians had shunned the cavern; but they knew of its existence, and elaborated the tale.

Confident of the truth behind the legend, The Shadow had risked that dive last night. The weight of his garments and his guns had helped him stay below the ledge. Finding the banks of the subterranean river that flowed out into Kewanee Springs, he had remained there.

The Shadow's cloak, though torn and mud-stained, was very nearly dry. Remembering that this was the drought season, when the flow of the Springs was at its minimum, Laura recognized that the underground channels could not be filled.

She pictured The Shadow's long, painful journey from the river channel along those of underground streams that flowed into it. He had preferred that venture, rather than a trip out through the Springs, where the crackers might be waiting. The Shadow had been looking for another outlet.

He hadn't found one, but he had recognized the sucking sigh of the Seminole Punch Bowl when he came beneath it. The intervals, too, must have told him where he was. Knowing that Laura brought Roger there, The Shadow had waited.

A longer wait than he expected. Because of the cloudy weather, Laura had not wheeled Roger to the glen until evening. Picturing The Shadow's long wait, Laura suddenly realized why his strength had weakened. He needed food.

Hurrying to the kitchen, Laura brought back a glass of fruit juice and sandwiches which she hastily prepared. Noting that Cranston's eyes were closed, she laid the food on a table at his elbow, then went out to the back door.

She was wondering about Roger; perhaps the long walk from the glen had overtaxed him. Lacking the wheelchair, the girl went along the path without the accustomed vehicle.

STIRRING in the wheelchair, The Shadow looked about the library soon after Laura had left. He saw the fruit juice and drank it; then began to eat a sandwich. He saw his slouch hat on the mantel.

Rising a bit shakily, The Shadow plucked the hat from its perch and clamped it on his head.

A whispered laugh came stronger. This was where The Shadow wanted to be—in the mansion where he had returned, after setting the brush fire the night before. Things seemed a bit disjointed, but The Shadow's laugh told that he expected them to clear.

His long journey through the underground caverns was a timeless expanse, that brought no definite recollection, until he noted a calendar that rested on Clenwick's desk. The rancher was particular about that calendar. The Shadow had noted, when calling as Cranston, that the day card was always correct.

The calendar said Wednesday, where The Shadow had expected Tuesday. Perhaps this night was nearly over, and Clenwick had changed the day card.

Glancing toward the mantel, The Shadow saw the clock. Its hands showed quarter of twelve. Clenwick wouldn't have changed the date on the calendar before midnight.

This *was* Wednesday!

It would be midnight in fifteen minutes—the time when Tony Belgo and his mob were due! Lost from the world, The Shadow had sent no message to his agents, nor had he given the planned tip-off to the sheriff.

There wasn't time to rouse men to action before the crooks arrived. Last night hadn't worked out as The Shadow wanted it. He had gained a peculiar status in this locality; one that might apply to Cranston, as well as to The Shadow. It would be difficult to reason matters with a mistrustful sheriff, even if The Shadow did manage to find the fellow.

Remembering the path that led up from the wharf, The Shadow resolved upon a swifter course. Every inch of the way could serve as ambush. It wouldn't take a squad to drive off Belgo and his hoodlums. A lone fighter could manage it. The task could readily be The Shadow's own.

His guns were dry; he still had ammunition. Pushing the wheelchair from his path, The Shadow strode out to the hallway and through the rear door into the moonlight.

Wavering as he passed the barn, he paused; then resumed his way toward the path to the wharf. He wasn't as steady as he hoped to be, but the night air would settle that problem. Nevertheless, it wasn't wise to hurry. The Shadow slowed his pace.

At that moment, Laura saw him, while helping Roger along the last stages of the trip from the glen. She pointed out The Shadow to her brother. As they saw the figure fade, they heard sounds from the house.

Clenwick had returned.

Leaving Roger, Laura dashed into the mansion, found Clenwick staring at the empty wheelchair. His look was puzzled, but it became an amazed one as the girl poured the story of all that had happened.

Hearing the details of The Shadow's return, Clenwick gazed toward the mantel, saw that the slouch hat was gone.

"He was delirious!" exclaimed Laura. "I could see him falter as he took the path toward the old wharf. We must find him and bring him back!"

Clenwick agreed. He told Laura to hunt for Cranston. Clenwick would hurry back to the ranch and assemble men to look for the wandering victim, in case Laura's search failed.

"We've *got* to bring him back," declared Clenwick, grimly. "If he runs into another crowd of crackers, it will be his finish! His senses certainly have left him, or he wouldn't be parading in that ghost masquerade of his."

ACTUALLY, The Shadow's senses were not at their best. He was stumbling badly along a path that had been easygoing the night before. When he paused to listen for sounds of a motorboat, he fancied he heard the constant, sucking gurgle of the Seminole Punch Bowl.

Reaching for his flashlight to help find the path, The Shadow was puzzled when the torch wouldn't glow. Dimly, he remembered that it had failed him earlier, when he had tried to use it in the caverns, following his deep swim through Kewanee Springs.

It took a close sound to make him listen. He could hear muttered voices, the scrape of footsteps. He saw a gleam, not from his own flashlight, but from one that was handled by a person farther down the path. He heard a savage command to "Douse the glim!"

Belgo's mob had landed at the wharf. They were on their way to the mansion, almost upon The Shadow, before he had even chosen the ambush spot he needed!

Galvanizing into action, The Shadow swished toward the palmettos. The ground was moundy; he tripped across a root. Tony's rasped voice came again, this time calling for lights. They appeared in plenty, large glares that swept the palmettos.

Whipping deep into those stalks, The Shadow had struck another mound. The palmettos were nothing more than a fringe that lined a hammock. He wasn't nearly set in ambush; he was in the open, with lights converging upon him!

Forced to open battle, The Shadow preferred it. His blood surged with the love for action. As often before in times of stress, The Shadow felt his whole strength and cunning sweep back into his veins. Better than any lurking spot, where his shots could be mistaken for another's, The Shadow had found the place that suited him.

He was on high ground, above the level of his foemen. To The Shadow, they were a bunch of skulking rats of the sort that he had often scattered in the past. They, on the contrary, were about to meet a foe that they never expected to find in this terrain; one whose power terrified them.

The Shadow!

The name, itself, was gulped half-coherently from choky throats as the joined beams of flashlights focused full upon the cloaked fighter in black. Those croaks were drowned by the rise of a fierce, strident laugh from the waiting master on the mound.

Puny pops of revolvers were likewise thundered under by the blasts that came from two huge automatics that appeared in The Shadow's black-fisted hands. Driving bullets straight for the flashlights, The Shadow obliterated those gleams before a single mobster could aim a telling shot in his direction.

Transplanted crooks, new to the Florida terrain, were finding a merciless treatment at the hands of the same foe who had so often driven them to cover along the sidewalks of New York.

The Shadow's hour of battle had arrived!

CHAPTER XIX
THE DOUBLE FIGHT

THE tune of blazing guns was music to The Shadow's ear: a harmony that wafted away all hazy impressions. From the moment that he began his rapid fight, he took to measures that promised to turn advantage into mastery.

His first step was a weaving retreat, necessitated by a simple reason. In his blind choice of the original position, The Shadow had placed himself between his foemen and the moon. The mound where The Shadow stood was still illumined, though the flashlights were gone.

To correct that situation, The Shadow swung across the mound. Crooks, urged by Tony Belgo, charged through the palmettos, only to be met by a devastating fire. Spreading, they took advantage of the darkness, to come in from the sides.

Their strategy failed. A shout from one gunner turned all eyes to another knoll. The Shadow was going across another hump, to entrench himself in a new position. Crooks followed warily, shooting a dozen times before The Shadow replied.

Even Tony Belgo did not guess The Shadow's purpose. Working from hammock to hammock, The Shadow was drawing the mob to clearer ground, where they, before they realized it, would be visible in the moonlight, too.

The speed of his retreat did not symbolize an urge for flight. The Shadow was simply preventing the crooks from flanking him—the one thing that might destroy his scheme.

Behind a hammock near the open ground, The Shadow viewed a darkened patch to the right. If any of Tony's followers had circled that far, they would be dangerous. The Shadow was keeping a set eye on the spot, as he made another rearward trip.

A flashlight shone. The Shadow burned a shot toward the patched darkness. He made a whirl across a broad, low hammock, to bring the flanking men into the open. He expected a few, who would give themselves away when they charged. Instead, a dozen came.

They weren't mobbies; they were ranch hands. Accepting the challenge of The Shadow's single shot, they were taking him for a foe. The guns that they eyed beneath the wide brims of their Stetsons were handled by capable trigger fingers.

Bullets were thwacking hard against the trees, as The Shadow reached the open ground. The whoops of the gunning cowhands joined with pleased snarls of the mobbies, who were swinging wide to cut off The Shadow at the other flank.

Chance had produced strange allies. Whether purposeful or blind, their efforts were united. Both factions were out to get The Shadow.

It seemed certain that he would be a target, until the converging battlers looked for him. The Shadow was gone, as suddenly as if the ground had swallowed him.

AS halted men stared through the moonlight, they saw the reason.

The open ground was jet-black. It was the wide strip that the brush fire had burned, the night before. More than a hundred yards in width, the sooty ground offered The Shadow the same cover as night. Flattened somewhere, he was crawling to a new position, his cloaked form rendering him invisible.

Black against black—a combination that no eye could detect. Blindly, Tony's mobbies and Clenwick's men were slashing the turf with their bullets, hoping to score a hit.

In the midst of that crazy fray, Laura reached the scene, to stare as helplessly as she had the night before. She was away from the range of fire, and she could venture a short way from cover, because her dress was dark and kept her inconspicuous.

She knew that gunners were looking for The Shadow, and that her shouts could not stop them. Even the ranch hands wouldn't listen, though Clenwick might be able to manage them when he arrived.

Probably, his men had heard shooting in the woods and had started there before Clenwick reached the ranch.

As for the group responsible for the trouble—Tony's mob that came up from the wharf—Laura had no idea who they might be.

Then into the search came a new type of weapon: a flare that exploded when it struck the ground. A flame bomb, that someone had thrown, it spattered a wide range of light.

Laura couldn't see the man who threw it; he was far across the blackened ground, up near the Giant Sinkhole. When they lashed upward, the flames whipped in the girl's direction, for tonight the breeze was toward the mansion, from the hammock ground above.

Lacking brush which they could kindle, the flames died rapidly; but Laura feared that the next puffy bomb might reveal The Shadow's position. Instead, The Shadow showed himself of his own accord.

Yells caused a score of men to look to the left of the sinkhole. Against the moonlight, they saw The Shadow, wrestling with a rangy foe. Cutting away from his first objective, the sinkhole, he had driven in upon the man who was tossing the flares.

Ironically, the fellow had been throwing those bursting objects beyond The Shadow. He had another fire bomb in his fist when the cloaked fighter pounced upon him. The flare left the hand that held it, but did not strike the ground.

Sledging his gun to his adversary's head, The Shadow plucked the bomb before it fell. The thing that hit the turf was the stunned form of The Shadow's surprised foe.

GUNS were ripping madly; men were on the move as they fired. The range was too great for them to score a hit, until a few came closer.

By then, The Shadow had almost finished a shortcut race to the sinkhole. Stabbing shots with one gun, he picked his nearest enemies while on the run.

Both parties were closing in upon him as he reached the fringing trees. Circling to the far side of the sinkhole, The Shadow could go no farther. He was being hemmed in by outspread enemies, who gradually closed in around the semicircle that marked the near side of the sinkhole.

The Shadow had chosen the little promontory that jutted into the wall of the great, steep funnel. His position was much like the one that he had held at Devil's Rock—a central spot upon a girdling brink, where enemies were ready.

Again, retreat was useless, for the ground beyond was barren and unburned. Unlike Kewanee Springs, however, the sinkhole offered no chance at self-rescue by a daring dive.

The scummy murk that lay far below offered no suitable outlet.

Prone behind a few low stones at the sinkhole's jut, The Shadow felt the breeze fan over him across the murky hollow. It was blowing toward the men who crouched beyond barbed wire. Hidden in the fringing brush, they were pumping shots that The Shadow could not answer.

One of his reloaded guns was emptied, the other held a few spare shots. But to lift his head would be suicide. Bullets were spanking the stones, only inches from him.

The Shadow's cause seemed gone. Soon, foemen would be working around from their present positions. Arriving, they would seal his doom through sheer power of numbers.

But The Shadow did not intend to have them reach him. Rolling half upon his back, he let his finger release the spring pin of the flare bomb that he had captured in his recent drive. With a toss that worked only from his wrist, he flipped the projectile over the sinkhole's brink.

The flare burst almost as it struck the scummy pool below. It was answered by a huge belch—a vast explosive rise of flame. The whole bottom of the sinkhole seemed to rise in fiery deluge, as if The Shadow had primed the crater of a volcano!

Roaring upward, like thunder from the earth, the mighty mass of flame lifted the scrubby brushwood with it. That blazing fuel became the kindling that ignited the half-dead trees around the brink. A titanic beacon, reaching for the sky, the sinkhole emitted gorging flames that lashed to lengths of fifty feet above the edge.

The conflagration did not dwindle. Pressed by the breeze, it spurted its fiery shoots around the half circle of the opposite bank, away from The Shadow's shelter. He could feel its scorch, but not the fury.

His foemen were getting the latter. Some never rose; the surprise had taken them all too suddenly. The rest fled, yelling, most of them with clothing afire, their guns dropped behind them.

As they ran, they heard a sardonic burst of mockery as chilling as the flames were hot.

The laugh that told the triumph of The Shadow! Single-handed the master fighter had scattered a horde of murderous foemen who had trapped him by doubling their forces.

Upon those enemies, The Shadow had launched a cataclysm. He had stirred up nature's powers, to make the final thrust. With that deed, The Shadow had shattered the riddle that involved a city of ghosts.

CHAPTER XX
CRIME'S LAST STAND

LEAVING his own vantage point, where the ground was becoming overhot, The Shadow reloaded his automatics as he went. Bodies were sliding down into the roaring pit, which still resembled a volcano. By the vivid glare, The Shadow could see scorched men rolling on the ground.

A scattered few were fleeing in opposite directions—the mobbies toward the wharf, the ranch men to their own preserves. None cared to return and resume battle with The Shadow. All wanted escape, but neither band was due to travel far.

Serving as a massive beacon, the blazing sinkhole was attracting new forces, who had heard the gunfire but had not managed to locate it.

At the wharf, The Shadow's agents were coming from a boat, in which they had followed Tony's mob. They were cutting off the kidnap crew.

Sheriff Harley and some deputies had heard the shooting from far away, and had driven for the ranch by car. Charged by an excited group of returning ranch hands, the sheriff's squad responded. Both factions that had battled The Shadow were finding new trouble that they couldn't handle.

Far off across the barren stretch, Laura saw The Shadow emerge from beyond the screening fire. She watched his actions, saw that he was checking on both frays, ready to join the one in which he was most needed. Realizing that she wasn't needed, the girl turned and ran back to the mansion.

Roger had dragged himself indoors, and was slumped wearily in his wheelchair. From the library window, he could see the flicker of the blazing sinkhole. He asked what it was about.

Wheeling him into the hall, where the rear door offered a better view, Laura began to relate all that she had witnessed.

Promptly, Roger stopped her. His eyes held a sharp look.

"You say that the ranch hands turned on Cranston?"

Laura nodded.

"Mr. Clenwick couldn't have reached them," she replied. "I was hoping that he would ride up—"

"But he didn't?"

Laura shook her head, very ruefully. She noted that an odd expression was tracing itself on Roger's face.

"What if Clenwick had *told* those ranch hands to go after Cranston?" said Roger, slowly. "Would that explain things, Laura?"

"Impossible!" exclaimed the girl. "Why—"

"Clenwick brought those crackers here last night," persisted Roger. "An accident that happens twice doesn't look so good to me."

Too hopelessly amazed to speak, Laura turned to stare out toward the fire. Roger, gazing in the same direction, suddenly smacked his hand against the wheelchair.

"I've got it!" he exclaimed. "The thing that Cranston knew last night. He was the one who started the brush fire!"

"But—why?"

"He wanted it to reach the Giant Sinkhole. He knew it would give Clenwick's game away. He had to postpone the job until tonight; that was all."

Rising half from the chair, Roger pointed.

"You know what the experts have claimed for years," declared Roger. "They've said that there's oil in Florida. That's what Terry Knight was looking for when he came here. Petroleum! He found it in that old sinkhole!

"He interested Clenwick in it, Terry did. The reason Clenwick started a ranch was to cover up the find. I can guess what happened to Terry. Clenwick got rid of him!"

An ugly voice spoke from the front hall. Roger caught a wheel of the chair and spun it. Laura turned with him; both Severns found themselves facing Graham Clenwick.

"YOU'VE guessed a lot, haven't you?" sneered the bulky man. "Yes, you've struck something, just like Terry struck oil! But that's not going to help you, or incriminate me! There's no law against a man finding oil on a ranch. It's happened often, in Texas."

Drawing a .38 revolver, Clenwick toyed with the weapon. As he proceeded, he emphasized his points by slapping the gun against his open palm.

"I turned Pomelo City into a ghost town," boasted Clenwick. "My men were the sappers who opened sinkholes. They spread the Medfly in the orange groves. They ran Betterly's car off the road. When the crackers blamed it on Bayne's accident, we started things in town."

Remembering the fire bomb that The Shadow had grabbed and taken to the sinkhole, Laura understood. The man The Shadow battled belonged to Clenwick's tribe. He had brought a supply of flares that they kept in stock for other uses.

"I even started a cattle plague," chortled Clenwick. "It made it look as if I had troubles, too. But it was worth the stock I lost. The local cattlemen went broke. I supplied them with new stock, and took over their mortgages as security.

"Just like the mortgage on this house. Any time I want, I can gobble the whole circle where the oil is! I don't want Kewanee Springs; it's outside the oil land. After tonight, though"—he glowered toward the glare of the fading sinkhole fire—"I won't be able to buy the rest of Pomelo City.

"A few weeks more, and Welf and Tilyon would have been all through. Only one man knew the answers; that was Cranston. He gave himself away too soon, by starting that brush fire last night."

As Clenwick paused, an odd smile played across his face. He was thinking in terms of The Shadow, and he evidently didn't think the cloaked fighter's triumph would last. Laura trembled when she saw Clenwick's expression, but Roger remained quite calm.

"You say that only Cranston knew," spoke Roger. "What about Roy Enwald?"

"Enwald guessed just one thing," returned Clenwick. "He suspected that I'd disposed of his friend Terry Knight. But if he figured that I had done Terry out of any oil, he probably supposed it was in Texas.

"He wanted revenge for Terry. First, he wanted to make sure he was right. Enwald pulled a smart one, that night when he was here. After I told him that I had invited Terry to Florida, he questioned Laura. She said that it was the other way around.

"That's why Enwald told a bunch of crooks they could come and get me. They showed up tonight, and Cranston—The Shadow, they call him—knew that they were coming. I didn't know it, but The Shadow was nice enough to stop them for me. He finished them like—"

Clenwick paused, still juggling his gun. With a sudden side shift, he planted his gun muzzle against Laura's side. The girl gasped, but remained motionless at a signal from Roger.

A figure had stepped in from the rear door—a black-cloaked visitor, whose hands gripped a pair of automatics. One weapon was lifted; but Clenwick had seen it in time to cover Laura, thereby insuring his own safety.

Cannily, the master crook had chosen to threaten another life, rather than risk battle with The Shadow.

VERY calmly, in a style more Cranston's than his own, The Shadow accepted the situation. In a sibilant tone, he picked up Clenwick's statement where the unmasked crook had dropped it.

"Yes, I finished Belgo's mob," spoke The Shadow, "somewhat as you disposed of Enwald. But you missed another opportunity that night, Clenwick. I was lying, half-stunned, in that hotel courtyard, with both these guns empty, when you fired from the darkness."

From Clenwick's lips spat savage oaths, denials of The Shadow's statement. The crook was trying to cover his chagrin at having missed a chance that The Shadow termed an opportunity.

In reply, The Shadow delivered a whispered, taunting laugh. Clenwick's sputters stopped.

"I labeled you that night," The Shadow told him. "I heard what you told Enwald, about Knight. I spoke to Roger afterward, and learned just the opposite. Later, when you came to town, you told another story that had flaws.

"You couldn't have gone to the ranch for your car. There wasn't time. Your car was here, but you were trying the same system that I was. You wanted to cover the fact that you had been busy around town."

Approaching Clenwick as he spoke, The Shadow watched the man's expression. He knew that Clenwick, though at bay, was dangerous. Three persons needed to die in order for the master crook to cover up his crimes.

Those three were Lamont Cranston, otherwise The Shadow, Laura Severn, and her brother Roger.

If Clenwick murdered Laura, as at present he was able, he would bring his own death. But if he could offset The Shadow, the crook would feel certain of success, for he would be dealing then with only a girl and an invalid.

Only one scheme could be in Clenwick's brain. The Shadow resolved to test it. He waited, knowing that Clenwick would soon speak. The crook's statement came.

"Suppose we make terms," suggested Clenwick. "Knight's death was really an accident. He fell down the Giant Sinkhole. With Terry gone, I just lost my head. Killing Enwald wasn't murder. You knew the fellow was crooked. So did I."

Though Clenwick's statements were mostly lies, The Shadow appeared to accept them. The features of Cranston were visible beneath his hat brim, when he spoke:

"State your terms."

"There's the front door," declared Clenwick, gesturing his free hand. "Walk on out, and go your way. I know that Laura and Roger will agree not to talk, when I give them a share of the oil property. Naturally, I won't harm them. I don't want to bring you back."

Both Laura and Roger saw catches in those terms, but The Shadow started to accept them. He walked toward the front door. Keeping Clenwick covered with one gun, he put away the other and reached for the knob.

Though Clenwick and Laura were both watching The Shadow, only Roger caught the commanding glint of the cloaked avenger's directed eyes. He understood the gaze. Graham Clenwick had forgotten one thing: that Roger Severn had learned how to walk.

INSPIRED by The Shadow's confidence, Roger did more than walk. He sprang, covering the distance to Clenwick in a single leap. He bowled the big man to the floor.

Startled completely by the attack, Clenwick didn't press the gun trigger until he struck. By then, his aim was far wide of Laura.

Sweeping the front door wide, The Shadow stepped out into the moonlight. On the lawn were the men that he expected—a score of crackers, all with shotguns. Clenwick had summoned them here, but hadn't told them why he wanted them.

Lifting his head, The Shadow delivered a long, weird laugh that stretched its defiant mockery above the topmost twigs of the huge oaks. With that challenge, the whole scene changed.

Men flung away their shotguns and fled. With the first break in the ranks, the rest followed suit. Clenwick had misjudged what would happen at that meeting; The Shadow had not.

Last night, The Shadow had proven himself a ghost, so far as the natives were concerned. Former suspicions became convictions, the moment they realized that the ghost had returned. No human being, so they supposed, could have survived last night's disappearing dive from Devil's Rock.

One gunshot sounded, not from the cleared lawn but within the house. Looking back through the door, The Shadow saw Roger rising, picking up a smoking revolver. Clenwick lay motionless on the floor.

The Shadow had held no doubts about that outcome. Graham Clenwick, on the verge of murdering Laura, had been easy prey for Roger Severn and the latter's powerful hands, the moment that The Shadow had given Roger opportunity to begin the fray.

Clenwick's crimes were bared. His death would bring credit to Roger, when the sheriff arrived to learn full facts. As for Clenwick's holdings, those properties and the oil they represented would revert to the actual owners.

Mortgages were held by Clenwick, but they could all be lifted. Tomorrow, Welf and Tilyon would hear from Cranston, offering loans to any persons who needed to reclaim their properties.

To Roger and Laura, such a loan would come from their old friend, The Shadow. As for the natives duped by Clenwick, they could regard their good luck as a "thank you" from their chance acquaintance, the ghost.

Reaching the wharf, The Shadow found his agents in a speedboat drawn up beside Belgo's deserted cruiser. Soon, the speedboat was gliding toward the Oklawaha River, with The Shadow at the helm.

As he steered a winding course by moonlight through the thick-walled river jungle, The Shadow gazed into the distance when the craft turned a low-banked bend.

His gaze was toward Pomelo City. The laugh that issued from The Shadow's lips was a token of departure to his two friends who lived there. A farewell to the city of ghosts, where life and prosperity would soon begin anew!

THE END

Spotlight on The Shadow
by Anthony Tollin

Walter B. Gibson was a prolific wordsmith long before he was recruited to chronicle The Shadow's adventures. "For nearly ten years," he recalled, "I had been a full-time professional writer, supplying daily features to the Ledger Syndicate in my hometown of Philadelphia. These included simple 'After Dinner Tricks,' 'Brain Tests,' 'Crossword Puzzles' and other items that ran into the hundreds and were sold to newspapers everywhere. For three years, I had done a 'Puzzle a Day' for the Newspaper Enterprise Association in Cleveland, along with various articles for other syndicates."

However, by 1930, much of Gibson's syndication work had dried up due to newspaper closures brought about by the Great Depression, and the prolific writer was searching for new markets.

One of those was America's largest publisher of pulp fiction magazines. "I had recently sold a short fiction story to Street & Smith for one of their detective magazines and Frank Blackwell, the editor-in-chief, had expressed a possible interest in a series of shorts on factual crimes." Gibson would also develop puzzles and short articles for Lon Murray, editor of the publishing house's *Headlines, Sport Story Magazine* and the new *The Shadow—A Detective Magazine*.

In December of 1930, the Philadelphia resident journeyed to Manhattan to finalize separate book contracts for *Houdini's Magic* and *Blackstone's Modern Card Tricks,* and finished the day with an unscheduled trip to the Street & Smith offices. That visit led to his being assigned to develop a mysterious hero for a new magazine. "Specifically, they wanted a character to be called 'The Shadow,' as a tie-in with an announcer's voice that was being used to introduce *The Detective Story Hour*, a weekly radio program that dramatized a short story from each new issue of *Detective Story Magazine*."

Gibson turned in his first Shadow novel a week ahead of deadline, and was told the novel would be published under a house name because "…it was customary for a writer to use two different names if he had two stories in the same issue of a magazine. It applied here, for 'The Green Light,' the short story that I had already placed with Street & Smith had been scheduled for the new magazine under my own name. *The Living Shadow* would have to be under another name unless the two could be switched about. But as a final point, the editorial staff had decided to treat The Shadow as the living character that the story title implied, in order to impress juvenile readers. So they wanted to play up the author as a raconteur who alone had access to The Shadow's annals and was too deeply engrossed in them to be concerned with anything else."

Sanctum Books begins our 2011 commemoration of the 80th anniversary of *The Shadow* by reprinting "The Green Light" from the rare first issue of *The Shadow—A Detective Magazine*, the story that launched Walter Gibson's career at Street & Smith and directly led to his being assigned to bring literary substance to radio's shadowy mystery host. •

Headlines
INC.
48 W. 16TH STREET NEW YORK CITY

January firstn 1931. 1932

Dear Walt:

Here is one from the London "Express." Has this been pulled in this country? If not, play with the idea a bit, and see if you can work out a good one on Contract for HEADLINES. Maybe you can make the stunt more graphic, more distinctive.

Would also like to revive puzzles in SPORT STORY. About 4 puzzles to make up one page; all puzzles to be closely associated with particular sports--- the type that ~~axixxaxfaa~~ will particularly absorb a sports fan.

The "Black Master" is being set. If you're coming over the early part of the week, it would be a good stunt if you could work in a little of this postoffice-anti-Fascist-bomb stuff. Just about half a chapter of the Easton, Pa. story to demonstrate how closely The Shadow follows current crime.

See you later --

Lon

THE NATIONAL NEWS REVUE

The Street & Smith Building at 79 Seventh Avenue

The GREEN LIGHT

By Walter B. Gibson

What was the portent of the light that was sometimes red and sometimes green?

GLOWING weirdly, high from the ground, came the rays of a green light from the house down the roadway—a house set back among trees as though seeking to be of itself alone, not desiring the company of other buildings or of persons.

The ghostly, unblinking light was the object of excited attention on the part of Bert Rogers who, with his friend Harry Wilson, stood outside the courtyard door of Bert's apartment house. Rogers was pointing toward the eerie green eye in the distance, his manner full of wonderment—and something of fear.

"Do you see it, Harry?" asked Wilson. "There, through one of the windows of that house among the trees. That light!"

"Yes," replied Wilson, a trace of amusement in his face at Rogers's quite apparent excitement, "but what of it?"

"There is something mysterious about it," said Rogers, "something positively uncanny. It gives me the shivers!"

"Shivers!" Wilson laughed softly. "A green light? Nonsense! It merely looks like an illuminated emerald in the distance; although it probably is only a light in a third-floor room—a light with a green shade, or possibly a green bulb. No use becoming squeamish over a thing like that."

But even as Wilson looked at the distant green glow, he was conscious of a creepy feeling stealing over him—a feeling which affected him queerly, yet one which he could not define. Was it possible that he, too, was beginning to fear this light which seemed to hang over the world, waiting and watching—watching—

No, reflected Wilson, it was not just an ordinary light—there was more to it than that. But, what? He found himself uncertain, hesitant, and he looked at Bert Rogers with serious eyes. The jovial light-heartedness was gone from Wilson's face and manner.

Bert's voice came to Wilson from a great distance, so it seemed.

"That house over there," said Rogers, "is old Alfred Saunders' place. You've probably heard of him. He retired from business some years ago; he's probably worth a few millions. But that light is what gets me. You can see it from the street, here, and most likely from various apartments in this building, even though the house is set back among the trees. I imagine, also, that it can be seen from the side road that leads by Saunders' front gate."

Without taking his gaze from the green glow which so strangely affected his friend, and which was now having a similar effect upon himself, Wilson spoke:

"Bert, just what is it that makes you feel that this light is uncanny, or perplexing and strange?"

Rogers did not reply immediately. His thoughts seemed to follow an unbroken course; his eyes seemed entranced by the bright dot of glittering green.

"I have seen that light every night, Harry," he said, finally. "It has fascinated me. But there is a reason why it particularly perplexes me now. Until tonight, it had shone red, like a ruby. Tonight, for the first time, it is green."

"Which could mean much—or nothing," replied Wilson.

"Standing by the window," continued Rogers, not noticing the interruption, "a rather complete theory has entered my mind. I know something about Saunders and his habits. That light, therefore, seems to me to hold a very definite meaning.

"Alfred Saunders is a widower. His house is almost a fortress, for it contains many valuables. He has five servants: two of them—his valet and his chauffeur—are the men-at-arms of his castle. The downstairs doors are massive and heavily locked. The windows, on both the first and second floors, are barred.

"Saunders rarely leaves his home. When he does, he goes away in the evening, and generally returns the same night. His two guards go with him, and that leaves the house virtually unprotected, for the other servants are simply an old butler, a female cook, and a housemaid."

"It's rather absurd," objected Wilson. "Why doesn't he leave the valet in the house?"

"Saunders has enemies," replied Rogers, "or at least he thinks he has. He evidently values his carcass above his worldly possessions. Furthermore, he makes his occasional excursions so unexpectedly that there is no way of telling whether he is home or not. It would be impossible to get near the place; the chauffeur is on the job every evening looking for prowlers, and I imagine it would be tough luck to be caught on the premises."

"What has the green light to do with it?" asked Wilson.

"I'm coming to that," said Rogers. "I think I have made it clear that Saunders' house must be a good nut to crack—even though it is certainly a hard one. The best way to get at it would be when Saunders is away, and it would be ideal if one of the doors should happen to be unlocked. Therefore, whoever might decide to enter the place would require an accomplice.

"I don't suspect the butler or the cook. Both of them, I believe, have been with Saunders for a long time. But I think the housemaid is in on some kind of a game."

"But I still don't understand about the light," said Wilson.

"Picture it this way, Harry. That light, with a red shade, is a warning. It means that Saunders and his two huskies are at home. The maid lights it every night. Someone goes by on the side road and sees it

"Tonight the light is green. Saunders is away. This, perhaps, is the opportunity that has been awaited. I'll guarantee that one of those formidable downstairs doors is unlocked, for the convenience of someone who wants to use it."

"You have even been in Saunders' house?" inquired Wilson.

"Several times. With friends. The place is quite unusual. It has an inside telephone system; you can ring any place from the cellar to the servants' quarters. There's a big old-fashioned safe in the living room. I don't imagine it would be hard to crack."

Harry Wilson yawned and consulted his watch. The mental effect of the ghostly green light had apparently worn off.

"Time for me to be along home," he said. "Before I go, I'll give you my theory on this mysterious light The housemaid is to blame, all right. She cracked the red shade while she was cleaning today, and replaced it with a green one. That solves the riddle. See you later, Bert." And with that Wilson stepped into his coupé and went his way.

BERT ROGERS stood on the sidewalk in front of the apartment, watching the departure of Wilson's car. It was after midnight; the spring night was extremely quiet. Rogers tapped one of his rubber-soled shoes on the curbing, and smiled in amusement.

He carefully buttoned his dark coat, glanced up and down the noiseless street and sauntered across to the high fence that surrounded Alfred Saunders' small estate.

He chose an obscure spot where a tree hid him from the street and swung himself over the fence. Then he strode easily along the silken grass, well concealed in the shrubbery that grew in haphazard spots about the lawn.

He stopped at a corner of the house and sidled behind a bush. The driveway was ahead; it led through a porte-cochère that was lighted from the archway.

The front of the house was dark, except for a very small gleam that showed from the edge of a drawn curtain in a first-floor window. The light from the porte-cochère was sufficient to distinguish the graystone walls, and Rogers noticed a small door by the nearest corner of the building.

Suddenly a form passed between him and the light; he hardly noticed the man before his figure had merged against the side of the house. Then he saw the black form against the white of the little door; the door opened inward and the figure was gone, so quickly that it might all have been hallucination.

Rogers slipped to the side of the house and touched the knob of the door. It was not even latched; it had been left ajar.

Tense, he entered the darkness of the hallway,

closing the door slightly behind him. There were steps to the left; beyond them, curtains and the dimly lit living room.

Sensing that this was the visitor's objective, Rogers tested the steps with his foot. The stairs were carpeted, and there was no sound as he mounted them.

Behind a broad curtain, Rogers saw the whole tableau. Just beyond the curtain, so near that he could reach it, stood a large table, on which was the room's single light. The intruder had laid his blue coat carefully on the table and was now at the far end of the room, his white shirt splotched against the blackness of the safe door.

The man was motionless for a moment; then he drew a handkerchief from his hip pocket and carefully placed it around the bell of the telephone box which was a few feet away from the safe. Then he turned back to the safe and placed his ear against the door. Bert could see his fingers working at the knob.

The man's work held a fascination. It was easy, deliberate, and almost noiseless. Though hidden completely behind the curtain, with only the slight space between the velvet hanging and the wall as a peek-hole, Rogers was apprehensive lest he should betray himself.

The safe door swung open. A tiny flashlight gleamed into the deep interior. The man removed various objects and set them carefully upon the floor. Then he paused as though examining something. The flashlight snapped out.

THE man turned from the safe and walked directly across the room, to the table where the coat lay. He was carrying a long envelope, from which he had removed a small pamphlet or folder which he held in his other hand. Leaning over so the light on the table illuminated the pages, the man ran noiselessly through the pamphlet.

His face was turned slightly away, but it was unmasked, and Bert was surprised to observe a clear-cut physiognomy which no character reader would have analyzed as a criminal type. The man was young, firm-jawed and businesslike. Most impressive was his calmness of expression.

Bert watched him replace the folder back in the unsealed envelope, and push the entire packet into the inside pocket of his coat, which was so turned that the pocket lay uppermost on the table. Then the intruder was on his way back to the safe.

Almost instinctively, Bert's hand went into his own inside pocket and gripped an advertising circular that had come to him in the afternoon mail. Peering through the slit between curtain and wall, Bert saw the man carefully replacing the articles he had taken from the safe.

Urged by sudden inspiration, Bert reached through the curtain and drew the envelope from the man's coat pocket. Although his hands shook clumsily and the darkness of the hallway was a handicap, he made the transfer. The mysterious document was safely in his own pocket; the advertising circular was in the envelope.

Bert drew a breath of elation when he had slipped his own envelope into the visitor's coat.

The door of the safe shut quickly. There was a short buzz from the telephone alongside. The man hastily drew his handkerchief from the bell-box and began to wipe the knob and tile front of the safe.

Bert combined silence with speed as he moved down the steps and through the door, which he opened as little as possible. He reached the friendly bush and waited.

Some seconds later, the outside door opened once more and the mysterious man came out, wearing his coat. He pulled the door tightly behind him;

There was a sharp click as the latch went in place. Then he strode across the lawn and dodged into the shrubbery, just as the bright headlights of an automobile shot up the driveway.

Bert shrank under the bush as the lights turned in his direction; then they curved away and the car rolled beneath the porte-cochère.

Alfred Saunders had returned.

Back in his apartment, Bert Rogers examined the former contents of the envelope taken from the safe. The little folder proved to be a most curious document.

It was a typewritten pamphlet of twenty-four pages, bound together for convenience. It consisted of long columns of words, in alphabetical order, each followed by a defining word that bore no relation to the original. The alphabetical words were uncommon ones—the list was headed by the word "abaca"—while the definitions were words of extreme simplicity.

There were upward of a thousand words in the vocabulary, and Bert soon realized that he possessed a codebook that was the key to a system of secret correspondence that could not be solved by any usual method.

He tossed the book into a drawer of his table and looked from the window. The green light still shone amid the distant trees.

"I wonder what Harry Wilson would say about this?" he mused softly.

Then he stuffed his pipe with tobacco, sat at the table and began to wonder over the situation. He smiled as he thought of the businesslike safe-opener and the envelope which that gentleman had in his pocket. Bert was sure the advertising circular would prove quite a perplexity to the outwitted burglar.

The events of the past half hour had merely added to the mystery of the green light. Obviously the man who had entered Alfred Saunders' house had wanted just one thing—the codebook. The housemaid was certainly his accomplice. She had set the signal light. She had unlatched the little door. Watching from upstairs, she had seen the lights of Saunders' car when it reached the front gates, and the chauffeur had stepped out to open the barrier.

The buzz of the telephone, a short ring from upstairs, had been the emergency signal. The burglar's handkerchief had prevented the phone from ringing.

There were other questions more important than why the man had taken the codebook. What would Alfred Saunders do when he discovered that it was missing? That was unanswerable. But there were two other very definite questions.

What would the safecracker do when he made the unexpected discovery of the advertising circular? He would hardly suspect the substitution; more than likely he would believe that he had made some unaccountable blunder and had carried away the wrong envelope.

The green light still shone, and Bert whistled softly. The safecracker would be back for another search. That would be his only course; and since Bert could see the signal as well as he, Bert would know when he was coming back.

The more important question was what Bert should do with the codebook. Two people evidently wanted it—Alfred Saunders and the unknown visitor.

Rightfully, Bert should return it to Saunders; but to do so would be an admission that he had committed a theft of his own.

For a few moments he considered destroying the pamphlet; then be laughed when he realized his own security. No one could possibly suspect that he had pilfered the much-sought codebook. He had gone to Alfred Saunders' house and had returned totally unobserved.

The best plan was to wait—but until when? Until tomorrow night, when the light would shine red or green—in fact, until whatever night it would be green; for then he would have an opportunity to discover the identity of the stranger; and that, more than anything else, was the intriguing question.

BERT ROGERS went to the city the next morning, and it was not until ten o'clock in the evening that he returned. He was about to open the desk drawer when his eye caught the gleam of the green light. Without hesitating, he hurried downstairs, scanned the street, and seeing no one, entered the Saunders' estate by the over-fence route.

Since Saunders was away again—the green light told that story—there was no time to lose. Treading a zigzag course over the lawn, Bert quickly formulated his procedure.

He would not enter the house tonight; instead he would shadow the expected intruder and do all that might be possible to discover his identity. Then, when he returned the codebook to Alfred Saunders, he would be able to give a satisfactory explanation—complete enough to serve as an excuse for his own trespassing.

He reached the bush that commanded a view of the little door and rested patiently. It was not yet late, but the house was silent and the whole scene was in readiness for the man of the night before.

But as the minutes moved by, Bert Rogers commenced to feel a cooling of enthusiasm. He realized that he was injecting himself into a troublesome matter; that there was no gain other than the satisfaction of useless curiosity.

Yet the remembrance of the codebook in the table drawer of his apartment kept him alert. After all, whatever the situation might be, he was already in it. The present opportunity would not come again. Tonight would surely bring another visit of the stranger.

A distant clock clanged eleven and a new and disconcerting idea surprised Bert Rogers. He recalled that he had not returned to his apartment until ten; that on the night before, the green light had continued to shine after the visitor had departed. Perhaps the man had come and gone!

That could be learned by testing the little door. So he crawled from behind the bush. made reasonably sure that the man he expected was not even then coming for the quest; and in another moment was trying the door. It did not yield this time.

There was no need for special secrecy. The stranger had made an unsuccessful visit; Alfred Saunders was away, as evidenced by the green light; so Bert could think of no better place for a one-man conference than by the door itself.

He listened for a few moments; tried the door again, and even made a little noise. Then, realizing the uselessness of further activity, lie turned away and strolled across the lawn.

Something landed on his back with a heavy jolt. He was pinioned on the ground, and rolled on his back like a barrel. Clumsy hands frisked his clothing, and he was dragged to his feet and urged along the driveway toward the porte-cochère.

UNDER the light of the archway he recognized the man who had so expertly handled him. It was Saunders' chauffeur. The front door of the house had opened and the owner of the estate, apparently aroused by the one-sided conflict, was standing in quizzical expectation.

"What have you there, Rich?" he demanded, in a biting voice. ''Bring him in. Another trespasser, eh?"

Bert was plunged into a chair in the living room. The bright lights shot on, and he gasped for breath as he looked at the two men before him.

"Too much excitement today," complained Alfred Saunders. "What do you make of it, Rich? The maid left this afternoon and never came back. And now we have one of these fellows who likes to go places where he shouldn't be."

Bert Rogers stared at the old man.

He had seen Alfred Saunders before, and had never particularly liked him. But now the smooth, yellowish face that confronted him seemed almost demoniacal; the bitter eyes that stared at him indicated a man who would not be satisfied to see a trespasser go unpunished.

"What were you doing here?" snapped Saunders.

Bert regained his breath with a long puff.

"I thought you were not at home," he admitted.

"No?" Saunders' smile was not enjoyable.

"I can explain matters, Mr. Saunders," said Bert. "But I must admit that my story is unusual. My name is Rogers—I have been here before—as a guest. Last night I came here, while you were away, because——"

Saunders held up a quivering hand.

"Watch him, Rich," he said. "No more from you, young fellow. You say you were here last night. Wait a minute."

He walked across the room to the safe. He opened the heavy door and fumbled among the papers. His search was brief; he turned sharply and strode fiercely back to Bert's chair.

"I've expected this," he rasped. "Ever since Anderson cleared out, I've been suspicious. See if he has any papers on him, Rich."

"I searched him outside, sir," said the chauffeur. "I thought maybe he had a gun. His pockets are empty."

"Well, you've got the code, haven't you," rasped Saunders. "Where is it? I want it!"

"I have it," admitted Bert. "It's in my apartment across the street. But I didn't steal it—that is, not from your safe."

"Has anybody seen it?" demanded Saunders.

"No," answered Bert.

"Good," said the old man with a sudden pursing of his lips that made Bert apprehensive. "That's very, very nice. We can go and get it right now. Then we'll attend to your case. Where's your apartment key ?"

The chauffeur fished it from Bert's pocket.

"What apartment?" demanded the old man. "Where have you hidden it?"

"Top floor front" was Bert's mechanical reply. "In the table drawer."

SOMEHOW the situation seemed hopeless. He realized that no explanation would appear logical to Alfred Saunders. The next statement from the old man was proof of this.

"When Rich gets the code," said Saunders, slowly, "it goes back in the safe; and you go to jail. Trespassing and forcible entry. As far as the world is concerned, that code does not exist. It is all supposition. Old Jonathan Blake wanted it, didn't he? Well, he can continue to want it. I'll fix him very soon. Meanwhile, you can pay for your smartness."

"I don't know what you mean, Mr. Saunders," pleaded Bert. "All I know is, I'm not the man you want——"

His words seemed useless. The old man turned to the chauffeur.

"Hurry over and get that code," he said. "I'll look after this fellow. Murray is here with me."

The valet had entered the room and was standing by the doorway. Bert found himself speculating which of the two would be the more dangerous in combat, the departing chauffeur or the other man-at-arms.

Five minutes passed—five minutes of troubled silence. Alfred Saunders had turned his back on Bert

Murray, but the valet, was patiently watching. Bert was still wondering over his strange, unexplainable plight. He began to feel that his only possible defense against these odd conditions would be his ignorance and the testimony of Harry Wilson relating to the conversation of the night before.

There was a knock at the front door. The valet looked questioningly at Alfred Saunders.

"Rich is back," said the old man. "Answer the door."

Bert thought wildly of escape. Then he gripped the arms of the chair and sat fast.

There was an argument in the hall; then a man entered the room, followed by Murray. Bert became suddenly alert. The arrival was not Rich, the chauffeur; it was the man who had entered the Saunders' house the night before—the calm young safecracker!

Without noticing Bert, the visitor walked up to Saunders. The old man stared sourly, and waved Murray aside.

"Well," he asked, "who are you?"

"Osborne is my name," replied the newcomer. "I'm a detective. Employed by Mr. Jonathan Blake. Just dropped in to tell you that Blake has your code. I cracked your safe last night, Mr. Saunders."

Alfred Saunders looked toward Bert Rogers.

"What about this fellow?" he asked. "He says he has it."

The detective smiled and turned to Bert.

"Your name's Rogers?" he asked.

Bert nodded.

"He *had* it," said the detective, turning again to Saunders. "I don't know how he got it, but I'm telling you where it is now. Jonathan Blake has it, and he's going to keep it."

"So there's two of you in it," said Saunders. "That means trouble for both instead of just one."

"Bluff," laughed Osborne. "You know where you stand now, Saunders. Blake has the goods on you; but he's a sport, and he'll call it quits. Read this. It's a note from Blake."

Saunders glanced at the folded paper which the detective gave him. For a moment his face was sour; then came a smile that was reassuring to Bert Rogers.

"I'LL have to give Blake some credit," he said. "The cards are all his way, now, but he's willing to drop it. Murray, you can go. When Rich comes back, tell him to forget that paper he went to find. And by the way, Murray, ring the butler's bell. I think I'll have a drink with these gentlemen."

The appearance of the refreshments produced an *entente cordiale*.

"Now that we're bordering on friendship, Mr. Saunders," said the detective Osborne, "I can tell you just what our camp has been doing. I don't think I'm making a mistake in enlightening Mr. Rogers. He is something of an unknown quantity that came into the matter unexpectedly."

"Tell your story," agreed Alfred Saunders.

"You and Jonathan Blake have been at odds for many years, haven't you?" asked Osborne.

Saunders nodded.

"Well," continued Osborne, "you worked a clever stunt when you subsidized Anderson, his secretary. Blake realized that you were getting information that would ruin him, and he figured that you were going to blackmail him after you had received enough dope from Anderson."

"Call it that," admitted Saunders. "I was out to fix Blake."

"You received your information," said Osborne, "and I found out that Anderson was sending it to you. All the letters went in code; we nailed the last one that Anderson sent. That's why he skipped."

"I knew it," said Saunders.

"We couldn't figure that code to save us. Then I had a hunch that the answer to it lay here, in your safe. It had to be a word code—a sort of junior dictionary, in which one word stood for another. So I decided to get it, and I had to crack your safe to do it. If we had the code as evidence, your schemes would be ended.

"That's where Myra came into the picture. She managed to get a job here as housemaid. I figured the job was impossible without cooperation from the inside."

Saunders grunted.

"So she was in it," he said. "Now I know why she left today. Did she let you in here?"

"She did," replied Osborne. "She had a red light in the third-floor hall. It burned every night for a week. I saw it from the front road. Then one night it was green, and I knew you and your two men were away. That's when I came in and swiped the code.. She left the side door open for me."

"Where does Rogers come into it?" asked Saunders.

"I SAW the light, too," explained Bert. "I figured its meaning. I came over here and spotted Osborne going in the door. I followed him and took the code-book while it was in his coat pocket, over on that table. I put an advertising circular in its place."

"But why did you come here tonight?" questioned Saunders.

"I wanted to find out who Osborne was. I felt sure he would be back tonight for another try. I thought you were away—for I saw the green light again in the window."

Osborne laughed.

"Myra skipped out this afternoon," he explained.

"She met me and I told her the job was done. She didn't change the green light back to red!"

Bert Rogers scratched his head, and Alfred Saunders grinned.

"But wait a minute, Osborne," said Saunders suddenly. "How did you get the code? You didn't see Rogers take it?"

"No, sir," replied the detective. "I was amazed when I found that mail-order catalogue instead of the code that I was so sure I had. I had no idea whatever that anyone had been in the house with me. It was the most complete surprise I ever experienced.

"It put me in a tremendous quandary when I discovered it. But this morning I went over to Rogers's apartment, opened the door, and found the code. It was very easy, because Rogers was away. I gave the code to Blake; he wrote the note to you and sent me over to see you this evening."

"But how did you know about me?" demanded Bert. "There are thousands of catalogues sent out by that concern. You didn't know I was the man who took the code. You had no clue—"

The detective smiled and drew the circular from his pocket

"I guess you didn't notice it when the circular came," he said. "Of course you couldn't sec it in the dark, when you made the switch. It looked like this when I pulled it from the envelope—"

He laid the circular on the table. The name of the mail-order house proclaimed itself in bold letters.

"—and then I turned it over. That was the only clue I needed. You must be on their regular mailing list, young fellow. Your name and address were made by an addressograph!"

THE END

THE MAN WHO CAST THE SHADOW

Walter B. Gibson (1897-1985) was born in Germantown, Pennsylvania. His first published feature, a puzzle titled "Enigma," appeared in *St. Nicholas Magazine* when Walter was only eight years old. In 1912, Gibson's second published piece won a literary prize, presented by former President Howard Taft who expressed the hope that this would be the beginning of a great literary career. Building upon a lifelong fascination with magic and sleight of hand, Gibson later became a frequent contributor to magic magazines and worked briefly as a carnival magician. He joined the reporting staff of the *Philadelphia North American* after graduating from Colgate University in 1920, moved over to the *Philadelphia Public Ledger* the following year and was soon producing a huge volume of syndicated features for NEA and the Ledger Syndicate, while also ghosting books for magicians Houdini, Thurston, Blackstone and Dunninger.

A 1930 visit to Street & Smith's offices led to his being hired to write novels featuring The Shadow, the mysterious host of CBS' *Detective Story Program*. Originally intended as a quarterly, *The Shadow Magazine* was promoted to monthly publication when the first two issues sold out and, a year later, began the amazing twice-a-month frequency it would enjoy for the next decade. "This was during the Depression, so this was a good thing to be doing. I just dropped everything else and did *The Shadow* for 15 years. I was pretty much Depression-proof."

Working on a battery of three typewriters, Gibson often wrote his Shadow novels in four or five days, averaging a million and a half words a year. He pounded out 24 Shadow novels during the final ten months of 1932; he eventually wrote 283 Shadow novels totaling some 15 million words.

Gibson scripted the lead features for *Shadow Comics* and *Super-Magician Comics,* along with

Walter B. Gibson in 1941, celebrating ten years of *The Shadow Magazine* and more than 200 novels.

Walter and Litzka Gibson on their wedding day, August 27, 1949

a visionary 1942 *Bill Barnes* comic story that foresaw the United States dropping a U-235 bomb to defeat Japan and end World War II. The following year, he organized Penn-Art, a Philadelphia comic art shop utilizing former *Evening Ledger* artists. Gibson later scripted numerous commercial, industrial and political comic books, pioneering the use of comics as an educational tool.

During the Golden Age of Radio, Walter plotted and co-scripted *Nick Carter—Master Detective, Chick Carter, The Avenger*, *Frank Merriwell* and *Blackstone, the Magic Detective*.

Gibson also wrote hundreds of true crime magazine articles. In his book *Man of Magic and Mystery: A Guide to the Work of Walter B. Gibson,* bibliographer J. Randolph Cox documents more than 30 million words published in 150 books, some 500 magazine stories and articles, more than 3000 syndicated newspaper features and hundreds of radio and comic scripts.

Walter hosted ABC's *Strange* and wrote scores of books on magic and psychic phenomena, many co-authored with his wife, Litzka Raymond Gibson. He also wrote five *Biff Brewster* juvenile adventure novels for Grosset and Dunlap (as "Andy Adams"), a *Vicki Barr, Air Stewardess* book and a *Cherry Ames, Nurse* story (as "Helen Wells"), *The Twilight Zone* and such publishing staples as *Hoyle's Simplified Guide to the Popular Card Games* and *Fell's Official Guide to Knots and How to Tie Them*.

No one was happier than Gibson when The Shadow staged a revival in the sixties and seventies. Walter wrote *Return of The Shadow* in 1963 and three years later selected three vintage stories to appear in a hardcover anthology entitled *The Weird Adventures of The Shadow*. Several series of paperback and hardcover reprints followed, and Walter wrote two new Shadow short stories, "The Riddle of the Rangoon Ruby" and "Blackmail Bay." A frequent guest at nostalgia, mystery, and comic conventions, Gibson attended the annual Pulpcon and Friends of Old-Time Radio conventions on a regular basis, always delighted to perform a few magic tricks and sign autographs as both Gibson and Grant, using his distinctive double-X signature. His last completed work of fiction, "The Batman Encounters—Gray Face," appeared as a text feature in the 500th issue of *Detective Comics*.

Walter Gibson died on December 6, 1985, a recently begun Shadow novel sitting unfinished in his typewriter. "I always enjoyed writing the Shadow stories," he remarked to me a few years earlier. "There was never a time when I wasn't enjoying the story I was writing or looking forward to beginning the next one." Walter paused and then added, a touch of sadness in his voice, "I wish I was still writing the Shadow stories."

So do I, old friend. So do I. —Anthony Tollin

Walter Gibson and Anthony Tollin